Hope Rises

BY DAVID BALDACCI

Walter Nash series
Nash Falls • Hope Rises

Travis Devine series
*The 6:20 Man • The Edge
To Die For*

Amos Decker series
*Memory Man • The Last Mile
The Fix • The Fallen
Redemption • Walk the Wire
Long Shadows*

Aloysius Archer series
*One Good Deed • A Gambling Man
Dream Town*

Atlee Pine series
*Long Road to Mercy
A Minute to Midnight
Daylight • Mercy*

Will Robie series
*The Innocent • The Hit • The Target
The Guilty • End Game*

John Puller series
*Zero Day • The Forgotten
The Escape • No Man's Land
Daylight*

King and Maxwell series
*Split Second • Hour Game
Simple Genius • First Family
The Sixth Man • King and Maxwell*

The Camel Club series
*The Camel Club • The Collectors
Stone Cold • Divine Justice
Hell's Corner*

Shaw series
*The Whole Truth
Deliver Us From Evil*

Other novels
*Absolute Power • True Blue
Total Control • The Winner
The Simple Truth • Saving Faith
Wish You Well • Last Man Standing
The Christmas Train • One Summer
Simply Lies • A Calamity of Souls
Strangers in Time*

Short stories
*Waiting for Santa • No Time Left
Bullseye • The Final Play*

Vega Jane series
*Vega Jane and the Secrets of Sorcery
Vega Jane and the Maze of Monsters
Vega Jane and the Rebels' Revolt
Vega Jane and the End of Time*

DAVID BALDACCI

Hope Rises

MACMILLAN

First published 2026 by Grand Central Publishing, USA

First published in the UK 2026 by Macmillan
an imprint of Pan Macmillan
The Smithson, 6 Briset Street, London EC1M 5NR
EU representative: Macmillan Publishers Ireland Ltd, 1st Floor,
The Liffey Trust Centre, 117–126 Sheriff Street Upper,
Dublin 1 D01 YC43
Associated companies throughout the world

ISBN 978-1-0350-3538-0 HB
ISBN 978-1-0350-3539-7 TPB

Copyright © Columbus Rose Ltd 2026

The right of David Baldacci to be identified as the
author of this work has been asserted in accordance
with the Copyright, Designs and Patents Act 1988.

All rights reserved. No part of this publication may be reproduced,
stored in a retrieval system, or transmitted, in any form, or by any means
(including, without limitation, electronic, mechanical, photocopying, recording
or otherwise) without the prior written permission of the publisher.

Pan Macmillan does not have any control over, or any responsibility for,
any author or third-party websites (including, without limitation, URLs,
emails and QR codes) referred to in or on this book.

1 3 5 7 9 8 6 4 2

A CIP catalogue record for this book is available from the British Library.

Printed and bound in the UK using 100% Renewable Electricity by CPI Group (UK) Ltd

This book is sold subject to the condition that it shall not, by way of
trade or otherwise, be lent, hired out, or otherwise circulated without
the publisher's prior consent in any form of binding or cover other than
that in which it is published and without a similar condition including this
condition being imposed on the subsequent purchaser. The publisher does not
authorize the use or reproduction of any part of this book in any manner
for the purpose of training artificial intelligence technologies or systems.
The publisher expressly reserves this book from the Text and Data Mining
exception in accordance with Article 4(3) of the European
Union Digital Single Market Directive 2019/790.

Visit **www.panmacmillan.com** to read more about
all our books and to buy them.

*To the memory of Leona Baldacci Jennings, my aunt and second mother:
You lived life big and touched the worlds of all those around you with grace and love.*

Hope Rises

CHAPTER 1

WALTER NASH WAS JOLTED AWAKE as the jet he was on en route to Hong Kong encountered some rough air. He turned to see his employer, Rhett Temple, sitting next to him.

Nash's now-alert gaze then moved to Lynn Ryder, who was asleep in a forward seat on the privately owned plane soaring westward toward Asia. Ryder was in her thirties with long white hair that was either colored or natural, he didn't know which. She was also an emissary for Victoria Steers, one of the most dangerous criminals in the world. They were currently aboard Steers's jet and were traveling to see the woman, at her behest.

He next glanced out the window and saw his image reflected back. That spurred Nash to *reflect* on his life. He used to be a mild-mannered, law-abiding business executive, tall and skinny, with no discernible muscle, a full head of hair, and nary a tattoo within a mile of him. Out of necessity Nash had shaved his head, grown facial hair, and transformed himself into a muscled and tatted fighting machine, complete with a new identity: Dillon Hope, personal security expert. No one—not even his wife, Judith—now recognized him.

He had gone from reviewing business plans and acquiring companies and flying on corporate jets, with not a whiff of intrigue or danger in his life, to playing a deadly game of cat and mouse and having to fool everyone around him into believing he really was Dillon Hope. Because he knew that Lynn Ryder and Victoria Steers wanted nothing more than to kill Walter Nash because he had been recruited by the FBI to help bring down the Steers criminal empire.

I truly am living in the upside-down world. And I seriously doubt I will ever get back to my world, if it even still exists.

He turned to Temple, the CEO of Sybaritic Investments, Nash's former employer. The man had been across the aisle when Nash first shut his eyes, and Nash wondered why he had changed seats. It was a small detail, but Nash sensed that even seemingly trivial acts clearly mattered right now.

As Dillon Hope, Nash had dexterously placed himself in a position to be employed as his old boss's personal bodyguard, without Temple having any clue as to Nash's real identity.

Speaking in the slow, deliberate tone he had adopted as Hope's voice, Nash said, "Is there a problem?"

Temple replied quietly, "Look, Dillon, it's delicate, but Victoria Steers is not...completely on the up-and-up."

"Okay," said Nash cautiously. "Meaning what exactly?"

"She's...well, dangerous. And I don't want you to slip up and get yourself in trouble when you meet her."

Nash thought it far more likely that Temple didn't want Nash to get *him* in trouble with the villainous Steers.

Though he well knew the answer, Nash asked, "Exactly how is she not on the up-and-up *and* dangerous?"

"She's into illegal drug distribution on a global scale. And she has people killed. *That's* how."

Nash stared back in feigned astonishment at his boss. "What the hell, Mr. Temple? Why is a rich guy like you involved with her?"

"It's a long story, Dillon. My father...he was working with her to recoup his fortune and he got me involved. I wish I had an out but I don't. I really don't. Trust me, I've tried."

"So she wants to meet? Why?"

Temple leaned in closer and said in a near whisper, "The FBI has tried to make some inroads at my company, finding a mole—a spy there to help them."

Nash let his jaw go slack. "The FBI! Jesus, Mr. Temple, I didn't sign up for this."

"Then you shouldn't have come," said a voice.

Both men looked up to see Ryder standing in the aisle, scowling at them. "In fact, as I made very clear, I did not want you to come."

Nash glanced at Temple before saying, "As his personal security guard, I insisted on coming because I was concerned with Mr. Temple's safety. But, frankly, I might have declined if I had known *all* the facts."

Ryder gave Temple a withering look. "And now that you have been provided *some* facts, we will see what happens when we arrive in Hong Kong." She walked back to her seat.

Temple glanced at Nash. "Dillon, I'm sorry you got caught up in all this. I really am."

He returned to his seat, where he closed his eyes and started taking deep, calming breaths.

Nash looked out the window, his heart heavy but his spirits coalescing around a possible opportunity. *Well, Nash, this might be the end of you. But if I go down, I'm taking others with me. Starting with Victoria Steers.*

CHAPTER 2

A MAN WAS WAITING FOR THEM in the airport with Lynn Ryder's name on an iPad. He led them to a large Mercedes passenger van in the parking garage. There were four men there in addition to the driver. Nash could see that all of them were armed. After their bags were loaded in they were driven off; one sturdy guard sat on either side of both Nash and Temple. They passed through a tunnel under Victoria Harbour and emerged into daylight on the other side. After negotiating a series of surface roads they reached a highrise building in the Hung Hom neighborhood, which was located in the southeast section of Kowloon Peninsula. Nash recognized the area because he had stayed nearby on a previous trip while working for Sybaritic.

The Mercedes parked in the building's underground garage, and a minute later a glass elevator was carrying them skyward.

Temple looked nervous, Ryder confident, and Nash, despite his anxiety level riding pretty high, did his best to appear calm.

The doors opened directly into an entry vestibule, where two armed men appeared. They efficiently searched Nash and Temple, and promptly confiscated Nash's two guns and both men's phones.

"I want those back," demanded Nash. However, nothing was returned.

They were escorted into a large room with floor-to-ceiling windows and sweeping views of the dazzling harbor. Ryder took a seat next to a large chair set in the center of the room, while Nash and Temple were directed to a pair of seats across from her.

Nash's gaze took in every aspect of the room, especially the armed men. What Nash was observing was not good, since he had no weapons and the exits were guarded by men who did. And he was in a foreign land that was controlled by China.

Your margin of error is basically zero.

Then she came into the room.

Prior to this Nash had seen only a photo of Victoria Steers, briefly shown to him during a meeting with the FBI. Steers was the product of a Chinese mother and an English father. Tall and lean, with long black hair and porcelain skin, Steers glided across the floor dressed in sleek dark clothing that covered all of her body except her neck, face, and hands. She carried no weapon and did not look particularly threatening, yet at her appearance every hair stood up on the back of Nash's neck. There was an aura around the woman that was undeniable; it filled Nash with a sense of foreboding that something violently destructive could happen without warning.

When he eyed Temple, Nash noted that his boss was staring at Steers with palpable fear.

Steers smiled at Ryder. "Thank you, Lynn, for all your good work."

"Of course, Ms. Steers."

Then Steers looked at Temple. "Mr. Temple, introduce me to your colleague, whom *you* insisted accompany you on this trip despite my objections."

Temple cleared his throat and said, "This is Dillon Hope, my personal bodyguard."

"Your personal *bodyguard*? Do you have something to fear, Mr. Temple?"

"Everyone has something to fear, Ms. Steers."

She glanced at Ryder before saying, "I also understand that Mr. Hope has been told some things?"

Temple's lips curled in displeasure in the face of Ryder's smug features. "He had to be told *some* things about our business, Ms. Steers. But he is a professional, and everything will be kept in the strictest confidence, I can assure you."

Steers's features turned even more stern. "You have revealed some of our *business* to a man I do not even know? You have, without question, performed an act that is *truly* unforgivable."

"I was told you had approved it," Temple added, with a sharp glance at Ryder. "And he can be a real asset to you," he added. "He's top-notch. I've seen that for myself."

"I have many *top-notch* people in my employ already, Mr. Temple. I require no others."

She slowly withdrew her searing gaze from him and swung it around to Nash. "However, Mr. Hope, now that you *are* here, it will be interesting to see if you *can* become an asset. I trust you understand all that this entails?"

"I do, Ms. Steers," Nash said in a casual tone, although every muscle in his body was tensed in the face of her threatening phrasing.

If I can just reach the man who took my guns...

As though she were reading Nash's mind, Steers held out her hand. One of the guards produced a Glock nine-mill and placed it in her palm. She gripped it, checked the mag, and racked the slide, loading a bullet.

As she looked at them Temple went rigid in his chair, and Nash felt his butt cheeks involuntarily clench.

"A good choice in a personal sidearm, Mr. Hope," she said. "However, I prefer a Norinco NP42 Mini. But then again, I like to buy local."

"The Chinese also make good weapons," Nash said.

"Indeed they do. They made *me*, after all. I also understand that three of my people are now in the custody of the FBI. That is a decided setback that I find unacceptable. Accountability must be served."

At this abrupt segue, Temple glanced anxiously at Ryder and blurted out, "I had *nothing* to do with that. That was not my call. I argued against it, in fact."

Steers said menacingly, "You disavow all responsibility for this debacle? Is that really what you are telling me?"

Temple sputtered, "I didn't mean...I just wanted to point out that…" He glanced at Ryder and saw her smug look deepen even as he squirmed.

Before he could say anything else, Steers raised the pistol, causing Temple to put up his hands and flinch backward. Nash prepared to leap at the woman before she could fire.

Steers then pointed the gun to her left, pulled the trigger, and shot Ryder in the head. The woman fell to the floor, blood and other bits of her spraying all over her clothing and white hair. Some of the blowback also dotted Steers's cheek, hand, and sleeve. One of the guards hustled forward and used a wet cloth to thoroughly clean her off. Two other men rushed in, wrapped Ryder in plastic, and carried her out. The chair in which she had been sitting was also removed and the marble floor underneath the chair thoroughly mopped. Temple and Nash sat there, stunned, while Steers had her eyes closed.

When all traces of the woman had been removed, Steers opened her eyes and studied the two men.

"Death can be awkward," she said quietly. "And unpleasant."

"Yes, it can," said Nash evenly, though he felt sickened.

"And also *necessary*," Steers added. She looked at Temple. "Decisions that led to my agents being in the custody of the FBI are… not… good."

"No," agreed Temple quickly. He still looked horrified by what had just happened.

Steers once more turned to Nash. "I trust that you understand the implications of what has just transpired, Mr. Hope?"

Nash said cautiously, "You mean Ryder's death?"

She shook her head. "You disappoint me. I thought it rather obvious." She held up the pistol. "You and your weapon have just committed a terrible crime in Hong Kong. And though Hong Kong does not have the death penalty, China does. It is done by lethal injection, or else they shoot you." She handed the gun to one of her men. "That choice will be theirs. But you also have a choice to make." She glanced at Temple. "And as an accessory, Mr. Temple, your fate will not be much better: life in prison. But again, you have a choice as well."

"You mean we can *choose* to work with you?" Nash said grimly.

She shook her head once more. "To work *for* me."

"And if we refuse?" said Nash, already knowing the answer.

"Then steps will be taken to demonstrate that my colleague's murder occurred in China, and all necessary evidence to implicate both of you in her death will be provided. The rest is assuredly known to you. One of you will be executed, and the other will spend his life in a Chinese prison." She added coolly, "I think I would prefer death, actually. The Chinese are often not kind to their own law-abiding citizens. And they are completely ruthless with respect to their criminals." She glanced at Temple. "And Americans in particular are not at all popular in China at present."

"To work for you doing what exactly, Ms. Steers?" asked Temple in a tremulous voice.

Nash thought he knew the answer. But it would turn out that he could not have been further from the truth.

She said, "My mother is being held in a prison in another country. And you both are going to help set her free."

CHAPTER 3

WALTER NASH STARED UP FROM his bed at a ceiling that was a frothy shade of seafoam green. It was so calming and neutral that he almost forgot he was in Hong Kong and that his life was in serious peril.

Almost.

It was two in the morning local time. He had been asleep for only three hours and now was wide awake. And it had nothing to do with jet lag. The reason was two floors above him in the penthouse, where, he assumed, Victoria Steers was sleeping just fine in *her* bed.

Nash had no idea what they'd done with Ryder's body, but he was certain that if he didn't do what Steers wanted him to do, he would be taken to China and charged with Ryder's murder.

But rescue her mother from a prison in another country? How the hell are we supposed to do that?

Yet he had one thing going for him: His Army veteran father had had an unstoppable motor, powering through every obstacle to reach his goals under the most hellish of conditions. And though he and his father had been estranged for over half of Nash's life, he had apparently inherited this attribute from him.

He listened for sounds from the adjacent bedroom where he knew Temple was sleeping. His boss had mentioned he was looking for an exit from this nightmare with Steers. However, Nash thought it far more likely that they would both leave Hong Kong in body bags.

But her mother being in a prison did answer the question of where Masuyo Steers had been all this time.

His thoughts next turned to his wife, Judith. She was in FBI protective custody after Nash had saved her life from Steers's killers. Judith had initially believed he had sexually abused and then killed their daughter, Maggie, until the FBI had released proof that he had been framed. This was a plan that Steers had come up with to destroy Nash's relationship with the FBI, who had recruited him to help bring down Steers's criminal empire.

Well, I might have a new goal now that is not aligned with the FBI's.

Killing Victoria Steers. And if I get the chance I need to take it. So my being here so close to the woman might be a good thing.

He slept fitfully for a few hours, rose from his bed, showered, changed into a clean set of clothes, and joined Temple in the small kitchen, where a breakfast had been laid out by a woman who never made eye contact or spoke a word. Both men ate their meals in silence, lost in their own dismal thoughts.

After Temple finished his coffee he said, "Jesus, I can't believe she just shot Ryder like that. And she seemed to *like* her. So God help us."

"You ever see her kill someone before?" Nash asked.

"I heard her order someone to be killed. And I've seen some of her *handiwork*."

"Don't know how you kept all that to yourself, Mr. Temple. Although I guess you had no choice."

"Look, Dillon, like I said before, I'm sorry you got sucked into this."

"I sort of insisted, Mr. Temple. Although I have to say I didn't foresee this."

"I...I never should have come, either. I should have run for it. But Steers would have found me. And she would have killed my stepmother, Mindy, and her kid, and my siblings, too. My father took the easy way out by jumping off his balcony."

Nash strongly suspected that Temple had killed his father, Barton Temple, but that didn't matter right now. Maybe one day the son would be held accountable for his father's death if he had indeed murdered him. But right now Nash needed to worry about himself.

One small misstep and his cover might be blown. He had done well up to this point in keeping the truth from Temple. But with Steers on the scene, tomorrow was simply another day to make a critical mistake. And then he would be dead.

"Any idea who the hell her mother is?" he asked.

Nash actually knew some things about the woman, only because the FBI had filled him in. But the extent of his intel was limited, and he wanted to know whatever else the other man did.

Temple said, "Steers has never mentioned her parents to me, but I found out some details from other sources. Her mother's name is Masuyo. Her husband was a Navy guy from England who stayed in Japan after he got out of the service. He wasn't any sort of criminal, at least I don't think so. But Masuyo had the connections, brains, and cunning that pushed the empire she created to a truly global level." Temple paused and then said, in a resigned voice, "You should know that Steers killed all her siblings in order to take over the business in some sort of survivor's contest. I mean, how sick is that?"

"She mentioned turning us in to the Chinese. Is she tight with them?"

"I don't know for sure," said Temple. "But I do know she's dangerous and all the guys who work for her could kill us with their pinkies."

Nash suddenly thought of something he should have before. He rose, grabbed a piece of paper and pen from a drawer, wrote something on the paper, and slid it across to Temple. When the man read it, he looked up, utterly terrified.

Nash had just suggested that the apartment was bugged. He said, "I guess we just wait until she tells us the plan."

"Right," said Temple as he tore the paper into strips and threw them into the trash. Then he put his face in his hands and moaned.

A knock on the apartment door a minute later caused both of them to jump.

"I guess it's time," said Nash.

CHAPTER

4

They were once more seated across from Steers in her penthouse. Nash found his eyes wandering to the spot where Lynn Ryder had died and felt some sympathy for the woman, even though she probably would have cheered if he had been the one to perish.

Getting your humanity back, Nash? Don't. It won't be useful now because no one around you has any.

His gaze finally landed on Steers, and he had to fight the urge to try to strangle her.

Steers said, "Gentlemen, what I am about to divulge will show the faith that I am placing in each of you. This mission that you will undertake is delicate and dangerous, but the rewards for each of you will be...enticing."

Nash thought the woman had an oddly formal way of speaking. But he assumed that Mandarin had been her first language, or perhaps Japanese. The FBI had told him that Masuyo, while she had purportedly been Japanese and had met her husband there, had actually been an agent of the Chinese Communist Party, and had been sent to Japan to undermine its democratic institutions.

Nash said, "We're listening."

Steers closed her eyes for a moment. When she opened them they seemed, to Nash, to sparkle with an ethereal force.

"My mother is Masuyo Steers. She is currently being held in a private prison facility in an isolated region in Myanmar near the Chinese border."

"A *private* prison in Myanmar?" said Temple. "I didn't know there was such a thing."

She gave him a superior look. "You and your father traveled extensively in what was then Burma."

"How did you know that?" said Temple in surprise.

"I always know what I need to know. And your father worked for me. I elicited this information from him because I knew it might be useful one day. And so it has become. Now enlighten me as to what you *do* know about the country."

Temple glanced at Nash. "That it's a very unstable place. I wanted to travel there last year on business. Like you just said, I'd been there with my father a number of times, when it was still called Burma. I even became passable in the language. But then Covid hit, and the State Department strongly advised Americans not to travel there because of the junta's coup and the presence of armed militia and insurgents. It's a chaotic hotbed with lots of different factions asserting authority over a patchwork of territories and cities. A real mess."

"Doubtless, you will not be surprised to learn that I am also aware of all that, Mr. Temple," said Steers. "But it is good that you are as well and have familiarity with the language. This will increase the odds of successfully bringing my mother home safely and was also the reason I constructed this plan with your involvement."

Steers now made a point of turning to Nash. "However, while your employer has some value to this mission and has long worked for me, you must think it somewhat curious that I would engage *you*, Mr. Hope, whom I know not at all, with the task of freeing my mother from her incarceration."

"Well, you can pin a murder rap on us. And we're in a foreign country, totally in your control. Our only chance of getting out of this alive is to do all we can to succeed in freeing your mother. I assume *that* is why you're entrusting *both* of us with this mission. It's not like we have a choice."

"I must congratulate you, Mr. Temple," said Steers.

"For what?"

"Your judgment in selecting bodyguards."

She said to Nash, "Lynn Ryder informed me that you had saved Mr. Temple and a friend from grievous bodily harm."

"I can hold my own and I did my job, yes."

"Good, because I believe that your skill set will be required. I will now explain in detail."

CHAPTER 5

"My mother has been imprisoned for many years now," began Steers.

"Why?" asked Nash. "What crimes did she commit?"

Steers said dismissively, "She has broken no laws. She is a political prisoner."

Temple said, "So she's a political prisoner of the Myanmar government? What did she do for them to imprison her?"

Steers said sharply, "That is *not* relevant. And the prison is not run by the government; it is private, as I said. Nor is it controlled by the various rebel groups."

"Then who does control it?" asked Nash.

"Again, irrelevant to the mission. What matters is my mother is not in good health, and I will not allow her to remain there."

Nash said, "I'm sure you have highly skilled people to do this for you."

"I have people who are well-known to the people from whom we will be extracting my mother. Whereas, you both are *unknown* to them, which makes you particularly useful to its success."

"Just so it's clear, I would do anything to help you, Ms. Steers," said Temple. "But two Americans trying to free your mother from what I assume is a heavily guarded prison in a hostile land in Asia does not seem a recipe for success."

"It's all in the details, Mr. Temple. I have thought through every conceivable possibility and have arrived at a bold plan that I believe represents the best opportunity for my mother's freedom. And you *both* will be critical to that success." She glanced at Nash. "At first, I was only going to allow Mr. Temple to journey there, Mr. Hope. But when Mr. Temple insisted you come, I queried Lynn Ryder and, as I alluded to before, she told me of your... strengths. I was intrigued, and thus here you are as well. I trust you will not disappoint me."

"And when do you plan on our executing this mission?" asked Nash.

"Very soon. Ideally, we would have more time, but there is nothing ideal about the situation. Thus, you both will have to learn most of what you need on the ground in Myanmar."

"This prison?" began Nash. "I assume you have someone on the inside who will help with the extraction?"

"You are thinking at a level which I appreciate, Mr. Hope. Yes, I do have someone on the inside. Otherwise, the plan would have little chance of success."

"How far is the prison from here?" asked Nash.

"Normally, the flight time is around four hours, but commercial service is not reliable and in some regions completely unavailable. The airspace around the prison is tightly restricted. And the junta, which now controls less than half the country, has taken to bombing the parts held by rebel factions. So it is decidedly risky on all levels. Thus, you will work your way to the prison from points north, where you will be initially dropped."

"Points north!" exclaimed Temple. "But to the north of Myanmar is China. And I don't think going across that border is a good idea."

"China is not the only country to the north of Myanmar, Mr. Temple," she chided. "I would have expected you to know this with your many trips to that part of the world."

"So we enter from the north and make our way south to the region where the prison is located?" said Nash. "How long will that take?"

"A week, at the very least. And you must ingratiate yourself with the people there using the cover provided by others in Myanmar who are working for me on this."

"And how do we do that?" asked Nash.

"Simply put, Mr. Temple is a businessman seeking commercial opportunities, which will work to his strengths. And you, of course, Mr. Hope, will be his personal bodyguard, which will be a natural fit for your skill set. Despite its political and governing challenges, and the hostilities unfolding across the country, Myanmar is opening up more to foreign trade. Locals engaged by me will be there to help you on your way."

"And what about my company, Sybaritic?" asked Temple. "I told them I was taking some time off and I'd check in periodically, but still, I can't just disappear for long periods."

"All in good time, Mr. Temple. My mother's welfare comes before all other things."

"And the enticing rewards you mentioned if we do succeed?" said Nash.

Steers turned her gaze to him. "You get to live, of course."

CHAPTER 6

Back in their apartment they found books and maps and other information on Myanmar with a note from Steers telling them to go through the material thoroughly.

Temple said scornfully, "Great, we're back in high school." He glanced at the sliding door leading to a small balcony overlooking Hong Kong, and motioned toward it.

Outside, the noises of the large metropolis cascaded over the men. They watched in silence as an Emirates A380 jet drifted by in preparation for landing at the nearby Hong Kong International Airport. They had left the door open and positioned a small clock radio near the door with the sound turned up high to cover their conversation in case there were bugging devices out here as well.

"I don't trust the woman any farther than I can throw her," muttered Temple as he leaned on the balcony and studied the cityscape below. "You believe her mother really is in a prison in Myanmar?"

"If she has an inside person, why not deploy a well-trained extraction team to do the job quickly and precisely, instead of us slowly making our way there?"

"Does she want her mother to die? And us along with her?"

Nash shook his head. "Why not just leave her in prison then? And if she wants us dead, she doesn't need an elaborate scheme to do so. Bang bang and we're done."

"Then she really must want her mother out of there. So I guess we're headed to Myanmar on an impossible mission," Temple said miserably.

They went back inside, where Nash started to go through the

materials left for them. Temple, however, walked past all of that and headed to his bedroom.

Nash called after him, "Hey, it would be a good idea if we knew some of this stuff."

"Yeah, brief me when you're done."

Nash shook his head and settled down to his *studies*.

Later that night, as he went to his room, Nash thought, *I've done the impossible up to this point. Maybe I can do it one more time.*

But then another thought occurred to him.

Why wait?

CHAPTER

7

IN PREVIOUS BUSINESS NEGOTIATIONS WHERE the outcome was anything but certain, Nash had sometimes sought to throw a scare into the other side, to get them thinking about things they could not completely control. Well, the time had come for him to do that here.

He opened the exterior door of their apartment. There was no one there. He walked toward the elevator at the end of the hall, and that was when two men appeared. They were both around five ten and wiry. He could see the bumps of the guns in their shoulder holsters as they walked toward him. He knew if he attempted to leave the floor these twin guards would not allow it. And he had no interest in fighting that battle, which he would undoubtedly lose.

"I'd like to talk to Ms. Steers," said Nash.

"What about?" said one.

"It's for her to hear only. But it's important. Very important to the reason we've been brought here by your boss."

Nash said this authoritatively and kept eye contact with the man.

"Stay here," the guard said. He moved away and pulled out his phone.

A minute later he came back and nodded at Nash. "This way."

He was led into the elevator and up to the top floor of the building. Steers was waiting for him in a small room. The walls and floor were dark in color and the light subdued to the point of near blackness. It was very unsettling at first, but the longer he was there the more calming the surroundings became.

The room had no chairs or other furniture, only tatami mats, and pillows and small colorful balls. The smell of incense tickled his nostrils. The man left him there alone with Steers, who sat in a lotus pose on one of the mats. Her eyes were closed, but she said, "Sit, Mr. Hope."

Nash sat across from her, his limber joints allowing him to easily duplicate her position.

She opened her eyes, observed this, and said, "You are a practitioner of qigong perhaps?"

"No, but I try to stay flexible. You live longer that way." He eyed her intently as he said these last words.

"That, of course, remains to be seen," she shot back. "And what do you want at this late hour?" she said, shutting her eyes once more.

"Just to be clear, I speak for myself, not on behalf of Mr. Temple."

She nodded. "Go on."

"I obviously came into this situation late in the game. I don't have the history with Mr. Temple that you seem to."

"Agreed. You do *not*."

"But he is my employer, and my duty is to keep him safe to the extent that I can."

"And your point?" she prompted, sounding impatient.

He looked at her long neck and his fingers tensed. He knew her guards were just outside, but Shock had shown him how to do it: prevent the target from calling out, then break the neck at the C1 or C2 vertebra. He edged a bit closer.

"Your point?" she said again, opening her eyes and perhaps, in his mind, noting his slightly closer proximity to her. She called out in what he recognized as Japanese.

A moment later the door opened and the same two men appeared, watching them closely, pistols in hand.

In that moment Nash realized that he had lost the opportunity to kill the woman. But that was the short game. The smart game was bringing her to justice and destroying her empire.

And you have to play it smart, Nash, no matter how much you want to end her life now, to avenge Maggie.

His gaze met hers. "So even if we are successful in rescuing your mother from this prison, you really have no incentive to let us go, or let us live, despite your words to the contrary."

She stared at him in a way that was deeply unnerving. But Nash had no time to let this intimidate him. This was a negotiation, and whether you were haggling over money or property—or your life—the principal framework remained the same: Your position was only as strong as what you could offer in return.

"So?" she said, no longer appearing to be in a meditative mood.

"Well, as you can understand, I'm sure, that matters to me and my boss."

"Once you stepped on my plane, Mr. Hope, you put yourself under my complete control. You do not strike me as a stupid or rash man, quite the opposite, so surely you know this. There is nothing you can say or do that will influence me one way or the other. I think you came here to negotiate. But one needs at least a single card in their hand to do that." She eyed his empty ones. "You clearly lack that."

This next part was tricky, and Nash had to play it to absolute perfection or he might not walk out of this room alive.

"I believe, if you think about it, Ms. Steers, there is a flaw in your plan."

"Such as?" she demanded sharply.

"We *do* have some control over the process. And if certain events occur, we will have more still."

"What events?"

But Nash had already risen from the lotus position and was now staring down at her. It actually felt good to be looking down on the woman who had had his daughter kidnapped and then murdered.

Deep breaths, Nash. Four in, hold for four, four out, hold for four. Repeat. Your chance will come to avenge Maggie.

This was a breathing technique his father had taught him when, as a child, Nash had been riddled with anxiety. The technique almost always worked, and it did at this moment as well.

He said calmly, "It would be foolish on my part, you would agree, if I were to explain in greater detail. Otherwise, you would immediately work to correct this flaw." He bowed. "I wish you a good night, Ms. Steers."

He turned and walked to the door, where the two men escorted him back to his apartment. He lay in his bed and stared at that ceiling painted seafoam green, wondering if what he had just done had worked. Or had sealed his and Temple's deaths.

It might be both. And maybe I'm okay with that so long as Victoria Steers goes down, too. So next time you have the chance to kill her, for God's sake take it.

CHAPTER 8

The next morning they were summoned to a room where Steers stood in front of a laptop with a projection screen hanging on the wall behind it. She motioned them to chairs.

"I am now going to explain the logistics of the mission to you."

She picked up a remote and clicked a button. An image appeared on the screen: It was video of a prison complex seen from an overhead shot.

"This is the facility where my mother is being held. It is roughly halfway between the towns of Katha and Bhamo, the latter of which is only forty miles from the Chinese border. Katha is in the Sagaing Region, while Bhamo is located in the Kachin State. Both towns lie along the Irrawaddy River."

"Who operates the prison?" asked Nash, his eyes on the double security fences, concrete block walls, armed sentries, and guard dogs set against a flattened landscape with absolutely no cover.

"I told you before that that is irrelevant," Steers said severely.

"Okay, how do we get there?" asked Nash.

"As is obvious, you must first get into the country. Once inside, travel for foreigners is...difficult, as I mentioned before."

Steers hit the remote and another screen appeared; she pointed to a spot on it.

"Myanmar is bordered on the northeast by China, but it shares a border on the north*west* with India and Bangladesh." She glanced at Temple. "Which answers your confusion about only China being to the north of Myanmar. There are two official border crossings through India that are open and do not require permits for foreign travelers." She tapped two spots on the screen. "Tamu and Moreh there, and Rikhawdar and Zokhawthar to the south, there. Moreh is considered the gateway to Southeast Asia and is the main point of exporting goods from India to Myanmar. You would traverse the Friendship Bridge at that point."

"But we don't want to enter at an official border crossing, do we?" asked Nash.

She glanced at him again, her expression unreadable. "No. Besides other problems, you receive only a day pass and must return by four thirty. Thus, neither Moreh nor the other location will work."

She clicked the remote and another picture came up.

"Now, 120 kilometers inside the Myanmar border from India is a place called Shingbwiyang. During the Second World War it was located within the China Burma India Theater, and consequently an airbase and runway were built here." She placed her finger on this spot. "It is lightly populated. You will fly from here to India to a location near the border with Myanmar. And then you will travel from India to Shingbwiyang, where the runway, with my secret funding, has been recently upgraded to accept a small private jet. The junta allows me to fly into this airspace for my 'business.' However, this time they will not know what my business is.

"You will be met there by two men whom you will stay with overnight. They will then drive you to a second location, where you will be met by three people. Their names are Thura, Zeya, and Amrita. Your initial destination is Myitkyina. Roads and trains are not really viable at the current time, too many checkpoints and other issues. And there are no flights available that will work."

"So how do we do it?" asked Nash.

She turned back to the screen and indicated a route with a laser pointer. "You will go overland across very rugged terrain along this path. Your guides are experienced with the lay of the land and will deal with the people that you may encounter. This part will take several days via dirt bikes, horseback, and walking."

"Horseback?" exclaimed Nash.

"You do not ride?" she said, a touch of amusement in her expression.

"No, I never have."

"The guides will give you all the help you require." She looked at Temple. "And you?"

"I can ride." He looked at Nash. "I was on the polo team at the country club college my old man got me into."

"Of course you were," said Nash dryly.

Steers said, "The guides will get you to Myitkyina, where you will hold meetings with local businessmen who are interested in exporting their goods to America. You will be fully briefed on this before leaving Hong Kong."

"Look, do we really have to waste time playing this *businessman* subterfuge?" said Temple. "It'll just allow mistakes to be made."

"On the contrary, it will allow you and Mr. Hope to avoid death. Two Americans traveling straight through to a highly restricted prison complex? You will be dead before you have any chance at all. The groundwork must be laid, gentlemen. The area you will be in is fraught with peril. The junta is not in control of the Kachin State, where both Myitkyina, the capital, and the prison are located. The KIA, the Kachin Independence Army, commenced its operations against the junta a few years ago. As a result KIA has taken back great swaths of land in the region, and also gained control of military bases and most of the police stations.

"The junta's Border Guard Force is now in tatters after this offensive. Of course the junta did not take this lightly, and they conducted bombing raids among some of the villages there. But the KIA and its allies pressed on, and they have largely driven the junta out of the region. But the junta's army, the Tatmadaw, is still a formidable force."

"So the KIA controls the prison?" asked Nash.

"I did not say that, did I?"

"Well, do they or don't they?" said Temple irritably.

"It is not a yes-or-no question," she replied smoothly before moving on. "The KIA are not fools, and even though you will enter the country in secret, do not think that your presence will remain unknown for long. But if we give you roles that could actually help the Kachin State economy, which they desperately need? Your odds of success are enhanced and there will be no suspicion about you traveling in the direction of the prison complex. Now, after your meetings in Myitkyina, you will fly to Bhamo. It is a short trip on Myanmar National Airlines, which still operates in the region because the KIA allows it."

"Won't traveling by plane raise uncomfortable questions?" said Temple.

"Not after your positioning as an American businessman has been established. Now, once in Bhamo you will be met at the airport by more of my operatives, and driven to the *vicinity* of the prison. There all of you will be met by another group of my associates."

"And then what do we do?" asked Temple, looking incredulous. "Jump the fence, fight off the guards and dogs, punch through concrete, snatch your mother, and, what, fly away like birds?"

"All in good time, Mr. Temple. I am giving you the big picture only at this point. *After* you secure my mother, you will travel south to Lashio, which is the largest town in the northern region of the Shan State, and which sits on a low mountain spur overlooking the Yaw River Valley. The population there is roughly 130,000, which will allow you to more easily blend in. Those seeking you for liberating my mother will almost certainly believe that you will attempt to take a river ferry from Bhamo to Mandalay, which is the most obvious initial escape route out of the country, but it takes a great deal of time."

"Are there no roads that we could take via car?" asked Nash.

"All surface roads in that part of the region are in deplorable condition, but the ferries are available, both slow and fast. But, as I just said, they will know this, and thus will commence their search on all boat traffic. But you will be transported from Lashio to Mandalay far more quickly than a ferry ride would provide. Mandalay is a city of over one million persons with an international-grade airport. Thus, while they are still looking for you on the water, you will be on a private plane and heading back here."

"Who will be looking for us?" asked Nash. "If the prison is in the Kachin State, will it be the KIA? But will they be able to pursue us into junta-controlled regions?"

She once more studied him with...fascination, thought Nash.

"It matters little who will be after you, Mr. Hope. Their goal will be to kill you and retake my mother. You will have the necessary monies, human support, and logistical wherewithal to be successful, I am confident."

"The only thing you haven't mentioned is how do we get in and out of the prison with your mother," said Nash. "And that's the most important part of the plan."

The next screen she brought up held the image of a heavyset man in a drab uniform.

"He is the principal guard of my mother. And this," she said in a reverent tone, "is Masuyo-san."

She clicked the remote and a picture of a woman in a gray sackcloth dress appeared. Masuyo Steers looked beaten down and exhausted to Nash, but when he focused on the woman's penetrating eyes, even as depicted in lusterless pixels, she appeared far more formidable.

"Is this guard your inside man?" asked Nash.

She nodded. "He is doing it simply for the money. That is the extent of his loyalty, but since it represents a treasure for both him and his family, we can count on him doing everything to make the situation successful."

"And the extraction plan?" prompted Nash.

"It is known there that my mother is not in good health. She will suffer a serious condition that cannot be dealt with by simply taking her to the medical unit at the prison. An ambulance will be ordered to take her to a nearby hospital. The ambulance will never reach that hospital with Masuyo-san inside. It will be overtaken and my mother will be transferred to another mode of transportation."

"And where do we come in?" asked Temple.

"You will be part of the group that overtakes the ambulance.

You will be with Masuyo-san when she leaves the country and comes back here. That is why I gave you no details on breaking into the prison, which would have been impossible. Now, of course, the ambulance will have guards. They will need to be quickly overcome and left unable to communicate afterward."

"You mean we're supposed to kill them?" said Nash.

"Not necessarily. If they can be bound in such a way that they cannot free themselves for at least two hours. But if there is no other way..." She didn't need to finish the statement.

She continued. "It is a one-hour-and-twelve-minute drive to the hospital. The overtaking of the ambulance will take place fifteen minutes into the journey at a particularly isolated spot. That means you will have just under an hour to leave the area before the hospital will contact the prison about the ambulance not arriving."

"Unless someone gets off a communication between the time the ambulance is ambushed and the time all of them are subdued," pointed out Nash.

"That is one of the risks, yes," conceded Steers. "But I believe that our plan of ambush will be so effective that no such opportunity will present itself."

"Can you tell us what that ambush plan is?" asked Nash.

She glanced at him. "You do not need to know that. Others will take care of those details. *Your* mission is to accompany my mother back here."

"Okay, but what is the transportation conveyance we will be on with your mother?" asked Nash. "I assume we need to know *that*."

"You will be picked up by a helicopter at a spot approximately a mile south of the ambush site. There a road intersects and you will turn left onto that road. The chopper will be waiting at a clearing a few hundred yards down. That is the much faster travel option I mentioned. This will all take place at night, of course. The assault team will already be in place to stop the ambulance, which is why you do not require knowledge of the actual ambush plan. The chopper will fly you and my mother to Lashio. The distance is roughly 160 miles. The chopper can easily do that in one hour and twenty minutes. A car will be waiting for you in Lashio and will take you to Mandalay, which is a 120-mile trip and on good roads. That car journey will take no more than two and one half hours. There a private jet will be waiting. You will be wheels up within ten minutes of arrival."

Nash said, "But why not have the chopper take us directly from the ambush site to Mandalay? I've studied the maps and other materials on Myanmar you provided us." He quickly calculated the distance and time in his head. "It's less than two hundred air miles. Your chopper could easily do that in less than two hours. We'll be wheels up in Mandalay and out of Myanmar in half the time you just cited."

"Very good, Mr. Hope, you show initiative and attention to detail. However, nothing is easy in Myanmar after the coup and the war that is currently going on between the junta and the various rebel factions. And the fact is that they will be searching for my mother immediately after the hospital notifies the prison of the ambulance not arriving. That will be less than one hour after your escape with my mother. They will immediately take steps to lock down all of the airports and ferries."

"Which makes it all the more critical that we are out of the country as quickly as possible," countered Nash. "They'll close Mandalay Airport for sure. And even if it takes us only two hours to get there by chopper rather than by car, which is your plan, they'll still have shut down the airport in *Mandalay* before that. So how the hell do we get out?"

"I didn't say you were flying out of *Mandalay* Airport, did I?" she said.

"You said we were driving to Mandalay and that it had an international-level airport!" retorted Temple, glancing at Nash.

"Mandalay is a large city, Mr. Temple. With a wide footprint, but, again, during World War II there were improvements made to further the movement of Japanese troops and equipment. A bit of additional clandestine enhancement on my part has made that long-ago improvement valuable once more."

Nash said immediately, "You mean another runway?"

She nodded, looking impressed. "One that the junta knows nothing about."

"But why not still have the chopper take us straight there? It will save time all around."

"A helicopter coming into Mandalay airspace at that hour will raise immediate suspicion. It will direct the authorities to the nearby airstrip and you will all be arrested."

"But it will be impossible to miss a jet lifting into the air," countered Nash.

"The runway does not appear on their airspace grid. And even if they detect the plane, it will be impossible to shoot it down at a moment's notice," said Steers. "For that you need certain equipment that is not currently in the vicinity of Mandalay, or so my high-level contacts tell me. And Myanmar is not a large country. By the time they scramble whatever aircraft they can, you will be outside of their airspace and in another sovereign's jurisdiction. And while my mother is important to some, she is *not* important enough to incite an international incident."

"But whoever operates the prison *is* important enough to the junta's and/or the KIA's interests," noted Nash. "Otherwise, why would they allow it to operate there?"

"You display an awareness of strategic elements that mildly surprises me, Mr. Hope."

"I guarded VIPs, Ms. Steers. People who were intimately involved in the world you are describing. I would be dull indeed not to have absorbed as much of that as I could."

She tapped the remote against her long leg and continued to watch him intently. Nash could feel his pulse spike and sweat accumulate in his armpits simply from the woman's glare.

"You leave in two days. If you bring my mother back safely, then you will have fulfilled your part of the bargain."

"And if we fail to save your mother?" said Temple.

"Then my people will bring you back from Myanmar and you both will be turned over to the Chinese government for the appalling murder of Lynn Ryder." She eyed each man in turn. "The Chinese do not dawdle when it comes to such crimes. It will not take years like it does in your country. It will take weeks. So I strongly recommend that you do...not...fail."

CHAPTER 9

Only one night later Nash was in his bed asleep when strong hands seized him and something was placed over his mouth and nose. A few seconds later he fell unconscious.

When he awoke he was lying on the floor in a darkened room, spreadeagled and bound to steel rings set into the floor, so he could not move. As his eyes adjusted to the darkened conditions and his senses began working normally, Nash jerked when Victoria Steers said, "Hello, Mr. Hope. Thank you for joining me."

"I didn't have much of a choice," he replied tightly.

She ran her eyes over his bare chest. "You are to be congratulated on your obvious physical discipline. And your skin art runs the spectrum from ordinary to...interesting."

Nash had had the scales of justice tattooed on his chest, a roaring lion on his back, a dragon running from his right delt down his arm to the back of his hand, medieval shields across both thighs, and one large die on each of his calves. She let her fingers dance over his shaved head. "This is the truly interesting one. The kinks in the chain? What is the meaning?"

Running from earlobe to earlobe and over the crown of his head was a long chain, kinked in three separate places equidistant from one another into a fairly indistinctive shape, but one that he knew to be a heart.

He cleared his throat. "Honor, devotion, and sacrifice."

This was a lie. But he could not tell her the truth without giving up a clue as to his real identity. They actually symbolized him, his wife, and his now-dead daughter.

Steers bent forward and let her long hair drift into his face. It smelled pleasantly of lavender and coconut. But he turned his head to the side.

Steers looked amused. "You do not like to be touched?"

"Not after being taken from my bed, knocked out, and bound, no."

She stood over him, straddling his body. He could see she had on a long white robe that covered her completely. Not knowing what was going to happen, but suspecting something truly unpleasant was about to occur, Nash closed his eyes.

"Open your eyes, Mr. Hope," she said softly.

When he didn't she put a bare foot on his crotch and started to press.

As it became more and more painful, he finally opened his eyes and was surprised that she had only drawn up the sleeves of her robe.

Seeing his look she said derisively, "Did you really think I would take off my clothes for *you*?"

"I..." But then he focused on her arms and drew in a quick breath. They were covered in what looked to be long-healed burns now cast as ripples of twisted flesh. When she turned, and lowered her robe to her waist, he saw that her back, too, had been burned in sections; the flesh was raw and looked exceedingly painful.

She covered herself and turned back around to face him. "This is *my* skin art, of a sort, although I did not choose to have this done, as did you yours. Tell me, Mr. Hope, what do you see in what I have just shown you?"

"I...see someone who has obviously suffered greatly."

Nash now believed that Steers might have been on the plane owned by the Steers family that had crashed, and perhaps killed her father. If true, he couldn't even contemplate how she had survived, or handled the pain. And then he thought of her meditation. The way she moved, slowly and gracefully. Had she the mental willpower to make the pain, if not go away, at least subside to a manageable level? She did not strike him as one who would control pain with medication, because that would mean Steers had to rely on some artificial means, when it was clear she preferred to rely only on herself.

If she has such mental strength, she is even more formidable than I thought.

She gazed down at her arms. "This was once something of significance to me, but no longer. I was advised to have operations, to cleanse myself of...it. To return to my normal self, or as normal as possible. But though some medical attention was required, I decided to let it mostly...lie, as it were. As a remembrance."

"Of what?"

"Of *defeat*, Mr. Hope. It is quite powerful. But if you hold it only up here," she added, touching her temple, "that memory will fade. And you may even convince yourself it did not actually occur because the mind, the ego, does not like to dwell on personal defeat. And thus you forget your failures, your vulnerabilities, and become weaker, not stronger. But I will never forget, because I see this failure of mine every time I look at myself." She turned her gaze to him. "What do you think of my logic?"

Nash chose his words carefully. "I think it is...unique. But I don't think many people would have the...strength to carry this reminder with them so...viscerally."

She ran her hand over the damaged skin on her right arm. "Most people are not me."

"We are in complete agreement on that."

"Do you know what I see when I look at you?" she asked, meeting his gaze once more.

"No."

Steers cocked her head slightly and her disappointment in his rushed response was clear to Nash, as were her subsequent words.

"A quick answer that is wrong, is as wrong as an incorrect answer delivered after substantial delay," she noted.

He collected his thoughts and an answer occurred to him with startling clarity. It was as though Nash and Steers were suddenly operating on intermingled wavelengths. That could be an advantage in all this, he knew. Yet it also rattled Nash that he could even approach thinking along the same lines as this woman.

He said slowly, and in a measured tone, "Your whole life is about understanding and thus controlling everyone you come into contact with. And yet in me you see only an...*enigma*."

She studied him for a long moment. "Much better, Mr. Hope." She glanced at her arm. "You are perhaps repulsed by my injuries?" she said.

"What does it matter what I am? I am nothing to you."

She stared at him as though he were a fascinating beast behind zoo bars. "If I cannot comprehend you, Mr. Hope, I can at least own you. That is something, is it not? Perhaps more important in the end."

He left this comment unanswered simply because he wanted to. And in that, at least to Nash's thinking, was conclusive proof that she did *not own* him.

"Is that why you brought me here?" he said instead. "To dispose of an...unwelcome mystery? So does that mean I'm not going on the trip to free your mother?"

"I have committed to your participation, and I never go back once committed."

"So where does that leave us?" he asked.

"It leaves me still wondering, Mr. Hope, and it leaves you with this."

Steers picked up a knife from the floor. She said, "I will not ruin your lovely dragon, as I am partial to them myself."

She squatted and placed the tip of the knife near his left wrist and proceeded to walk it up his arm, careful not to sink the blade too deeply or hit an artery or a large vein. She kept her focus on her work, but when she was finished, with the end of the incision right below Nash's shoulder capsule, she moved herself squarely back over his torso and looked him in the eyes, her expression impressed.

"You barely flinched," she said breathily, from the effort of slicing him. To Nash, her gaze now held the conflicting emotions of disappointment and admiration.

Nash, in truth, had known what she was going to do to him, because the FBI had warned him that Steers sometimes sliced up her underlings, including, probably, Rhett Temple.

While the blade had bitten into him Nash had held the mental image of a painting he had seen in Rhett Temple's home back in America, depicting a young girl and a dog running in a field. During a conversation Temple had been having with a detective concerning his daughter Maggie's death, Nash had seized upon the painting as a mental refuge. His friend Shock had told him how Ty Nash, his father, while a POW in Vietnam, had used the memory of himself as a teenager riding a beloved horse in Mississippi where he had grown up, to survive the torture inflicted upon him by his captors. It was all about separating your mind from the present. And if you did that, the pain, while still there, could be managed. Nash was glad that he had practiced this technique over and over. Otherwise, he would have been screaming in pain while Steers carved up his arm.

"Mr. Temple was not nearly as stoic when it was done to him," she said, confirming what Nash had long suspected.

As his mind left the girl and the dog behind, Nash let out a long breath and felt the spread of blood across his skin.

"What good would that have done?" he said quietly. "If you can't change something, the waste of energy is unforgivable."

She wiped the bloody knife off on his bare chest, smearing, perhaps symbolically and intentionally, the tattoo of the scales of justice. "And are you saving your energy for something important, Mr. Hope?" she asked, her expression holding an air of expectation.

"Aren't we all?" he replied smoothly.

Then Steers leaned down and kissed him on the lips. When she pulled away and looked at him Nash noticed the strange expression on her face, as though she was surprised by her action. Her lips parted and he glimpsed strong, white teeth and a flicker of tongue.

She started to lean back down, perhaps for another touch of his lips, but then stopped. The woman rose and was quickly gone.

A few moments after that men were all over him. One injected him with something in his other arm, and Nash fell unconscious once more.

When Nash awoke he was back in his bed. He would have thought it was all a dream but when he moved his arm, he realized it had all happened, painfully so. He lifted his limb and looked at the wrapped and bloodied bandages. He had the same brand that he now knew Temple carried.

We're both owned by that woman, or at least she thinks so. But if I survive Myanmar her life will be over, even if it costs me mine.

CHAPTER

10

Speers sat on her tatami mat with a large mirror hanging on one wall in front of her. Her mother was Chinese, her father of English descent, but culturally she was Japanese, and her possessions, interests, and lifestyle reflected that upbringing.

With her white robe off she ran her gaze over her naked reflection. Steers's eyes passed along her face, her chest, her flat belly, her long legs. The flames had not reached there. In those areas she looked "normal."

The clothing she typically wore concealed everything that she wanted hidden from view. This was not from embarrassment. She could walk naked through her people and no one would ever make a comment, or even flinch in revulsion. Not because they cared about her, but because they cared about living. *That* was the power she held, and it was an intoxicating thing.

Sometimes too intoxicating. Sometimes too...

No, Steers kept her damaged flesh away from everyone because it belonged to her and no one else. Steers had been running the business for years when the *accident* had occurred.

The plane they were on had suffered an explosion of some kind while in the air. Her father had looked upon her in horror, as, afire, she screamed in her plane seat across from him. This was moments before part of the plane's interior dislodged from the violent impact with the ground, and crushed his life away.

The only other person to survive the plane crash had been her loyal Hiroko, who had been with Steers since birth. Hiroko was a woman whom Steers revered, and loved. This woman, then over seventy years of age, had managed to pull a critically injured Steers from the wreckage and roll her over until the flames were extinguished.

Hiroko had tended to her as best she could and then alerted authorities, who had taken the unconscious Steers to the nearest hospital. Steers had then been airlifted, along with Hiroko, to an acute trauma facility, where a number of operations had taken place to stabilize her health. Hiroko's miraculously minor injuries had been treated there as well. Two years of more surgeries and intense rounds of physical therapy had followed as Steers regained the use of her arms and normal range of motion in her back, shoulders, and arms. She had then endured additional surgeries to repair and clean away more damaged flesh. Hiroko, the only family she really had left, had been with her for every moment of this hellish journey.

Steers had resisted calls from her doctors to completely fix the damage to her skin. As she had explained to Nash, what remained was the most powerful incentive she had to survive.

Because I almost didn't. And my father did perish. That is all I need to understand how precious what I have truly is. And how deadly even one mistake can be.

After she had recovered, Steers had thanked Hiroko profusely and rewarded the woman for her courage and loyalty. Hiroko, now long since retired, lived in peace with all her needs taken care of in an apartment in Steers's building.

During her recovery, with her father dead and her mother imprisoned, Steers had nearly lost her empire. But the loss of her father and her own miraculous survival drove every small step she took in her recovery. There were many tiny victories and more sweeping, grander moments that, at the end, saw her reassume her perch at the top of the Steers organization.

She now rose and stood before the mirror.

They thought they had beaten me. But in the end, I survived.

She smiled at her reflection as she thought of this. Then the smile wilted away, like a rose in the frost.

She had, for years, *not* succeeded in her other lofty goal: the liberation of her mother. Now Steers sensed that this was her last chance. And not only for Masuyo, but Steers's final opportunity as well, for her empire and her life were more precariously situated than they appeared. She had long suspected that enemies of the Steers family had sabotaged her plane, hoping to take out both her and her father. Then with her mother behind bars in another country their empire would be ripe for conquering. But from her hospital bed Steers had not allowed that to happen, taking decisive action while she was in excruciating pain to ensure that her business remained intact. Now the only thing lacking was her mother.

She had not told anyone who it was that actually ran that mysterious prison. He was also the man who had met her on the airplane tarmac and ordered her to destroy Walter Nash. This man was not her partner but her *master* in crime. The very same man who had finally allowed her a visit with her mother. He had not done so out of kindness, for he possessed none. He had allowed the visit simply so Steers would understand that he had complete control over her. That he had all the leverage necessary to dictate the remains of her life. *This* was his message to her. And it had been effectively if subtly given.

Well, I am preparing my message back to him. And I will either be free of him, or I will be dead.

She flexed and stretched for one hour, allowing her stiffened skin to push and pull in remarkable ranges of motion that not a single one of her doctors told her would ever be possible. Finished, she put her robe back on, sat down, and stared once more at her unblemished face in the mirror.

Dillon Hope is a most interesting man. Perhaps the most interesting of my current acquaintance.

Temple was not remotely fascinating to her, largely because she had divined everything held within the man's heart and soul within five minutes of meeting him. The same had been the case for his father. Barton Temple had been smarter, cagier, more ruthless than his son. But he, too, had been quite transparent in what drove him to do what he did in life: money, greed, and power. Sought by so many and, in the end, meaning absolutely nothing at all.

I have money and power. But I do not possess greed. What I desire is survival. And then to die on my own terms. That is all.

Dillon Hope was a different matter altogether from the Temples. She did not really know why he was here, since she did not believe that he was simply Temple's bodyguard. Paid mercenaries did not blindly walk to their deaths for men they barely knew. Money was never a great enough incentive, and she did not see in Hope a man obsessed with wealth. So he was here for another reason.

Friend or foe, Mr. Hope? I saw how you looked at me yet I could not read what your gaze truly meant, although most men are so easy to understand. But we will have to see with you, won't we?

But even as she thought this, Steers's spirits faltered and she pulled her gaze away from her reflection.

Dillon Hope said that he is nothing to me. But, in reality, I am nothing, too. I have been that way for a long time. And I see no way back to where I truly began. Which is a defeat that no discipline, no effort, no sheer willpower on my part can possibly overcome.

Steers rose and walked unsteadily to her bed.

CHAPTER

II

In the darkness the seven-passenger Cessna twin engine jet took off from a runway in India and landed at the old WWII-era runway near Shingbwiyang in Myanmar less than a half hour later, after never going above five thousand feet. Nash just prayed that the pilots had filed a flight plan so they wouldn't be dodging or slamming into other aircraft, but they touched down without incident. They had been provided expertly crafted IDs and other credentials in case they ran into any trouble, which Nash feverishly hoped wouldn't occur. However, he also couldn't see how such trouble wouldn't happen on such a perilous mission.

Nash and Temple were met by two toughened men with dark hair and muscular builds. Temple's Burmese was good enough to allow sufficient communications with the pair. Now they climbed into an old all-terrain Jeep with their backpacks and enormous amounts of uncertainty.

After a long drive over backbreaking roads, they arrived at a hut southeast of Shingbwiyang. The four men ate a simple dinner of ngapi, thoke, rice, and ginger. It was one of the coolest months in Myanmar, but it was still a comfortable sixty-eight degrees and no fire was needed in the small, primitive fireplace.

Nash said, "We've only been told some of the plan. Can you fill us in?"

The men looked at each another. One said in English, "We get you to a place. Then, we forget we ever see you. That is *our* plan."

His friend nodded. "It is good for us this way."

"What about good for *us*?" groused Temple.

The men grinned and went back to their meals. When they were finished the pair settled on mats laid out on the floor and quickly fell asleep.

Nash and Temple remained sitting at the small, rough-hewn table.

"This is nuts," said Temple in a furious whisper. "I thought her plan was going to be super detailed and bulletproof. Not two clueless guys dropping us off somewhere and forgetting they ever saw us."

Nash rubbed at his injured arm and winced.

Temple noted this. "Wait a minute? Did she…?"

Nash had to play dumb since he wasn't supposed to know what had happened to Temple's arm. "Did she what?"

In answer Temple slid up his sleeve to reveal a long, jagged scar on his arm.

Nash nodded. "They knocked me out, and when I came to I was bound and she cut me up." He decided not to tell Temple what else had happened between them. Indeed, Nash was having difficulty processing it.

Temple said, "The bitch did it as a way of telling me that at any time she wants, she could carve me up, cut off my balls, slit my throat, and there's not a fucking thing I could do about it."

"You mean she owns us now?" said Nash.

"You bet she does. And now we're in one of the most dangerous places on earth with those two guys, who either know jack about shit, or have been paid to cut our throats as soon as we close our eyes tonight. God, I would give every damn cent I have to be back in America."

Nash said, "Steers is treating us like throwaway money. So we have to make ourselves critical to the success of bringing her mother back safely."

"Right, but how the hell do we do that?" whispered Temple. "And let's just point out the elephant in the room, namely, we don't even know if there is a prison, or if her mother's really in it. So if this is all bullshit, what then? Why are we here, Dillon?"

Nash had no ready answers to any of these questions.

But he had one thing going for him. As Temple's bodyguard he had been given back his weapons. His Glock was in a shoulder holster, his backup Beretta at his ankle. It wasn't much in the grand scheme of things. But it wasn't nothing, either.

He and Temple settled down on mats as far away from the two men as possible. Temple, despite probably his best efforts, quickly fell asleep. Nash did not close his eyes fully until he heard the deep snores of the other men.

As he drifted off to sleep he wondered what tomorrow would bring.

He doubted it would be anything good.

CHAPTER

12

The next morning the men drove them southeast into the foothills of ruggedly mountainous territory, then had Nash and Temple get out. Next, the Jeep turned around and sped away.

Nash and Temple stood there in the middle of nowhere looking helplessly in all directions until they heard the sounds of another vehicle approaching.

A battered box truck came into view and pulled to a stop a few feet from them.

Three men got out of the front seat and walked to the back of the truck. Two of them pulled out a metal ramp from a recessed pocket above the back bumper. They angled it to the ground and locked it into place.

As they were sliding up the rear cargo door Temple and Nash heard a powerful engine start up. When the door fully opened, a dirt bike roared out and down the ramp, then skidded to a stop. The rider took off their helmet, revealing a tall, slender woman in her early thirties with long dark hair and skin, and an intense look.

Nash noted there were four other dirt bikes in the back. He also saw that each bike had an extra fuel tank attached. After they were all brought out, along with five gear packs, two of the men and the woman came over to them.

The bigger man, who was taller than Nash and about 230 pounds of solid muscle, said, "I am Thura. We all speak English, so no worries." He pointed to his companions. "This is Zeya. He is Burmese like me. Amrita is Indian. In her language that means 'immortal.'"

Temple quipped, "Well, let's hope that rubs off on us."

Thura pointed toward the formidable range of mountains. "That's the way we're going, and it's going to get rough. But just follow us and all will be good." He handed each of them a gear pack. "Water, bedding, some food, and other essentials like toilet paper. There are no toilets the way we are going, man," he added with a grin.

Nash eyed Zeya, who wouldn't look at him, while he noted that Amrita watched him curiously. The third, unnamed man hung back by the truck.

Amrita said, "Let's roll. It gets dark early here. And cold in the mountains."

Thura said, "With that in mind…" He walked back to the truck, reached into the cab, and pulled out two thick leather jackets and warm-looking gloves. He passed them over to Nash and Temple. Then they loaded the ramp back into its slot and closed the cargo door. The third man climbed into the driver's seat, started the vehicle, and sped off without saying a word.

Nash hadn't been on a motorcycle since college, but he got the hang of the clutch and throttle by doing a practice run along the road.

They put the gear packs in their own backpacks and rode off. They kept to the road for a few miles but then turned off onto what amounted to a dirt path that switchbacked its way upward.

Thura dropped back and over the sounds of the comingled engines barked, "Roads have checkpoints. Not good for us. We are better going this way. They think no one is stupid enough to do this," he added with a laugh.

"We understand that the KIA controls the Kachin State," said Nash.

Thura nodded. "The junta is not welcome here, but that does not mean that KIA is any easier." He eyed Nash closely. "For people like you."

As the elevation rose the temperatures dropped, and Nash was glad of the jacket and gloves. The condition of the trail continued to deteriorate, and he found himself bounced all over the place, barely able to keep his seat or both wheels on the ground. His forearms and legs ached with the effort. Thura, Zeya, and Amrita showed no signs that this persistent beating bothered them in the least.

He glanced over and saw that Temple was struggling more than he was. Temple looked over and gave a feeble thumbs-up. They rode for well over five hours before they stopped by the side of the road for a meal unpacked from a saddlebag that Amrita carried on her bike. It was traditional local food, they were told, and it was good. But Nash would have eaten anything at that point.

They started up again, cleared the pass, and headed down. By the time they reached the bottom it was pitch-dark, and their way was illuminated only by their collective headlights.

They reached a rotting shack under a stone overhang and inside it had their final meal of the day, which both Nash and Temple inhaled.

As they sat in a circle on the floor, Thura pulled out a bottle of whisky and five shot glasses wrapped in plastic from his backpack.

"Surprised you made room for that," said Temple.

"There is always room for liquor, man. Now, this has been a good first day. We shall drink to an even better second day."

He filled up the glasses and they all drank. The whisky was strong, but Nash welcomed its warmth going down.

Thura eyed Temple. "So you are businessman looking for riches here?" His eyes twinkled, showing that he probably did not believe this.

"Hopefully, I will be when we get to Myitkyina," replied Temple with a forced grin.

Amrita looked at Nash and said bluntly, "And you guard him? From what?"

Nash nodded. "I'm sure something will come up, aren't you?"

Thura smiled at this, but Amrita just stared at Nash with even greater curiosity.

Later, they spread out their bedding on the floor, and one by one they fell asleep. Around two in the morning Nash awoke to see Amrita staring at him from her spot on the floor. The only light was from a small battery-powered lantern. The others were sleeping soundly.

"Not tired?" said Nash quietly.

She shrugged and then slid her bedding and herself closer to him. "You have a gun," she said quietly. "I saw it inside your jacket."

"Goes with being a personal bodyguard."

"Does your boss have a lot of money?"

"Not on him, if that's what you mean. Why?"

She shrugged again. "So, your boss has business in Myitkyina?"

"He does, yes."

"Where are you from in America?"

"All around."

"Have you been to New York City? And Hollywood?"

She said the latter with a starstruck giddiness that made Nash smile.

"I have."

"And are they as amazing as people say?"

"They're never boring, that's for sure. When did you come here from India?"

"Four years ago."

"Why?" he asked.

She said sharply, "Why not? Oh, you think this place is for shit?"

"No. But it's not exactly the easiest place to live, either."

"I...I got into some trouble in my country. I came here to get away from it."

"Do you plan to stay here much longer?" he asked.

"Not if I don't have to. Look around, this place *is* for shit. At least this part of it. And there is no government or law, just bullets and bombs."

"Well, I hope you are being well paid to escort us."

"I'm sure Thura is. Me and Zeya maybe not so much."

"So you work for him?"

She inched closer. "I want to work for myself. But sometimes it doesn't *work* out that way, you know?"

Nash thought of his relationship with Temple and nodded. "I can understand that."

"What does an American really want from this place?" she said.

"I'm just the hired help, Amrita. I go where my boss tells me to."

"Have you killed people with your gun?"

"Would it matter to you?"

She shrugged. "I do not believe you are simply here on business."

"Well, you'd be wrong because unfinished business is the only reason I'm here."

Nash caught himself and prayed he had not just made a big mistake. He stared at Amrita, trying to read her reaction to his statement.

"You Americans are very...different," Amrita said slowly.

To change the subject, he asked, "Where did you learn your English? It's excellent."

She smiled at the compliment and it made her look less hopeless. "In India. Many there want to learn English so they can go to America."

"Do *you* want to go to America?"

"Will you take me?"

He gaped. "I'm not sure how that would work, Amrita."

"You could make it work," she said.

"Let's see how things turn out."

"Which means, no, you will not take me."

She turned away from him and went to sleep.

CHAPTER 13

Another day of body-slamming dirt-biking that was even more arduous than the first gave way to the horses on the third day. The horses were sturdy beasts, Thura told them, and possessed sure footing.

He said this was most critical due to the rugged terrain they would be encountering, where even nimble dirt bikes would not work. Plus, he said, even with the extra gas tank they did not have enough fuel for the bikes to make the full journey.

"Horses find their own fuel in the grass," Thura said with a grin.

He and Zeya gave Nash a tutorial on riding while the horses were still in the corral. After an hour Thura pronounced him good enough. They set off, and for the first few miles the land was relatively flat. Then the ground started to rise rapidly, with more towering mountains ahead.

Thura looked at Nash and Temple and said, "Those are the Northern Mountains of Burma, the eastern ends of the Himalayas really. Hkakabo Razi is the highest peak here, but *only* twenty thousand feet tall." He grinned. "Luckily, we do not have to cross it to get to where we're going. Breathing up there would be very hard without oxygen," he added with a smile. He spurred his horse in the ribs and said, "Come, let us head to the clouds!"

For the most part the horses moved methodically with a rocking motion that kept making Nash drowsy. But as the heights advanced he felt his adrenaline pick up, and he kept a tight grip on the reins. However, the horses seemed to know what they were doing and where they were going. He rode next to Temple for a while until

Amrita let her mount slow down to where she roughly paralleled Nash. Temple, after giving Nash a curious glance, moved up to take her spot in the column.

"Forget what I said the other night," Amrita told Nash in a fierce tone. "I was tired and not thinking clearly."

"You didn't say anything wrong," noted Nash. He wondered if Thura might have overheard the conversation between them and given her hell about it later.

To supply proof for this theory, she aimed an angry glance in Thura's direction and whipped her head around, sending her long black hair flying in the stiff swirling wind coming off the mountain ridges.

"Forget all about it. Forget about *me*. This is just a job. For us both!"

She spurred on her horse and moved in front of Nash.

As Nash headed along the narrow trail, he reflected, and not for the first time, how extraordinary it was that he was currently on a horse with three strangers and his former boss crossing over mountains in Myanmar on a mission to free the mother of a global criminal from her prison.

Five years ago I went to Fiji with Judith and sat by the pool reading a book and having a daiquiri. And I thought that was adventurous.

They camped that night on a reasonably flat plain amid the shadows of far higher ground. It had become still colder as they had risen in elevation, and they built a small fire and ate around it, and afterward slept close to it for warmth.

It was Nash who was first to hear something amiss. The horses, tied up in a makeshift pen, were snorting and shuffling their hooves.

Nash's first thought was of a deadly mammal or a venomous reptile, both of which were in abundance in Myanmar.

He slid his gun from his holster and racked the slide. Then Nash slowly sat up and let his eyes adjust to the poor light.

He heard Thura say softly, "Bandit, man, to the right, by the horses."

Nash nodded. He quietly rose and kept his gaze in front of him.

He saw a glint of light and recognized it as the illumination coming from perhaps a phone or flashlight. Whoever was holding it was very near the horses, as Thura had said.

He edged toward the light and drew a bead on it with his Glock.

Then the light went out. A few moments later, Nash saw muzzle flashes and heard the sounds of two gunshots. Nash then heard someone cry out behind him.

He fired back and he must have hit his target because someone screamed in pain.

Thura ran past Nash and leapt onto the intruder, who had fallen to his knees next to the whinnying and rearing horses.

"Got him," shouted Thura. He flipped the man over and shouted in Burmese, "Trying to steal our horses?"

Nash ran forward, and Temple and Amrita, roused by all the noise, joined them.

When they reached him, a terrified-looking Thura had risen off the fallen man and stared at Nash. "You killed one of the KIA's soldiers."

Nash felt his heart race as he looked down at the uniformed man lying dead in the grass. "What was he doing here?"

"He can be wherever he wants to be," said Thura, looking wildly around. "Wait, where's Zeya?"

Nash remembered something: the sound he'd heard when the soldier had fired.

He raced back over to the dying fire and saw Zeya lying face down on top of his sleeping bag.

Nash knelt down and felt for a pulse. There was none. He rolled the man over and saw the bullet hole in his face.

"Shit!"

This came from Thura, who had hustled after Nash and seen his dead comrade.

"We are fucked!" roared Thura.

Temple and Amrita raced up to them.

"What do we do?" she exclaimed in a frightened voice.

"We get the hell out of here," replied Thura. "We leave now. The horses will find the way even in the dark. Come on, let's go. Now."

"And leave the bodies here?" said Nash.

"We can't take the time to bury them. One soldier means others are close by. And if you don't bury them deep the animals will get them anyway. Come on!"

He started rolling up his bedding and kicked dirt onto the fire. Amrita watched for a moment and then grabbed up her belongings.

Temple muttered to Nash, "We're gonna die in this shithole."

They saddled their horses, with Thura tethering Zeya's horse to his. By dawn they were far away from the dead men.

CHAPTER 14

THEY SPENT ANOTHER NIGHT OUTSIDE in the mountains, but Thura told them they would turn the horses in the next day and make the rest of the trip to Myitkyina on foot.

After Temple and Thura were asleep Amrita whispered to Nash. "You killed the soldier."

"I didn't even know it was a soldier. I thought it was somebody trying to steal our horses, or worse."

"Here that does not matter. They will kill you. They will kill all of us."

"I never intended for any of this to happen, Amrita."

"You may get out of here alive because you are American. But I will not. They will find me and kill me."

"You don't know that."

Amrita's face flushed. "I *do* know this. Do not tell me what I do not know." Thura mumbled in his sleep and she glanced anxiously at him before turning back to Nash.

"I know I told you to forget about me wanting to go to America, but now it is different. With the KIA dead it is all changed. So can you help me?" she said urgently. "Can you take me with you? You and your boss? I am smart. I know the language. I can help with your… business."

Nash was about to say no, but then he noted the woman's desperate expression.

"I'll talk to my boss. Maybe we can work something out. But what about Thura?"

"For me he cares nothing, but he will take care of himself. You will talk to your boss? You promise me this?"

"I promise you," he said firmly, but his thoughts did not match his tone. Nash had always been at his best when he could think things through. Ever since boarding Victoria Steers's plane for the flight to Hong Kong, he had only had time to be reactive.

Amrita gave him a searching look and then turned away. A few minutes later he could hear her gentle snores.

Nash looked up at the hazy sky and wondered what planet he was actually on.

Because it no longer feels like earth.

* * *

The hike was long and difficult, and it left them at varying points covered in sweat or chilled to the bone. Nash could not imagine what it would be like during the monsoon season when the rain would fall in feet rather than inches. As he glanced at Temple, who was trudging next to him, Nash could tell his boss was feeling the full effects of the journey. But Temple's grim expression also told Nash that the death of the soldier was probably also weighing heavily on him.

For himself Nash expected a chopper to roar over one of the mountain peaks and land with men holding automatic weapons pouring out of it, and his life would end either in a prison or with a wall of bullets.

He wondered if Thura had communicated to anyone what had happened. Had word reached Steers about the death of the soldier?

Even if we get back safely with her mother will she declare the deal null and void and kill us anyway?

These glum thoughts followed Nash until they made their last camp.

After a dinner that consisted of the remnants of their provisions and filled none of their bellies, Nash drew Temple aside and talked to him about Amrita and her request.

"Are you nuts, Dillon?" Temple had exclaimed. "It's highly doubtful *we'll* get out of this alive, much less with a third wheel. It's out of the question."

All of this made sense from a logistical point of view, Nash knew. And also from a commonsense perspective. But when one threw empathy into the equation it was not so simple. However, he knew that Temple, as usual, was concerned only with his own survival. The man clearly had no qualms about what might happen to Amrita.

That night around the campfire Amrita positioned herself near him and Nash knew what was coming.

Around one in the morning she whispered, "Did you talk to him?"

"Yes."

"And what did he say?"

Nash decided to tell the woman the truth. "He said no."

A sob escaped the woman's lips. "I knew it, in my heart I knew that he would refuse to help me. He is American. They only care for themselves. It is why you all are so rich." She spat on the cold ground.

"What were you planning to do once we got to Myitkyina?"

"Why do you care?" she shot back angrily.

"My boss said no, but I haven't. Tell me. And it might help me make a case to my boss to help you after all."

In the light of the campfire Nash could see that her expression grew calm, and when she spoke her tone was more measured. "We were told to get you to Myitkyina so that you can hold your 'business' meetings."

"And after that I understand we are taking a short flight to Bhamo where there will be others to meet us?"

Surprisingly, Amrita shook her head. "I spoke with Thura. He said that after what happened the plane will not work. The KIA will surely be checking."

"So you think they've found the bodies then?"

"Thura believes so. He has been on the phone, and even though reception is not so good here, he was able to get through to someone. He did not say in so many words, but his face told me that things are not good."

"He should have told us that then," said Nash irritably.

"Thura cares only for Thura. I have *told* you this!"

"Okay. When we get to Myitkyina do you know where we are to meet the local businessmen?"

"Yes, at the hotel where you will also be staying. We are to leave you there but remain in the area. Then we are to escort you to the airport in three days' time, and then we will have finished our job."

"What were you planning to do after that?"

"I have no choice but to continue to work for Thura. I am not even supposed to be in this country."

"So if we can't take a plane to Bhamo, how do we get there?"

"I know that one may travel by either a minibus or a car. The car will take around three hours at least. The minibus will be twice that long with a stopover in a village called Sinbo. But the thing is, the roads are not always safe or allowable for foreigners, and the bus service is very spotty. From day to day it might not run. And after the death of the soldier, the KIA will have set up checkpoints all along the roads. So, I do not think it is a good plan to take a car or bus."

"How about a fast ferry on the Irrawaddy?"

She thought about this and nodded. "Yes, it is possible. But they will look for foreigners on the fast ferries, but not so much on the slow ones. Americans in particular do not like the slow ferries. They are...primitive and full of locals and animals, and the toilets are... not nice. And you sleep on the deck."

"How long will the slow ferry take?"

"It is around two hundred kilometers on the Irrawaddy between Myitkyina and Bhamo with many stops in between. It could take a whole day."

"We don't have that much time. We were supposed to fly, which would only take a half hour, and the people meeting us aren't going to wait a full day."

"Is your business that important?"

He studied her, reading suspicion in every facet of her features. "Yes."

"Then contact your people and tell them of your delay."

A very sensible idea, thought Nash. Only they had not been allowed phones.

"We can't count on that," he said. "If you can aid us in getting out of Myitkyina ahead of schedule then I could help you get out of the country."

"But nothing I can do is as fast as a plane."

"But we can cut short our business meetings by a day and get on a slow ferry, and still beat the plane. Do you really think this provides us a better chance of evading the KIA?"

She brightened. "Undoubtedly it will."

"If we change plans, what about Thura?"

"I think that once you get to Myitkyina you should lose Thura as soon as possible."

"Why?"

"It is because he will see turning you in as the only way for him to escape responsibility for the soldier's death."

Nash took this in and nodded. "Okay, let me talk to my boss about all of this and ditching Thura, and we'll go from there. But you need to get us on that ferry, okay? Whatever it takes. We have money."

"As soon as we get to town I will work on this with all my passion, I swear," she said. She then took his hand and kissed it. "Thank you."

All this was done so earnestly that he almost smiled, until he realized that for her this was truly life and death.

As it is for all of us.

CHAPTER 15

They reached Myitkyina the next morning. Thura had not spoken the whole way, but he kept shooting furtive glances at Temple and Nash.

Amrita said, "Myitkyina is the capital of Kachin State. It translates to 'near the big river.'" She pointed to the water. "*That* is the Irrawaddy. It goes all the way to the Andaman Sea. Its delta is one of the biggest in all the world."

"What, are you a tour guide now, Amrita?" said Thura snidely.

They looked up when a jet plane flew over as it ascended into the sky.

Thura said, "The daily flight to Bhamo."

Nash said, "So we'll be on that flight when we've completed our business here?"

He had told Temple about Amrita's suspicions of Thura, that the bodies of Zeya and the soldier had almost certainly been found, and also about the likely impossibility of taking a plane to Bhamo. He had also told Temple of the plan to take a slow ferry with Amrita instead. But Nash wanted to hear Thura's take.

"That is right," said Thura, without looking at him. "A very short flight. The fastest way between here and Bhamo. Very easy." He now looked at Nash. "The easiest part of the trip."

Okay, it seems that Amrita was spot-on in her analysis, thought Nash.

As they walked along with their backpacks over their shoulders, they noticed piles of burned objects along the roadway.

After seeing Nash's questioning look, Thura explained, "That is how they get rid of their trash and other waste. They burn it, usually starting in the afternoon and early evening." He took a shallow breath. "That is why the air is not too good. Even if you do not smoke, you smoke in Myitkyina." He tacked on a brutal, exaggerated laugh that Nash interpreted as coming from fragile nerves.

"And it's safe for us coming into the city now?" said Temple.

Thura nodded. "No government restrictions here for foreigners. At least not now."

"Then let's make sure they don't know we were responsible for the death of the soldier," said Temple. "I assume your employer is paying you well enough to keep all secrets. And would be displeased if something happened to those in your care."

Thura gave Temple a dark look, but Nash looked at his boss approvingly.

Nash said, "In fact, Thura, I'm not sure we need your help anymore." He looked at Amrita. "Or yours." But out of sight of Thura he winked at her.

Thura said, "My orders are to get you on that plane."

"Give us the tickets. We can get ourselves on that plane. And this way you can avoid being with us if the KIA do find us. Isn't that best for you? Or is there something I'm missing?"

Thura looked at Amrita and then back at Nash. He reached into his pocket and took out two pieces of paper. "Your tickets." He looked at Amrita. "Let's go!"

They trudged off, but Amrita looked back and smiled.

Nash and Temple cleaned up at a hotel that neither man would have looked twice at back in the States. But after their ordeal in the mountains, they welcomed its meager comforts like it was the Ritz.

After changing into a fresh set of clothes, Nash and Temple met downstairs in the lobby in a private nook to discuss their next steps.

"Amrita could also be lying about Thura so you'll help her get out of the country," Temple pointed out.

"I considered that," said Nash, who did not trust anyone

anymore, including the man sitting across from him. "But did you notice how Thura is behaving? He's worried. And to tell the truth, I always thought it ridiculous that after having us grind through the mountains on dirt bikes, horses, and finally on foot that Steers would think it perfectly fine to get on a government plane. It just doesn't add up."

Temple shot Nash a glance. "You really think she's setting us up then? But why not just kill us in Hong Kong, or turn us over to the Chinese as murderers with all the proof necessary?"

"Because I think she's actually setting us up to take the blame somehow when Masuyo is freed from that prison. I mean, what does she really need us for? She said it was because her people are known here. How does that make sense? Her people are coming *here* to help us free Masuyo. They could easily do it without us and then fly back to Hong Kong with her."

"You're right, Dillon. So we're the American patsies in Myanmar?" added Temple bitterly. "But Steers probably doesn't know about the soldier dying."

"And maybe we can use that to our advantage."

"How?" asked Temple quickly.

"Let me think on it." Nash checked his watch. "You have your first meeting in five minutes." He glanced toward the front doors of the hotel where three men in khaki suits had just entered, sweat lining their faces in the morning heat and humidity. Two of them carried briefcases. "And I think your potential partners just showed up."

Temple rose, adjusted his cuffs, and buttoned his jacket. "At least *this* shit I know how to do," he said firmly. He walked off with a confident swagger while Nash followed.

CHAPTER 16

Over the next two days Temple met with a number of Myanmar businessmen who had traveled far, and with some risk, to meet with him. They had been told that he had a large international import-export business that would enable them to market products such as rare earth minerals, gemstones, and rice on favorable terms to new markets around the world. They were prepared, informed, and enthusiastic. Nash, who knew the men would be ultimately disappointed, felt more than a tinge of remorse when he looked into their hopeful faces.

His former boss at Sybaritic had handled each of the meetings with skill and tact. Nash, an accomplished businessman himself, had nodded approvingly at the strategies Temple had used with each group. The men had all gone away excited by the future prospects.

When the last meeting on the second day had been concluded, only Nash and Temple were left in the small, private room they had used for the meetings. Temple said, "Let's go get a drink. God knows I need one."

They sat at a table in the hotel bar.

"It's a pretty town," said Nash, who between meetings had walked around Myitkyina and gone down to the river where the ferries came and went. "Obviously lots of history, but it has a modern edge to it, too."

Temple leaned forward over the small, knee-height table. "So talk to me about Amrita and how we get out of this place by ferry. You've had enough time to come up with something."

"I've seen the ferries heading out of here. I also met up with Amrita in between your meetings and we've talked to the ferry people, with her translating for me. Amrita has confirmed that the three of us can get on a slow ferry early tomorrow morning and it will get us to Bhamo tomorrow night."

"But Steers's people will expect us to be on that plane, Dillon. They're to meet us there and take us on the next phase of the trip. If we're not on that plane, Steers will know that we've screwed her over."

Nash scrutinized his companion. "This is where the rubber meets the road, Rhett."

Temple drained his drink. "Meaning what exactly?"

"Meaning we need to start taking control of this situation. If I'm right about this being a setup, the closer we get to the prison phase the closer we get to her double-cross. I think we're meant to be where that ambulance is going to be with Masuyo inside. And I think a rescue attempt will be made. Only we won't survive it, or else they'll leave us behind to be arrested and punished for everything that happened, like I talked about before."

"So they free Masuyo and get her out of there and we take all the heat? Patsies, like I said? But how do we get out of the country then?"

Nash had given this a great deal of thought and he had come up with a plan that was as ambitious as it was perilous. However, he had not come all this way to avoid risk. His mission, unlike Temple's goal to survive, was far broader and deeper. He was here to bring Steers and company down. And this situation had presented him with potentially powerful leverage to do just that.

"We get out of Myanmar *without* Steers's rescue team, and with the biggest bargaining chip possible: Masuyo."

CHAPTER 17

THAT NIGHT AMRITA APPEARED AT their hotel and the three walked to dinner at the Green Bird, which the sign outside said provided traditional Kachin meals. The roof was thatched, and the walls were made of sturdy bamboo poles. The staff, all dressed in dark blue slacks and light blue shirts, were uniformly friendly and energetic. Inside the restaurant, walkways were bracketed by low stone walls backfilled with river rock. Teak poles supported the ceiling, where a large light fixture was featured with a round wooden backing and basket lights aplenty illuminating the space. In another section of the restaurant, fixtures shaped like mushroom heads and made from wicker hung from the ceiling. In one corner a small, thatched tiki bar housed plates, cups, and serving baskets.

They were given a private room framed by bamboo and latticework walls and a table with a red tablecloth and wooden chairs set around it. Here the ceiling was open with the rafters showing and vines growing over and around the planks. The pine-scented humid air enveloped them as they sat down.

There were no English menus, so Amrita explained the offerings to Nash and Temple.

Amrita said, "Shat Jam and Si Pa are very good. But I favor a dish called Silu, because it is a curry, like I am used to back in India. Bamboo shoots are served with every dish. It is like your French fries," she added, grinning.

"But a lot healthier for you," observed Nash.

They ordered, and when the food and drinks came, they took their time over their meals. There was an abundance of poultry, fresh fish from the Irrawaddy, leafy greens, balls of rice, and tangy onions.

Nash peered through an opening in the bamboo to the outside. After the mountains they had traversed, he had been surprised, and pleasantly so, at the lush evergreen surroundings of Myitkyina. It reminded him of both Colorado and the Pacific Northwest. The forests here were enormous and, combined with the rugged mountain ranges, formed a fascinating and unique topographical mix.

Amrita said to Temple, "Your meetings went well?"

Temple shrugged. "No deal is guaranteed. You only hope that you win more than you lose. I have to say that the men I met with spoke English far better than I do Burmese."

"English is the language of business," said Amrita confidently. "So the men here learn it. They want to become rich, too. And maybe buy a penthouse in New York." She shot Nash a telling glance.

"They're dealing in rare earth minerals, gemstones, and rice, the exports of which I would imagine the junta or KIA strictly control," said Temple.

"All governments control everything having to do with money, not just in Myanmar," voiced Amrita. "They take the dollars and leave the little cents to the rest. It is not fair but they do not care."

Temple said, "And do you care about money?"

"Yes. Because I must eat. Just like you."

Temple said, "Do you really think they've found the bodies?"

Amrita pulled a newspaper from her jacket and dropped it on the table. They looked at the grainy photo of two bodies lying on the ground with policemen and soldiers all around.

"There is your answer," she said.

"What does it say?" asked Temple, picking up the paper.

"There is a reward for information about the killers. One hundred million kyats."

"What's that in dollars?" asked Temple.

"Around fifty thousand bucks," noted Nash, who had looked up the current exchange rate before they had left for Myanmar. He eyed Amrita. "Where did you get this?"

"Thura had it. He is still in town. I took this paper from where he is staying. I think—"

"You think he may want to earn the reward?" said Nash.

"It is far more than what we are being paid," replied Amrita. "And Zeya was Thura's good friend. He is very angry that he is dead." She looked at Nash. "He blames you."

Temple said, "So he's lurking around and wanting to earn fifty thousand bucks and avenge his dead friend. Great." He looked at Amrita. "Does he have a gun?"

"Here anyone can get a gun if they need it."

Temple eyed Nash. "We have to watch our asses like nobody's business."

Nash said, "He believes we're going to be in town for one more day and night and then we get on the plane. With luck, we'll be out of here before he knows it."

"You just have to make it through tonight," said Amrita.

Temple looked at Nash and said warningly, "Unfortunately for us, nights can be very long."

CHAPTER 18

It was late when they made their way toward their hotel down an alleyway. The only illumination was from the moon as it drifted behind hazy clouds. The sounds of a few cars and motor scooters rumbled in the distance, but other than that it was quiet.

Temple said, "Where is Thura staying?"

Amrita glanced at him. "At a hostel nearby. He is not happy about your telling him to leave. I think he's afraid you will blame him or tell the police that he was involved in the soldier's death."

"So he plans to kill us and not turn us over to the police?" said Temple as they entered an especially darkened section of the alley.

"I think he will kill you and then show the police the gun that killed the soldier," she said, looking at Nash. "*Your* gun."

"And he collects the reward and leaves no witnesses to dispute his account of things," added Nash. "Nice plan."

"Shit." Amrita had stumbled over something and banged her shoulder into a wall as she fell to the ground, moaning and holding her arm.

Nash bent down to help her as Temple turned to look.

"What the—" began Nash, as Amrita rose, holding his gun and pointing it at him. She had slipped it out of his holster when he had gone to her aid.

"What are you doing?" barked Temple.

"I am making a hundred million kyats," she shot back.

Eyeing her warily, Nash said, "The plan you said was Thura's was actually yours."

She smiled. "With that much money I can go to America."

"Fifty grand won't get you a penthouse in New York," pointed out Temple.

"But it will get me out of here."

"We were going to help you do that, Amrita," said Nash.

"You lie! You were never going to help me. Men always lie to women. It is how you think." She spat on the ground. "So which first, you, or you?" she said, oscillating the muzzle between the two of them.

"The police will arrest you for murdering us," said Temple.

She smiled. "In America maybe, but not here." She pointed the pistol at Nash. "I choose you to die first." Her finger went to the trigger and she started to pull it.

The woman then flinched, her eyes bulged, and her mouth collapsed. As she fell forward, Nash saw a knife sticking out of her back.

He bent down to check her pulse. There was none. It looked like the blade had pierced her heart. Nash retrieved his weapon and then they heard footsteps.

Nash rose and pointed his gun as Thura walked into view.

He stopped next to Amrita and shook his head. "It is sad what I had to do." He looked up at Nash. "I do not know you. Her, I knew. Her, I called a friend. But I had to kill a friend to protect those I do not know. It is messed up, man."

"So why did you do it?" asked Nash.

Thura bent down to free his knife from Amrita's body. "Because it is not right to kill somebody like that. Amrita was wrong. You do not just shoot someone who stands without weapons in front of you."

He wiped off the blood on her jacket and put the knife in a holder under his coat. "I know I said it was all good, but you do not want to get on that plane, man," he said.

Nash said, "Amrita told us she could get us tickets on the slow ferry. But obviously that was a lie," he added, looking down at her body.

"I can get us on the ferry. I will get you to Bhamo, and then my job is done."

"Is that why you stayed around?" asked Temple. "You suspected her?"

"When I saw the reward offered, yes, I thought there might be... a problem."

Nash said, "I misjudged you. I'm sorry."

Thura shrugged. "Life and people, not so easy to figure out."

Temple said, "What do we do with her body?"

"She will be taken care of. I will see to it. We will meet at the ferries at dawn." He looked them over. "I will bring you some other clothing. You will not stick out so much."

"Thank you, Thura," said Nash.

"It is my job, American. And I do my job." He glanced sadly at Amrita's body. "No matter what."

CHAPTER 19

Early the next morning Nash and Temple were standing on the deck of the ferry, gripping the rail and staring out at the water. Thura was asleep on the deck, using his backpack as a pillow. The air was crisp on the water, and they turned their faces away from the biting wind as the sun rose.

Thura had been true to his word, getting them on the slow ferry and providing them with hooded cloaks.

When they boarded the ferry Nash had told him, "We need transportation when we get to Bhamo, preferably an all-terrain vehicle."

"I'll see what I can do," he said. "What do you need it for exactly?"

"To pick someone up and take them someplace else."

Thura raised his eyebrows at this cryptic comment. "I know a guy."

"I thought you might."

Thura had taken out his phone and gone over to a corner of the ferry to make a call.

Now Temple, after glancing over at the sleeping Thura, said, "What do you think he did with her body?"

Nash eyed the water where perhaps creatures that ate corpses lurked. "I don't even want to go there. You ever travel on the Irrawaddy on your previous trips here?"

Temple shook his head. "My dad and I were in other places. Yangon and Mandalay primarily, where the money was back then. Yangon has these fabulous gilded pagodas, temples that go up, up into the sky. I mean, they look like they're solid gold. And then there're modern skyscrapers and this beautiful lake, I forget the name. It also had this ship shaped like a dragon. It was pretty cool. We came over to develop some opportunities while I was still in college. Nothing came out of it, but it was a learning experience."

"I take it this was pre–Victoria Steers?"

Temple smiled bitterly. "My old man hadn't become involved with her. Yet." He stared down at the water and said in a contemplative voice, "He was an asshole back then, too, Dillon, but nothing like what he eventually became. I looked up to him. I really did," he added, as though to convince himself. "He was the most confident person I've ever met in my life. He'd walk into any room, any meeting, didn't matter where the hell in the world it was or who it was with, and just take over the room by the sheer force of his personality. I've never seen anything like it. Biggest balls in the world."

"Must have set a pretty high bar for you," noted Nash, who had seen the elder Temple do that very thing many times.

"An *impossible* bar," growled Temple. "And you know how parents usually want their kids to do better than they did?"

Nash thought of his own father and nodded. "Yeah?"

"Well, not my old man. He beat me down every chance he got. I didn't know it at the time, but after he hooked up with Steers it got really bad. I think he was pissed at himself for losing his wealth and needing to get bailed out by her. And he took that anger out on me. And worst of all he got me involved with her. And I only found out about it shortly before he died."

"How?"

"He came right out and told me. He did it to shock me, play mind games, and also to stick it to me." He paused. "But he did say something…that I wanted to believe was true, only I'm not sure I can."

"What was that?" asked a genuinely curious Nash.

Temple held up his scarred arm. "He told me he was the one who suggested to Steers that she give me this little souvenir."

"Damn, your own father?"

Temple glanced at him. "But the thing is, Dillon, my dad told me that Steers had originally wanted to kill me, for some mistake she claimed I made. And maybe I did. So...so my old man suggested that she just hack up my arm instead." He stopped talking and stared down at the Irrawaddy.

"So your father saved your life, Rhett. That means he must have—"

"What? *Loved* me?" said Temple, with a snort tacked on. "No, he didn't love me, Dillon. But I guess he didn't want me to get murdered by that woman, either. In his mind it probably would have made him look bad. And we couldn't have that, could we?" He stopped talking for a moment and then reached into his pocket, pulled out his wallet, and produced a photo. He handed it to Nash. It was a picture of a lovely woman in her forties with abundant brown hair, hazel eyes, and a warm smile, who resembled Temple.

"That's my mother, Amanda. I lied to you before. I came up with the name for Mindy's daughter." Temple looked out to the water, his expression unlike any Nash had ever seen on the man. It was reflective, somber, containing depth, all things he had never associated with Rhett Temple before.

"She was a wonderful person, loving, nurturing, to me and my little sister. But my half-sister Angie's mom? She took off when Angie was a little girl, and Angie had serious developmental issues. And my dad didn't like that one bit, let me tell you. You see, he never understood Angie, never. But when my mom married him? Well, she took care of Angie, really wonderful care, like Angie was her own flesh and blood. And she taught me to always do the same. And...and I have, because, well, other than my mother, Angie's probably the only person I ever really loved." He drew a long breath, glanced at Nash with an embarrassed expression, and said, "Jesus, I know, TMI, right?"

"It's okay, Rhett," said Nash quietly. "It speaks well of you."

Nash had met Amanda Temple several times before she and her husband had divorced. He had liked her, a lot, and wondered how such a nice, kind, and loving person could be married to a man who was none of those things.

Temple looked back at the water swirling past. "I…I guess I always connected with Angie on certain levels. And I think I know why. Wanna hear my theory?"

Nash nodded, absolutely amazed by this string of personal revelations. "Yes, I do."

"Because neither one of us ever grew up. Angie couldn't. And I guess I wouldn't. It gave us sort of a bond." He wagged his head, as though trying to swirl around all the thoughts running through his mind. "When my father was going through financial hell he was panicked, out of his depth, raging at everyone. But my mom stood by him. Even when it looked like he was going to lose it all. Hell, she even went out and got a job. It was more symbolic than anything. She couldn't exactly earn the billions of dollars that he needed. But she did it. And then when he got back on top—with Steers's help—do you know what he did?"

"What?"

"He dumped my mother. Divorced her. Fought her tooth and nail in court over every dime. Worried and depressed her so much that…that she ended up taking her own life."

"My God, Rhett, I'm so sorry." And Nash truly was sorry. He had never heard this story before.

"My dad covered it up, of course. Accidental overdose. But I know better. She saw me right before she did it."

"Did she tell you that…?"

He shook his head fiercely. "No. I would have stopped her. I would have…" He glanced at Nash. "I loved my mom. She was… everything to me."

"But you still ended up working for your father?"

Temple's expression turned grim and then resigned. "Yeah, after all that. Money-grubbing SOB that I am. Daddy had the dollars, so that's where little old me went. The easy route, you know. Instead of being a real man and telling him to go fuck himself even if it cost me every penny." He paused. "So that's my long-winded sob story. How about you? Were you close with your father?"

"Let's just say that we didn't see eye to eye on a lot while he was alive. But after he died things became clearer how he actually felt about me."

Temple nodded. "Shouldn't be this damn complicated, should it?"

"Family is actually more complicated than quantum physics, least I've found it so."

"Speaking of family, what do you think of Steers and her mother? I mean, from what I've heard they seem tight. She had older brothers and sisters but she beat them all out to get the top spot. And now she's trying to break the lady out of jail."

"She said her mother's imprisonment was political," noted Nash.

"You believe that?"

"Right now, I believe nothing." Nash looked around at some of the other passengers who were sleeping on the deck, or else sitting and eating and drinking some of the provisions they had brought on board. Other travelers had animals with them: goats, chickens, dogs, sheep, pigs, and a couple of critters Nash didn't recognize.

He said, "Who else other than the military junta, or one of the regional crews Steers mentioned, could run a prison like that?"

Temple replied, "It's near the Chinese border. So maybe Beijing? They seem to be involved in everything."

Nash knew from the FBI that Steers was actually working with the Chinese. But he had a thought. *Maybe that's their leverage over her: Masuyo.*

"So if the Chinese control the prison, does that mean they're actually an enemy of Steers and her family?"

Temple looked uncomfortable, something Nash was quick to pick up on.

"You have another theory?" he asked.

Temple shrugged. "Just scuttlebutt I heard."

"Tell me."

Temple glanced around at some of the other passengers, who did not appear to be paying them any attention. When he spoke his voice was so low Nash had to lean in to hear.

"The thing is, Dillon, most people think Steers's mother is Japanese."

"You mean she's not?" Nash knew this but he wanted to hear Temple's version.

"No, she's Chinese."

"How do you know that? Did Steers tell you?"

"Hell no. She never talks about stuff like that, at least not with peons like me. No, I was at this huge facility in southern California used for processing and distribution of the drugs Steers brings into the country, when I overheard two of her associates talking. They were speaking a mix of languages, Thai and English and Mandarin. Now, I've traveled to Asia more times than I can count and I've got a passable talent for linguistics, so I was able to interpret some of what they said. Anyway, *Masuyo* is a Japanese name, but I heard these men refer to her as *Dai Lu*, which is a Chinese name. I looked it up, and it means 'lead the way,'" added Temple. "Makes sense, right?"

"Yeah, it does," said Nash. The FBI had previously told him about Masuyo actually being a Chinese agent, but they had not known her Chinese name; or if they did, they had never shared it with Nash.

"But they gave their daughter the name Victoria, which, I guess, comes from her English father," pointed out Nash.

"Exactly," Temple said in a scornful tone. "Queen Victoria. Fitting, since the bitch acts like royalty."

Nash thought of the woman with the burned flesh standing over him that night. "From what you told me before, the kingdom wasn't handed to her. She had to fight for it."

"I'm not saying she's not tough, she is. And ruthless and a killer. Which means since we have now gone off-grid from her plan we have giant bullseyes on our backs."

A few hours later Temple plopped down on the deck and, like Thura, used his backpack as a pillow before falling asleep.

Amid all the noise, including sheep bleating and pigs grunting and the related odors that assailed him from all corners, Nash stood by the railing and looked out at the Irrawaddy, which flowed north to south, roughly cleaving Myanmar in half. There were a lot of boats out there, from big ferries to personal craft to a single fisherman balancing on what looked like a few boards as he cast his line into the water looking for food to either eat or sell. It seemed like every few minutes the ferry put into shore, where some got on and others got off. The slow rocking of the boat combined with the growing heat finally overwhelmed Nash, and he sat with his back to the railing and closed his eyes. He jerked awake when something touched his arm.

Temple and Thura were both staring down at him. As Nash looked around he could see that night had fallen.

Thura said quietly, "Bhamo is the next stop. About five minutes."

Nash nodded and stood, stretching out his cramped limbs and trying to forget about his empty belly. They had left too early to get a meal at the hotel, and they'd had no provisions to bring on board.

"Hopefully, we can get something to eat in Bhamo," he said as his stomach rumbled.

Thura nodded. "There's a place we can walk to. Good food."

Five minutes later, as they were trudging off the boat and onto land, Temple said, "I hope you have a plan for tomorrow, Dillon. Or else this might be our last stop in Myanmar."

The thing was, Nash did have a plan. *Now I just have to see if it works.*

But he needed one other thing, and he asked Thura if it was possible.

"For a price," said Thura. "Like the vehicle. I know another guy in Bhamo."

"Good," said Nash. "In tight spots it's always fortunate to know guys who have the things you need."

CHAPTER 20

They ate a filling meal at a café near the river, and later walked to a small hotel where they made up half of the guests. Temple and Nash shared a room, while Thura had his own. Before they separated for the night, Thura told them, as Nash had requested, that he would take them to the airport early the next morning in the vehicle he had managed to acquire.

Neither Nash nor Temple slept well that night. It was hot and humid and there was no air-conditioning. And leaving the windows open was not an option because they had both seen the size of the bugs flitting around outside.

Thura came for them the following morning. He led them outside and over to a forest-green 4WD Jeep. It was old and dented and dirty, but as Thura said, "The engine works and the wheels turn."

Temple said, "You're a genius, Thura. I can use resourceful guys like you in my business."

Thura glanced at Nash but did not comment on this. He then handed Nash the second item he had requested: a phone. "Charged and ready to use, with a new SIM card and enough bars to do what you need it to do."

As they drove to the airport, Nash sat in the back seat and loaded onto the phone the things he needed. By the time he was finished, they had reached the airport, which was in a large field and consisted of a small building blotched by the weather and painted, in part, white and aquamarine. A small tower with radar gear sprouted out of the structure.

"It is also called Banmaw Airport," Thura said, pointing at the sign hanging on the building.

There were a few locals and some tourists, probably awaiting the arrival of the plane. Other folks were lined up with their bags to board the aircraft for its return flight to Myitkyina.

Thura told him where the jet would land and deplane its passengers on the single runway. After looking over the area, Nash directed him to park well away from the building, but in a spot that still provided a good sight line of the road leading into the airport.

"I suppose you will tell me who is coming to meet you at the plane," said Thura, with a glance at Nash in the back seat.

"I'm not sure we know any more than you do."

"Were they supposed to take you somewhere?" asked Thura.

"Yes, only we don't know exactly where." Nash had an idea. "Thura, you obviously know this area well. Have you heard of a prison installation roughly halfway between Bhamo and Katha?"

Thura shot a look out the window before answering. "Why do you ask that?"

"Because we'd like to know," interjected Temple. "Can you help us out?"

Thura said, "I know about it. I had a cousin who used to work there as a guard."

"Who operates it?" asked Nash.

"No one knows, really. But I can tell you that the junta leaves it alone. And the KIA does the same."

"That's very strange, isn't it?" asked Nash. "Allowing people to do something in your own country and you just let them get away with it?"

"I do not think that is what is happening."

"Then what?" asked Temple.

In reply Thura rubbed his thumb and forefinger together.

"You mean they're being well paid not to do anything about it," said Nash.

Thura nodded. "Money talks here just as good as any other

place. All I know is, it is a place to give a wide berth to. That is the smart thing to do." He eyed Nash in the mirror. "But something tells me that you two are here to do the opposite of that."

"I'm not sure we have much choice in the matter," said Nash.

Thirty minutes later Nash, who from the middle of the back seat was keeping his eye on the Jeep's side mirrors, said, "Looks like our friends are coming."

As they slid down in their seats, a black four-door Toyota 4Runner pulled into the entrance to the airport and parked as close to the runway as possible.

Two men got out and Nash ran his eyes over them. They were tall and well-built, and he could tell from the bulges under their jackets that they were armed. He eyed the Toyota and thought he could see two other people sitting in the rear seats.

They all looked at the clear, windless sky when the sounds of a plane approaching reached them.

Thura said, "That is the plane you were supposed to be on."

As it came closer, Nash could see that it was a relatively new-looking Boeing 737 model with the Myanmar National Airlines name on the side of the fuselage.

The plane's landing gear deployed, and it descended rapidly and thumped onto the tarmac. The jet then slowed dramatically, and came to a stop near the terminal. All three watched as the forward door opened and portable steps were brought to the side of the aircraft and lined up with the door.

The two armed men drew nearer and watched as the passengers deplaned. When the last of them came off and the grounds crew signaled for the cleaning team to board the 737, the two men hurried across the tarmac and spoke to the grounds crew. Then one of the men dashed up the steps and into the aircraft. When he came back out he was not looking happy. He quickly rejoined his comrade and pulled out his phone as they hustled back to the 4Runner.

Nash said to Thura, "Okay, where they go, we go."

Thura said, "My job was to get you to Bhamo, and you are here."

Temple took out his wallet and handed him a wad of American currency he had brought with him on the trip. "Think that'll cover it?"

"There is not enough money in all the world if I lose my life over it."

"We won't force you to come, Thura," said Nash.

Thura gave him a harsh look. "I told you this before, when I have a job to do, I finish it." He took the offered money and began to follow the Toyota as it left the airport. "And now I have a *new* job to finish."

CHAPTER

21

Later, the 4Runner pulled to a stop in front of the Friendship Hotel in downtown Bhamo. It was a multistory structure, white with blue trim; circular balconies sprouted off one wing, and AC units rested on metal shelves bolted to the exterior walls.

Thura pulled to a stop where they could see the Toyota clearly.

The two men got out, then a young woman emerged from the back and assisted another woman out of the other rear seat. The second woman moved with the slowness of either age or ill health, or perhaps both. Her head was covered with a scarf and her body was wrapped in a bulky cloak, despite the warmth of the morning. All four walked inside while a hotel attendant collected their bags from the SUV.

"Nice place," noted Thura. "Not cheap."

Temple said, "Who do you think the women are?"

Nash eyed Thura. "Since they were meeting us at the plane they must have descriptions of us. You want to go in and see what you can find out?"

Temple handed Thura some more cash. "Payment for any bribe you might need to make. I'm assuming U.S. dollars work here."

Thura snorted. "They work everywhere."

"Tread cautiously, Thura," warned Nash. "These people do not play around."

Thura put the money in his pocket and got out of the Jeep. They watched as he crossed the street, dodging a motor scooter with three boys hanging off it, and entered the hotel.

"You think those guys are part of the ambush team?" asked Temple.

"They look it," said Nash, who was staring down at his phone to check the time zone difference in connection with the email he had sent while they waited at the airport; it was late in Nash's old hometown.

But supposedly the FBI never sleeps.

However, after a half hour he had not received a reply back.

"Here comes Thura," observed Temple.

Nash looked up to see the man sauntering out of the hotel like he didn't have a care in the world. A newspaper was under one arm and he stopped at a market stand and bought some fruit. He was chomping on a banana when he climbed back into the Jeep.

He passed a mango to Nash and a passion fruit to Temple. He held up a knife.

"For the fruit. Don't worry. It is a different knife than with… Amrita."

Temple looked down at his passion fruit and said, "I'll save it till later, thanks."

"What did you find out?" Nash asked Thura as he took the knife from him and cut into the mango.

"I was told they are from Pakistan. Here on holiday, two brothers, their sister, and their mother, who is quite old and not very mobile. The receptionist said she could not do the stairs, but took the lift instead."

"How long are they booked in for?" asked Nash.

"Three nights. Paid in cash."

"Names?" asked Temple.

"Your money did not get me a peek at their passports."

"You think they're really from Pakistan?" asked Nash.

"I went up to their floor and actually passed them in the hallway. Many languages are spoken in Pakistan. I am passable in Pashto and Urdu, but the fact is they were speaking in English, which many Pakistanis do."

"What did they say?" asked Nash.

"Something about people on a plane not being on the plane. So I suppose they were talking about you two."

"Thura, do you have your passport?"

Thura touched his shirt pocket. "Always. You never know, man, when you need to *jump*."

Temple glanced at Nash. "So what do we do now? They've probably already told Steers that we were no-shows."

"There could be lots of reasons for that," pointed out Nash. "We could have been killed, or arrested. She won't necessarily conclude that we willingly did not get on the plane."

"But she won't necessarily conclude that we didn't, either."

Thura said, "So what do we do now?"

"We keep eyes on the hotel and wait," said Nash. "Those men have a mission coming up. And they're going to do it, regardless of whether we're there or not."

"Do you know when this mission will take place?" asked Thura.

Nash said, "Actually, we have the day and time, but not the *location*. For that, we'll need to follow *them*. But I want eyes on the place to see who else they might meet here."

Temple shot him another glance. "You think she—?"

"I don't know. That's why we have to keep watch."

"This is getting really dicey," noted Temple.

"It's been *dicey* ever since we got on that plane for Hong Kong," countered Nash.

"Who is this *she* you keep talking about?" asked Thura.

Nash glanced at Temple, who said, "Trust me, Thura, if you never meet her in your life, that will be a great thing. For you."

CHAPTER 22

They left Temple at the hotel to keep watch, and Nash and Thura drove off in the Jeep.

Nash said, "I'm going to need some more things, Thura."

"What things?"

Nash told him the items and then said, "I'll also need access to a stovetop and an oven."

"You need to cook some things?"

"Yeah."

"But not food?" said Thura, with a sharp glance aimed at Nash.

"No, not food."

Thura took him to two places where he got what he needed or close to it. And for ten dollars American, Nash got the use of a small, makeshift kitchen tacked onto a building on the outskirts of Bhamo for a few hours.

"You make no drugs here," warned the owner. "For sure," he added firmly.

"No drugs for sure," replied Nash.

After the man left Thura said, "Why did you want stump remover?"

"Principally because it has potassium nitrate."

They mixed the stump remover with white sugar. Nash put it in a plastic bottle and had Thura shake it vigorously.

Then Nash heated up a frying pan, put some water in it, and sprinkled in the mixture of sugar and potassium nitrate. He had Thura continuously stir the concoction with a spatula until it dissolved.

"The water will boil off," said Nash. "And then we'll have what we need."

While Thura watched the pan, Nash grabbed some shoelaces they had bought and tied them together to make one long strand. He then put the lace in the pan and, with Nash holding on to one end of the lace, they took turns using a spatula to move the single lace around until the entire strand was equally coated with the slurry.

He instructed Thura to get a baking sheet from a cabinet, and then Nash placed the single lace on it in a sine configuration. He had Thura heat the oven to three hundred degrees, and they cooked the lace for twenty minutes until it had assumed a golden tinge. They then let it cool for five minutes, leaving the lace very stiff. Nash cut off four short strips from the lace and left the rest intact.

"Okay, part one is done," said Nash. "Time for part two."

At Nash's request, Thura had looked for and found in a recycling bin an old battery pack for a cordless drill.

Nash unscrewed the housing and took out the cell pack.

"Batteries?" said Thura. "But these are no good."

"I don't need the batteries," replied Nash. "I need their *casings*."

He removed the four tubes from the battery pack, pushed out the electronics, and was left with the four casings. He had previously cut four pieces of cardboard into circular shapes, and set one casing on each. Using a glue gun they had purchased, Nash affixed each casing to a separate piece of cardboard. He then poured the remaining slurry from the pan into each of the casings. He finished it off by sticking one short strip of shoelace into the casings, leaving about two inches of shoelace free of the slurry.

"It'll harden and then we're good to go."

"I don't understand any of this, but if you say good to go, okay."

Nash pocketed the long lace and thought, *I hope to God we're good to go.*

* * *

Late that night Thura came to their room and showed them the newspapers, which said a search was ongoing for the persons who had killed the KIA soldier. Thura told them that they had not yet identified Zeya.

"He carried no ID. But once they do find out who he is, they will find out we were friends and worked together. Then they will start looking for me."

Nash said, "What will you do?"

"For me, it is time to leave Myanmar. To search for a new life."

"Where will you go?" asked Temple.

"I know Amrita wanted you to take her to America. I do not want to go to America. They do not like people like me, I've heard. I'm not white and I take jobs from Americans. No, I will go somewhere else. India, maybe South America. I will fit in better there. Much better. I can work and have a little house and grow old without bullets flying around."

"How will you get there?" asked Temple.

"I will find a way."

"Look, you help get us out of Myanmar and I'll pay your way to wherever you want to go," said Temple.

Thura looked at him closely. "Is this bullshit or the truth?"

"I mean it, Thura."

"Okay, I will hold you to that."

And they had left it at that.

They took turns surveilling the Friendship Hotel, where the four people were staying. The only time anyone had ever left was when the young woman went to a pharmacy. Thura was coming on duty and Nash off, but Nash followed her while Thura settled in to keep eyes on the hotel.

Wearing his hooded cloak, Nash went into the pharmacy and bought some mosquito repellant and gum. The woman was getting a prescription filled. Nash drew close enough to overhear the pharmacist confirm in English that the prescription was for digoxin.

Nash didn't know the term, but he searched for it on his phone.

Another name for digitalis. Probably for the elderly woman, who must have a heart problem of some kind.

While pretending to look over some headache medications Nash studied the woman's reflection in a mirror set up on one wall. She was in her late twenties or early thirties, he estimated, tall, wiry, fit, and focused.

After she departed he took his time leaving, paying for the gum and repellent. He knew where the woman was going back to, and if she was suspicious of his presence in the pharmacy, his not following her back would hopefully alleviate that concern.

When he returned to the hotel Thura told him that no one else from the party had left the hotel. Nash filled him in on the digitalis, and Thura said, "My mother took that before she died. Big heart problems." He tapped his thick chest. "I might have them, too, who knows?"

"Surely you've been checked for it," said Nash.

"Of course! I go to doctor every week to make sure I am good to go," said Thura with heavy sarcasm.

"Sorry, I didn't mean it like that."

"Not to worry. I hear your health care is not too good, either. What is it you Americans do with all your money anyway?"

"It mostly goes into the pockets of a few, and the rest get the scraps."

Thura's expression screwed up in confusion. "Then why not change it, so the few don't get so much?"

"Ever heard of the term *lobbyists*?"

Thura shook his head.

"Well, I wish I hadn't, either." Nash paused. "You're taking a risk helping us. You don't even know what we're here for."

"Life is always risky, at least for people like me. And I know you are interested in the prison and the four people in that hotel. Do I need to know more?"

"With the money my boss will pay you, how will you get out of here?"

"How will *you* get out of here?"

Nash eyed him and a possibility that had already occurred to him solidified in his mind. "Maybe we can go together."

"Okay, but you have to think ahead, my friend, to all the bad that can happen and say to yourself, 'What can I do if the shit goes down?' I don't mean when it goes down. I mean before it blows up in your face."

"I agree with you."

Thura laughed. "I will tell my children that. You agree with me."

"Wait, you have children?"

"No, man, but maybe someday. If I live long enough to find a good woman."

Nash wondered if Amrita might have been a good woman for Thura.

Thura's eyes narrowed. "Good women are hard to come by, for men like me."

"That's something else you can tell your children that I agree with you on."

Nash left him there, drove the Jeep to a gas station, and filled its tank and then half filled a five-gallon metal canister that he'd had Thura procure. He then drove back to where they were staying. He woke up his boss and explained his plan to him.

Temple said, "It sounds crazy as hell. In fact, crazy enough to work."

"Let's hope so, because there ain't no Plan B."

CHAPTER

23

On the third day the two men and the two women rose from their beds. However, the young woman left her companions at the hotel, and the two men and the older woman later drove out of Bhamo in the 4Runner. It was now evening, and Nash, Temple, and Thura, who was driving, followed.

Nash said, "What else, if anything, do you know about the prison?"

"It was built maybe twenty years ago by the old regime. Then, about ten years ago, it was sold to a private company."

"Do you know to who?" asked Temple from the back seat.

"No. But whoever it is must be very rich. Prisons, even here, do not come cheap."

"You said your cousin used to work there. What sorts of prisoners are kept at the place?" asked Nash.

"I can tell you that when the prison was sold, all the prisoners there at that time were sent to other places within Myanmar."

"But why buy a prison with no prisoners?" said Nash. "As a private company you make your money by charging per prisoner, don't you?"

"Oh, they have prisoners now. But where they come from?" Thura shook his head. "Nobody knows. They're not from Burma. It is wild, man. My cousin told me that while he was there after it was sold, private jets came and private jets went. And on those jets prisoners come and prisoners stay, and the jets go back to where they came from."

"Private jets?" said Nash.

"There's an airstrip nearby. It is only for those who have permission. You do not have permission, man, they shoot your ass out the sky. Boom! My cousin finally quit last year because he said it was too stressful."

"He must have seen the prisoners?"

"Yeah, but he was told to never talk about it. They were serious about that, real serious."

"I suppose whoever owns the prison wants to keep all that a secret?" said Nash.

"Oh yeah. He can do what he wants, I guess. It is his place."

"You know it to be a man?" said Nash sharply.

"No. I never tried to find out. It would not be good for me."

"And yet here you are helping us," said Temple.

"You promised to get me out of here if I did," said Thura, eyeing him in the mirror. "And you had better keep your promise... If we make it out. If we don't, no worries, right? Because the dead have no worries." He grinned.

Two hours later they parked off the road and behind some large bushes after killing the lights. Adjacent to the bushes ran a field of grass nearly six feet high. Using a pair of night binoculars he had brought with him from Hong Kong, Nash got out of the Jeep and watched from behind some of the bushes. The SUV they'd been following had pulled off the road but on the other side. Twenty minutes later Nash sank down as another vehicle passed by and stopped parallel with the SUV. Four men got out of the second vehicle, and the two men from the SUV joined them. There was a brief discussion, and Nash watched as one of the four men opened the back of their vehicle and drew out some substantial firepower. He passed out these weapons to the other men.

Nash looked at his watch. It wouldn't be long now, he thought.

A minute later the men climbed back into their vehicles. They pulled well off the road and hid them behind thick underbrush and high grasses across the road from Nash. He continued to watch as two men from the second vehicle reappeared and placed something dark and flat in the roadway. He then hurried back to the Jeep and told the others about what he'd seen, including all the weaponry they'd be up against.

"Okay, Thura, an ambulance coming from the prison is going to appear along this road on its way to the hospital. There are six men up there who are going to stop it. There will be a woman in the ambulance. The guards will be subdued and the woman will be freed. The men believe they will be taking her to another location in a planned chain of stops prior to getting out of this country."

"But you will not allow this?" said Thura.

Nash said, "We *will* allow it, up to a certain point. What the men there don't know is that *we're* going to take the woman and get her out of here. And *they're* going to be left behind."

"But how will we get her out of here?" asked Thura nervously.

"You can leave that to us. But you'll be coming along for the ride," added Nash.

"You said those men have heavy firepower," Thura pointed out. "And there are six of them."

"Seven, counting one prison guard who's on their side and will no doubt be in the ambulance."

"Okay, seven. I only have a knife and you have two pistols. Not a fair fight."

"We'll have to level the playing field then," said Nash as he pulled out his guns and checked their loads, making sure each was racked with a round.

"How?" asked Thura.

"By putting our finger on the scales when it's best for us," replied Nash.

"But how will you do this?" Thura wanted to know.

"You'll have a ringside seat. But when we leave, you need to drive like a bat out of hell."

Thura smiled. "I do not know what that means, but it sounds like something I would like to do."

CHAPTER 24

A FEW MINUTES LATER NASH CHECKED THE TIME and told Temple and Thura, "Okay, they'll be here soon."

Thura looked at him and said, "Leave me one of your guns."

Nash eyed him, glanced at Temple, who shrugged, then handed his Beretta to Thura. "Aim straight and true," advised Nash.

"What other way is there to kill someone?" replied Thura.

Nash ducked out of the Jeep. Carrying the can of gas and a knapsack with the four casings of slurry, he threaded his way completely hidden through the high grass on his side of the road. He stopped when he was roughly parallel with the device that the men had laid over the road. He set the can down and inserted his homemade shoelace fuse through a hole he had punched into the can above the level of the gas. Making sure the gas cap was screwed on tight, he then splayed out the rest of the fuse along the ground. Leaving that spot, he placed the four casings about three feet apart, mentally gauging the location of the two hidden vehicles across the road as he did.

He checked his weapon a final time, did his four-and-four breathing, and tried to push from his mind how many ways his rather primitive plan could go wrong.

But it's not like I had much to work with.

As he crouched in the high grass Nash texted Thura and told him that when the ambulance approached he was to wait for the signal from Nash before starting the Jeep.

Now Nash awaited the arrival of the ambulance.

Ten minutes later Nash turned to the right when he heard the vehicle approaching. He slipped back to the first of the casings he had planted on the edge of the high grass, took out a lighter, and waited.

When the ambulance hit the spike strip the ambush party had placed across the road, all four tires were ripped to shreds, the driver lost control of the vehicle, and the ambulance ran off the road and onto the edge of the high grass.

Several prison guards emerged from the ambulance with their guns drawn. However, automatic gunfire erupted from the high grass and all of the guards were killed. Then the heavyset guard, the inside asset that Steers had shown them during their planning session back in Hong Kong, climbed out of the back of the ambulance.

Peering through the high grass, Nash watched as the guard hurried to the driver's side of the ambulance. Nash flinched when the man fired a round through the window.

The guard then opened the ambulance door, and the dead driver fell out onto the road.

The men with the automatic weapons who had dispatched the other prison guards quickly emerged from cover and rushed over to the vehicle.

Two of them slipped inside the rear of the ambulance and carried out an elderly woman in shackles. Nash had never seen Masuyo in person but had to assume that it was her. The prison guard briefly talked to the other men, and then the other elderly woman appeared from the corner of the bushes, escorted by one of the men from the first SUV. The guard unlocked Masuyo's shackles, and two of the men worked quickly to assist the women in exchanging clothes. With that finished, the guard shackled the other elderly woman and she was put into the ambulance.

Okay, thought Nash. *That was the reason for the other old woman. They're doing a switch so it'll look like the prison break wasn't successful.*

He had to admit, it was pretty damn brilliant.

Nash quickly lit the fuses on the four casings. He counted off seconds in his head as he flitted over to the long fuse that was connected to the half-full can of gas.

Smoke started pouring out of the casings and quickly rose above the high grass.

Nash heard people crying out, and he heard feet running toward the side of the road he was on.

He lit the long fuse and moved far away, lying flat on the ground. Some of the men fired shots at the smoke. Nash crawled to the edge of the high grass and peered out. The only man left by the ambulance was the guard. Masuyo stood beside him.

Nash sunk as low to the ground as he could and put his hands over his ears.

Five...four...three...two...one.

The lighted fuse reached the closed gas can and the concentrated vapor housed there, and the resulting explosion, equal to about thirty-five sticks of dynamite, was far more than even Nash had anticipated. He mouthed a silent prayer of thanks that he had moved so far away from the blast site. People screamed, and a flame ball soared into the sky, joining all the smoke that had been released from the four canisters. As the smoke billowed across the road, Nash heard Thura start the Jeep because the explosion was his signal to do so.

Nash jumped up from his hiding spot and ran out from the high grass. Two of the ambush team lay dead, their bodies dismembered from the explosion. Another member of the team ran screaming out of the high grass, flames dancing all over his torso. He saw Nash, who raised his weapon and shot him in the chest. The man dropped to the ground, dead. It was as much an act of mercy by Nash as anything.

A fourth member of the ambush team, blackened and gagging, hurtled out of the brush right in front of Nash. He attacked Nash with a knife. Nash blocked the multiple thrusts of the blade and then gripped the man's wrist, torqued it back and up, tripped the man with his ankle, and drove him hard into the dirt while using the knife to strike multiple blows into his side and neck. The man was dead before Nash rose off him.

Nash's gaze darted to the left as the fifth member of the ambush team raced across the road heading for the ambulance. The confused guard struggled to unholster his weapon, while Masuyo cowered behind him.

Nash rolled to his right, grabbed his pistol where it had fallen, came up in a crouch, took aim, and fired two shots. Both of them hit the man, one in the neck and one in the back, and he went down. Nash ran across to check on him. When Nash turned him over, the man let out one final gasp and grew still.

Nash sat there on his haunches for a few seconds, surveying all the death and destruction he had caused.

I've come a long way from crying over killing a cricket with my BB gun. It's not progress. Actually, it's the reverse.

But Nash had made a strategic miscalculation. The sixth and final member of the ambush team now emerged unscathed from the high grass. He took aim at Nash just about the time the Jeep bore down on them. A shot was fired and the sixth man took the round in the head.

Nash whipped around at the sound. Sitting in the Jeep's driver's seat, Thura lowered his gun and called out, "Straight and true; you're welcome, man."

Nash quickly searched several of the dead men and found an envelope stuffed with Burmese currency in one of their pockets. Then he sprinted across the road to where the guard was standing, still paralyzed. Masuyo was staring at Nash curiously but was now showing no sign of fear. Nash next looked in the rear of the ambulance and saw the elderly woman in Masuyo's prison uniform and wearing her shackles. He looked between the two women and could find no discernible difference. He could imagine that the substitute had been chosen for her natural similarity to the other woman and then perhaps she had undergone plastic surgery to make their appearances indistinguishable. Otherwise, the plan wouldn't have worked.

Thura pulled the Jeep to a stop next to them.

"When do I drive like a bat out of hell?" he said to Nash.

"Soon."

Temple poked his head out of the window. "That was some serious shit back there, Dillon. Good job."

"Come and get her," Nash said to Temple, as he indicated Masuyo.

Temple jumped out, helped the woman into the Jeep, and climbed into the rear seat next to her.

Nash looked at the guard. "Do you speak English?" The man looked at him blankly. Nash said to Thura, "Tell him that the men who we killed were not part of the plan. We were the ones hired to free Masuyo, and the other men ambushed us and then got here before we did with the other woman, who they took from us. They were trying to kidnap Masuyo for their own purposes."

Thura slowly translated all of this to the guard, whose face showed increasing levels of astonishment.

Nash said, "Now tell him he is to drive the prisoner on to the hospital in the Toyota hidden in the bushes. He's to report in and let them know about the ambush attempt and that the kidnappers have all been killed. The substitute will be returned to the prison as Masuyo. He will be hailed as a hero."

Thura conveyed all of this. The guard looked across at the smoke and flames and dead bodies. He told Thura that he understood and it was good that they came along when they did. Nash found the Toyota's keys in the pocket of one of the dead men and handed them to the guard. Nash then seized the man's gun, pointed it in the air, and fired off the remaining bullets.

"Tell him I did this so they will believe he shot and killed the other men."

Thura translated, and the guard smiled and nodded. Nash handed him back his empty gun.

"Tell him good luck." Thura did so. When Nash handed the man the envelope full of cash the guard even shook Nash's hand and said some words that Nash did not understand but deduced were probably "Thank you."

Nash climbed into the Jeep and said to Thura, "*Now* you can drive like a bat out of hell."

While Thura drove, Nash turned and looked at Masuyo. His time had been consumed recently with the mission of freeing the woman, and now seeing her in the flesh Nash concluded that he was underwhelmed by her appearance.

But then, when she glanced at him, he saw, just behind the eyes, something he had seen before. In the daughter. A level of extreme ruthlessness, coupled with a haughty superiority that made his skin crawl. He shot Temple a look, and the man shrugged and glanced nervously at Masuyo.

Nash gave further directions to Thura. They made the turn at the crossroads, and after a short drive down that road they saw the chopper parked in a cleared field.

They left the Jeep, hurried across with Masuyo, and climbed aboard. The pilot asked no questions, but upon seeing Masuyo he nodded, powered up the bird, and they were soon aloft. The flight to Lashio was swift and uneventful.

When they landed in Lashio, a vehicle was waiting and they were immediately driven off toward Mandalay. No one would be searching for them because the prison officials would believe the attempt to free Masuyo had failed and the kidnappers had all died at the scene. If they investigated carefully some holes in the story would emerge, of course. But Nash could do nothing about that. And they'd be long gone by then.

He did wonder about Steers's carefully timed getaway plan. He hadn't known about the plot to switch Masuyo with a manufactured twin. If things had gone according to plan, the only way the substitute plan would have worked was if the guards had all been killed, save the inside guard, but the kidnappers would have either all been killed or else fled without Masuyo. That seemed convoluted, thought Nash.

But if we were supposed to die, then Steers's plan had to be that we were the only kidnappers. We would be found dead there, having failed to free Masuyo, the other guards would have been killed, and Steers's paid-off guard would be the only one left to explain what had happened. Which was why he had to kill the driver. So we really were the patsies.

Right before they arrived in Mandalay he finally got a reply to his days' earlier message to Agent Reed Morris.

Can you make it back to Hong Kong? We can arrange to meet you.

Nash texted back, We'll be heading there shortly in Steers's jet. But no need to intervene. We are delivering Masuyo to Steers.

The FBI agent's reply was fast and terse: Are you out of your damn mind?

Nash texted back, Maybe.

He had debated whether to get the FBI involved at this point and bring Masuyo into their custody. But what would that do? It was highly doubtful the FBI would be able to leverage Masuyo to get to Steers. And then Nash would have no more access to Steers and thus no possibility of bringing her down. He would just have to go into hiding for the rest of his life with no justice for his daughter.

Or for me.

When they reached the private airstrip Steers's sleek jet was waiting, its door open and the jetway down. Two pilots and a flight attendant stood at attention.

The flight attendant came over to them, bowed to Masuyo, and handed her a passport. The elderly woman's fingers clutched the object like it was gold. And for the first time since her freedom had been secured she smiled. Nash and Temple already had the necessary documents to clear entry into Hong Kong. However, Thura's presence had not been planned for. When Nash explained that they needed to get him into the country under Steers's orders, the attendant nodded and said that on the flight she would communicate the information to Steers's people in Hong Kong, and the necessary entry documents would be awaiting them there. She took Thura's passport and then hurried onto the plane to begin this process.

Nash glanced at the jet and thumbed in another message to Morris, giving the man the jet's tail number. That way the Bureau would at least be able to track it to Hong Kong.

Thura said, "You gonna be mixing up more stuff that goes boom?"

"You never know," replied Nash as they all headed on board.

Five minutes later the jet rocketed eastward into a clear sky over Myanmar and back to a woman who had tried her best to leave them dead in the very same place.

CHAPTER 25

AFTER AN EXHAUSTED MASUYO FELL asleep in the jet's bedroom, Nash held a meeting with Temple and Thura in the main cabin.

Temple said, "Look, when you first told me your plan was to return the mother to the daughter, I thought you were out of your mind. But then I realized I didn't want to be looking over my shoulder the rest of my life. So, it seems to me that even though she probably wanted us as scapegoats, the fact that we got her mother out? She'll owe us. Now, I know the lady kills people and I wouldn't trust her as far as I can throw her. And believe me, I'd throw her into a fucking dumpster fire in a heartbeat, but she obviously loves her mother, so that's got to be in our favor. Right?"

Nash nodded. "Let's hope. But now we have to get our stories straight for when we get back. And we have to have an explanation for why Thura is still with us."

"Do you *have* an explanation?" asked Temple anxiously.

"I think so. A good one."

"It needs to be better than good, Dillon. Her bullshit meter ranks right up there with a basset hound's nose."

They spent the next several hours working through all the details. Nash allowed extra time with Thura to go over what to say and not say.

"If you get in trouble with a question, just blame it on the language barrier, okay?"

"This woman is…?" said Thura nervously.

"Yeah, she is," replied Nash, who knew exactly what the man meant.

They all caught a couple hours' sleep before the plane began its descent into Hong Kong.

The jet taxied to a stop at a private facility on the periphery of the main airport. They deplaned and were shuttled over to the main terminal to go through passport control. There a man approached and provided Thura with the papers he needed to enter the country legally.

Once they cleared customs and walked out into the arrivals section, Nash saw a man holding up a sign in Mandarin. When Temple had told him Masuyo's actual name was Dai Lu, a curious Nash had looked it up in Mandarin. Thus he could recognize the characters on the sign. For obvious reasons, Steers had not had her people use the name Masuyo.

Nash led the others over to the man and introduced Masuyo as Dai Lu. They were escorted out of the airport and into what looked to be the same Mercedes van that had picked up Nash and Temple when they had initially arrived in Hong Kong.

They followed the same route, taking the tunnel under the harbor and finally pulling into the underground garage of Steers's building. They rode the elevator up to the penthouse suite and when the doors opened, Steers was standing there.

Nash announced matter-of-factly, "Here's your mother, Ms. Steers, safe and sound."

"Mission accomplished," added Temple in a grander fashion.

Steers ignored this, looked at her mother, and bowed so deeply her long hair touched the floor. She straightened, took her mother's hand, and gently led her into the apartment.

Masuyo said something in Mandarin and Steers answered her in that language.

Masuyo turned and looked at Nash, Temple, and Thura. While Steers thumbed a message on her phone, her mother bowed her head slightly and said to them, "Thank you, gentlemen."

A female attendant quickly appeared in response to Steers's text, and Masuyo was escorted away.

Steers watched her go and then turned to them. "Come," she said, and led them into the next room.

They sat in chairs across from her. Nash noted that Steers's guards had appeared from the shadows and encircled them.

Steers opened by saying, "I was told that you did not get on the plane to Bhamo. Why was this?"

Drawing on his plan Nash said, "We were ambushed. Twice. First, we were almost killed in the mountains and had to run for it, which threw off our timing. Then one of the people you hired, Amrita, tried to kill us in Myitkyina, but Thura here saved our lives."

She glanced at Thura, who seemed to shrink under her gaze. She looked back at Nash. "Why would she try to kill you?"

"I believe she was paid off by the same people who tried to kill us in the mountains. There must have been a leak somewhere," he added, staring at her resolutely. His implication was clear: The leak must have come from her side.

"Go on," she said, her look unreadable.

"We left Myitkyina early and took a ferry to get to Bhamo because we figured we'd be sitting ducks if we flew on that plane. We tracked down the men you hired and saw the woman who was to take your mother's place."

Steers interjected, "I did not tell you about that element, so how did you know that was part of the plan?"

"You showed us a picture of your mother and they could have been twins. It became obvious that your plan was to rescue your mother, but not have the prison even realize she was gone." He added, in genuine admiration, "It really was a brilliant plan, Ms. Steers."

"Continue," she said tersely, but her expression showed that his praise had pleased her.

"However, without the men knowing, Thura overheard them

saying that they were going to kidnap your mother and hold her hostage. They were planning to blackmail you into paying a hundred million in U.S. dollars for her return."

Steers once more looked at Thura. "You heard this?"

He nodded, keeping his gaze on her. "Yes. Their passports said they were Pakistani. But they were speaking English at the hotel where I overheard them. They were stupid to do so. Everybody speaks English in Burma, but Urdu or Pashto, not so much."

"So you still call it Burma?" questioned Steers.

"Yes. What is this 'Myanmar' bullshit? I was born in *Burma*, not this other place."

Steers actually smiled warmly at the man's heartfelt words.

Nash was surprised at how much this changed the woman's overall appearance. *She seems...human. Well, almost.*

Nash then gave Thura an appreciative look and took up the conversation. "So we decided not to meet up with them, but to follow them instead. We got there before the ambulance. The team you hired shot all the prison guards when the ambulance arrived and were about to shoot your guy on the inside when I set off some homemade bombs. We managed to kill all of them and save your mother and the guard. We gave him the monies we found on the kidnappers. They obviously had no intention of paying him. We told him about their plan and then had him drive the woman substituted for your mother on to the hospital in one of the kidnappers' vehicles. The woman is no doubt at the prison, the guard is a hero, and the other guards and the ambulance driver and the kidnappers are dead. So they can't tell anyone about the substitution. Your plan, as modified by conditions on the ground, worked to perfection." Nash added, "And Thura here went above and beyond the call of duty, so I told him that he would be taken care of, too. He has earned a just reward."

Steers glanced at each of them before settling her gaze back on Nash. She said nothing but studied him for several uncomfortable moments. Nash felt like his mind was being x-rayed by the woman.

But he kept his expression calm and stared earnestly back until she finally said, "Thank you for successfully bringing my mother to me."

Nash said, "And thank *you* for your faith in us."

She looked at him again, conjuring in Nash that x-ray feeling once more.

Fortunately Temple said, "So where do we go from here, Ms. Steers?"

"I think showers, fresh clothes, food, and sleep are the obvious next moves for each of you," she said, running her eyes over their dirty faces and hands, soiled clothing, and wan features. "We will reconvene when you have sufficiently recovered." She took up her phone and sent off various messages. Within a minute more attendants had entered the space and led the men away.

Nash looked back at Steers as she sat in her throne chair, staring off. He knew her suggestion that they reconvene later had been made more to buy herself time to process all this than it had to do with concerns over their personal comfort.

Yet where it went from here, Nash did not know.

Perhaps now, with her actual plan foiled, neither does Victoria Steers.

CHAPTER 26

The next day, bathed, rested, and fed, and wearing clean clothes, Nash and Temple stood outside on the balcony of their apartment. As before they had also turned on the radio to disrupt any sort of electronic eavesdropping.

Thura had been ensconced in another apartment on the same floor.

Temple yawned, stretched, and said, "I have to say I'm happy as hell to be out of Myanmar, but I'm not sure we're any safer here, really."

Nash nodded, his look absent, his thoughts far away.

His voice as low as possible, Temple said, "And you played it really well turning the tables on the other guys and letting *them* be the scapegoats."

Nash kept his gaze on the cityscape below. At the airport in Hong Kong he had surreptitiously thrown away the phone Thura had given him. He didn't like not having communication capability, but he knew that Steers would search all they had, and if she found it the woman would demand that he unlock it. And while his communications with the FBI were secure, the app he was using to communicate with the Bureau would be impossible to explain. And if she demanded that he show her his messages, and he refused?

I'd be dead, regardless of my having saved her mother.

He couldn't be candid with Temple, either, since his goal was to take him down too. So his thoughts were his own for now, and his counsel as well.

He said quietly, "What interests me far more are how things will be now between mother and daughter."

"You're thinking maybe the queen is no longer the queen?" noted Temple.

"I'm just not sure how it plays out, Rhett, now that there are *two* queens in residence."

"Look, we need to be thinking about our exit strategy, Dillon. I don't believe our chances are going to get any better than they are right now. Gratitude only lasts so long."

Nash had been afraid of this. He knew that at some point his and Temple's goals would no longer align, and maybe they had abruptly reached that crossroads.

Temple said, "In that vein, I'm going to do a little negotiating with the woman today."

"You think that's a good idea?"

"It's a better idea than hanging around until she decides to kill us once and for all."

Temple went back inside, and Nash looked down over the bustling city. His time in the corporate world had been spent on the proverbial hamster's wheel. Before one deal was done you were already looking for the next one on the horizon and the next one and the one after that. It was Pavlov on steroids, only Nash wasn't a dog. At least the canine had the excuse of being domesticated.

He went to Thura's room and found him finishing his breakfast.

A big smile on his face, he looked around at his luxurious surroundings and said, "Man, I got sheets on the bed and a proper toilet that actually works. And the food?" He finished his eggs and toast and washed it down with the remains of his coffee. "And the bath? Dillon, it has a tub. I soaked in a damn tub, man!"

Nash sat down across from him. "Glad you're enjoying it, Thura. So let's talk about the future. Where do you want to go from here?"

Thura's smile diminished and he put the empty cup down. "I got no work visa for this place. So I can't stay all that long. At passport control I had to show my return flight ticket back to Myanmar that your people got me. But I ain't going back there, man."

"Any place you'd *like* to go?"

"Why?"

"Thought I'd put in a good word on your behalf to Ms. Steers." Nash put a finger to his lips, then pointed to his ears and glanced around.

To his credit, Thura picked up on this quickly. "Well, I hear London is nice, with lots of folks from everywhere. Or maybe France. If I could find work."

"How about the U.S.?"

"I told you that is not a good place for me. And I hear they've shut their borders."

"There are always ways."

"That might be nice then. Big country. I'm sure I can find something to do."

"You have any family left?"

"No parents. Had a brother. Think he's dead. Had a sister. I buried her. Covid."

"I'm sorry."

He shrugged. "Lots of people die, man. So, no, I ain't got nobody."

"Okay, let me talk to her and then I'll get back to you."

"You don't have to take care of me, Dillon, but it is nice that you think to."

"I wouldn't be here if it wasn't for you, Thura. Debts like that never really get repaid."

CHAPTER 27

Steers looked sternly at Temple as they sat across from each other in her office.

"How is your mother this morning?"

"Fine," Steers said tersely. "You wished to discuss something?"

"Yes, namely where we go from here," said Temple.

"Meaning?"

"Meaning what role, if any, do you see for me in the future? Also, I would like to get back home," he added, before she could respond.

"What role are you seeking?"

"Well, if you want the truth, I'd rather just go about my business and you go about yours."

"Meaning no more involvement with me then?"

"Look, Ms. Steers, I'm not going to try to bullshit you, because you're way too smart for that. I just want to get out of this now and go live my life. But you can continue to use Sybaritic for your purposes."

"How, without you there?" she interjected.

"I control the board of directors. I can name anyone you want to be the CEO. And I will. You just say the word."

She sat back and considered this. "And why should I allow this?"

"I would hope that my risking my life to get your mother back here safely would be worth something to you."

"So you can simply run along and enjoy your father's billions?"

"You knew my father. I hope you would agree that I earned every dollar as the son he loved to belittle at every opportunity."

This statement seemed to take her aback. "I will give your proposal full consideration and give you a decision by tomorrow."

"I appreciate that. I really do." He rose to leave.

"And Mr. Hope?"

"What about him?"

"What will be his fate?"

Temple sat back down. "I just assumed that he would travel back to the States with me."

"I do not like people making assumptions about things that concern me."

"I'm sorry, Ms. Steers, I wasn't aware that he concerned you in any way. I mean, he's just my bodyguard."

"And if I wish to retain him here?"

"Look, feel free to make him whatever offer you want. He's a good man. I'd hate to lose him, but it's not a deal-breaker for me."

"So you simply leave it up to him?"

Temple looked startled. "I...I'm not sure what you mean."

"You are unwilling to make the decision to have him stay here?"

"I'm not sure I have the power to do that. It's a free country. He's an independent contractor. He can go and do what he wants."

"*This* is not a *free* country, Mr. Temple."

"I...I don't know what you want me to do."

"You can order Mr. Hope to remain here."

"But regardless of what I tell him, he doesn't have to stay here." He paused. "Unless you...unless you force him to. So what does it matter what I do or don't do?"

"The point is, Mr. Temple, I want you to order him to remain here. Once you do that I will take care of the rest, and you may leave. I will fly you back on my jet, and I will send to you the name of the person I want to become the next CEO of Sybaritic. Then *our* business is concluded. *That* is my decision. You have no need to wait any longer for it."

Temple looked relieved but also wary. "So let me get this straight.

All I have to do is order him to stay and then you will make him do so? And then I'm free to go on with my life?"

"After the new CEO of my choosing is appointed, yes."

Temple took a few moments to think all of this through. However, he could think of no downside for him. "I'll order him to stay with you right away."

She gazed at him disdainfully. "I knew that you would. But there is one more thing that I require of you."

He looked at her anxiously. "What?"

"You never found Walter Nash."

"Look, I tried—"

"You clearly did not try hard enough. That is your assignment, if you truly want your freedom. And I will be checking." She waved her hand in dismissal.

Temple immediately left. Out of her sight he had the broadest smile on his face.

I can string her along on Nash. So I am fucking free at last.

He never gave a thought to the fate of Dillon Hope.

Yet he was the son of a narcissist, and the apple had apparently fallen right next to that warped tree.

CHAPTER 28

The next morning Masuyo emerged from her room to find an attendant waiting.

"Do you require anything, ma'am?" said the woman respectfully.

Masuyo glanced over her and said bluntly, "My daughter. Her I require. Tell her to come to me. I will be in the dining room where I will take my breakfast. Now."

The woman took out a phone, texted a message, and hurried off as Masuyo made her way slowly to the dining room. She was dressed all in silk, which felt cool and soft against her skin. She admired the costly furnishings and artwork and sculptures that were arrayed around the penthouse. Each servant and bodyguard she passed bowed solemnly to her.

My daughter has done well, because I trained her correctly. This is how it should be.

Masuyo entered the dining room, where her place setting was being laid out and her tea poured by another attendant.

"Excuse me," said Masuyo imperiously. "You will set my place at the *head* of the table."

The attendant froze, but only for a moment. Then she quickly rearranged the setting so that Masuyo would be at the demanded spot.

The chair was then held out for her. She sat down and the napkin was placed in her lap. She lifted the cup of tea to her nose, took a sniff, and nodded her approval. Masuyo then gave her meal order. The attendant scurried off.

Masuyo drank her tea, set the cup down, and pressed the napkin against her lips. Each of her movements was slow and deliberate because she wanted to relish each moment.

Masuyo looked up when her daughter entered, dressed all in black.

"Good morning, Māma," she said. "Did you sleep well?"

"Much better than I have slept for years, my child. Please, sit with me."

From her expression, it seemed that Steers had just realized that her mother was seated in the chair she would normally use. She sat down next to her and took her mother's hand in hers. "You look better already."

"I feel better. Much better. You did well, in all things, Victoria."

"Thank you, Māma."

"The men you sent, especially the tall, white one. He killed many men to save me."

"Please tell me about it, Māma. It would be most useful to me."

Masuyo did so, speaking slowly and clearly. After describing her leaving the prison and her journey to the hospital she said, "They had just put the other woman into the ambulance after shooting all the guards save one."

"The guard who was assigned to you: He was my person."

"And the tall man with no hair...?"

"Yes, his name is Dillon Hope."

"He handled himself admirably. Quite resourceful and brave. And lethal. The rest of the night was helicopters and cars and jets. Quite the exciting time, Victoria."

"Yes, perhaps too exciting." Steers kissed her mother's hand. "You wished to see me?"

"Yes. Now that I am back, I require certain information."

"Such as, Māma?" asked Steers.

"I need to be brought up to speed on all the various business operations that you have. I also need to understand the parties involved."

Steers started to say something but then seemed to catch herself.

"Of course, Māma, this will be done. We can meet after dinner tonight. Before that you will have all that information at your disposal to go over."

Masuyo clutched her hand, pulling Steers toward her. "I do all this in your best interests, my child. I have been out of your life and out of this business for a long time. But that does not mean that I have not thought of both in great detail. I had nothing else to do with my time, you see. And such thoughtfulness, from an outside perspective as it were, can be invaluable."

"I believe this too, Māma," agreed Steers.

Masuyo withdrew her hand and said, "Now, show me."

"Show you what?"

Masuyo tapped her finger against Steers's sleeve. "That. I saw a hint of it in the prison when you came to see me, which is why I drew back your sleeve that day. You said it was only some damage. Now I need to understand how much."

"It is not something that you would want to see *more* of."

"I carried you in my body for nine months, Victoria. There is nothing about you that I cannot see."

Slowly, Steers drew her sleeve up, revealing the damaged skin underneath.

"How far does it go?" her mother asked.

"Both my arms, and parts of my back."

"You may cover yourself, my child."

Steers did so.

"Who did this?"

"I was never able to find out."

Her mother nodded. "Such actions must have consequences or else they will think you are weak."

"It has been a long time, Māma. It will be very difficult. And I have clearly shown that I am *not* weak."

Masuyo smiled sadly. "I know it is a high bar I hold you to, my beautiful daughter."

Steers bowed her head. "Of course. I expect nothing less."

When her food came Masuyo asked Steers to sit with her while she ate. As she did so, Masuyo said, "The other men with Mr. Hope? Explain."

"One is Rhett Temple. He is the CEO of Sybaritic, an American investment company. It is through his firm that I conduct some of the business."

"And what will you do with him now?"

"He wishes to return to the United States. He will place one of my people as CEO of his company and then he wants to live off his quite large inheritance."

"And will his plan work for you?" asked Masuyo.

"Yes, with some additional conditions attached."

"And Mr. Hope?"

"I wish him to remain here. Along with the other man, Thura. As you know, he helped with your liberation."

"And why do you wish Mr. Hope to remain here?"

"I want him and Thura to be *your* bodyguards."

Her mother sipped her tea and pursed her lips. "You do not already have enough bodyguards for me?"

"Hope is exceptional. You saw that for yourself."

"Am I wrong in thinking that you already have exceptional protection?"

"Hope is different."

"Tell me how he is different."

Steers frowned at the woman's obvious persistence. "Is it important?"

"I do not have enough information to answer your question."

"I...he is an interesting person. An enigma. I have yet to... figure him out. I wish him to remain here while I do so."

Masuyo ran her gaze over her daughter. "All right, Victoria. We will leave it there for now. But does he know you wish him to remain?"

Steers looked toward the doorway. "He will know soon enough."

"And if he does not wish to remain here?"

"He does not have a choice, Māma."

Masuyo gazed sternly at her daughter. "Are you sure that *you* have a choice in the action you are taking with this man?"

Steers averted her gaze. "I do not know what you mean."

Her look flinty, Masuyo said, "Your lies worked with many, your father included. But not with me, Victoria. Never with me."

Steers rose and said, "I have business to attend to. We will talk tonight. Continue to rest, Māma."

"I have had years to 'rest,' daughter. I require no more."

Steers hurried from the room while Masuyo turned back to her meal.

CHAPTER 29

"You're actually ordering me to stay here?" said Nash.

He and Temple were out on the balcony of their apartment.

"Look, when I met with Steers earlier, she said I had to tell you to stay. I didn't want to do it. I thought of every conceivable argument against having you stay, but she wasn't buying it. The lady's mind was made up."

"Why?" asked Nash. "Why does she want me to stay here?"

"She's nuts, in case you hadn't noticed."

"And are *you* staying?"

Temple glanced away, his expression one of guilt. "Um, no, actually. I'm returning to the States. Fairly soon."

"So she didn't want *you* to stay?"

"Obviously not."

"And you're just leaving me here?"

"No, Dillon. I'm going to get you out of here, but I can't do that if I'm stuck here, too. Once I get back home I'm going to work to get you out of here. I promise."

Nash observed that Temple was rubbing his thumb and forefinger together, a tell that he had seen the man do over the years when stressed or lying.

"And Thura? Is he staying?"

Temple fixed his gaze on Nash. "I don't know. She didn't mention him. If not, he can fly home with me. But if he wants to stay, it's up to him. If he doesn't, I'll get you both out. I promise."

Temple looked away again, Nash noted. That was another tell of the man's deceit.

"So you really have no idea why she wants me to stay?" asked Nash.

"If you want a spitball opinion, I think you've impressed her, especially with all you did back in Myanmar. I'm sure her mother told her everything. She likes having the best around her. It's actually a compliment to you, Dillon. And she will probably pay you, like, a fortune. This actually could be an excellent career move for you to make," he added, looking hopeful.

Yeah, so you can forget all about me, thought Nash. He said, "Sure, being a bodyguard to a global criminal, always on my bucket list. And she already has a world-class protection team, so what do I do?"

"Maybe she's sweet on you. You know, the tatted, muscled bad boy and all. And she's actually good-looking, and her body looks pretty rack."

"Right, she's a real catch if you overlook the homicidal element. Okay, so now what?"

"I would expect a visit from the woman to follow up. It seemed like a high priority."

"And if I tell her I want to leave and go back home?"

Temple shook his head. "I would not advise that, Dillon. Steers does not take no for an answer. I know that better than most. And she already cut both of us up. And we saw her shoot Ryder in the head. She will not let you live if you cross her."

"So I'm out of luck?"

"I will get you out of here. You just have to hang on, that's all. So when she talks to you, tell her you'll agree to stay on, for some period of time. Leave it open. Then I get back to the States and start working on getting you home."

"And how exactly will you do that?"

"Hell, I'm worth billions now, Dillon. I can hire the best guys. I'll take care of it, don't you worry. It'll be my top priority. I swear to you."

He slapped Nash on the shoulder and went back inside.

Nash looked down at the streets of Hong Kong all those stories below. It would be easy to jump. In sixty stories it would all be over. Yes, that would be the easy way out. The hard path would be to stay here and finish what he came here to do. And Nash knew which course he would be pursuing. Every time his confidence failed him, all he needed to do was conjure up the image of his dead daughter, and it supplied his spine with necessary steel.

He thought things through, particularly his conversation with Temple. It didn't bother him that the man had just lied to him. He had expected nothing less now that their goals were no longer aligned. Yet he wondered why Steers had given Temple an out. He had either agreed to go back and run Sybaritic as before and let her continue to use his platform for her illegal business, or else he had offered to put one of Steers's people in as CEO.

So Steers wins, Temple wins, and you lose, Nash. But do you really? This is actually what you wanted. To stay here and keep working it from the inside. And then when the opportunity arises, kill her and end this whole thing.

He turned when he saw one of Steers's bodyguards appear at the sliding glass door.

"Ms. Steers wishes a word with you. Now." He said all of this with a grimace, as though something distasteful was in his mouth.

Nash reluctantly followed the guard to the elevator. *Okay, here we go for round two. And I thought surviving Myanmar was hard.*

CHAPTER 30

Nash was taken to a large study that held a gas fireplace. This struck him as odd, since even in its coldest months Hong Kong never got much below fifty degrees Fahrenheit.

But perhaps because of her injuries Steers feels the chill more? Ironic if fire could make you cold.

There was a large desk with a closed laptop on it. The shelves held many books and some small sculptures and photos. As he waited for Steers he wandered the room looking at the books and pictures.

Reading-wise she seemed to favor business books, but there were also a number of spy classics from John LeCarré and Eric Ambler.

He pulled one book off the shelf and glanced through the pages. It was full of handwritten marginalia and underlined sections. It was *The Art of War*, attributed to the fifth-century BC Chinese military strategist Sun Tzu.

Nash read through the notes carefully before he put the book back on the shelf and turned his attention to the array of photos displayed on a waist-high counter of one of the built-in shelving units.

In one photo were seven people: a far younger and regal-looking Masuyo; her presumably English husband, Joseph Steers, who was short and beefy with reddish hair; and in between them, five children, also presumably theirs. The oldest was a boy who looked to be around fourteen. There were two more sons, and a daughter who looked to be about eight. The youngest, who was standing next to her mother, was Victoria Steers, and she looked to be around five. She was already tall for her age while the other children seemed to have taken after their diminutive father.

Masuyo was staring directly into the camera with an imperious expression, while Victoria shyly glanced off to the side, with her ankles crossed, and fingers hovering near her mouth. Victoria was dressed in a frilly white dress with black ballet flats. Her hair was done in pigtails, and though she wasn't looking directly at the camera, the one eye visible seemed full of mischief. She actually looked quite cute and...normal, thought Nash grudgingly.

So what the hell happened to transform the woman into a monster?

As he looked at her four siblings he answered his own question.

The competition happened, instigated by her mother, and she killed her three brothers and one sister and took control. And the cute little shy girl was gone forever.

Nash was surprised, considering their fates, that Steers had even kept photos of her siblings.

"I did not mean to keep you waiting."

Nash turned to see Steers standing in the doorway. She seemed to move with the silence of a ghost.

"That's okay. It's an interesting and *enlightening* room."

Steers glanced sharply at the photo he'd been looking at and a frown creased her face. Steers walked behind the desk and sat, motioning for him to sit across from her.

"It is quiet in here and I can think," she said tersely. "Everyone needs such a space, even if it exists only in their minds."

"I see you're a reader."

"I value books, yes. They broaden horizons and they also allow one to learn from the mistakes of others."

He nodded and sat back. *And now to business*, he thought.

"I presume that Mr. Temple spoke with you?" she said.

"He did."

"Then you are aware of how things lie?"

"I'm aware, but that's not the same as understanding."

She let her gaze slowly roll over him; Nash found her penetrating look to be disquieting.

"My mother told me of your bravery and skill in rescuing her." She paused and glanced down at her hands. "She seemed quite taken with you, in fact."

"I did my job. I'm glad she was unharmed, and I'm happy that the two of you have been reunited. And I would be dead except for Thura. He saved my life over there."

"She wants you, and Thura, to be her personal bodyguards. And I agree."

"I'm sure your current protection detail is more than adequate."

"That is irrelevant," she said brusquely. "My mother desires the two of you, so that is how it must be."

"And I have no choice in the matter?"

Her lips formed a firm line. "You either work for me in protecting my mother, or you do not go on existing. The same for your comrade."

"And yet Rhett Temple gets to go home?"

"But he still works for me."

"How long will this arrangement be for?"

"At the very least it will be for the lifetime of my mother, and though she is old, she is remarkably resilient."

"So years," said Nash dully. "And we stay here then? As prisoners?"

"You will be amply paid. Amply paid," she repeated, her imperial manner dissolving somewhat and her gaze softening. "Your every need will be fulfilled. That includes women, when you want and however many you want, day or night. Quite beautiful women who know how to please men."

"That's quite a strange offer for a job interview," noted Nash.

"You are a man," she replied simply. "Men need these things. I'm sure your friend Thura will not complain. He looked quite *robust* in that regard." She paused. "As do you."

This comment made Nash look away. He was inwardly trembling with rage. On the one hand he had achieved what he desired: a way to stay next to Steers and company in the hopes of bringing her to justice or, as a last resort, killing the woman. But the manner in which he had gained this access, by becoming her pawn and prisoner, angered him to his absolute emotional and mental limits. He composed himself, conscious that she was watching him closely, and said, "I will let you know when and if I require such…services. I will tell Thura as well."

"You will be paid two million American dollars per year. Thura will be paid half of that. Accounts will be set up and the monies deposited on a biweekly basis. You will have full access to the funds. And you will live here for free."

His eyes widened. "That is an extraordinarily generous compensation package."

"You saved my mother. I am feeling generous."

"Do I get a telephone as one of the perks?"

"You will be provided one, yes. For your *job*."

Right, one that will have surveillance software embedded in it, so you'll know everyone I call, email, or text, every site I access, every keystroke I make.

"You will also be fitted for new clothes, shoes, accessories, and whatever else you may need. The same for Thura. Your meals will be prepared for you, and your apartments cleaned by my staff. There is also a gymnasium on the basement level. My protection detail trains there. You are welcome to use it." She ran her gaze over his physique. "In your profession, I know that you need to keep fit."

"I'll need my weapons returned. They took them when we arrived back."

"Of course. You shall have them."

The two stared at one another. All Nash could visualize was raising a gun, aiming at her forehead, and pulling the trigger.

With that thought in mind he asked, "Is there a gun range where I can maintain my shooting skills?"

"Yes. Now, is there anything else?"

"I suppose not."

"I am most happy to welcome you to our family, Mr. Hope. I will be in touch soon with further and more precise details regarding your protection of my mother."

"And how is she doing after her long ordeal?"

Nash saw just a flicker of the eyelids that seemed to represent a brief short-circuit in the woman's synapses.

"You will find that my mother, above all other things, is indomitable. She can survive anything. And after doing so, she then thrives."

She waved her hand at the door in a gesture of curt dismissal.

As Nash rose to leave he was wondering if the daughter wished her mother was a bit less indomitable and far less *thriving*.

CHAPTER
31

"ONE MILLION *AMERICAN* DOLLARS? JUST to guard the old lady? And we get to live here? And I can have women whenever I want? You're shitting me, right?"

Nash had had Thura come up to his apartment and they were standing out on the balcony to avoid being overheard. He had told him about their being hired to be Masuyo's security team and the details of that arrangement.

"I take it you don't have a problem with any of that?" said Nash.

Thura stared at him in confusion. "Why would I? I am in nirvana, man. And I'm not even dead!"

"I suppose we'll need to coordinate with Ms. Steers's protection detail."

Thura's smile faded a bit. "Them dudes do not like us, not one little bit. I seen it with my own eyes." He perked up. "But for a million bucks they can hate me all they want." Thura laughed but then noted Nash's stern expression. "You don't look happy, man."

"I don't like being told what to do."

"Wait, you did not have a choice?" said Thura.

"No, and neither did you, for that matter."

"So we can't, like, quit if we want to?"

"I wouldn't advise it, no," said Nash.

"That woman?"

"What about her?"

"She scares the shit out of me, just...being, man. Just by being."

"Well, I don't think her mother will be any easier," replied Nash.

"So when do we start?"

"I'm sure we already have in some ways. But officially, soon."

"And the other guy, your boss? Does he get to leave?" asked Thura.

"Yes, he's heading back to the States."

"So he's free then?" said Thura.

"I didn't say that, because he's not."

"What is really going on here?"

"Just keep your head down, do what you're told, and don't rock the boat."

"I am good at not rocking the boat. In Myanmar, I never rocked the boat."

"Until I came into your life," Nash pointed out.

Thura grinned. "Yes, you speak the truth there, man. So, the daughter, you think she'll treat us okay so long as we do our job?"

Nash rubbed his arm where the blade Steers wielded had cut him. "I hope so. But she can be difficult to read at times."

Thura went back to his apartment, and Nash looked in on Temple in his bedroom, where he was packing his things.

"Everything good with Steers?" Temple said, looking up.

"As good as they can be," replied Nash. "So, you going back to running your business?"

Temple shot him a glance. "Why, did Steers say something?"

"No, she just said that you two were still going to be doing business."

"Yes, that's right."

"So, I guess even though you're going home, you really won't be free of her, either."

"Keep that up, Hope, I might forget my promise to you," snarled the other man.

"Safe travels," said Nash before going to his room.

CHAPTER 32

Masuyo met with her daughter to go over the business. Then Masuyo spent the next two weeks conducting numerous phone calls with her daughter's business associates, from very important to very junior. She also spoke with Steers's attendants and security detail. She took all this data in, and the information she received filled out some thoughts in her mind.

My mission now is clear. I need to move forward in the most effective way possible. I now know what she is capable of, but more important, I know what she is not *capable of.*

The next day Masuyo had her first meeting with Nash and Thura.

Her daughter had provided her mother with her own suite of rooms in the penthouse; one space was a well-appointed office-study, where she sat across from the two men. Dressed in a colorful pantsuit with her hair styled and her makeup done to perfection by one of her attendants, Masuyo looked radiant, confident, and ready to conduct business.

Nash and Thura sat side by side in the new trim Armani suits that had been fitted to their bodies by an accomplished Hong Kong tailor and his team. Their white shirts glistened as the two men waited for Masuyo to speak.

Masuyo studied them in the same deliberate manner that her daughter employed. She finally said, "I welcome the both of you, Mr. Hope and Thura, into our family."

"Please just call me Dillon, Mrs. Steers."

"Thank you, Dillon. And you too, Thura, for all that you have done in the past, and all you will do in the future to protect me from harm."

Thura nodded and said quietly, "Yes, ma'am."

The friendly look faded from her expression and when she spoke next, the woman's speech matched her new sternness. "Now, we must get a few things straight, gentlemen. You both work for me, and no one else." She stared first at Nash and then at Thura, and repeated, "No...one...else."

Nash sat straighter, glanced at Thura, and said, "Um, does that mean—?"

"If you are referring to my daughter, yes. You are to report to me only. If you are unable to do that, I see no future for either of you in this organization, because the only person who detests disloyalty more than my daughter is me."

Nash realized that they had just been put into a classic catch-22: If they were loyal to Masuyo they would be disloyal to her daughter, and vice versa.

Masuyo seemed to sense his ambivalence. "Is there a problem, Dillon?"

"No, ma'am. I understand perfectly."

"Now, I have been cooped up in this building long enough. I need to stretch my legs, as it were. So I will be going out on a routine basis. And where I go, you go."

"Yes, ma'am," said Nash. "But we need to keep in mind that—"

"That I am supposed to be in a prison in Myanmar? Yes, Dillon, I am aware of that. But I think you will agree that I look nothing like the filthy hag who once dwelled there."

"No, you don't. But—"

"But my daughter is well known to these people, and if they suspect for a moment that a substitution has been made they will be watching her and those around her for any sign of me?"

"Yes, ma'am, that is my concern."

"And I say to that, I have my life to live, especially after years of it were taken away. And I intend to live it. And I intend to right some wrongs."

"And what wrongs are those?" Nash asked.

She said dismissively, "I do not answer questions posed by a mere *bodyguard*."

"No, ma'am, I'm sorry. I was just curious."

"Curiosity is not a virtue in someone like you."

"Yes, ma'am."

"I will advise you in advance of my travel plans and you will take appropriate precautions to see that I may do so safely."

"Of course."

She studied Nash. "You killed many people that night."

"I did what needed to be done."

"The guard you left alive?"

"He posed no threat, and he was part of the effort to free you."

"He did so only because of money. I would have preferred that you killed him. He did not treat me well."

"I'm sorry. But if we had killed him the plan wouldn't have worked. However, if I had known—"

She cut in, "Next time I will make sure that you *know*, Dillon. And then you will take the action I order you to take."

Nash glanced at Thura, who sat there frozen.

"Yes, ma'am," said Nash again.

"You both may go. I am done with you, for now."

As they rose to leave Masuyo added, "Oh, Dillon, I do have a question for you."

"Yes?"

"At the airport here you led us over to a man who was waiting for us."

"Yes, ma'am."

"He was holding up a sign in Mandarin with the name Dai Lu, I recall."

Nash felt his gut start to burn. "Yes, ma'am."

"I was not aware that you knew my real name."

Temple had told Nash that that was her Chinese name and he could have simply informed Masuyo of that fact. But if Masuyo then went after Temple for knowing that information, that might disrupt what Nash and the FBI were trying to accomplish.

"I do my due diligence and I listen. I find it increases the chances of success."

She stared at him and he wasn't sure if she believed him or not, but Nash had to be somewhat vague in his response.

"I see," she said.

He could feel her watching him as he left.

Did I just blow everything the hell up?

As they were heading to the elevator, Thura looked at Nash and said fearfully, "You know what I am thinking, Dillon?"

"No, what?"

"That we're gonna earn every damn dollar we're paid working for that woman."

CHAPTER 33

After a time Nash and Thura had been allowed to go out by themselves in Hong Kong. Nash knew the city fairly well, having been there on business when he worked at Sybaritic.

Hong Kong was one of the most densely populated places on earth, and the influence of its Chinese master was felt everywhere. And yet it was also energetic and exciting. Once or twice Nash almost forgot that he was a prisoner of Victoria Steers.

He and Thura had walked through some parks, taken in some shows, and ridden on the sightseeing boats. They had eaten at good restaurants and had even taken a ferry to Macau and gambled some dollars away. The fascinating tram tours and the delicious dim sum had particularly delighted Thura.

And Thura had been provided with women, or so he told Nash one day in Nash's apartment. Lots of them.

He'd exclaimed, "Oh my God, man, unbelievable. The most beautiful women. And they'll do anything you want. Anything."

"Thura, I really don't need to hear the details, okay?"

"Have you had women?"

"No."

"Do you not like women?"

"I don't like women who are provided to me, because they don't have a choice."

Thura's enthusiasm had drained away. "Not a choice? This I did not know."

"What, you thought they were all in love with you?"

Thura had leaned against the wall, his features perplexed. "I…

maybe next time I will just talk to them, you know. Just talk. Or we could listen to music, or dance. Get to know each other. Then…if they want to…"

"Sounds like a good plan," Nash had told him.

As the months went by they had escorted Masuyo on many trips into the heart of the city, mostly shopping and dining and some sightseeing. The woman seemed to absorb every detail of what she was seeing, and then she would glance at Nash and seem to perform the same deeply penetrating appraisal that her daughter performed so effortlessly.

She would order them around with terse commands, and then when they returned home she would dismiss them with a curt, imperious wave of her hand.

The queen really has come home to roost, Nash had thought. *Well, the other queen.*

He had also been summoned by the woman for various tasks while she had been in her office with a computer in front of her and stacks of files on either side of her. She was apparently scrutinizing every aspect of her daughter's business empire.

And now maybe her *empire once more*, Nash had also speculated.

He had seen little of Steers lately. At certain times some of her protection detail was gone, so he assumed the woman was traveling. They had been given phones, but Nash knew they would be closely monitored, so he could do nothing personally with his. And he could not buy a burner phone without it showing up on the credit card statement, since it was a card provided to him by Steers.

He could access the accounts where he had parked the monies provided to him by the FBI, and use that to buy a phone. But then there was the problem of hiding it somewhere that it could not be discovered, but where he would still have access. He was still thinking that one through.

During one of these excursions, while Thura had visited a cigar shop, Nash *had* taken a risk and finally managed to find, after much effort, a public pay phone. He had used it to call Agent Morris, but it had gone to voicemail. He had left a detailed message telling the agent everything that had happened, including the murder of Lynn Ryder and more details of what had transpired in Myanmar and their supporting role in Masuyo's escape from the mysterious prison. When Nash had put down the receiver he had looked around and hoped that he had not been seen.

But if he took no risks at all, Nash knew he would accomplish nothing.

He was sure that at some point Masuyo would want him to do something that went against Steers's interest. And Steers might, at any time, demand information about her mother's actions. If he refused to answer or, worse yet, lied? And she found out? But if he did tell the truth, would Steers see that as a betrayal to her mother?

Damned if I do and damned if I don't.

Since he knew it would seem normal to Steers, on his phone he had constantly scrolled the American business news and had learned that the board of Sybaritic, meaning Rhett Temple, had appointed a woman named Neisha Mirza to be the CEO of the company. And Elaine Fixx had once more taken over Nash's old job. He'd wondered if Agent Morris had followed up on his suggestion to try to recruit Fixx to their effort.

One day Nash was instructed through an email that Masuyo wanted to go out. Nash was also told that accompanying her would be her daughter's former nanny, Hiroko, whom Nash had never heard anyone mention before. And another thing that was different: The email had come from Steers, not her mother.

He had Thura get things prepped after they received the travel itinerary. It was only shopping, and then afternoon tea at an upscale café that they had taken Masuyo to many times previously.

Nash received another email from Steers asking him to retrieve Hiroko and bring her to Masuyo's suite.

He knocked on the apartment door that was situated on a lower floor, and instantly heard the sounds of shuffling feet. The door opened and an elderly Asian woman appeared there. She couldn't have been more than five feet tall and a hundred pounds. She wore a dark jacket and slacks with a creamy blouse, and her white hair was cut in straight lines across her forehead and down the sides. Her powdered face was heavily lined; her smile at the sight of Nash seemed genuine.

"Mr. Hope, it is so nice to finally meet you. Please come inside and wait for a moment while I finish my preparations for our journey today."

Nash stepped inside, smiling at the formal language used by the woman. They weren't *journeying*, really, just taking a drive barely twenty minutes away.

"Yes, ma'am. Take your time. There's no rush."

She scuttled away, saying, "I haven't been out in ages. So much fun. Tea, I understand?"

"Yes, with Mrs. Steers."

Hiroko abruptly stopped and turned. "*Mrs.* Steers? Not…not Victoria-san?"

Now Nash was unsure. "No, um, what were you told, ma'am?"

"I was told nothing other than shopping and tea, I thought with Victoria-san. I know she is so very busy but she comes to visit me quite often. And we have the most wonderful talks about…the old times."

"Um, well…"

Nash whirled around when the voice said, "You will be going shopping and having tea with my mother, Hiroko-san."

Steers stood in the doorway dressed, as usual, all in black except for a pair of white lace-up shoes. She barely glanced at Nash.

Hiroko looked surprised. "Your mother? Your mother is… here? You…you never mentioned…"

To Nash, the elderly woman did not seem very happy about this development.

"Yes, I'm sorry that I did not tell you. She has come home. I want you to see her. To spend time with her."

"If you wish it, Victoria-san. I will do whatever you want me to do."

Nash glanced at Steers and was surprised to see her lips

trembling. "You honor me with your faith, dear Hiroko-san," she said. Then Steers bowed to the woman.

Hiroko returned the gesture and rushed off.

Nash eyed Steers. "Is there anything I should know?"

She would not look at him. "Hiroko-san has taken care of me since I was born. She is an honored member of my family. She worked hard all her life and now she has her just reward."

"So she and your mother know each other then?"

"They *know* each other," replied Steers.

"Okay," said Nash, looking confused.

Steers now glanced at him. "It is sometimes difficult for mothers to appreciate others whom their children adore."

"Oh, okay, sure, I get that."

"Hiroko-san is kind and sweet and would never think of harming anyone," said Steers, now staring at the wall.

Nash wondered if the woman had left unsaid, *Unlike my mother, who is not kind or sweet and will destroy anyone she believes she needs to.*

"She seems to be all of those things." Nash glanced around at the neat confines of the apartment. "And she keeps a really spic-and-span home."

Steers smiled at this remark and, to Nash's eye, when she did it softened all the hard edges of the woman; indeed, she looked far more like the shy little girl in the old photo. "When I was a child Hiroko-san would have me make my bed every morning before breakfast. She told me that if I did so I would always have a clean place to return to that night. And that all things in between those times would be better off because my mind would be focused and organized. I have followed that advice all my life."

"I can see that."

She gazed at him but still seemed distant. "Can you, Mr. Hope?"

"You have no need to call me Mr., Ms. Steers. I work for you."

"Unwillingly," she said, then seemed to regret that comment. "I prefer to keep things formal between employee and employer."

"As you wish," he replied.

"I want Hiroko-san to enjoy her outing."

"I'll do all I can to make it pleasant and safe. That's my job."

"And my mother?"

"My job obviously covers her as well. You and she made that very clear to me."

"I'm sure *she* did."

Nash now wondered if Steers was going to grill him on any special instructions or demands her mother might have made on him. And he wasn't sure what his reply would be.

But, thankfully, she didn't. Instead, she said, "You should become acquainted with Hiroko-san, Mr. Hope. She is a good person to...know."

"With your permission, I will."

"You have it," Steers said curtly. She turned and walked off.

As she was walking down the hall, Nash's hand went to his gun. An easy kill shot. Back of the head. All he had to do was—

Hiroko appeared behind him. "Mr. Hope, I am ready."

He let his hand fall back to his side, turned, smiled at her, and said, "Then off we go."

CHAPTER

34

It was clear that Masuyo did not know that Hiroko was coming along on the outing. But when Nash told the woman that her daughter had organized it, Masuyo questioned nothing. However, she was dismissive of the other woman and showed her displeasure for Hiroko's presence the entire time they were out. For her part, Hiroko seemed nervous and excessively ill at ease, and Nash didn't think it was simply because of the way Masuyo treated her.

Hiroko just seemed afraid to be around the other woman.

The shopping and tea completed, they drove back in silence to Steers's building. Thura escorted Masuyo to her part of the penthouse, while Nash took Hiroko back to her small apartment.

"Ms. Steers advised me to get to know you better, Ms. Hiroko."

"How wonderful. If you have the time, come in then and we can chat, Mr. Hope."

"You can just call me Dillon."

"I will call you Dillon-san. And please call me Hiroko-san. I had my tea, but would you like some?"

Nash brightened at the offer. "Thank you, yes."

While she put on a kettle and got the tea ready, Nash looked around the living room. On some shelving there were a number of framed photos. Almost all of them were, presumably, pictures of Hiroko and Steers, the latter from the time she was an infant in a blanket to a fully grown woman. And there were numerous drawings of Hiroko that spanned many years. They were mostly done in pencil and pen and ink, but there was also one in watercolor.

Hiroko brought the tea in, poured out a cup, and handed it to Nash, who took a sip and smiled appreciatively.

"Excellent, thank you."

They sat down in her small living room with impressive views of the city.

"Victoria-san has always been so good to me," noted Hiroko.

"She said you have been with her since she was born. And I see that in the photos."

Hiroko looked at the shelves of pictures and her face crinkled into a smile. "Yes."

"And those drawings of you?"

"Victoria-san did those. She said she wanted to capture her Hiroko-san as I aged."

"She really did those?" Nash said in surprise.

"Oh yes. She maintains a studio here where she paints and draws. She is very talented."

"They're really exceptional."

"She was the youngest child, so it was in some ways easier and in other ways harder for her. The other children…they had their own people to care for them, and my job was to look after little Victoria-san."

"I'm sure she was a handful," noted Nash.

"I do not know what…?"

"Stubborn?"

Hiroko tittered. "Oh yes, she had that way about her. She would wave her little fists and would want to do things only her way."

This intrigued Nash. "What did you do when she did that?"

Hiroko said quietly and precisely, as though reliving a cherished memory, "I would get down on the floor so that I was eye to eye with her. I would tell Victoria-san that true wisdom was not thinking that only you had all the right answers in your head, but to draw upon all the knowledge that was out there and then judge for yourself what was worthy and what was not. If you did so, you would be smarter than everyone else."

"Did she listen?"

"Not so much when she was very young, no," said Hiroko with an amused expression. "But as she grew older, yes, Dillon-san, she *did* listen. And she indeed grew much wiser."

Nash thought of the competition against her siblings that the FBI had told him about, a deadly battle spurred on by her mother.

He wasn't sure how to frame it, but he wanted to hear Hiroko's impression of it. "I understand that she is the only one of the Steers children still living?"

Hiroko's features instantly crumpled and she put a hand to her mouth.

Nash said nothing. He just sipped his tea and waited.

"That is true," she finally said.

"Was there an accident? Or was it some sort of illness that was contagious?"

"I...I do not wish to speak of it, Dillon-san. It is sad, a very sad business."

"I'm sure. I'm sure everyone was sad."

"Not everyone," said Hiroko, who then seemed to catch herself. "Would you like some more tea, Dillon-san?"

"Yes, thank you." He held out his cup for her to fill. Next he said, "I...saw the burns that Ms. Steers has. How terrible."

Hiroko looked stunned. "She showed you?"

"Yes."

"She must trust you very much, Dillon-san. And she has spoken highly of you when she has come to visit me here."

"I think she does trust me. I hope you can, too," he added.

"Victoria-san is a wonderful judge of character, so I *will* trust you." She paused and kneaded her fists into her small thighs. "We were both on a plane that came down from the sky," she said in a trembling voice. "Victoria-san's father died. Everyone died except for Victoria-san and me. But she was so badly burned. I...I pulled her from the wreckage."

"When was this?"

"Nearly eight years ago."

Nash looked at the small, elderly woman in amazement. "That must have been very difficult for you. Especially after having just survived a plane crash."

"I could not let her die. Somehow, I found the strength to do what I needed to. She was in hospital for quite a long time. They wanted to do many surgeries. Many more, I mean. But…"

"But she wanted the injuries to remain, as a reminder"—he stopped to think of the right words—"to never let her guard down?"

Hiroko nodded. "Yes, that exactly. Oh, it grieved me to see her in so much pain. To the bone, right to the bone she was burned. The smell of the fuel, her screams, her father dying right in front of her." She paused and bowed her head, her small chest heaving with emotion. She sat back up, her face streaked with tears, and continued, "But her strength was beyond all my experience."

"Did they ever find out what happened to the plane?"

Hiroko said, "I have heard…that it was not an accident."

"Not an accident? What then?"

In a lowered voice she said, "Victoria-san has enemies."

"Well, from what I've seen I can understand that."

"I know what some say about her. I know what…" She looked up at him. "She is a good person, Dillon-san. She cares very much, sometimes too much. She adored her father. He…he was not like his wife." She stopped and looked frightened.

Nash said hastily, "I know exactly what you mean. I have met the woman, after all. And I will never share with anyone anything you tell me."

Hiroko smiled nervously and then her expression turned somber. "You asked about the other children?"

"Yes?"

"The Steers family has great wealth, and in such families there is always a…contest to see which child will carry on the running of this…great wealth."

"And is that what happened with the Steers family?"

Nash was hoping that he was getting close, finally, to learning the details of Steers murdering her own siblings.

"In a way, yes."

"And Ms. Steers is the only one left, so I assume she won this... struggle?"

But Hiroko shook her head and looked at him fearfully. "Dillon-san, do you care for Victoria-san?"

This query shook Nash, who had not been expecting it. "I...I work for her. My job is to protect her. So, yes, in that way, I *do* care for her," he said slowly and, he hoped, convincingly.

"I have never told anyone this."

"What?" he said quickly.

At that moment Nash's phone buzzed. It was Thura.

"Lady wants you, right now," said Thura.

"What lady?"

"Who you think? Masuyo. Something about going out again without the *baggage*."

Shit. "I'll be right there."

He put his phone away and looked at Hiroko. "I have to go now, but may I come back and talk some more, Hiroko-san?"

"I would like that very much."

"Is there anything you need? Anything I can bring you?"

Her face brightened. "I am quite fond of chocolates. Lindt? And Ferrero Rocher? The gold packaging symbolizes good fortune."

"I'll get both."

"Thank you, Dillon-san. And thank you for caring for Victoria-san. There are few who know her well. But for those who do, she is...different than one may think."

Nash didn't know how that could possibly be, since he had seen the woman blow the brains out of Lynn Ryder, and she had killed her siblings and God knew how many other people. But for her old nanny, *Victoria-san* could apparently do no wrong.

He rushed to the elevator and headed up to deal with another female Steers, and he was not looking forward to it at all.

CHAPTER 35

"JUST YOU, DILLON," SAID MASUYO. "Not him." She gave Thura a derisive look.

Thura took the insult with good humor, giving Nash a mischievous glance.

"Yes, ma'am," said Thura. As he walked off he added in a voice only Nash could hear, "Watch your back."

"Where would you like to go, Mrs. Steers?" Nash asked.

"Let us venture to Kowloon Park."

"All right, but, as we discussed before, there might be people out there looking for you after your escape from prison. They would know that your daughter lives in Hong Kong."

"And as I told you before, I look nothing like I did in that place, and I have my life to live and I intend to live it. It is your job to make sure I am not harmed. So do your job, Dillon, and let me worry about everything else."

"Yes, ma'am."

Nash was going to order a car, but Masuyo insisted that she wanted to walk.

His comm pack in place and his earpiece in, the armed Nash felt like a Secret Service agent on protection detail. *When I'm actually quite the opposite of that.*

The park was filled with walking paths, water features, and statues of serious-looking men in contemplative poses. But there were also whimsical sculptures of colorful cartoon and superhero characters, graffitied steps, racks of vending machines, and, jarringly, a

McDonald's. There were fountains of different sizes and legions of strutting flamingos, and large turtles swimming in pools.

And rising above all of this were the massive skyscrapers of Hong Kong.

They passed an ice cream shop, where Masuyo had Nash purchase her a cup of soft serve vanilla. "The weather is warm and I am a bit overheated," she explained, though there was no need to do so.

As they moved along Masuyo really looked at nothing. She just walked with a firm step and stared straight ahead while she slowly spooned the ice cream into her mouth. She had to use a public toilet and Nash offered to hold her ice cream for her, but she refused. When she came back out she led him down a set of steps that opened into a quiet area where there was seating. She settled on a bench and ordered Nash to sit beside her.

For a few minutes she said nothing, and Nash was not compelled to break the silence.

At last she said, "It was my daughter's idea, the outing with *her*."

"Was it?" asked Nash.

She glanced at him. "You are a smart man, Dillon. You know that it was."

"I suppose she wanted you to spend time with someone from the past. To help you resettle into your new life."

"I would never have chosen a mere *servant* with whom to do so."

"I thought Hiroko was an honored friend of the family's."

"Ridiculous. She was a paid caregiver to my daughter. That is all."

Nash wondered if the woman did not know about Hiroko pulling Steers from the plane's wreckage and saving her. "I'm sorry, I just assumed."

"Never assume. It is not a good tactic, for *anyone*."

"Yes, ma'am," said Nash, recalling that Steers had once said something similar to him.

"Now to your knowing my real name, Dillon, let us discuss."

"I thought we had, ma'am."

"You did no research. No one connected with my daughter told you. You came by this knowledge another way clearly."

Nash started to tell her, despite the risk to what he was trying to do with the FBI, that he'd heard it from Temple.

But before he could she added, "And your making up lies or excuses now is neither helpful to me nor beneficial to *you*."

Nash closed his mouth. Too late to try to explain, he concluded.

"What we must discuss is loyalty, Dillon. Where does yours lie?"

"I thought it obvious."

"Not to me. So explain it to an old woman who has been out of the world for so long that her senses are not where they should be."

I think your senses are far better than most, thought Nash. "I work for your daughter, but my mission is to see that no harm comes to you."

"From any source?"

"From any source."

"So you are loyal to me above all others?"

Nash knew this question was coming. It was like college debating, which Nash had actually done, where your opponent sought, by one logical statement after another, to box you right into a corner.

"Dillon?" she said when he did not answer.

"You place me in a difficult position, Mrs. Steers."

"Where else did you expect me to place you, Dillon? Please do not make me believe you are not up to this. I would hate to have you *replaced*."

She said the last word in a way that sounded to Nash like *killed*. And he could see very clearly how Masuyo had built a criminal empire. He now focused on how immensely difficult that must have been, since the woman would have had formidable opponents all around.

"If I have to make a choice, Mrs. Steers, I would have to say that my loyalties lie with you, because your daughter instructed me so."

He hoped he had done enough table turning on the woman to let that statement suffice against his being *replaced*.

He got an answer when she glanced away, but not before he saw a disappointed look on her face. Not disappointment in his answer being a bad one, just an unwelcome one, because it seemed to be sufficiently nuanced to prevent further interrogation.

"Then, to sum it up, you are loyal to me. You report to me. My daughter does not come into the equation. If I find that she does, then you will go away, forever, are we clear on that?"

She stared at him, her eyes like twin knife blades looking to pierce him.

"I am very clear on what must be done going forward, Mrs. Steers."

"If I do find that you have been disloyal, then my daughter will learn that you knew my real name to be Dai Lu. I wonder what she will do with that information."

Nash didn't have to wonder for a single second.

As they got up Masuyo left her ice cream container on the bench. When Nash went to retrieve it, she barked, "Leave it, Dillon."

He followed her to the steps they had taken down to this spot.

When he glanced back a few moments later, the ice cream container was gone. He gave a searching look all around but he couldn't see who had taken it.

What in the hell had just happened?

CHAPTER

36

NASH HAD FINISHED A GRUELING workout in the basement of the building. It was an elaborate space with everything the most fitness-minded person could desire. On several occasions he had ventured down here with Thura while various members of Steers's protection detail had also been working out. These men, who looked chiseled from stone, had enviable flexibility, nimbleness, quickness, and power that truly belied their average statures.

And each time they had glanced arrogantly and dismissively at the pair as they went through their workouts and close-quarter routines. However, Nash silently watched, and absorbed everything he was seeing.

Once, when he and Thura had gone back to their floor after working out, Thura had said, "Damn, those guys are unbeatable, man."

Nash had thought that as well until he had started to note their tendencies and weak points. He approached it like game film for football players. Even one small observation could provide an advantage that might be worth its weight in gold later. Nash had done the very same thing in business and found it to be a highly successful tactic.

Now Nash toweled off and sat on a bench after cooling down. Right from the start he and Thura had applied for and received gun permits to go along with their work visas. They had also been taken to a nearby gun range twice a week since they had been here. Thura was a good if undisciplined shot, and Nash had given him some pointers that the man had thought were excellent.

Considerable time had gone by, and he had heard nothing from Rhett Temple, not that he expected to. The man really didn't have the means to contact him except through Steers. And Nash wasn't under any delusion that his former boss was doing anything to fulfill his promise to bring Nash home. That wasn't what Nash wanted anyway.

As he got up to leave he noted, for the first time, a door at the far end of the room.

He walked over to it. The door was locked, but there was a glass panel in the top section of the door that allowed him to see inside.

What he saw startled Nash. It was pretty much the same boxing dummy that he had used at Shock's facility back in the states. It even had tape markers on the various strike points. He wondered who used this room. He knew it wasn't Steers's men. They had their own boxing dummy, which Nash used as well.

Puzzled, Nash left the workout room. He would normally turn left and head to the elevators to go up to his apartment. Now, after having stumbled on the room inside the workout space, his curiosity got the better of him. And since no one was around, he turned to the right and walked down the corridor to the end. There were three doors down here; two of them were unlocked and empty. But one was secured. When he heard voices behind this door, Nash slid behind one of the other open doors, but kept it ajar just a sliver so he could see out.

Two men exited from the secure doorway. Nash recognized them as part of Steers's protection team.

They turned away from him, and he noted that the door of the room they had just exited was a self-closing one.

If he timed it just right…

As the men walked off, Nash was able to slip through the gap before the door closed. He waited until he could no longer hear their footsteps and then, using his phone's flashlight feature, he looked around the darkened space.

There were shelving and tables with cardboard boxes stored on them. Each box had writing on it, but it was in Mandarin. He looked inside a few, thinking he might find drugs or even body parts. But some contained clothing, others books; still others held some framed pictures that were very old, and he recognized no one in them.

One box did contain things of interest. The items looked like ceremonial garments of some kind, very colorful, made of silk with unusual markings down the sleeves and across the chests. There were also hats and jewelry and handbags that looked old but well-preserved.

He kept searching until he found one box in a far corner. When his phone light flashed over the box's front and he saw the lettering in the English alphabet, his blood felt like it had frozen in his veins: MN.

With trembling fingers, Nash slowly opened the box and shone his light inside.

His heart skipped when he saw the velour warmup suit his daughter was wearing when she had appeared online to accuse him of sexually abusing her. Then he found her shoes. The tears trickled from Nash's eyes as he conjured the image of his deceased daughter. Smiling, happy, full-of-life Maggie Nash.

Now her entire remaining physical existence had been banished to a box in the basement of a building in Hong Kong, a place she had never even visited.

Nash wanted to pull everything out of the box and take it with him, but that would have been a death sentence for him. He picked up the velour jacket and pressed it against his face, trying with all his might to detect her scent. And he thought he had; he felt her right next to him.

At least I want it to be so, even if it never will be for real.

And down at the bottom of the small box, his light glinted off something. He reached down and picked it up. It was the ring that he and Judith had given their daughter when she'd graduated from high school. She'd loved it and almost never took it off. She'd been a September baby, so it was a sapphire. He thought back to the bones they had found in that field. Some had been the bones of her hand. Perhaps the hand that had worn this ring.

He held the ring for the longest time, trying not to think about what had happened to his daughter, but, in truth, that was all Nash could think about.

Although it was risky, he took photos of everything, put the items back in the box, and closed it up. He left the room after making sure no one was about, and rode the elevator to his floor. And all the way, Walter Nash thought only about killing Victoria Steers.

CHAPTER 37

For months afterward Nash accompanied Masuyo to Kowloon Park twice a week. And each time she had him buy her ice cream. She also went to the bathroom during each trip and then left the container on the same bench, as always. It was as though she was defying him to question her actions.

However, Nash held his tongue and just watched. On the third time this happened, he was able to walk slowly enough behind her to see a young, slim man dressed in a dark suit rush up from somewhere and take the container off the bench. On the fourth time, Nash managed to surreptitiously snap a picture of him with his phone.

When he got back to his apartment he looked at the image. The man resembled a million other youths in Hong Kong.

Nash enlarged the photo as much as possible to examine the ice cream container. When he got it to its highest magnification, he thought he could see an edge of a piece of paper sticking up from the napkin that had been wound around the outside of the container.

Okay, she goes into the restroom with the container, writes her message, hides it behind the napkin, and leaves it on the bench for this guy to retrieve.

The only problem was, whom did Masuyo know to send messages to? She'd been in prison in another country for years. It made no sense at all unless it was someone from her past who now resided in Hong Kong.

* * *

A few days later Nash got a message from Steers. She wanted to meet. He had seen very little of her recently.

He took out his gun, checked that a round was in the chamber, and rode up to her penthouse, accompanied by a member of her protection team. The man looked at Nash like he was a piece of bird shit that had fallen on the floor of the elevator.

When the doors opened, the man said, "Get off, now."

"Getting off now," Nash shot back. He looked at the man as the doors closed.

The look on the man's face was clear. He wanted to kill Nash.

That's okay, the feeling's mutual. And after I kill your boss, I'll do you next.

He turned back around to find one of Steers's female attendants standing there. Then he realized he was not on the penthouse floor.

"This way, Mr. Hope," she said, her gaze downcast.

"Where are we?" he asked.

"This way, please."

He followed her down a hall, and she stopped at a large, intricately carved wooden door.

The attendant knocked, and Nash could hear Steers say to come in. The attendant opened the door, bowed, motioned Nash through, and closed the door after him.

Nash looked around and felt like he was in a top-tier museum, with walls so tall he knew two floors of the building had been combined to created the extra height. The windows were all covered with shades to prevent sunlight coming in. The artwork hanging on the walls ranged from Renaissance to Baroque periods to more abstract Jackson Pollock–style themes. Nash knew this because his wife, Judith, had minored in art history in college. In helping her to study for exams he had learned a fair bit about that world.

Steers was standing near the far wall. She was dressed, as always, in black. Her hair hung straight down. She was not looking at Nash, but at a massive painting hanging in front of her.

"You asked to see me?" said Nash stiffly. After finding Maggie's belongings in the box, Nash was finding it hard to stay civil in front of the woman. He eyed a small statuette on a pedestal that he could use to bludgeon her. That might be better than his noisy gun, actually. It would give him and Thura time to make a run for it. He edged closer to it.

She turned to him and his look must have made her curious because she said, "Are you all right?"

"I'm fine."

"My mother is treating you well?"

"No complaints."

"She can be...difficult."

"It's all good," he replied in a tight voice.

She cocked her head, clearly still perplexed by his brusque manner.

Not wanting her to focus on this he looked around and said, "I feel like I'm at the Met or the Louvre."

"Have you been to those places?"

"Guarding clients, yes," he lied, but he had gone to those places as a tourist.

"Do you enjoy art?"

"I know what I like." While he recognized many of the paintings on the wall he didn't want to say so, because Steers might know that his wife knew about art, and she might eventually make the connection despite his vastly altered physical appearance. He pointed at a foreboding painting of a group of men in seventeenth-century garb gathered around a table. "Most people would know that's a Rembrandt. And next to it, I think, is a Warhol," he added, indicating a silkscreened print depicting stacked Brillo boxes. He stopped and looked at one painting consisting of colorful loops and polka dots. "But I don't know that artist."

"Yayoi Kusama. She is Japanese. She's now very old, but still at work, I believe."

He studied her, putting aside for the moment his plan to kill the woman. "Hiroko told me about your artwork, and that you have a studio here. I saw the drawings you did of her. They were really good."

Steers looked embarrassed by his praise. "It allows me time... away from other things."

Also in her expression he saw, for the first time, an infinite... *sadness* was the word he was looking for. It was actually quite startling to him because the woman always seemed to be in steadfast control of her emotions. He glanced once more at the statuette. Yet now Nash reasoned that it would be unfair to Thura for Nash to kill Steers and then force Thura to flee with him as well, with the most likely result that both men would be killed by Steers's guards.

Damn.

Nash refocused and then gazed at the painting she was standing in front of. It was quite large in scope, a full fifteen-by-fifteen feet, he estimated. It was literally bursting with shapes, images, colors, an amalgamation of concentrated power and fluid whimsy, but somehow still compellingly disciplined in its composition and execution.

"I don't know that artist, either," he said.

She turned once more to look at it. "Julie Mehretu. She's Ethiopian. I first saw her work at an exhibit in Australia. I was so moved by the collection and watching the video of her life, what inspired her, the meanings behind what she does, that I bought this piece when it became available."

As Nash studied the work he said, "It's...hypnotic."

"Yes, I find it so. Quite powerful and moving despite its seeming subtleties."

Curious, he drew closer. "What impressed you the most about her work?"

In a wistful tone Steers said, "She...paints in the abstract, as do many other accomplished artists, but she does so with great *clarity*, if that makes sense. Mixed mediums, hand drawings, silk screening, air brushing, so much complexity, so many layers to what she has created. She said that her work was meant to defy description, or pigeonholing or labeling. But what she was really talking about, I think, was not so much her work, as...people, the individual that is embodied in all artwork because it is the individual that creates and also inspires the art. She seems repelled by the universal habit of reducing us to bodies, or skin, or faith, or wealth, or occupation, or where we live, or our language. She refuses to accept that as an identity for others because I believe she thinks individuality transcends such triviality. She draws inspiration from Chinese ink paintings as well as literature, Japanese manga, music, so many subjects that she brings to bear to create...this." She motioned to the painting as Nash moved closer to her. Despite his guilt over probably condemning Thura to death if he killed Steers, Nash's hand moved a few inches closer to the statuette.

"What do *you* see in it, Mr. Hope?"

He glanced at her and thought that she had put his daughter in a little box in a crummy room of this building. *Just grab the statuette and kill her, Nash. Do it now.* But he had never had such an internal fight as he was having right now.

"I see...possibilities."

"What sort of possibilities?"

"I agree that people wrongly label others all the time. They do so based on what we look like, as you just said." He ran his hand over himself. "For instance, what do you see when you look at me?"

She slowly turned to face him.

He smiled. "Muscles, tats, bald head, gun. Easy to label, right?"

Surprisingly, she shook her head. "No, Mr. Hope, not so easy. As you correctly pointed out before, I see you as an enigma. I still do. But I am figuring some things out."

"Like what?" He wasn't asking to be polite; he wanted to know, for many reasons, most of all his survival.

"You are logical, calm, secure in your abilities, not quick to judgment. But above all else, I believe you are one thing. And it is perhaps an incongruous element in contrast to your physical appearance, which was Mehretu's whole point."

"Really, what's that?"

She reached out and touched his arm before quickly pulling it back.

"I've seen how you interact with other people: Thura, Hiroko-san, my various attendants, even my mother. You are *kind*, Mr. Hope. No, you are more than that. You are *empathetic*. Which is the best of all human attributes, because it leads to all the other goodness of which human beings are capable."

She looked away, and Nash thought he saw a blush creeping to her cheeks.

"I suppose you find such lofty words starkly hypocritical coming from someone like me," she said.

"Someone like you?"

She looked up at him and her expression grew defiant. "You know exactly what I mean."

"Hiroko-san thinks that you are misjudged."

A sad smile now spread over Steers's features. "Hiroko-san is biased in my favor. She believes I can do no wrong. That I am perfect." Her smile faded. "But no one is perfect, least of all me. I am as far from perfect as it is possible to be, in fact."

Nash was growing more and more confused by her words. Where had the global criminal who killed with ease gone to? He forgot about murdering the woman.

"What do you see when you look at me, Mr. Hope?" she said abruptly.

He didn't answer right away. Not because he feared his answer would upset her. But because he wanted to figure out what he actually thought.

"I might have answered your question differently before our meeting today, Ms. Steers. But I see someone who would have... preferred a different life than the one she has. And perhaps that is the 'possibility' that I spoke of before."

Steers held his gaze for a long moment before she glanced back at the Mehretu piece. He thought he glimpsed a tear sliding down her cheek. She made no move to brush it away.

"Am I wrong?" he asked.

"On the contrary, your perspicacity does you justice. But why would your answer have been different before today?"

He looked around. "Because I had not seen this room yet and your interest in art. It…provides a facet I had not known of you before. Like Mehretu's work, people have many different layers and they do not always easily blend together. And sometimes it might seem that more than one person resides in a single body."

And don't I know that? added Nash to himself.

She now looked at him for a long time and he really could not read her expression.

He thought, *Did I go too far? Did I say something I shouldn't have?*

"I wish to go to dinner tonight, Mr. Hope. You will accompany me."

"And not your usual protection detail?"

"You are coming as my *guest*. Be ready to leave at nine. Thank you."

She turned and left the room, leaving Nash alone with priceless paintings and his own terribly conflicted thoughts. He glanced at the statuette, his mind now on the box in the basement that held some of his daughter's belongings.

You're a coward, Nash. With all your muscles and fighting skills, and desire to avenge your daughter. Just a fucking coward.

CHAPTER 38

Later that afternoon, Nash rode the elevator to Hiroko's apartment. He had arranged for this visit immediately after his meeting with Steers in her personal art gallery. Hiroko greeted him with enthusiasm and made each of them a cup of tea. He had brought with him a box of Lindt chocolates and a bag of Ferrero Rocher delectables that he had picked up for her. She thanked him profusely. They sat in the same chairs as before and had their tea and a chocolate and delectable each.

Nash said, "I'm sorry we were interrupted last time. And I'm sorry it's been so long since I've been back to see you. You were talking about Ms. Steers and the competition with her siblings?"

She looked at him warily. "Dillon-san, you said that Victoria-san showed you her...injuries?"

"That's right, she did."

"Would you mind telling me where they are on her body?"

"You don't believe me?" he said, feigning offense.

Her look deepened and in that expression Nash saw not a bubbly, cloistered, honored servant living out her retirement in quiet style. But rather he was observing an astute and cagey individual who had survived all these years in the Steers empire, which was no easy task, he well knew.

"I want to believe you, Dillon-san," she said slowly. "But that is not the same as whether it is wise to. You see, there are reasons to mistrust people. I do not trust all of the people who are around Victoria-san."

"Including her mother?"

"Just tell me where her injuries are, Dillon-san, if you can."

"Both arms and her back," he replied promptly. "Nowhere else that I could see. Frankly, I don't know how she withstood the agony."

"She must think very highly of you, Dillon-san," she said. "To my knowledge, other than myself, no one has ever seen them."

"I hope that means you can trust me, Hiroko-san."

She gathered herself, sat forward, and said, "People believe awful things about Victoria-san, truly awful things."

"Like what?"

"That she killed her siblings."

He acted surprised by this, "My God, why would they believe that?"

"Because people lie. People place blame on innocent people, like Victoria-san."

"So she didn't kill them?"

Hiroko shook her head fiercely. "No, oh, no."

"Then what happened to them?"

Hiroko looked pained, and she took a moment to compose herself. "You told me before that you care for Victoria-san?"

Nash had to glance away for a moment. "Yes, yes, I did."

"Well, she harmed no one. It was...it was..." The woman apparently could not bring herself to say it.

Nash had a sudden idea. "It was Masuyo?"

Hiroko burst into tears and left the room. Nash heard water running and a few minutes later the woman slowly walked back in, her face very pink and her eyes and nose reddened. He rose and helped her to sit down.

"Are you okay?" he said anxiously after retaking his chair.

She nodded and pressed her fingertips together. "You must understand that I have never spoken of this to anyone."

"I understand. I hope you feel you can trust me enough to tell me about it."

"I do, Dillon-san. I truly do after what you have told me. Because it is clear to me that Victoria-san trusts you."

"Go on," he prompted.

"Victoria-san was always her mother's favorite. I have my thoughts on this."

"What sorts of thoughts?"

"I have known Masuyo a very long time. I served her before Victoria-san was born. I know things about her that many do not. I have seen things—" She broke off and nervously studied her hands.

"What are you trying to say?" prompted Nash.

Hiroko seemed to summon up her courage. "Masuyo did not love her husband, Dillon-san. She is actually Chinese, not Japanese. I am Chinese like her. She came to Japan to...do her duty to her country."

Nash had learned this from the FBI, but he acted startled. "You mean she was, what, some sort of spy?"

"I do not know the correct term. But what I do know is that she quickly turned to the bad. She did terrible things. She married and she began to do even more terrible things. I wanted to leave. I tried to separate myself from all of it, but she would not allow it. She would have killed me, I am sure of that."

"My God, Hiroko-san."

Hiroko wiped her eyes with a tissue and eyed him closely. "There is something else."

"What?"

"I am not sure I can tell you. Even though I do trust you."

Nash thought quickly. "Hiroko-san, you say that there are people here you do not trust. They may wish Ms. Steers harm. If I can prevent that, as her bodyguard, I need to know all you can tell me. Please."

She considered this and finally nodded. "All right. What you say makes a great deal of sense. As I said, she did not love her husband. But she did love another man. A tall, handsome man from our country. And this man, and not her husband, was Victoria-san's father."

Nash nearly dropped his teacup. "Jesus, does she know?"

Hiroko shook her head. "Never one word has been spoken about it. You see, Masuyo believed her other children to be unpure, their father being a white man. But Victoria-san is wholly Chinese."

"I wondered about that. From a picture I saw she didn't seem to take after Masuyo's husband, and now I know why. But I'm actually very surprised you're telling me all this."

She looked at him wistfully. "Victoria-san visits me here, as you know. She speaks highly of you, Dillon-san, as I told you before. So very highly. I have never known her to speak of another man as she does you. And I am an old woman. My light grows dim. But since you proved to me that Victoria-san trusts you, I needed to reveal to you what I know. I cannot tell Victoria-san because I know it will break her heart. But I felt I could tell you, in confidence. I know you will do the right thing. And that you will never tell her."

"I promise," said Nash. "But you say Masuyo killed her own children?"

"Yes, they were the offspring of her English husband and thus unpure. She did not love him, and she did not love them." She paused. "But that is not the worst of it, Dillon-san."

"How could it get any worse?" Nash exclaimed.

In a trembling, halting voice Hiroko said, "Masuyo convinced... Victoria-san that she indeed... vanquished her siblings."

Nash gaped. "What, that *she* killed her siblings? How is that possible?"

"Masuyo is very experienced in such things. In manipulating others."

"What, you mean hypnotism?"

"No, that is foolish and ineffective. Masuyo used certain medicinal herbs."

"You mean hallucinogens?"

"That is what Westerners call them, yes. But it was not only that."

"What else?"

"Masuyo used her mind and her words to convince her daughter that she committed these terrible acts. Over and over she told Victoria-san lie after lie until my dear Victoria-san believed every word."

"How could she do that to her?" Nash asked. "Ms. Steers is too smart."

"I saw her do it, Dillon-san. I watched her destroy Victoria-san's will. I saw her rid her mind of all truth and logic and replace it with her lies, her cruel lies. And that knowledge? It changed Victoria-san. She was no longer the shy little girl that I knew. And I simply stood there and did nothing to stop it. Nothing," she added quietly.

"You could have told her later—the truth, I mean."

"I was…afraid, Dillon-san. That…she would not believe me. And if her mother had found out I told her? I…I am ashamed at my cowardice." She began to quietly weep.

He reached out and gripped her hand. "I understand how incredibly difficult that would have been. But what about her husband? How could he possibly—"

She interjected, "He was a kind man, but he did not have what it requires to stand up to a woman like Masuyo, Dillon-san. But after she went away, he came out of his shell. He began to be a better influence on his daughter. I believed things were turning for the good with Masuyo gone. And I also knew that Masuyo would not like that at all. Which is why I am so distraught that she has returned."

"Why did she even marry him?"

"Because no one would suspect that she worked for the Chinese if she had an Englishman as a husband."

"I see," said Nash.

Hiroko said thoughtfully, "I believe Masuyo's mother was Japanese. She knew the language and took after her mother in her physical features. That is why she was selected to go to Japan to do her duty. But then she became what she is. A…terrible, merciless person."

"If what you say is true about Masuyo, why would she want her daughter, or anyone else, to succeed her?"

"In our culture, Dillon-san, we prepare the next generation for the responsibilities of family. Masuyo was no different in this. And she had many enemies and one of them could vanquish her. But she would not allow the empire, which she had so painstakingly built, to topple. She could name Victoria-san as her successor *and* still control her."

"But then Masuyo went away. How did that happen? I know now that she ended up in a prison in Myanmar."

"All I know, Dillon-san, is that she went on a trip and never returned. Soon after that, the plane Victoria-san and I were on fell from the sky."

"So someone was trying to topple the Steerses' empire. But you don't know who?"

"No."

Nash leaned forward. "Hiroko-san, I know that you say Ms. Steers would not hurt people. But I witnessed her kill a woman right in front of me. In her penthouse. Lynn Ryder. Did you know her?"

Hiroko gave him a whimsical look, unlike any she had expressed so far. "Dillon-san, you are a very intelligent man, I am sure. But what you must always remember is that no matter whether a cow looks like a cow, and moos like a cow, and gives milk like a cow, there is no guarantee whatsoever that it is indeed a cow."

Nash glanced at his arm where Steers had cut him and wondered how that was not a cow.

"She wants to have dinner with me tonight. As her guest. What should I know, Hiroko-san, before I sit down with her?"

Hiroko reached out and slid her soft, aged palm against Nash's cheek.

"Dillon-san, in encounters such as that, you must follow your heart. No amount of pondering will provide you the guidance that you seek." She touched his head. "The mind thinks too deeply and will play you false when you most need it to be true." She then touched his chest. "But your heart will lead you to where you need to go, Dillon-san. It always does."

Later, as Nash got ready to go out with Steers, he wondered whether his heart was up to the task. Because no matter what had happened to Steers to change her, the fact remained that she had killed his daughter and destroyed his life. There was no going back from that.

That cow was indeed a cow.

CHAPTER 39

Nash appeared in the penthouse foyer five minutes early. He was dressed in a dark suit and white shirt with no tie. He had showered, shaved his scalp, and trimmed his beard and goatee, and he felt terribly self-conscious and uneasy about all of it.

Earlier, Thura had given him some good-natured ribbing. "Dating the boss, man, you better be careful." But then he'd lost his jocularity and said, "All kidding aside, Dillon. Be careful. She is the dragon lady for sure."

As he stood waiting for her, Steers's protection detail emerged from various nooks and crannies. They stood arrayed around him, and the grim expressions on their faces told Nash all he needed to know. The only thing keeping him upright and alive was the fact that these men feared Steers. As Nash thought about it, such power was tenuous and might be undermined by certain things. And those things might already be in play.

When Steers appeared, right on the dot of nine, Nash felt his mouth ease open in surprise. He had grudgingly conceded that Steers was quite an attractive woman. And yet there had always been a hardened edge to the beauty that had managed to diminish it to a state where he saw only the hard—and not the lovely—woman behind it.

Now the hair had been swept back into a ponytail, giving off a casual vibe that Nash found difficult to associate with the woman.

Her makeup was muted, but the red on her lips was bold against the pale skin.

Her clothing choice was perhaps the most astonishing.

It was the first time that Nash had ever seen the woman wearing a dress, and in a color other than black. It was a striking shade of orange, and it contrasted pleasingly with her dark hair and red lips.

She swiped self-consciously at her hair, and with that motion Nash realized that she was probably as nervous as he was.

"Are you ready, Mr. Hope?" she said, not looking at him.

"Yes, Ms. Steers."

They rode down in the elevator alone, the protection detail having gone on ahead.

As the floors swiftly passed by he said, "You look very nice, Ms. Steers."

She shot him a quick, sideways glance. "You as well, Mr. Hope."

For an anguished moment Nash felt like he was back in high school on his first date. *The only thing is this* date *killed my daughter.*

The car was waiting in the garage and they climbed in. When Nash tried to hold the door for Steers, one of her men beat him to it, giving him a surly look as he did so.

They sat in the back of the Maybach and didn't speak for the whole ride. A car rode in front of them and one in the rear with her men housed inside both.

Twenty minutes later they walked into a small restaurant in a suburb of Hong Kong. It was expensively and tastefully decorated, and it was also empty.

The hostess escorted them to a table and quickly left.

Some of Steers's men were clustered near the entrance and another two guarded the rear.

"Nice place," said Nash. "I'm surprised there aren't other customers."

"I made arrangements. I do not like...people all that much. They tend to...stare."

"I understand," he said, though in truth he was surprised.

"I am certain you are wondering why I invited you to dinner."

"Yes, it did cross my mind," replied Nash.

She looked over his shoulder and nodded.

A few moments later the hostess came forward with two small glasses and a bottle.

"Baijiu," said Steers. "The light variety, for you. It is a very high alcohol content."

The woman poured out small quantities and left them.

Steers raised her glass. "It is commonly used to toast, Mr. Hope."

He raised his glass. "What are we toasting?"

"Perhaps a new understanding between you and me?"

"How so?" he said warily.

"I will be frank. I have no friends, Mr. Hope. I have people who work for me. And people who work against me. I have people I pay, and pay off. I have people who hate me, despise me, want to kill me. I only have one who loves me, truly, and seeks nothing from me in return."

Nash knew she was not referring to her mother. "Hiroko is a good soul," he said.

She smiled—a bit sadly, Nash thought.

"Your intelligence shines through once more. And Hiroko-san is also a *wise* soul."

"What do you want from me, Ms. Steers?"

"I will call you Dillon-san if you would honor my request to refer to me as Victoria-san."

This stunned him, but then the dinner invitation and her words were clearly leading up to something changing between them. Apparently, whether he wanted it to or not.

Which I don't.

He said, "I'm not sure how your protection detail will take that. They hate me enough already."

"This does not concern them at all. Now, my mother does not call me Victoria-san even though it is expected between a mother and her daughter. Hiroko calls me that because I want her to. As I want you to, Dillon-san."

He said, "All right... Victoria-san."

"You, I am sure, have thought of the reasons why I had you

remain here. Why I pay you so much money. Why I have you guard my mother."

"You want someone you can thoroughly rely on. Not just because of the money. Not just because they fear you." He glanced over his shoulder at her protection detail. "You want someone around who has your best interests and who can't be bought off."

"Then we understand each other, yes. Loyalty is a fragile thing if its foundation is precarious."

She looked down at the liquid in her glass. She tipped the glass to the left and right and watched as the baijiu swirled and pitched in the small vessel.

"When one's existence is stable, it is flat, like when I set this glass down and the liquid settles." She tipped it again. "But when one's existence is uncertain, then nothing is settled. Everything is moving, and no one knows whether it will ever settle right again."

"I guess that's why life has to be lived. To find that answer."

"But life can be very short, Dillon-san."

"You are a young, healthy woman."

"Looks can be very deceiving."

Nash was taken aback by this surprising comment. "You're not ill, are you?" he said.

"My illness does not come from within me. It comes from without." She lifted her glass higher. "So if you would honor me by becoming someone who has my best interests at heart, who is loyal for the right reasons, who is my...*friend*, I would be in your eternal debt."

But even as she said the words, Nash couldn't help but think of the box in the basement with his daughter's belongings. He didn't want to be loyal or have Steers's best interests at heart. Or be her friend. He wanted to make her feel the same pain that his daughter had. The pain that he was still suffering. But Steers was, like Rhett Temple before her, giving him the perfect opportunity to place himself exactly where he wanted to be: in her inner circle.

I could kill her and let the rest of her empire go on hurting countless people. Or I can bring it and her down at the same time, if I just let this go on a little longer.

He raised his glass. "To a new understanding of loyalty."

And they drank together.

CHAPTER 40

Their meals were served and most of it was seafood, some of the best Nash had ever had. A bottle of rice wine helped wash it all down. When Nash chose not to have dessert, Steers said, "A little treat will not ruin your intimidating physique."

She flicked a finger at something behind Nash, and he was startled when a waiter appeared carrying a small cake with a single candle in it. He placed it in front of Nash, lit the candle, and retreated to the kitchen after giving Steers a fearful look.

"What is this for?" asked Nash.

"Today is your birthday."

It *was* Nash's birthday. He had wished himself a happy one that morning, but he believed no one else knew.

"How did you know?"

"Your passport gives the date."

Nash smiled. "Of course."

But then he thought that it was a mistake to give Dillon Hope the same birthday on his alternate passport. *If that had made her suspect...*

"Now, I think it customary in your culture to make a wish and blow out the candle."

He did so.

"Did you wish?"

"I did."

"I will not ask for what. That is yours and yours alone."

"Thank you. The dinner and the cake were very kind." He handed her a fork. "Will you do me the honor of joining me?"

They ate the cake together, talking about matters unconnected to anything of importance.

They left the restaurant as her protection detail converged around them. The cars had already been brought around and were lined up in front of the restaurant entrance with their engines running.

Nash did not like how the security detail was clustering, because the men had given up their point and surveillance positions by looking inward instead of outward. He had seen arrogance and complacency in these men before now. Even the driver of their Maybach was out of the car and looking at Nash and Steers.

But at this moment he was seeing something else: the glint of a knife blade held by Hao, one of her men, as he seized Steers by the arm and slashed at her neck.

Nash had seen Hao work out in the basement gym numerous times. He was the most powerful and, to Nash's mind, the most arrogant of the crew. But he had one weakness in that when striking out at a combatant, he tended to let his knee edge out over his foot too far, creating a slight imbalance.

Using this knowledge, Nash gripped the man's knife hand and jerked, pulling Hao further off balance and away from Steers. Using his grip strength to keep the knife locked in Hao's hand, he shifted his weight and ripped Hao's hand up, and the blade bit deeply into the center of Hao's chest, once and then twice. Then Nash let go of Hao and watched the dying man fall to the pavement.

He glanced at the other guards, who looked stunned by what had happened.

So maybe Hao was the only traitor?

"Eyes outward and set the perimeter," Nash barked. "He won't be alone."

Then he grabbed Steers and threw her into the Maybach's back seat. "Stay down," he told her.

He slammed the door shut and pulled his gun just as automatic weapons fire came at them from the alleyway off to their right. Nash dropped to the pavement as the bullets struck the men in front of him. Within seconds the remaining protection detail members were wiped out.

Nash emptied his mag in the direction of the shots, then crawled forward and snatched weapons from two of the dead men. He opened fire even as he propelled himself toward the car on his back. He took return fire and then finished off both mags, spreading his shots in a wide arc before jumping into the driver's seat of the car. He shifted into gear and slammed down on the gas, then dodged around the empty lead car in front.

The Maybach flew down the once-quiet street as bullets pinged off the metal hide and bulletproof glass. The tires were also struck but they were run-flat, he knew, and kept rolling. But one heavy round hit the passenger's side window with such force that it nearly shattered.

"They've got explosive rounds," Nash called out to Steers. "Stay on the floorboard. Do not sit up!"

As more bullets banged off the car, Nash turned right at the next street and then blew through a red light. He hung a left that probably pushed the Maybach to the limits of its handling capability. He then orchestrated another turn so extreme that Nash had to use all his strength to maintain control of the heavy vehicle. This was not the way back to Steers's building, but he wasn't sure he wanted to go there. There had clearly been betrayal in the ranks, and he had no idea how deep it went.

He called Thura, told him what had happened, and instructed him to check on Masuyo and Hiroko. He next called the Hong Kong police and told them what had occurred.

Then Nash drove until he came to a park and stopped the car. "Okay, I think we're safe."

When she didn't answer he looked over the back seat.

"Victoria-san!"

He jumped out of the car, opened the battered rear door, and peered inside.

Steers was on the floorboard, covered in blood.

He turned her over and he could see the slash on her neck.

"Oh my God."

How the hell did I miss that when I put her into the car?

He popped open the glove box, grabbed the first aid kit there, and treated the wound as best he could. He sat back on his haunches, hovering over her. She was going to die if she didn't receive medical attention. And quickly.

As he stared down at the critically wounded woman, Nash's mind filled with the images of his daughter, happy and safe, and then he imagined her bones lying in the dirt. And then the memory of the box in Steers's basement crept into his mind.

I can do nothing and just let her die right now. I can't be blamed. I can make a statement to the police and then go home. And my nightmare will be over and Maggie will be avenged.

When the groans of the injured woman reached his ears, Nash knew he could not just sit by and watch Steers die.

And if I ever get to that point, I'm no better than she is.

He drove to the nearest hospital and carried the unconscious Steers into the emergency center, where he screamed for help. Her blood now also covered him.

Doctors and nurses converged to aid them.

Nash told them what had happened, and they quickly triaged Steers's neck wound. A minute later she was rolled away on a gurney, leaving Nash standing there helpless.

As the swing doors closed behind the medical team with Steers, his phone buzzed. It was Thura.

"All good here, man. You saying one of them tried to kill her?"

"Yes, Hao. I neutralized him, but the rest of the detail is dead. They didn't appear to be in on it. But it was an ambush all the way. So keep your eyes and ears open, all right?"

"You got it. Think she's gonna make it?"

Nash looked toward the doors through which they had whisked Steers away. "I don't know."

He clicked off and hung his head. *Part of me wants her not to recover. But another part of me? After what I've seen and what Hiroko told me?*

He waggled his head, the inner debate in his mind beyond his ability to process it.

"Sir?"

He looked up to see a nurse standing in front of him.

"Yes?"

"You are injured."

"What?"

She pointed to his forearm. Where his jacket sleeve had been ripped open there was blood, his blood.

"Come with me."

He rose and she led him over to a small cubicle. The nurse had him take off his jacket and roll up his sleeve.

"It is not too bad," she said. "But it could become infected."

He looked at the damaged flesh and immediately thought of Steers.

"Does it hurt much?" she asked.

"Well, considering I didn't even know I was wounded until you pointed it out, I guess the answer is no."

As the nurse worked on him she shot Nash curious glances. "I do not see a ring, so was that woman your girlfriend?"

Nash, who had been staring at the floor, looked up. "What?"

"The woman you brought in? Your girlfriend?"

"No, she's...my...boss."

"Oh, I see." The woman did not look like she believed him.

After she was done, Nash returned to his seat and kept an eagle eye on the doors leading into the emergency center. Whoever had ambushed them might have managed to follow them, intending to finish the job. Nash had already reloaded his Glock, and he still had his Beretta. He had also called the police again and told them where he and Steers were.

An hour later Nash jerked upright when a number of officers entered the building. One of them, who appeared to be in charge, looked around and spotted Nash, who rose and hurried toward him.

"Are you the one who phoned?" said the officer, who glanced over all the blood on Nash's clothes.

"Yes. Ms. Steers is with the doctors. She was badly wounded."

"We have found the dead men. I need to know exactly what happened. And I need to see your identification."

Nash showed him his passport, and for the next half hour he went over all the details as best as he could remember them, while one of the other officers took down his account on a laptop.

"So one of her own people tried to kill her?" said the officer.

"Yes. I used his knife against him. That's when the gunfire opened up. The other men were killed. And we got away in the car. I didn't notice she was wounded until we stopped."

"And you were wounded as well?" he said, noting the bandage wrapped around Nash's arm.

"Just a nick."

The officer nodded and looked sharply at Nash, his expression suddenly unfriendly. "So you work for *Victoria Steers*?"

"Yes. As part of her security detail."

"And she is unable to speak to us presently?"

"She's unconscious. Lost a lot of blood. She's probably in surgery right now."

The man looked at his assistant, who was taking notes, and shook his head. The assistant closed the computer.

"In Hong Kong the police well know of Ms. Steers," said the officer.

"Okay," said Nash dully.

"She has many enemies."

Nash said nothing.

"And they could very well be the ones who tried to kill her tonight."

"Looks to be the case," replied Nash.

"And the fact is, Ms. Steers is a criminal, but we have yet to prove this. She..." He paused and looked around. "She has friends in high places."

"I know nothing about that," lied Nash.

"Your passport says you are an American?"

"Yes, I am."

"Then how did you come to work for her?" asked the officer.

"I was employed by someone else and she liked how I did my job," replied Nash.

"But she only uses other Asians for protection. This is because she trusts them."

"Well, that trust didn't work out so well tonight, did it?"

The officer rose. "We will see what we can do. But we have much to work on right now. So results on her case may not be forthcoming quickly. If at all. But then again, she may die and no investigation will be necessary."

The man smiled and suddenly Nash felt defensive of Steers.

"No one should get away with murder," he said.

"I completely agree," said the officer, his expression once more serious. "And that includes your boss."

CHAPTER

41

Steers slowly opened her eyes. However, the lights were intense and she closed them reflexively. She was tired, in pain, and desperately confused.

She opened her eyes once more, and then Steers turned her head from one side to the other. The hospital room was cluttered with machines buzzing and chirping. She tried to sit up but felt restrained. She tried again but her strength failed her. She could hear voices from somewhere but could not make out what was being said.

She lifted a hand and touched her neck, feeling the large bandage there and then the tape over it.

They tried to kill me. My own people tried to kill me.

She remembered the knife striking her, the gush of blood, and then Dillon Hope had killed her attacker, hurled her into the car, and then bullets started coming from everywhere. Then more shots were fired. And then they had driven off, rapidly. Her body had been flung around with the force of the car maneuvers Hope was employing. He had said something as things kept hitting the car and windows with incredible force, but she could not hear him clearly.

And then her mind had turned off and Steers remembered nothing more. Until she had opened her eyes just now.

"Victoria-san?"

She looked up to see him standing over her. His face and white shirt were bloodied.

With my blood?

She slowly eased her head from side to side, trying to...She closed her eyes.

Nash looked down at her. She was alive, and he was terribly conflicted about that.

If she had died, it would be so much easier. My nightmare would be over. So why is part of me so relieved that she survived?

He pushed these thoughts from his mind and said, "The doctors stitched you up, filled you back up with blood, and your vitals are strong."

"You brought me here?" asked Steers as she once more opened her eyes.

The same nurse who had taken care of Nash's wound walked up to the bed. "Yes, he carried you in himself. Otherwise you would not be alive now." She checked the wound, dispensed some meds into a port they had placed in Steers's forearm, and left.

Nash sat in a chair next to her.

She looked at him and said, "He cut me."

"Yes, it was Hao. I—"

"You killed him. This I remember seeing."

"I didn't know you had been wounded. I would have driven you straight here if I had known. It was my mistake. I'm sorry, Victoria-san. You could have died."

She reached through the bed's side bars and gripped his hand. "You saved my life. Like the nurse said, I would be gone but for you."

Her touch suddenly maddened Nash. The police officer had been right. All murderers should be punished.

And yet cows, Hiroko had said. Cows are strange beasts indeed, then.

"You were hurt as well!"

He looked up to see her staring at his bandaged arm. "Looks far worse than it is."

She relaxed and said, "I am happy it was nothing more."

"Hao must have been working for one of your enemies."

She released his hand and lay back. "The fact that this caught me unawares pains me even more than this," she said, touching the bandage on her neck.

"But you're still here and he isn't. Which means we can find out who's behind this."

"My other men? They are dead?"

"Yes. All of them. They were obviously not part of it. Only Hao."

"Only Hao," she repeated dully. She glanced at him. "You are now my protection."

"Me and Thura, yes. Until you hire a new team."

"I do not wish a new team, Dillon-san. You *are* my team."

"What, why?" he said in surprise.

"Because you have more than proven your loyalty."

And here I had almost let her bleed out in the car. And part of me wanted her to die. "You need to rest. And then you can make decisions."

She closed her eyes and, probably due to the meds put into her port, was soon asleep.

And not for the first time since his nightmare had commenced, Walter Nash had no idea what he was supposed to do.

He had previously bought a burner phone with cash. He now slipped out of the hospital room and left a voicemail for Agent Morris, telling him about the assassination attempt.

Over time Nash had made recordings of discussions he'd overheard with Steers and her associates. In addition, he had chronicled his observations, including Masuyo's information drops in the park. Using the burner phone he had sent all this, and the photos of Maggie's things in the box, to Agent Morris via the secure portal the man had provided. He'd then deleted everything, including the portal, from his phone in case anyone tried to force him to reveal what was on it.

As soon as he returned to the hospital room his phone buzzed. It was Thura.

"We got a package delivered here, Dillon. It showed up in the lobby. The reception guy said some dude left it and then rushed out. Weird as shit. And with what happened to Ms. Steers I called the police. They scanned the exterior for bomb stuff and it was clean, so they left without opening it. They couldn't tell me what was inside from the scan. So what do I do?"

Nash gave him the address of the hospital and told him to get here as soon as he could. When Thura arrived a half hour later, Nash instructed him to remain in Steers's room until he got back. "Eyes on her at all times. You never leave."

"Right."

Nash grabbed a cab back to the penthouse and rode up in the elevator. He was met by one of Steers's young female attendants, who had clearly been crying.

"Has...will she be all right?" the woman asked.

"Yes, she will. Where is the package?"

She led him into a small room off the dining area where a sturdy box with a lock sat. On top of the box was a letter and a key.

He read the letter. The message was brief: "We are returning your property, Ms. Steers."

It was unsigned.

Nash looked the case over. It was black with chrome hinges and a clasp lock.

He figured since it had already been checked for any explosives, there was only one thing to do. He took the key and inserted it in the lock.

He counted to three, and then, ready to jump if the thing contained a snake or some other danger, he opened it. When Nash looked inside he saw an object but couldn't tell what it was because it was wrapped in opaque plastic and tied off at the top.

He lifted it out and set it next to the case.

Drawing a long breath he gingerly undid the tie and pulled the plastic free.

He had to fight back the urge to vomit.

Staring back at him was the severed head of the elderly woman who had been substituted for Masuyo at the prison in Myanmar.

CHAPTER

42

Steers sat very stiffly in the chair in her office while Nash sat across from her.

She had been home from the hospital for several days, much of the time either asleep or in pain. She was now rested, but the ache was still with her.

And the fear.

Nash had disposed of the severed head before she had returned, but he had told Steers about it.

"That is most...unfortunate," she said, her mouth seeming to have difficulty forming the words.

"The people who operate the prison must have figured out the switch."

"Clearly."

"Did you know the woman?" he asked.

She nodded. "She was old and very sick. She had little time left. She had children that needed help. I gave them enough money for the rest of their lives, and in return she agreed to do what she did. The children know nothing of it—only she did."

"She looked exactly like your mother."

"Yes, which was why she was selected. Although small things were altered through one surgery, but it was done delicately because of her fragile condition. She was schooled on information having to do with my mother so that if they questioned her, she would be able to pass any sort of test conducted by them. But I suppose it was inevitable that our charade would be found out at some point. Only

I hoped she would die of natural causes before they discovered the truth."

"Well, Hao betrayed you. It could be that these people also found out about the substitution from him or another source within your camp."

"Hao knew nothing of the plan." She looked up at him. She wore a neck scarf to hide the bandaged wound. "Which means we may yet have another spy among us."

Nash thought of Masuyo and her cryptic messages left in an ice cream container on a park bench.

"The police spoke with me while you were in surgery," said Nash.

"I am aware of this, because they came and saw me while you were arranging for the car home."

"What did they say to you?"

"I believe that they are quite unhappy I survived."

"I don't think they will do much to find out who tried to kill you."

"Why should they help someone like me?"

"Well, murder and attempted murder are against the law."

"The law is not for people like me. They wanted me to die. They are glad my men are dead. I can understand this completely."

"You're being brutally self-honest."

"Honesty must always be brutal or it grows dangerously close to self-deception and then on to lies, and that helps no one, least of all the liar."

"Okay, what do you want to do now?"

"In Hong Kong we are not safe."

"So we pick up and go somewhere else then?" he asked.

"You have wanted to return to the United States?"

"Yes."

"Then we shall go there. All of us: you, Thura, my mother, and Hiroko-san."

"Where will we go?"

"I own a home. It is actually near the estate of Rhett Temple. It is secluded. We can...feel safer there until I can regroup and think things through."

"And your enemies?"

"Trying to kill me and sending me the poor woman's head was only the beginning. They will obviously keep trying until I am dead. But then we shall see what we shall see. I have survived much."

"Victoria-san?"

"Yes?"

"I have been guarding your mother, as you know, although now Thura has taken over that role while I watch over you. She has demanded absolute loyalty from me above all others, including you."

"That has always been her way."

"But I am now guarding you. So my loyalty is to you. It is complicated, but I want you to understand what I'm grappling with."

She said wearily, "There is no need to contort yourself. I am *aware*."

"No, with respect, I don't think you are. You see, she has gone to Kowloon Park twice a week for quite some time now. She always buys an ice cream, she always goes to the restroom, and she always leaves the container on the bench and—"

Steers held up her hand. "I *know* this. My mother leaves messages for the man to pick up."

"You knew about it?"

"I know about anything having to do with me or my mother."

"But this could be tied to the attack on you."

"We will not speak of this now."

"But you almost died. I don't understand."

Her features became rigid. "I understand that you do not understand, Dillon-san. But if it makes you feel better, I am the only person alive who truly understands *my* world. Now, if there is nothing more, I need to complete some...tasks." She touched her neck. "And...rest. This has taken more out of me than I originally thought."

"Of course." He rose and bowed slightly. "If you need anything?"

"Yes, thank you."

He turned to leave.

"Dillon-san?"

He turned back to her, and now Steers's expression was softer, calmer, and sadder.

"Yes?"

"I truly thank you for your friendship and your loyalty. It means a great deal to me. Especially now when one feels alone above all other things."

Nash bowed again, more deeply this time, and left, his mind full of confusion and his heart full of foreboding.

CHAPTER 43

Weeks later a warm day led to a thunderstorm and a chilly night. Finally gaining Steers's approval, Nash had retained temporary security personnel and posted them around the clock at the elevators in the lobby. He and Thura had moved to the same floor as Steers and her mother. Hiroko had also been moved here, via Steers's order. They were circling the wagons until they would leave for America, which Steers had told him would be soon.

Now Nash rose from his bed and checked his watch. He was not on duty for another six hours, but he just couldn't fall asleep. He got dressed and decided to go for a walk since the storm had passed. He checked in with Thura, who patrolled through the penthouse every thirty minutes and also was in contact with the security in the lobby. No one was allowed up to the penthouse or the two floors below it without Steers's express permission. He and Thura were splitting the security shifts with one of them on for twelve hours and the other off.

"Anything going on?" he asked Thura.

"All quiet. Hey, you sure they gonna let me in?"

"In where?"

"America, man."

"Ms. Steers will take care of the paperwork, I'm sure."

Thura looked at him questioningly.

"What?" said Nash.

"Been meaning to ask you: When you went to dinner with her, what did she want?"

Nash shrugged. "I think she wanted a friend."

"Why does someone like that need a friend? That woman is so rich, she can buy whoever she wants."

"Well, she bought the guy who tried to kill her."

"This is true," Thura conceded.

"So that sort of 'friendship' is only good until someone comes along who's willing to pay a higher price."

"Money, man, it does bad shit to people. Look at Amrita."

"She said you were the one who was greedy. That you wanted us dead to collect a reward and throw off suspicion."

"I told you, man, I get paid for a job, I do the job."

"You proved that."

Thura grinned. "And that lady is paying me so much. I am rich, Dillon. What else do I need? I mean, come on."

"Just wait until you get to America. You see, there the richer someone is, it's actually the case that they want even more money. It's an addiction, like meth or heroin."

"So what did you say to her when she asked about you being her friend?"

Nash didn't answer right away. "I told a vulnerable and lonely woman that I would be her friend. You think I did the right thing, Thura?"

"Look, Dillon, sometimes you got to do and say stuff. I don't mean you don't mean what you say. Life throws you some crazy shit. Amrita turned up one day in my town, scared, hungry, all alone. She told me her story. She had nothing. She needed a friend. So I became her friend."

"But then you ended up having to kill her," pointed out Nash.

"That's what I mean when I said life throws you some crazy shit. It was my turn to get hit with it. I did not want to do it. I wished I didn't have to do it, Dillon. But..."

"But I'd be dead if you hadn't."

Thura looked away and shook his head. "That will go with me to my grave."

"Don't beat yourself up too badly. We all have things like that we carry around. Phone me if anything comes up."

He slipped on a raincoat and headed down the elevator. He checked in with the guards in the lobby. They had come from a licensed agency and seemed to be real pros, but Nash didn't trust any of them. If one of Steers's longtime people could be corrupted, anyone could be.

Except for me, and I'm already working against her.

His head suddenly throbbing, he headed out into the drizzle and got a cup of flat white coffee and a croissant from a café. Even at this hour, large groups of people were out and about, and many places were open for business.

He ate and drank, lost in his own thoughts. Nash being back in his hometown would make it easier to communicate with Morris and the FBI. And being back on American soil would probably make him feel better. He could even drop by Temple's home or office and check up on his efforts to liberate him.

Right.

But it also came with complications.

As he was walking back to the penthouse at around three a.m., Nash saw the woman get out of a cab in front of the building.

And received the absolute shock of his life.

CHAPTER

44

Nash immediately slid into the shadows as the woman looked all around before heading into the building.

He quickly followed. When he got to the lobby she had already been cleared to go up in the elevator.

He asked one of the guards in the lobby about it and was told that they had checked with Thura, and Steers had approved the woman's admittance.

Nash rode the elevator up, got out in the foyer, and spied Thura, who was coming into view from one of the halls, probably after finishing his rounds.

"Did you see her?" asked Nash.

"The woman who just came up? Yeah. She went to Steers's office. Boss is working really late."

Nash stole down the corridor and drew near to Steers's office.

It made sense. At least the visitor showing up when she had.

Because I'm not supposed to be on duty but asleep in my bed.

He waited in a niche down the hall. Twenty minutes went by and then thirty.

Finally, the door opened. And Steers and the woman stepped out into the corridor.

Nash didn't hesitate. He walked out from the shadows and stood there.

The supposedly dead Lynn Ryder spotted him and said, "Fuck."

Steers eyed Nash and then turned to Ryder. "Leave us."

Without another word, the woman walked off.

Now it was just Nash and Steers staring at each other across a five-foot space that might as well have been the width of a continent.

"Well, that cow was definitely not a cow," commented Nash.

"What?" said a startled Steers.

"Nothing, just something Hiroko-san once said. So Ryder is alive and kicking?"

"You believe that you deserve an explanation?" she said.

"I'll let you answer that, Victoria-san. But I will say that trust and friendship should be a two-way street."

She bowed her head. "You humble me, truly."

"Does that mean I get an explanation?"

She motioned for him to enter her office.

They sat in chairs inches from each other. She had removed the bandage and the scarf. The wound was healing nicely, Nash observed. But it would always be visible. *Another* reminder for the woman, he thought.

"Lynn Ryder and I met nearly ten years ago. She was outside of my business then but became part of it soon thereafter."

"Okay, but you also shot her in the head. Or so I thought. With *my* gun."

She now looked at him in triumphant fashion. "One gun looks much like another. And when I intimated that the gun I used was yours, you readily accepted that fact. It is what magicians refer to as sleight of hand and psychological manipulation. I use that often in my business."

"But the blowback on you, the blood everywhere? That wasn't magic."

She touched her temple. "A patch under the hair, triggered by the wireless remote in the fake gun. A harmless charge that detonated a small package, contained in the patch, of what looked to be blood and other things. Like they do in the movies. It was all prearranged, you see."

"It was very well done. But why?"

"You needed to be persuaded that you had no choice but to stay and do my bidding. Otherwise you would be charged with murder. Or so you believed."

"And your reputation as a heartless woman would remain intact?" He held up the arm that she had cut. "But *this* wasn't an illusion. And neither is the one on Rhett Temple."

She glanced away and crossed her legs. "I am not a good person, Dillon-san. You more than most should know this." She shot him a curious look, and Nash interpreted it as Steers perhaps thinking about the fact that she had also kissed him, but he could be wrong about that.

"What you are is perplexing as hell," he replied.

"I have ordered people to be killed. I distribute drugs that kill many people. There is nothing perplexing about that."

"And yet you didn't kill Lynn Ryder."

"She is a valuable asset who had done nothing to harm me."

"Neither did the people who take your drugs."

"As I said, I am not a good person. I am the opposite."

"But you have some conscience, clearly." As he said this, Nash realized the significance of his words.

How can this woman have a conscience?

She exclaimed, "I have no conscience. I killed my own brothers and my sister. I am a sociopath. I have looked this term up. It fits me precisely in every way. I…"

An open-mouthed Steers stopped and looked astonished that she had made such a stunning admission.

She said hesitantly, "I am sorry. I…that is not for…your ears. Please do not—"

"But did you really kill your siblings?" Nash interjected before he could catch himself.

She looked at him strangely. "Do not try to make me into something I am not, Dillon-san. It is a fool's errand. It makes you look weak."

"Okay, so how did you kill them?"

"You do not need to know anything about that," she said sharply. "I never should have spoken of it."

"But you did speak of it. So just tell me how you killed your oldest brother, and I'll stop asking."

"You will stop asking now, if you are truly wise."

"Are you going to kill me if I don't?"

In answer she walked around to her desk, opened a drawer, and pulled out a pistol. She pointed it at him. "Yes, I will kill you."

"Answer my question about your brother and then you can shoot me." He pointed to the center of his forehead. "Right here, kill shot ten times out of ten."

"You are mad," she cried out, the pistol wavering in her hand.

"No, I'm just curious. I want to know how you killed your brother. That's all. One answer and we're done."

She pointed the gun at his head. "We are already done."

"Then give a dead man his last wish. Answer me."

"I will not."

"You don't remember because you didn't do it."

"You are a fool," she snapped.

"I don't think so."

"I hate you," she shouted.

"That may well be true, but you didn't kill your family."

"You know nothing about it."

"I apparently know more than you do."

"You bastard," she screamed.

"I'm not doing this to hurt you, Victoria-san."

Tears trickling down her cheeks, she said in a pleading voice, "Then why are you doing this to me? I do not understand."

"I'm actually trying to save you."

"From what?" she exclaimed.

"Maybe from yourself."

Her hand slid to the gun's trigger and her voice regained some resolve. "You cannot save me. You cannot save yourself because I am going to kill both of us. We end tonight."

"Then go ahead, Victoria-san. Go ahead."

Then she did something unexpected.

She placed the gun's muzzle under her chin.

"No, you will not die, Dillon-san, but I shall. It is better this way. For everyone."

The tears were now streaming down her face and the pale skin had a sheen of red from the blood pulsing through it.

"Taking your own life will solve nothing," he said.

"It will solve the dilemma of *me*," she retorted.

"You are a *person*, not a dilemma."

"I am a person who does not deserve to live."

He watched as her features calmed and her finger curled to the trigger. But he couldn't let it end, not like this.

"If you kill yourself, you will leave behind many unanswered questions, to be sure. But you will be leaving behind people who care for you."

"Who? Who cares for me!" she screamed, her features twisted. "My father is dead. My own mother, I now realize, does not care for me. She only cares for the *business*. For power. So *who* do you speak of?"

"He speaks of me," said the voice.

Nash turned to see the diminutive Hiroko standing there in her robe, though at this moment she seemed to loom far larger than her physical self. She was not looking at Nash, but rather her focus was directly on Steers.

"Hiroko-san," Steers said in a strained voice. "I do not wish you to see me like this. Please go."

Hiroko did not go, but came forward. "I have seen you in many ways ever since you were born, Victoria-san. I have seen a happy, shy, and curious child grow up into someone else. But that child is still inside, hoping one day to come alive again."

Steers looked at Nash and said in an imploring tone, "Will you tell Hiroko-san that she speaks nonsense? I am what I have always been." When Nash said nothing, Steers screamed, "Tell her."

"I can tell her but she won't believe me," said Nash. "So what's the point?"

Hiroko walked over to stand next to Steers. She gently took the gun from her and passed it over to Nash.

"You will come with me, Victoria-san. You will sleep in my bed while I watch over you. Like when you were a little girl."

"I am no longer a little girl," Steers said dully, all the fight in her now gone.

"In years, what you say is true. But in other ways, we will see. Now come with me. Please."

Steers allowed herself to be led out of the room by her former nanny, leaving Nash alone and holding the gun that might have been the weapon of both their deaths.

He slumped back in his chair, as spent as if he had run a marathon.

This simple case of revenge and justice had taken on far greater complexities.

And Nash wasn't sure how much more of this he or Steers could take before they both would become permanently broken.

Or dead.

CHAPTER 45

The spacious Bombardier Global 8000 jet lifted off from Hong Kong International at ten p.m. heading east.

On board were Nash, Thura, Hiroko, Masuyo, Victoria Steers, and three personal attendants along with four pilots. There was also a flight attendant on board to cater to their needs.

Steers had immediately gone to her private cabin in the rear of the plane. Masuyo sat up front near the flight attendant. The three personal attendants shared a divan, where they could watch a large-screen TV.

Nash and Thura sat in the middle section close to Hiroko. The elderly woman looked nervously around the cabin, and Nash could understand her anxiety, what with Hiroko having once barely survived a horrific plane crash.

Masuyo made a series of demands to the flight attendant while they were still climbing out of Hong Kong. When the woman rose to respond, Nash stopped her and said, "Stay in your seat until we've finished the climb-out."

He called out to Masuyo, "Ma'am, we *all* need to stay seated until it's safe."

Masuyo turned in her seat and gave him a glare, but did not dispute his instruction.

Two hours later, after meals and drinks had been consumed, everyone settled in for the rest of the long flight over the Pacific, and then on to Nash's hometown.

An hour later Thura was snoring lightly and Hiroko also was dozing. Nash looked up at Masuyo and she seemed to be asleep as well. The flight attendant was doing some paperwork in her seat and facing away from Nash.

He rose, went toward the back of the plane, past the sleeping personal attendants on the divan, and tapped lightly on the door to Steers's cabin.

"Yes?" she said through the door.

"It's Dillon. Just checking to make sure you're okay."

She opened the door, dressed in a long robe. He saw her bare feet poking out from under it.

"Come in," she said in a monotone.

She shut the door behind him and he looked around the luxurious cabin, which resembled a high-end hotel room, with a club chair and a cabinet with a TV inside, and a private bath with walk-in shower.

She sat on the bed, her legs in a lotus position.

Nash perched on the chair opposite her. "How are you feeling?" he asked.

"You mean after I made a spectacle of myself the other night?"

"You said things that you were obviously feeling. Why keep them in?"

She glanced up at him. "Foremost, because I am not supposed to have feelings. Do you not know? I am made of steel. I am supposed to be in control, at all times."

"No one can do that, not even you."

She looked away from him. "I am fine. Going to America will rejuvenate me."

"And your mother?"

"What of her?"

"I told you about the messages in the park," said Nash.

"And I told you that I already knew."

"So you also know about the young man who retrieves the messages she leaves in the ice cream container?"

"My mother was away for a long time. What would be more

natural than for her to evaluate how the business she created and ran for decades is doing? And whether I am a good steward of what she had built?"

"Is that what she's doing?"

"The man in question works for a third party with which I do business. My mother has been seeking information about our dealings with this party. She has, I assume, been doing the same with other parties as well."

"Why not just ask you?"

She shrugged. "It is not her way."

"Is the business not doing well?"

"I do not think that is any of your concern," she said sternly. "You are a bodyguard, not a businessperson."

"Well, I have dealt with wealthy people all over the world. You pick up stuff."

She folded her arms and said, "Such as?"

Nash knew he was treading a fine line here. He *was* a businessman, a highly successful one, but he was also masquerading as a bodyguard, a pretense he desperately needed to keep up.

"Such as cash flow is king. Customers are fickle, the competition ruthless. And everybody wants to knock off the king. Or in your case, the queen. You don't have just the cops watching your every move, but a host of politicians dreaming about using you as their next campaign slogan. You know, 'I brought down Victoria Steers. Vote for me.'"

She looked at him with fresh respect. "And how do you feel being involved in an enterprise that you wanted no part of?"

"I'm in it now regardless of what I want."

"And you know if I go down those around me go down as well?"

"I understand."

"No, I don't think you do. I will do everything in my power to ensure that you and Thura suffer no consequences."

"And why would you do that?"

"You are not criminals. You were simply in the wrong place at the wrong time, but the right place at the right time for me. You should not suffer over that."

"That does not sound like something a sociopath would do, if you don't mind my saying so," noted Nash.

"Even evil people have moments of good."

"I appreciate you offering that. It speaks well of you."

"And you will no longer worry about my mother and her little trips to the park?"

"I can't promise you that."

"But I have told you—"

"Yes, you have told me," he said. "But can I make a frank observation?"

She sighed. "Go ahead."

"Your mother is smart, cagey, ruthless, sees the whole chessboard, correct? I mean, it's how she's wired."

"I don't see where—"

"Correct or not?"

"Yes, correct," she exclaimed, looking tired.

"Then can I ask a question?"

"Would it matter what I said?"

"It would. I work for you."

"Go ahead and ask your question," she said resignedly.

"Then why would such a woman be so blatantly obvious about what she is doing? So obvious to use a clumsy maneuver like notes in an ice cream container picked up by someone who I could easily spot? Does that strike you as something Masuyo Steers would do? Because it could easily have been the police watching her. Why not just pick up the phone and call the person about your business with them instead of playing these stupid spy games?"

Steers blinked rapidly three times and then she looked far more engaged. "And what is *your* answer to this, Dillon-san?"

"Remember what you said about your ruse in using what I thought was my gun to 'kill' Lynn Ryder."

"What of it?"

"You said a magician's tricks of the trade were sleight of hand and psychological manipulation."

Steers's lips parted. "You...mean...?"

"Maybe your mother made us look to the right with this 'ice cream in the park' subterfuge, when what she was actually doing was occurring on the left."

CHAPTER 46

Steers's home was situated in the hills about two miles from the Temple estate along a winding road. Nash had been in Hong Kong for a long while, and when he'd left America he hadn't been certain he would ever return.

When they passed through the estate's broad gates in a passenger van, Nash asked her how long she had owned it.

"Sixteen months, Dillon-san," said Steers. "It required renovation, which is now completed."

Neither of them noted that Masuyo appeared jolted by her calling him Dillon-san.

"Why so close to Rhett Temple?" he asked.

"Because he and I have further business. And I like to watch most carefully over my *investments*."

Nash had never observed this estate while he lived with Rhett Temple at his home because it was well hidden off the road behind high walls and mature trees. The place had a Tuscan feel to it, with a stone exterior, towers and turrets, and a cobblestoned motor court. In the rear was a large pool, a tennis court, an outdoor grilling area, a sprawling guesthouse, and several smaller cottages serving as staff quarters. There were also sculptures, fountains, and waterfalls, and outdoor spaces with seating areas connected by flagstone pathways arrayed around the manicured grounds.

The plants and shrubs were in full bloom, lovely and fragrant.

Nash and Thura were assigned to the luxurious five-bedroom guesthouse. When Thura walked into the place he spread his arms wide and cried out, "I am in America. No shit." Then, like a kid, he went into his room, jumped on the bed, and just lay there beaming at the timbered ceiling.

Along with the attendants they had brought with them, the estate came with a staff that Steers told Nash she had thoroughly vetted. However, he and Thura intended to keep their eyes and ears peeled for any sign of a traitor in the ranks.

Nash swam in the heated pool early each morning and then ran around the grounds until his shirt was soaked and he was breathless. Thura often came with him, to both keep in shape and tell Nash what a fabulous place America was, until Nash had grown weary of hearing about it.

Nash also walked the grounds admiring the hardscapes and fountains and secluded areas, where there were inviting benches and the sounds of water falling softly. He had seen Steers several times tucked away in one of these nooks, with a canvas on an easel, and painting away. He never disturbed her during these moments, but he did linger and watch her. She usually wore a loose-fitting smock but always with her arms fully covered. Sometimes she also wore a wide-brimmed straw hat, which made him smile because it looked so incongruous on her, or at least the person the world saw as Victoria Steers.

But then his mind would go to that box in the basement with his dead daughter's things in it, and his happy expression when observing Steers the artist rapidly turned hard and bitter.

He had been given a vehicle to drive—a Range Rover, ironically, like the one he had owned as Walter Nash—and he would drive into town some days when Steers and Masuyo did not need him. Either he or Thura always remained on guard. Nash had continually pressed Steers to let him hire additional protectors who could also stay in the guesthouse or staff quarters, but she had steadfastly refused.

"I do not know if one of them will contain another Hao," she had said, referring to the man who had tried to kill her. "This is a worry I do not have with you and Thura."

Her comment had made him feel guilty, since he was working against her. But then he had told himself that Steers had brought this on herself. He certainly hadn't asked for any of it.

Since he'd gained Steers's trust she had been less restrictive on his actions, and now as her head of security he had even more freedom.

Driving into town one day he called Morris on a burner phone, and the agent answered.

"So you're back in America?" Morris said.

"Come on, Reed. I'm sure you tracked our movements every step of the way."

"Of course we did."

"I'm actually surprised you didn't arrest her when we were going through customs."

"While we *might* be able to get an indictment on Steers with what we have now, the rest of her partners would go free. The Bureau has decided it's all or nothing on this sucker."

"I can understand that." He paused. "How is . . . Judith?"

"She's adapted better than most to being in protection."

"Can you tell me where she is?"

"I don't even know. That's US Marshal jurisdiction. But I can tell you it's nowhere near your old home." Morris paused. "By the way, she knew it was you."

"Excuse me?"

"That night when you killed those men in your home. She knew it was you."

"How do you know that?" asked a stunned Nash.

"I said you were quite capable and she said something like, 'What do you expect from a fucking Eagle Scout?' I take it you *were* an Eagle Scout?"

"Yes, but why didn't you tell me this before?"

"What good would it have done?"

Nash couldn't come up with an adequate response to that.

Morris said, "But there has been a development that you need to know about. I have no idea how you might be able to use it, or us either, for that matter."

"What is it?"

"It's good news for the country overall, but it needs a deeper dive for our purposes."

"I'm all attention, Reed."

"I don't know if you've been following this, but over the last eighteen months, fentanyl and related deaths have plummeted in this country. And over the last six months or so the decline has really accelerated."

"That *is* good news. Do you know why?"

"Lots of reasons. Some really depressing, like so many have died there aren't that many users left. But on the positive side treatments have helped, as have counseling and public awareness campaigns. Making Narcan free and widely available has also been a real boost. Lots of people who would be dead aren't."

"That is really great to hear."

"And young people, thank God, aren't using drugs like older generations did. And those that do are doing it smarter. Smoking instead of injecting, for example, and not using it alone so there's someone to bring them back from the dead if they OD. Related to this development, China has started to be the supplier for cursors and precursors as opposed to the finished fentanyl. We believe China has begun exporting the raw materials to the Steers organization, probably to evade detection and to also allow themselves plausible deniability. Smoke-and-mirror sort of things."

"But when they put all the stuff together you still get a drug that can kill people."

"The other reason, which has been borne out by testing of seized shipments of pills, is that the use of pure fentanyl in pills coming into this country has fallen through the floor."

"What are they using instead? I mean, don't they need some drug like fentanyl to make the product work and give addicted people the jolt their brain tells them they need?"

"They do. And what we've been finding lately is the presence of animal tranquilizers like Xylazine and Medetomidine. Now, they are toxic to humans but they are also not as immediately lethal as fentanyl. Still gives the user the pop they want, but the risks of death are less. And law enforcement in this country has been putting the squeeze on Mexico and China to get fentanyl out of the illegal drug supply chain, with mixed results. It's still there, but not as much as before. Now we're seeing more complicated street cocktails with less fentanyl. The Mexican cartels still churn out meth and cocaine and make a lot of money off that, but they don't give you the pop that the synthetics do. But the synthetics are ever evolving. When we think we have a handle on what's out there, they throw new, more powerful ones into the mix. It's like Whac-A-Mole, only with deadly results."

"So fatalities are going down. But you said the Chinese controlled that market and they want to use it to destroy this country from the inside out. That's why you recruited me."

"That hasn't changed, according to our sources, even with the law enforcement squeeze I talked about."

"Well, stop beating around the bush. If China still wants lots of dead Americans, but the drugs aren't as deadly, then something has changed. What?"

"Apparently, Victoria Steers has. Over the last fourteen months or so drug trafficking that we suspect is tied to her operation has heavily invested in labs in Mexico and Central America, as opposed to ones in China and Southeast Asia. That's where we are seeing the less lethal synthetic opioids and animal tranquilizers being used to make the pills. It could be that she is addressing the cartel's concerns of killing their own clients or it could be something more. Do you know anything about that?"

Nash thought he might. "Around that time she left Hong Kong for an extended period. I mean, well over a month. When I asked one of her protection detail where they had been he wouldn't tell me, but later I saw one of them had a box of Padrón cigars."

"From Nicaragua, right. And one of her jets landed in Guadalajara and Ciudad Juárez in Mexico, and León and Managua in Nicaragua around that time."

"But clearly the Chinese don't want less lethal drugs out there. So what's going on?"

"We believe Steers has gone rogue and the Chinese are not happy about it."

"Was that why the attempt was made on her life?" speculated Nash.

"Could very well be. The Chinese have been working hand in glove with the Steers org for a long time. Well before Victoria took over."

"Well, considering her mother was a Chinese spy, that makes sense."

"But why the change with Steers now? Any ideas, Walter?"

Nash thought about some things that alone didn't mean much, but together might mean a lot. "Let me dig into that before I give you an answer."

"Fair enough. Now, you emailed me about the box with your daughter's things?"

"Yes, including a ring we gave Maggie for her high school graduation."

"But why would she keep that stuff? I mean, it's evidence!"

Nash had given that a lot of thought too and had never arrived at a good answer. "I've been with Steers for long enough to discover that she is...a complicated person, Reed. Far more complex than I initially thought. Like I told you before, I believed she had shot someone right in front of me, but turned out it was a setup to fool me."

"Right, Lynn Ryder. You messaged me about that before."

"But she sells drugs around the world, and I know people *have* died on her watch, including three people who worked at companies I acquired while I was at Sybaritic."

"I sense another *but* coming."

"But there's another side to the woman. I let you know what her former nanny, Hiroko, said about Steers's mother, Masuyo, convincing Steers that she killed her siblings in this insane competition to succeed her in running the empire. I mean, that has got to screw you up big-time. But Hiroko also told me that Steers was a very different person growing up. She wanted no part of this criminal empire stuff."

"This Hiroko person might not be telling the truth. And she no doubt cares for Steers, so she might be trying to paint her in a favorable light."

"Even Steers said that Hiroko thinks she can do no wrong. But Hiroko also said she saw Masuyo manipulating Steers. And I've found that she can be kind and empathetic and sensitive. But she can also get depressed about her life. I told you about her nearly killing herself."

Morris didn't reply right away. When he did, his voice was tight. "Which shows the woman is not stable. But regardless who is saying what, Walter, Steers *is* a criminal that we need to bring to justice. She had your daughter kidnapped and murdered."

Nash barked, "You think I don't know that! You think I've forgotten about my own daughter and what happened to her?"

"Well, then? What are you going to do about it? Because I thought we were working together to bring Steers to justice."

Nash was about to snap back at the agent again, but he reconsidered. "I'm on my mission to the end."

"Okay, but whose mission, the Bureau's?"

"*My* mission. If that coincides with your agenda, so be it."

"Walter, we made a deal."

"No, you roped me into this whole nightmare and it cost me everything. Now I'm out here alone trying to survive and get this done. So don't tell me how I'm supposed to do it, or what I'm supposed to think. That part is over, Reed. Over."

He clicked off and stared down at his phone. His hands were actually shaking. Then he closed his eyes tightly, which forced his face into a grimace.

Okay, I just cut off the FBI, which means I've got nobody to support me.

So, I'm really alone in this now. But hell, in reality, I've always been alone.

Nash drove on, feeling as hopeless as he ever had.

CHAPTER 47

A MONTH LATER, STEERS CALLED HIM to her office at the estate and informed him of some men who were coming to meet with her.

"They are from Mexico, Nicaragua, and Honduras," she said. "They are business associates who are here to listen to a new proposal of mine."

"I assume they'll be bringing their own security?"

"They will be bringing a small army, but discreetly."

"How is it possible that these men can travel so freely in the United States?"

"Dillon-san, they are not on watch or detain lists and neither am I, or else I would never have come back here. At most they would have to endure some secondary screening."

"But the authorities must suspect them of criminal activity. And they'll know they are coming here? Is that smart?"

"I still need to conduct my business. And the police have no adequate proof that I or any of my business partners have done anything wrong. And this needs to be done in person. Electronic meetings can be intercepted. This is why I do not 'zoom.'"

Nash thought about the evidence he was compiling against her and wondered what she would think when the hammer came down.

Not as smart as you thought you were.

"But wouldn't it make more sense for you to go to them? That way the police here wouldn't know of the meeting."

"You think the police from different countries do not share information? And your CIA? You, I am sure, will not be surprised to learn that they have long been interested in my affairs around the world. There is no way to escape their scrutiny, but I have learned to live with it and survive it. Now, some of the ones I do business with can no longer enter the U.S. And I do not visit them when I go to their countries, because that would place me in a precarious legal position. I deal with them discreetly through intermediaries."

"Well that makes sense."

"But people suspect me, of course. Like the police in Hong Kong. They would have arrested me if they had the necessary proof. But they do not."

"But would China even let them?" asked Nash.

When she looked at him suspiciously, he said, "I'm not stupid, Victoria-san. I pick up on things, and it was clear when they met with me that the Hong Kong police's hands are tied. I assume that is why you made your home there."

"I have what you Americans call belts and suspenders on that score. No evidence the police can use, and also powerful allies in case such evidence materializes."

Until you turn on the Chinese and they then turn on you, thought Nash. *And maybe that's already happened.*

"But you mentioned that the FBI had tried to get people inside your operation."

"They continue to do so, of that I am sure."

Nash knew he shouldn't, but he had been at this for a long time and needed to make a breakthrough.

"Rhett Temple told me about one of them: Walter Nash?"

She glanced up at him from behind her desk. "It is a complex game that I have to play, Dillon-san. And I play it as well as I can. But there is no room for mistakes. And the less you know of the matter the better off you will be."

"Okay, but I heard that the FBI said that Walter Nash had been framed, and that he hadn't killed his daughter. She was what, nineteen?"

She took a few seconds to respond. "It is a hard world and I do not make the rules, but I have to live by them."

"I guess innocent young people dying is just the price of doing business?"

She looked sharply up at him. "What do you care about any of this?"

"I care because I'm an honest man. I was forced to become part of this world."

"And yet you have never tried to leave, have you?" she retorted.

"How? I was in a foreign country and you were holding a murder charge over my head."

She eyed him coolly. "Well, there was no murder, as you now know. And you are no longer in a foreign country. *I* am."

"Do you want me to leave?" said Nash.

Now her superior look faded. "I.... What I want is to no longer discuss any of this."

She then waved him away, and Nash reluctantly obeyed.

It had all been a surprisingly candid reveal by her, Nash thought later.

And by me as well.

* * *

The motorcade pulled through the gates of the estate while Nash and Thura stood guard by the front entrance. As the large SUVs, looking more like tanks than civilian vehicles, stopped and the armed men piled out, Thura glanced nervously at Nash.

"Shit, these muthers look serious."

"They *are* serious," Nash said. "As serious as they come."

Nash could only imagine the situations these men had to deal with in their world, where someone was gunning for you every second of every day. It made men into something less than human.

In fact I'm looking at a pack of wolves coming right at me.

But then he thought about his own transformation.

Who am I now: Walter Nash or Dillon Hope? When I look in the mirror now, I don't see Walter anymore, I only see Dillon. And I'm not sure how I feel about that.

Pushing these troubling thoughts away, he stepped forward to greet the man who appeared to be the leader of this crew. He looked like a carbon copy of Nash: tall, built, shaved head, and tatted.

He introduced himself as Gabriel Aguilar and wanted to know where all exterior entrances in the main building were, and Nash told him. When he asked how many personnel Nash had, Nash lied and said, "Two on the point, a dozen you'll never see unless there's a problem, and CCTV on every speck of this place."

Aguilar nodded approvingly. "Ms. Steers came to see us a while ago, now we reciprocate."

"She told me," said Nash. "I'll take you to the meeting place."

As the men walked through the house Aguilar said, "You have many problems with your police?"

"Not so far. But tomorrow's a new day."

"Your days sound very much like mine. But in my country we maybe have the cops better in line. But that can change. *Muy rapido*."

"Yes, it can," said Nash. *And don't I know that.*

There were seven men in the meeting with Steers. Lynn Ryder dropped in at the last minute and took a seat at the large rectangular table inside what had once been the home's ballroom. Interestingly enough, Masuyo was not in attendance. Nash wondered if that was by the woman's choice.

Or her daughter's?

The staff served drinks and snacks and then quickly left. Aguilar had his men arrayed strategically around the property, while he took up a post with Nash right outside the double doors leading into the room.

"The place has been swept for bugs?" asked Aguilar.

"Right before everyone settled in," replied Nash. *And I planted my bug right after that.*

With his earpiece in, he settled against the wall across the hall from Aguilar and commenced listening as Steers called the meeting to order.

CHAPTER 48

Dressed in a black tunic and matching slacks, Steers surveyed the men around her before saying, "Gentlemen, first let me thank you for journeying here today. I promise that it will be worth your while."

"It had most assuredly better be," said the older man to Steers's immediate right. "Things are difficult right now in my country. I need help, not new problems."

Steers nodded. "Yes, Señor Ramirez, I completely understand. Things are difficult everywhere for people like us. That is why I called this meeting. My proposal has the blessing of being simple: We combine, centralize, and streamline. Too many back offices, too many distribution centers, and too many middlemen in the mix provide numerous targets for both the authorities and our competitors to both hinder and then undo all that we have built. I have experienced this recently, as I know each of you has."

"But all eggs in one basket also does not make sense to me," Ramirez countered.

Steers gazed at the other men to see their reaction to Ramirez's words. She saw agreement and disagreement and some clear hesitancy.

"No one is proposing that, Señor Ramirez. What I am proposing is having one hierarchy controlled by one committee."

"And who controls the committee, tell me that?" barked Ramirez.

One of the other men, younger with slicked-back hair and a

clean-shaven face, and wearing a ten-thousand-dollar custom-fitted suit, said, "Enrique, let her speak. Then we ask our questions."

Ramirez glared at the other man but sat back and fell silent.

"Thank you, Señor Tecú," said Steers.

She glanced at Ryder, who said, "A detailed plan was distributed electronically to your secure portals. It provided all essential information for the formation of the structure about which Ms. Steers is now speaking."

Tecú said, "My people have already been over it. They say it was well thought out and shows much promise."

Steers said, "Thank you. But to answer your question, Señor Ramirez, the head of the committee would be on a revolving basis, serving only for one year before rotating to the next person."

"And who shall serve as the initial chairman, I wonder?" said a disgusted-looking Ramirez. "Or more likely, chair*woman*."

"I was actually going to recommend that *you* be our first chairman," said Steers smoothly.

"See, I told you that she—" Ramirez broke off and looked at Steers. "Me? Me as first chairman?"

Tecú smiled and said, "Did not see that one coming, did you, Enrique?"

The other men laughed, and Ramirez finally joined in.

Steers glanced at Ryder and allowed herself a brief smile before turning back to the others.

"The backroom operations cost us all far too much, and there are too many gaps that allow others to take what is ours. I have undertaken an intensive study, and it shows that each of us lose up to twenty-five percent of our profits to this sort of thievery."

"It *is* a problem," agreed Señor Tecú. "And the young, they do not want to work anymore. They just want to be rich on day one. Then the idiots go on Instagram and brag about it, not thinking through the consequences. Then the police show up and there goes a dozen of my men and a chunk of my business."

The other men nodded their heads and muttered about this in low tones.

Ramirez snorted. "The Americans complain and complain about all the drugs coming into their country. But do they ever think about supply and demand? Over seventy million Americans are drug users. What do they do about that? Nothing. And it is Americans who bring the drugs across the borders. It is Americans who distribute it on the streets. Do they think if they stop the drugs coming in these seventy million people will suddenly no longer want drugs? Ha! This is moronic. And it is Americans who bring all those weapons into our countries and they do nothing to stop it. But no, they do not want to acknowledge that. Bullshit, I say. And why do people take drugs in America? I will tell you why. It is because they have nothing. In the richest country on earth they have not the means for a good life. And why? Because Americans are big shots. They go it alone. There are winners and losers. But there are very few winners in America. These few have all the money and the power, and the rest of the people, they get the scraps. And dogs cannot live long on scraps." But then Ramirez smiled. "Not that I am complaining. It has made me very, very rich."

The other men laughed.

Steers said, "You are right, Señor Ramirez, in all that you say. However, returning to the business matters of importance, that twenty-five-percent loss represents billions of dollars to each of us. Billions," she repeated. "But by combining skillfully our operations with great care, and the exercising of hypervigilance, along with the very latest AI and biometric technology, I am confident that we can virtually wipe out these losses, and thereby increase our profits with great substantiality. It is true that the monies necessary to do this are not insignificant by any means, but my calculations indicate that we will be made whole in less than three months and that far greater profits will flow thereafter. However, we have one other matter of importance to address, and I believe it to be one of critical significance."

"You speak of the Chinese, your people, your country?" Ramirez said bluntly.

"I am *not* speaking of the Chinese. I am addressing fundamentally what we will do with our profits. Now that the United States and other countries are leaping helter-skelter onto the mania of cryptocurrency, it is time for us to seriously consider withdrawing our assets from these exchanges and returning them to more traditional assets. They tout crypto as the next global currency, but that, to me, is a lie. It is actually a sham with nothing behind it, is my true belief. It will never really be used as currency, for the price fluctuates too much. Stablecoin, the one such currency that fluctuates far less, is almost exclusively used to purchase cryptocurrency."

"But it kept the authorities at bay," pointed out Tecù. "This blockchain ledger bullshit which I still do not wholly understand," he added, to guffaws from the others.

Steers did not smile or join in the laughter. "Its complexity is one reason not to trust it. And yes, you are correct that this asset base was fine for people like us because it made it that much harder for the authorities to track down our funds. But my chief worry now is that there will come a time soon when there is a run on crypto, because everyone is buying it, but its only value is that there will be a finite number of coins created so that those behind this scheme will tout the fact that it continues to go up in value. But they will have already cashed out by then and taken their profits, as they always do, leaving the unsophisticated holding what remains, which will be nothing. And then there will be other such coins created with, again, a finite number, and the whole absurdity begins again. It is like children collecting Pokemon cards. But we are not children. And this does not even take into consideration that advances in both AI and quantum computing could pose serious threats to the sanctity of the blockchain. And if that is pierced or disrupted in any way, the whole house of cards, so to speak, will collapse."

"I agree that crypto is getting out of hand, particularly since so many greedy billionaires have their hands all over it," said Tecú. "But why do you think there will be a run on it?"

"Because of myriad global factors, consumer prices will continue to go up and credit card and car loan debt will increase along with it. People will run out of savings and need to cash in. Then, with the rich having already obtained their obscene profits out of the affair, and when no one else will buy the crypto, there will be a panic. There are Bitcoin ATMs, but you can withdraw only minimal amounts from them. More and more people will attempt to sell, not wanting to be caught with a worthless asset. And that is what it will become, worthless, as always happens when sellers far outnumber buyers. Just recently, because of an escalation in the tariff wars, Bitcoin lost 20 percent of its value in one day! That is unacceptable. There are no laws and regulations regarding it. The rich who created it have bought off all the politicians so they can take advantage of everyone else, and so they have."

"Then what do we do with our money?" asked Ramirez.

"I propose we turn to hard currency, gold, real estate, and high-quality stocks and bonds. The accounts will be segregated, of course, and encrypted and walled off to such a degree that I have been told that even quantum-computing assaults will be futile. And these are assets capable of appreciation based not on whim or manipulation but on verifiable market conditions and performance. And the bonds will throw off significant cash flow, particularly in the current high-interest-rate environment. It is a market condition that is unequivocally favorable to those with the means to invest. Comparisons of performance that I had undertaken, and that have been shared with your financial people, show that our returns will be more than double what we could expect from crypto, even without the inherent uncertainties and downsides of which I have already spoken. It is the steady tortoise that wins the race over the mercurial and undisciplined hare. *That* is my plan."

The men looked at each other and nodded approvingly.

Tecú said, "You have done well, Ms. Steers. But we would have expected no less."

"We are in a precarious moment in time, gentlemen," she said. "United we can survive, of that I am convinced." She glanced at Ramirez, who was drumming his fingers on the table and looking distracted. "Do you not agree, Señor Ramirez?"

He jerked up. "What? Oh, yes, yes I do." He made a fist. "United."

"As all of you know, I have worked with those from China on many of my endeavors. But that is no more. I cannot countenance pursuing an agenda that has, as one of its principal outcomes, the utter destruction of our customer base."

"About time someone said that to them," barked one of the other men.

"How did they take this change in your position?" said Tecú.

Steers stared at him. "As you probably know, they tried to kill me in Hong Kong."

Tecú glanced at the others. "There were rumors to that effect, but we know of no details."

Steers pointed to the still-visible wound on her neck. "Here are all the details you need, gentlemen. If it were not for the head of my security who now stands guard out there, I would not be here today to suggest anything. And I can guarantee that none of you would be better off having no buffer between you and the Chinese. You all are tough, smart men who have been through much, as I have. But none of us has a three-million-soldier military, plus nuclear weapons and a twenty-trillion-dollar economy with tentacles that run to every country on earth, do we?"

There were mumblings among all the men now, along with nervous looks.

Ramirez said, "What you say is true, Ms. Steers. And my first act as chairman of the committee will be to present you a substantial reward for what you have brought to us today."

Steers smiled warmly and bowed. "You do me too much of an

honor, Señor Ramirez. I trust this will be a defining moment in all of our lives."

* * *

After the men had left to fly back to their respective countries in their private jets, Nash asked her, "How did it go?" He had heard the clear, concise presentation that Steers had laid out, but he could not admit being privy to it.

"It went well, I think. But it is only a first step."

"So there are other steps?"

"There are always other steps. Until each one of us takes our final breath."

"I was surprised that your mother was not in attendance."

"Were you? After telling me what you did about her?"

"So, you suspect something is up there?"

"I *suspect* nothing," she said cryptically.

"Okay, will those men be back?"

"Doubtful. Implementation of my changes will begin shortly. But we will have another visitor, and soon."

"Oh, who is that?"

"You really must keep up, Dillon-san," she said, and not in a joking way. "I thought that would be rather obvious."

"Sorry. Who's coming then?"

"The gentleman who imprisoned my mother and sent us the severed head, of course."

CHAPTER 49

Nash was in the guesthouse watching the security console that controlled and showed footage from all the surveillance cameras arrayed around the property. He was surprised when he saw on one of the screens a Porsche pull up at the front gates. The driver honked.

It was his former boss, Rhett Temple.

Nash hit a button on the console. "Can I help you?"

"Dillon, is that you?"

"Alive and kicking, Rhett."

"Um, can you let me in? Steers called and said she wanted to meet."

"Okay, give me a sec." Nash texted Steers to confirm this was actually the case and received an immediate reply of yes.

He opened the gates and Temple pulled through and got out of the Porsche.

"Hey, Dillon, real glad you made it back to the States. I was working on it, I swear. But I hadn't reached the end zone yet."

"Yeah. Ironic that we're just right down the road from you now."

"Yeah, ironic." Temple looked the place over. "Damn, this is about the same size as the monstrosity my old man built. I knew something big was back here—just never had a reason to check."

"It might be big, but it's home sweet home to us."

Temple glanced at him sharply and then, sensing Nash was joking, he grinned. "So, where're the ninja dudes? Out dismembering somebody?"

"No, they're not here right now, but their spirit will always be with us."

"Shit, Dillon, you sound like you drank the Asian Kool-Aid."

"It's not like I had a choice—unlike you, right?" said Nash.

Inside the house Nash led him down the hall to Steers's office and knocked.

"Come."

Opening the door Nash said, "Ms. Steers, here's Mr. Temple."

"Thank you."

When Nash turned to leave, Steers said, "You are part of this meeting, Dillon-san."

Temple shot him a glance, presumably over what she had called Nash.

"Yes, ma'am," said Nash, and he took a seat next to Temple.

Steers sat at her desk and placed her hands in front of her. "Now that I am back in the United States, there is unfinished business."

Temple said, "I put the CEO in place. She's working out great."

"I speak not of that, Mr. Temple. Let me finish."

"Of course, sorry." Temple glanced worriedly at Nash.

"The outstanding item is the whereabouts of Walter Nash. I spoke to you about this before you left Hong Kong and told you that finding him was a top priority. However, *nothing* has been accomplished though much time has passed."

Nash hunkered down in his chair and glanced at Temple.

"I've been trying," whined Temple. "The guy just vanished like smoke. None of my PIs can find one damn thing. They've looked everywhere."

"That is not good enough," replied Steers in a sharp tone. "He *must* be found."

"Why is this so important?" asked Temple. "The guy's on the run."

"Ask yourself this question, Mr. Temple: If Mr. Nash has been exonerated from all crimes, why is he still, as you say, 'on the run'?"

"Well, because..." Temple turned to Nash, who kept his gaze

rigidly on Steers. "Um, well, I guess that doesn't make sense, now that you mention it."

"I think it makes sense in that Mr. Nash is still working with the FBI to bring me down. And if he brings me down, you go down, too, Mr. Temple—which is why I asked you here, as we have mutual interests in this matter. I have given you much leeway. Too much. That ends now." She stood and looked down at the men. "I will give you one month to find him, Mr. Temple. And if you do not, then I cannot guarantee that something irreversibly painful to you will not occur." She glanced at his cut-up arm. "Something immeasurably more than you have already endured."

A tense Temple sat up straighter and said, "Well, I could use some advice on where to look. It's been scorched earth and still nothing, other than the fact that he was at that place owned by his father's friend."

Steers glanced at an iPad on her desk. "This Mr. Isaiah York?"

"Right. But he's gone underground, too. No one's laid eyes on the guy in like forever."

"You think they're connected still?" asked Nash. Having been around the woman long enough, he instinctively knew that Steers did nothing without good reason. And since she had asked him to attend this meeting, she must desire his input.

"I think it obvious, Dillon-san."

"Then if we find York, his only last known contact, we may find Nash, that's your reasoning?"

"Correct."

"Look, we're chasing our tails here," said Temple. "They have both vanished from the face of the earth."

Steers said, "Not entirely true. While Mr. Nash has come close to achieving that status, Mr. York has a condo here in town and there is also his business facility, which you searched, but long ago. He has financial accounts, friends, and clients. These may furnish new leads." She glanced at Nash. "You can vet and bring in new security to assist Thura in protecting me, my mother, and the estate. I want you and Mr. Temple to focus full-time on finding Walter Nash. And failure is not something that I will countenance in this matter, to make myself perfectly clear."

Temple looked confused. "Why do you need a new security team?"

Steers glanced at Nash and nodded appreciatively. "I see you did not tell him. That was good. But I will." She turned to Temple. "I had a traitor in the ranks. He attempted to kill me. Dillon-san saved my life. The rest of my security team was slaughtered. Dillon-san and Thura are all that remain."

"Jesus," exclaimed Temple. "There was nothing in the news about that."

"I know. If I had died, no doubt it would have been newsworthy." Steers leaned forward and said, "I have given you more flexibility on this matter than was good for either you or me. But now accountability will be applied. Do you understand me?"

"I understand you," said Temple meekly. "You have made it crystal clear, Ms. Steers."

"Then you may go. Dillon-san will be in touch shortly with next steps."

Temple rose and quickly exited the room.

Nash said, "Why the sudden interest in Walter Nash?"

"I believe I just revealed my reasoning. Did you find a fallacy therein?"

"No. But you have a lot going on, what with your business partners, your mother, almost being killed. I just wondered why this floated back to the top."

"Your job is not to wonder, it is to execute my orders. You will follow up the leads I mentioned pertaining to Mr. York."

"Of course." Nash paused, sensing an opportunity, a risky one. "You do raise an interesting point about Nash: Why not just come out of hiding and accept everyone's apologies?"

"He is working with the FBI. It is the only explanation."

"No, I think there's another one."

She looked up from her iPad. "Such as?"

"Well, you set him up and ruined his life. Yes, he was exonerated from all that, his innocence established, his reputation intact. But there's one thing that you took from Nash that he cannot get back."

"And what is that?"

Nash took a moment to steel himself. "His daughter. You took his daughter. Now, I don't have children, but if I had? Well, I can't imagine a more powerful incentive for revenge."

She said slowly, "So...you believe Walter Nash has gone underground because he wants to kill me to avenge his child?"

"And now that you're back in his hometown you just made yourself an easier target."

"Perhaps I have," she said in a way that Nash did not quite understand.

"And if we find Nash—"

She interjected, "*When* you find him."

"When we find him, what do we do with him?"

"You will bring him to me."

"And then what?"

"And then I will deal with Mr. Nash. Once and for all."

CHAPTER 50

"WHAT ARE WE REALLY DOING here, Dillon?" said Temple.

They were parked outside of Isaiah York's condo about a mile from Nash's old home.

"Waiting for York to show up."

"And if he doesn't? Which he hasn't, ever since Nash went on the run."

"Then we move on to something else. Another lead."

"Back to the place we already searched, you mean?"

"Have you had eyes on it this whole time?"

"Not me, maybe Steers."

Nash nodded. He had contacted Shock about Steers's new focus on her people finding him and through him... *me*, he thought.

But now I am her people, so there's that.

Temple said, "So how was your time in Hong Kong? It went by fast."

"Maybe for you, it did."

"Look, I know you think I just left you there."

"I don't think it, Rhett, I *know* it. So let's not discuss it anymore. Steers was very clear. We get this done or else." He paused. "At least for you it is."

"Right, I get that I'm in the crosshairs, okay?" He looked off for a moment. "So what's this 'Dillon-san' junk?"

"It's an expression of friendship, of honor."

"Because you saved her life?"

"She actually started calling me that *before* I saved her life."

"Look, don't answer this if you don't want to," began Temple.

Nash gave him a sideways glance. "No, I'm not sleeping with her, and I have no intention of doing so."

"So you don't want to?"

Nash barked, "For fuck's sake, what part of 'focusing on the task at hand' don't you get?"

"I'm just trying to have a discussion here. We have a lot of ground to catch up on."

"Friends who have been apart have things to catch up on. We have never been and will never be friends."

"Hell, we went through a lot together over in Myanmar."

"That was a job. That's it." He glanced at Temple. "And why would you want to be friends with me? You're a billionaire. Everybody wants to be your friend. I'm a nobody."

"Yeah, they all do want to be my friend, but only because I have money. How can I tell if someone wants to be around me just for the real me?"

"Well, you might want to answer another question first."

"What's that?"

"Do you even know who the real you is?" asked Nash.

Temple started to say something, stopped, and looked off again. "I don't think the guy's coming back here. Why don't we go to the facility we searched before? We can take my jet." He added excitedly, "I got the latest Gulfstream, the G800. It's like the Taj Mahal at forty-one thousand feet. Set me back sixty million after my trade-in, but hey, it's just money. Can't take it with you, right?"

Nash shook his head. "No, let's do a road trip instead."

Temple looked startled. "A road trip? It's a long drive."

"Well, maybe along the way we can rekindle the *friendship* we never had."

"You are one strange dude, Dillon."

"Well, maybe I have every right to be," said Nash.

He put the car in gear and drove them off.

* * *

It was well past midnight. In two days' time Nash and Temple would be heading to Shock's training facility in a neighboring state. But Nash needed to meet with someone first.

He drove into the alleyway, blinked his lights, then killed the engine.

He had told Thura that he was going to snoop around Nash's old home to see if he could find out anything.

Shock got out of the SUV parked in the alleyway and walked toward Nash, who had also climbed out of his vehicle. The two men met midway between the two cars and shared an impromptu hug.

"Damn good to see you, Walter. Didn't know if I'd ever get the chance again."

"It's great to see you too, Shock. How's Byron doing?"

"No problems there. But, man, the shit you've been doing and in the places you been to that you told me about when you called? Damn miracle you still standing."

"You built me to survive, Shock. And I have, so far."

"So the lady is hot to trot to find you again?"

"She's made it my and Rhett Temple's sole mission on earth."

"So how you gonna play it?"

"I'll go along to get along, stall for time, and continue to discover all I can about her operations. I've already passed a lot along to the FBI. She had an all-hands meeting with her cartel partners. Now she's going to meet with the guy who put her mother in prison and probably tried to kill her."

"So the lady is playin' both sides. Risky, but show's she got some balls."

"She has the biggest pair I've seen on anyone, Shock. But her risks are always calculated. Only this one I can't figure out. Yet."

"What do you need me to do?"

"We're driving to your training facility in two days' time. Is there any way you can get the tattoo binders out of there? Keeping in mind that they might have eyes on the place?"

"Consider it done, Walter. Got a cleanin' crew goes in weekly, so if they got eyes on it, that won't raise no flags. I'll put Byron in as part of the team tomorrow. Old Black dude takin' out the trash ain't gonna get nobody suspicious. He'll bag the binders and get 'em out that way."

"Thanks, Shock. I…I know I could have put this all in a text or told you when I phoned, but—"

"It's good to see you, too, Walter," said Shock. "And Judith? You told me she was okay?"

"She's in protective custody. I killed three men who were going to kill her, and I did it by following your advice of using whatever was at hand, not fighting honorably, and doing what I needed to do to survive."

"Only way this shit works, Walter, and don't let nobody ever tell you different."

"I sometimes wonder what my father would think of all this."

"Well, *I* can tell you. First, it would be a bigger shock to him 'bout who you are now than when I came out the closet. And, second, he would be as proud of you as he was of anybody."

"You really think so, Shock?" said Nash uncertainly.

"Hell, Walter. You reinvented yourself to get the job done. No, you went even farther than that. You became the opposite of who you'd always been. You overcame every obstacle I threw at your ass. All the other guys I trained? They broke. Them muthers just quit. But you didn't. So take it to the bank that your old man, who never quit nothing in his whole damn life, is either lookin' up or down at you with a big-ass smile on his face."

"Thanks, Shock, that means a lot coming from you. No one knew my father better."

"Now, where do you see this all headed? Steers and everythin'?"

"I still want to bring down her empire and avenge Maggie, but…"

Shock looked at him funny. "But what?"

"You ever gone into a situation where you thought for sure you knew what someone else was all about? No gray, just black-and-white?"

"Hell, Walter, that's what I did with your ass!"

"But you were wrong about me."

"I prejudged you, sure. But how the hell you havin' that problem with someone like Victoria Steers? She killed your daughter, man."

"And I will hold her accountable for that."

"But?"

"But having come to know her after all this time together... and I know this will sound... weird."

"Just get it out in the open, son," advised Shock, looking seriously apprehensive.

"But part of me feels sorry for her."

Shock stared at him for a few moments. "All right, Walter, let me give you some advice."

"Okay."

"You may know the woman better now. And maybe there're things in her past that made her what she is, made her do what she does. I get that. Evil folks are created in lots of different ways. We all have choices, but some folks have a lot fewer than other folks. And sometimes the reason has nothin' to do with them, really, it's how other people perceive them. For me it's the color of my skin. But at the end of the day, Walter, you have to remember that Steers made her choices. And if push comes to shove, she will kill you if she perceives *you* as a threat to her. Just the way people like her are wired. You remember I told you about Peanut?"

"The most dangerous man you knew other than my father."

"Right, and I also told you what made him dangerous."

"He basically had no conscience and wouldn't waste a second debating whether to kill someone. It gave him just enough of an edge to be pretty much unbeatable."

"And with that, Walter, you just described Victoria Fucken Steers to a T. And don't you never forget that, son."

CHAPTER 51

On the way to Shock's training facility Temple turned to Nash, who was driving his Range Rover, and said, "Mindy wants me to marry her."

Nash shot him a look. "Jesus, Rhett? Your stepmother?"

"Yeah, I know," he said, looking miserable. "It was a big mistake letting her stick around. I guess I'm too kind-hearted for my own good. She loves living in the big house, and even though she has plenty of her own money she wants the ring and status that comes with being married to a Temple. Again."

"Yeah, you are quite a catch," Nash said drolly.

"And you know her kid?"

"Yeah, Amanda. What about her?"

"She's not my father's child."

Nash gave Temple an eye roll. "Really? What a surprise."

"What, you mean you knew?"

"I *suspected*. When I first met her I thought she looked a lot like you." Nash obviously couldn't tell him that years ago Temple Senior had bragged to Nash about his vasectomy, and his relief in not being able to help conceive, or having to support, any more children.

Temple said, "She's a good kid, she really is. I...I actually like being around her. I never thought I'd have children. I wanted complete freedom to do what I wanted to do because under my father's thumb I never got that chance. But the thing is, if we get married, people might start assuming Mandy is mine, and maybe they start thinking my father didn't kill himself."

"Do you *know* that he didn't?"

"No, I mean, no. I...look, he jumped, okay? He was dying from cancer and took a shortcut. But the police may think otherwise if Mindy and I get married. You know, bump off the old man so we can get together and inherit the money."

"Okay. But more to the point, do you *want* to marry her?"

"No, I don't. She was married to my dad. It...it would be weird as shit. And I don't want his sloppy seconds."

"You already slept with her, Rhett," Nash reminded him.

"That was an impromptu romp in the hay because my old man dropped a bombshell on me. Marriage means being faithful till death do us part."

This made Nash think of the adulterous Judith. "For some people it doesn't."

"You know what I mean."

"Then tell her no and your problem goes away."

"I've tried, but she won't take no for an answer."

"She can't make you marry her." Nash glanced sharply at him. "Can she?"

"I...she...look, just forget I said anything."

They drove in silence for a bit before Temple said, "Hey, in your line of work, do you know anything about disappearing?"

"What do you mean by that?" Nash asked.

"I mean, maybe you encounter people on the run, or in hiding. That's why they need security."

"So you're really asking me how you can disappear to get away from Steers? And Mindy?"

"No, I'm asking for a friend. Yes, I'm fucking asking about me! I got all this money and my own jet, and I'm still trapped by these women. It's driving me insane. I could be golfing in Scotland right now or bedding hot chicks in Thailand, but instead I'm going to that dump of a place to look through the trash cans. And when I get home, there's Mindy. *And* the kid. With Steers looking over my shoulder like some homicidal big sister. It's freaking me out, it really is."

"You made your bed, Rhett."

"I'll pay you. Name a price."

"And if Steers found out, I'd never get a chance to spend the money. Look, you left me behind with that woman. So don't ask me to liberate you, okay? That's going way over the line."

Temple slumped back, looking defeated. "Okay, okay, I get your point."

"But if we can find Nash, maybe she'll cut you loose."

Temple scoffed, "Fat chance of that. I'll be tied to her until I'm dead or she is. Thanks a fucking lot, Dad," he screamed out the window.

When they reached Shock's training facility, they used some tools they had brought along to allow them to get in the same way they had before.

"We have to be careful that we don't trip that alarm again," warned Temple.

"Yeah, we'll need to be really careful," replied Nash, who knew that Shock had remotely triggered the sirens that had driven them away from the place the first time.

They spent hours searching the facility from top to bottom.

Later, they sat side by side near the front entrance, Temple looking dejected and Nash looking relieved, because the tattoo binders were gone.

"Well, that was a big waste of time," groused Temple.

"But it shows we're trying."

"Steers doesn't give a shit about *trying*, Dillon. She wants results. And she gave us a month. The clock is ticking." He perked back up. "You said someone tried to kill her? Who?"

"Not sure. Probably the same person who runs that prison. I forgot to tell you one thing. That elderly woman they used to switch Masuyo with?"

"Yeah? What about her?"

"They sent her head back to Steers via DHL."

Temple looked like he might throw up. "My God, these people are animals, they really are." He suddenly glared at Nash. "So why the hell didn't you let them kill Steers? Both our problems would be over if you had. I really can't believe you passed up that opportunity, Dillon. I would have let them fill her full of bullets."

"First of all, my job is to protect her. Second, I don't care who it is, I'm not going to stand by and watch a defenseless person get gunned down. And third, do you really think they were going to let *me* live?"

"Yeah, yeah, I get it," Temple conceded. "We can't catch a break, can we?"

"Well, since you weren't there when the shooting started, I'm not sure your statement is accurate. And Steers and I *did* catch a break. We came out of it alive."

Temple, who obviously wasn't listening to Nash, said, "You think they'll try again?"

Nash thought about Steers now planning to host the person who owned the prison and had perhaps tried to kill her. "Anything's possible."

"You better have an army guarding her, then. Any person who can own and run a prison in the middle of Myanmar must have both big bucks and a lot of pull."

"No argument there."

"And on top of that sending a head by express delivery? I mean, that's Godfather shit. How did Steers take it?"

"She wasn't happy about it, obviously. But she took it in stride."

"The lady has ice in her veins. She is vicious and vindictive. Look what she did to Lynn Ryder, not that I'm crying any tears over that bitch."

Nash chose not to enlighten the man about Ryder being very much alive. He thought it better that Temple believed Steers had no compassion or conscience.

And, despite what I've learned about her and seen, does she, really? That's what Shock was trying to tell me. That, in the end, it's a binary choice: me or her.

CHAPTER 52

They drove for a few hours on the way back, then stayed the night at a hotel. They were back on the road at the crack of dawn.

Later, as they sat idling in the middle of a traffic jam, Temple said, "Next time we take my jet. My body's stiff as a board and I'm sick of breathing in gas fumes and wasting time."

"Must be nice to be a billionaire," muttered Nash.

"It should be. But I'm not there yet." A few moments later, he exclaimed, "Hey, I just got an idea about finding Nash."

"What?" said Nash.

"The woman who was with Nash's dad at the end? What was her name again?"

"Rose Parker? What about her?"

"When we went to her house she was acting funny. I didn't believe what she said. I think she knows more than she told us."

Nash felt the acid building in his gut. "I didn't see it that way. She seemed clueless."

"Not to me. And what other lead do we have? And like you said before, we need to show Steers we're trying."

"So what do you want to do?"

"Let's go see her."

"What, now?"

"Yeah, now. What else do you have to do?" Temple shot him a suspicious look.

Nash had no choice but to say, "Okay, but when we come up with zilch, I *will* tell you I told you so."

Later, as darkness fell they pulled into Nash's old neighborhood.

The house looked the same, but the neighborhood was perhaps a little grungier. Nash spied a VW bug parked in the driveway and thought that either Parker had a visitor or she had used some of her inheritance from his father to buy a car.

He pulled to a stop and they got out.

Temple knocked on the door while Nash stood behind him and off to the right.

When Parker opened the door, she glanced at Temple with a startled look and then saw Nash, who mouthed one word: *Sorry.*

"Yes?" she said to Temple.

"You remember us?"

"You were here asking about Walter Nash. I still have no idea where he is. Apparently nobody does."

"Look, we're sorry to bother you again, but could we come in and ask you some questions? You might remember something and it's really important."

Nash glanced over Parker's shoulder and was relieved to see that the picture of his father and Shock had been removed.

Parker looked at Nash, who nodded, and then said, "Well, all right. But I have to head out soon to meet someone."

"Sure, sure it won't take long. Hey, is that your car?" Temple added, pointing at the VW.

"Yes, it is."

"Fun set of wheels."

She led them into the small front room, where they sat down.

Temple glanced around the space. "So this is where Walter Nash grew up. Who'd 'a thunk?"

"It's a nice house," said Parker defensively.

"Oh, sure, I know. I just mean that he really moved up in the world. Before he moved down again."

"He was innocent of everything they accused him of."

Temple eyed her intently, and Nash did not like that look at all. "Sounds as though you like the guy even though last time we were here you said you didn't even know him."

"I *don't* know him. I just know what I saw on the news. And I would feel sorry for anyone that went through that and who turned out to be innocent. It's just not right."

Temple nodded. "We agree with you, it wasn't fair."

"So why do you want to find him?" she asked.

"We think we can help him," said Temple.

"How?"

"Well, that's really something we need to talk with Nash about directly."

"Well, I have no way to help you."

"So, he never visited this place after he grew up?" asked Temple.

"I don't know. He never came here while I've been here."

"Now, see, that's strange," said Temple.

Nash suddenly realized what was coming and tensed.

"What do you mean by that?" said Parker nervously.

"Nash Senior left you this house, correct?"

"Yes."

"What else?"

"I'm not sure that's any of your concern."

"But he did leave you the house?" asked Temple again.

"Yes!"

"Okay, now, I know for a fact that Nash was the executor of his father's estate. And I was told that he had come by here to pick up some of his parents' things. So how could that have happened and you getting the house and maybe some money that you used to buy the VW out there without at least talking to the man?"

Parker's features turned even paler than normal, and Nash inwardly berated himself for not thinking of this possible trap.

"Well, Ms. Parker?" said Temple.

"He might have come by here before I had access to the house."

Nash added, "And did you maybe speak to a lawyer about all this other stuff?"

Parker shot him a glance, clearly realizing he was throwing her a lifeline, and said, "Yes, Ty's lawyer dealt with me on all that. I had to sign some documents and he told me I have a life estate in the house. And I did get some money from Ty."

"So you dealt with this lawyer and not Nash directly?" asked Temple.

"Yes," said a relieved-looking Parker.

"And the lawyer's name?"

Nash had known that was coming, but Temple would see any signal he could make to Parker.

"I don't remember offhand."

"I'm sure you have it on some piece of paper somewhere. We'll wait."

Parker rose unsteadily, and with a furtive look at the man she hurried off.

Temple immediately said, "She's lying her ass off. She knows the guy. Right?"

"She's definitely uncomfortable," Nash said quietly.

"This might be our big break."

"But what can the lawyer tell us?"

"Who knows? But we'll let Steers know what we think, and she can have her guys tear this place apart and interrogate Parker. They'll make her spill."

"Rhett, you want to unleash Steers's goons on that poor woman?"

"No, I don't *want* to. But I'm not looking to end up in the water with concrete shoes or have Steers do to my neck what she already did to my arm." He added spitefully, "And she doesn't call me *Rhett-san*, Dillon. You may be in her good graces, but she'll crush me."

"Well, let's at least talk to the lawyer first before we unleash the hounds of hell."

"Fine, but the lawyer will probably tell us nothing. Attorney-client privilege crap. But Steers can make him talk, too."

"Don't you think the police have already talked to both of them?"

"Maybe. And both of them could have lied." He eyed Nash with a look of distrust. "If I didn't know better, I'd start thinking that you don't want us to find Nash."

"You knew the guy, I didn't. I have no skin in that game. But what I don't want to do is give Steers a lead and an expectation of success that goes nowhere. That would not be good for either of us, regardless of the 'Dillon-san' stuff."

Temple's suspicious look faded. "Yeah, she can be a real bitch about things like that. Expecting the impossible and if you come up a bit short, you lose an arm or a leg or both. We'll talk to the lawyer first."

Parker came back in with a piece of paper and handed it to Temple, who looked at it.

"Morton Dickey? Okay, great, thank you." He took out a wad of cash and held it out to her. "For your troubles."

"No, I...I don't want your money."

Temple looked at Parker like she had lost her mind. After glancing around once more at the modest interior he said, "O-kay, your choice."

They walked out and got back in the Range Rover.

Temple said, "Let's go see the lawyer."

"Rhett, it's after eight. He won't be at his office."

"Oh, I lost track of time. Okay, drive me back to my place. You can have some dinner and say hello to Mindy and the kid."

Nash drove over to the Temple estate and followed the man inside.

"Time for a drink," Temple remarked. "I sure as hell need one. A big one."

CHAPTER 53

"Nice to see you again, Dillon," said Mindy. The three of them were in the library having cocktails before dinner.

"You too, Ms. Temple."

"Please, it's Mindy. You don't work for Rhett anymore."

He nodded and looked her over. She was as lean and fit as ever, but there was puffiness in her face that he hadn't noted before.

"How's your daughter?"

"Mandy is fine. Growing like a weed. She's already in bed." She glanced at Temple. "Rhett told me that you know about…?"

"Yes. I'm glad she's doing well and has *both* her parents around."

Temple had just swallowed some of his scotch and almost coughed it back up.

"Yeah, lucky little kiddo," he said, giving Nash an unfriendly look.

A minute later dinner was announced, and they went into the dining room.

The conversation was listless if amiable.

"This place is so big that our toddler Mandy gets lost sometimes," said Mindy as they were finishing dessert.

"Hell, so do I," groused Temple. "It should have its own fucking zip code."

"Rhett, I told you before about your language. Mandy can pick it up."

"But Mandy's not here now, is she?" countered Temple. In a low voice that probably only he could hear he added, "Thank God."

Mindy turned to Nash. "I never really saw myself as a mother, but now? I really can't see myself as anything else."

Nash almost slipped and said something about his wife feeling the same way.

"Being a mother is the toughest job in the world. But probably the most rewarding."

Temple poured himself more wine. "Okay, can we talk about something else? I feel like I'm in a Hallmark movie, and in case you didn't know, I'm not a fan."

Mindy said, "Where did you and Dillon go? You just said a road trip."

"We had some business we were conducting on behalf of a third party," Temple answered vaguely, glancing at Nash.

"Is the business done then?" asked Mindy.

"Work in progress," Temple said casually, sipping his drink. He looked around the grand room. "You know, I like my penthouse a lot better. This place actually gives me the creeps. It's like a museum."

"We can move into your penthouse," Mindy said quickly. "There's plenty of room for Mandy and her things. And there's a separate suite for her nanny."

"No, nope. The penthouse is my escape place. Where I get to be, well, me."

"I just thought—" began Mindy before Temple cut in.

"We are not married, Min. And we are never going to be married, okay?"

Mindy shot Nash an embarrassed look. "Please, Rhett, this is not the time or place."

"Well, you just don't seem to take *never* for an answer. With capital appreciation you now have well over 300 million bucks in an investment portfolio that throws off nearly ten million a year just in interest and dividends, and a lot of it tax-free. You can go anywhere, buy anything. You'd be a great catch for some guy looking to score an easy life."

"That is *not* how I want to find my life partner," replied Mindy primly, shooting Nash another embarrassed look.

"Your *life partner*?" scoffed Temple. "I told you to knock off the meditation voodoo books, but you do you. And I'll do me. Now the meal's done, why don't you go check on Mandy? Dillon and I have some things to discuss."

"Just like that?" said Mindy coolly.

"Just like that," he replied, his mouth easing into a snarky grin.

She got up and stalked out while Temple watched her with a widening smile.

After she'd gone Nash said, "She's going through some complicated things right now, Rhett. You could be more supportive."

"I could be, but the fact is I don't want to be. And you haven't lived with her. It's hell. But forget that. This lawyer, Dickey, how do you want to handle it? I mean, he's going to want to say zilch. But we can't leave it there."

"I don't think siccing Steers's goons on him would be the right thing to do."

"Why the hell not?"

"They might kill him for all we know."

"Look, Dillon, you have to understand that this is dog eat dog. And while I don't want this lawyer to die, I don't want myself to die even more. So get with the program. There are winners and there are losers and there is nothing in between. Why do you think a few guys who look and act like me and my dad own this country? Because they are strong. And they don't care about anybody but themselves, okay?" Temple waved his arms wildly around. "I'm not saying that's how little old Jesus would have done it. But the tech bros would eat Jesus alive today. Take care of the poor? Treat everybody the same? Love everybody for who they are? Give me a break. No, you crush the opposition. You love your brother so long as he does what you tell him. The second he goes rogue, you throw him under the bus. You gotta be a killer, like my old man was in business. And we're killers like that, right? You and me. And, hell, you killed for real back in Myanmar."

Nash stared at him for a few seconds, considering how to respond to this barrage of a word salad. Temple was a man who had earned really nothing that he had, but had acquired it by simply being the son of a rich man.

He said, "Let's talk to Dickey. He might open up more than you think."

"If he's smart, he can be bought, and I'm willing to dump a truckload of cash on anybody who can get us to Nash." He paused and looked thoughtful. "Why do you think he hasn't surfaced? He'd get a hero's welcome."

"Well, his daughter is dead and so is his wife. Maybe he thinks he doesn't have anything to come home to."

Temple looked surprised. "Huh, I never thought about it like that. You might be right."

"By the way, what's with Mindy's face?"

Temple glanced at him sharply. "What are you talking about?"

"It was all puffy."

"Oh, she had some dental work done," he said quickly.

CHAPTER 54

AFTER NASH LEFT, TEMPLE WENT upstairs to go to his bedroom, bypassing where Mindy and their daughter were now staying on another floor in a two-bedroom suite.

As he got to his bedroom door his sister Angie opened hers. "I saw that man."

He turned and looked at her. "What man, Ang?"

"That man who used to live here. That man with all *these*." She jerkily moved her hands over her head and body.

"Oh, right, the tattoos. Yeah, Dillon Hope."

"I saw him."

"Yeah, I'm sure, he was here for dinner."

Angie shook her head vigorously. "No, no, I mean, before."

Temple glanced over at the door of the bedroom Dillon Hope stayed in when he had worked as his bodyguard.

"Well, he *was* staying in that bedroom, across the hall from you."

Angie shook her head fiercely again. "No, no!"

"Whoa, don't get upset. Deep breaths. What are you trying to say?"

"Not that door."

"What then?" said Temple, looking both confused and impatient.

"Not that door!"

"Okay, Ang, whatever you say. Look, I'm tired and you need to go *night-night*."

"Not that door," Angie persisted.

He said wearily, "Fine, what door? You mean downstairs?"

She marched across the hall and tapped the door next to her brother's bedroom. "This door!"

Now Temple didn't look impatient, but he still looked confused. "This door? You saw him come out of *this* door?"

Angie nodded vigorously.

His interest now piqued, Temple said, "When, Ang? Can you remember?"

Speaking fast and firmly she replied, "When that lady was here. With the white hair."

Lynn Ryder, thought Temple. "Okay, what else did you see?"

"She came out of your room and walked down the hall, and that man came out of this room and I asked him in for tea. And he had some and a cookie. But then he told me to go night-night."

Temple gaped. "Wait, hold on. He told you to go *night-night*?"

Angie vigorously nodded her head up and down. "Night-night, and so I did. Then he was gone. But I didn't go night-night." She smiled and then giggled. "I just pretended." She gave him a sly look. "I do it sometimes with you, too."

"Okay, so you didn't go night-night. Did you hear or see anything else?"

"I saw that man out my window."

"You mean he was outside?"

She nodded.

"What was he doing?"

"He opened the gate and then he pushed his car out it."

"He pushed his car? You mean he didn't start it?"

She thrust her arms out. "Push. Push! Then, I heard the car go vroom-vroom."

Temple took this all in and said, "Okay, Ang. Now this time, really go night-night, okay? I've got stuff to do."

"But Et—"

He exploded, "Jesus, go NIGHT-NIGHT for fuck's sake."

Her face crumpled at his harsh words and tone.

Temple saw this and his anger faded. He walked over to her. "I'm sorry, Ang, okay? I'm sorry. I'm just…I have a lot going on. I didn't mean to say that, okay? I will always take care of you, okay? I'm... I'm not Dad. I...I love you, Angie."

And then Angie did something she never had before. She wrapped her arms around her brother and hugged him. And he hugged her back, his tears leaching into her gray hair.

"Uv you too, Et."

And then Angie went into her room and closed the door.

Temple stood there breathing hard and trying to get his emotions under control. He finally managed that, and then he crossed the hall, opened the door to the room next to his, and studied the wall that both spaces shared. He closed the door and pulled out his phone and called one of the private detectives he'd used in trying to track down Nash.

Into the phone he said, "Look, it suddenly occurred to me that I didn't ask a basic question about all this. Namely, that place operated by this Isaiah York guy? What *exactly* does he use it for?"

Temple listened intently for a couple of minutes.

"Okay, it would have been good if you had briefed me on that without my having to ask, but better late than never. And just to show my displeasure for your total incompetence, I'm not paying your last bill. No, I'm not fucking kidding. Sue me, asshole."

Temple clicked off.

Talk about hiding in plain sight. But I've got to be sure.

He had a sudden thought and raced down the stairs. In the dining room one of his staff was starting to clear off the table.

"Don't touch that glass! Get me a dishcloth and a big plastic baggie," he ordered the young woman. "Now!"

She raced off and shortly returned with both.

Temple used the cloth to lift up the glass that Nash had drunk from. He put it in the plastic baggie, sealed it, and walked back to his bedroom.

Along the way he smiled and said, "Okay, Dillon Hope or whoever the fuck you really are, your ass is mine."

CHAPTER 55

"Dillon?"

Nash turned to see Mindy hurrying out from one of the home's exterior doors. He'd been checking his emails and was about to leave.

"Yeah?"

She stopped in front of him. "I...I could use some advice."

"Mindy, full disclosure, even before he brought it up at dinner, Rhett had mentioned what was going on with you two."

"Did he also mention that he hit me?"

"What?" Nash exclaimed. When she pointed to her swollen face, he added, "I asked him about that and he said you'd had some dental work done."

"The only dental work I'll have done is to fix a loosened tooth from when he slugged me."

"Did you call the cops?"

"I can't."

"Just because he's rich doesn't mean he can use you for a punching bag. It's against the law. He assaulted you, that's a crime."

"But I can't prove it."

"You don't have to. You can tell the police your story and then they can investigate. It's *their* job to prove it."

She started to cry and Nash put his arms around her. "Mindy, it's okay. Look, I can drive you to the police station if you want."

"I *can't* go to the police."

"Why not?"

She stepped away from him and wiped her eyes. "Because if they come out here they might..."

"They might what?"

"Start snooping around and asking questions about other things."

Nash looked down at her, his eyes narrowing. "What other things?"

"Rhett would kill me if he knew I was talking to you about this."

"He won't hear it from me. But what other things are you worried about?"

"Mandy needs her mother."

"Are you planning to go somewhere without her?" said a confused Nash.

She looked back at the house. "I can't say, Dillon. You might… tell someone."

"I'm not looking to hurt you, Mindy. Or your daughter. But I think you both should leave here and get away from Rhett. You have the money. And if he's beating you, who knows what he might do to Mandy?"

"I know that he feels trapped. And he… he might lash out." She picked nervously at her nails. "You were always very kind to me when you were here. Even when I came on to you, you, well, you handled it like a gentleman."

She looked back at the house again before facing him with a determined expression. "Rhett's father?"

"What about him?"

She blurted out, "He didn't kill himself. Rhett pushed him off the balcony."

Nash didn't react in surprise because he had long felt this was the case.

Sensing this she said, "You… you don't seem shocked."

"I know Rhett. And his story about what happened to his dad seemed lame to me. And even the police thought it was homicide. They just thought this guy Walter Nash had done it. But then he was exonerated. That left only Rhett as a suspect."

Mindy shuddered. "No, it… it left me, too."

"What exactly happened, Mindy?" he said quietly.

She told him all the details of Barton Temple's last minutes on earth.

"So he knocked out his father in an argument and then basically blackmailed you to help get him out to the balcony, where he finished him off?"

"But I knew," exclaimed Mindy as she teetered on her feet in her anxiety. "I'm an *accessory* or something. I looked it up."

He put his hands on her shoulders to steady her. "You told him to call an ambulance and were going to when he didn't. Then he scared you into participating in his scheme. I call that coercion."

"But I would have been stuck with the shitty prenup if Rhett hadn't fixed it so I got all that money. I'm as guilty as he is."

"No, Mindy, you're not. He killed the guy, not you. Okay, maybe you made a poor choice, but you were under immense pressure. Lots of people would have done the same."

She said tearfully, "So that's why I don't want the police around. For all I know Rhett will tell them I did it. I can't go to prison. Not with Mandy and all."

"Look, you don't have to call the police. But you can't stay here if he's beating you. If you make arrangements to go somewhere else, even temporarily until you have more permanent plans, I'll ensure you get there safely."

She hugged him. "Thank you, Dillon. You're really so kind."

"It'll be okay, Mindy. You and your daughter can start a new life together."

"Would... would you want to come along, at least for a bit? Until I got settled."

"Mindy, my employer would not allow that. She's counting on me for some important work and I committed to doing it for her. I can't go back on that."

She touched his right cheek and then kissed him on the other one.

"You really are one of the good ones, Dillon. I hope I find someone like you."

"Just don't jump at the first guy, and if your radar buzzes, run away, fast. You don't need to settle for anybody, Mindy. There are good ones out there. You'll find somebody."

He gave her his phone number and told her to keep him in the loop. "And if you need me to drive you somewhere, or just want to talk, okay?"

"Okay."

"And if he does anything to you again, you call me. And I'll deal with him."

"I will, Dillon, and thank you."

She went back inside and Nash eased into his car.

He looked up at the façade of the Temple mansion. And Nash could have sworn he saw Rhett Temple staring down at him from an upper window.

CHAPTER 56

There was no motorcade this time.

There was only an ultramodern and spacious helicopter that made a landing on a wide patch of grass on the rear grounds of Steers's estate. The bushes around the chopper were nearly flattened by the blades' wash.

Nash watched all this from an open doorway that led into the rear of the house.

The chopper was a Mercedes-Benz Eurocopter EC145. He googled the aircraft and found that the starting price was around nine million bucks.

Okay.

He was sure that Steers was watching the arrival, too, probably from the window of her office.

The chopper's engine wound down and the rear door opened. Only one man got out of the EC145, which could carry ten passengers plus two pilots. He was of medium height with slicked-back dark hair. His suit was quietly expensive. His manner was unhurried, Nash observed, and he did not seem impressed by the estate's lavish home and grounds. Though they were costly and luxurious, this man might be used to something still more costly and even more luxurious.

And he didn't need an army of armed men around him, it seemed. Which was even more impressive than the cartel entourage, for perhaps an unobvious reason.

This man is unafraid that anyone will attempt him harm because they will know that the consequences will far outweigh the benefits.

That was a rarefied position to be in, and one that clearly not even Steers enjoyed.

Nash stepped out of the shadows and said, "Welcome, sir. Right this way. She is waiting for you."

"Thank you," the man replied politely.

As Nash led him inside, the newly recruited security team lurked in the shadows. They had no idea who this person was. Indeed, Nash did not recognize him, either, which meant nothing, really. He didn't keep a mental dossier of global criminals in his memory.

They walked up the stairs and down the hall to Steers's office. Nash knocked once and received the command to enter. He got the visitor settled, nodded at Steers, and withdrew. He took up his post outside her office door and placed his AirPods in. His bug was behind a book on her shelf.

And so it began.

* * *

"Thank you for coming," said Steers to her visitor as he sat down, but she remained standing. She had on a milk-white tunic with Mandarin script running down one side of her top and done in a bright red, and black slacks.

"I had business in the vicinity, you see, such that it worked out," replied the man. "I also understand that you had other visitors some time back. I trust that the meeting was successful?"

"*They* believe that it was," said Steers. "And I believe that it was as well. But I do not think our respective beliefs stem from the same reasons."

"That is intriguing enough to justify my visit." He glanced at her clothes and the Mandarin characters. "'The spirit of one can walk through fire'?" he translated.

"I find it both inspirational and true, do you not?"

"I do not know, Ms. Steers. I have never walked through fire."

"But I have, quite literally."

He nodded. "And may I say that the skillful extraction of your mother from her accommodations in Myanmar was truly something to behold."

"That is a compliment I will treasure. However, I would have hoped that her replacement would have been allowed to die a dignified death. She had no blame in this."

"There is always blame to parcel out," he countered. "But do not distress yourself in the least. She did die in peace and dignity. Her head was therefore of no more use to her. And its receipt by you, I thought, was also beneficial. To you and to me. It provided information that needed to be...*received*."

"Your message was powerful. I trust it must have been a coincidence that it came about the same time that an attempt was made on my life. An attempt that would have succeeded except for the actions of the man who escorted you in here."

"He looked capable enough. And your line of work does encourage such things, Ms. Steers. As it does to us all. We must always be on our guard."

"Not all of us," she said. "You come here with no security, but you know that you are perfectly safe with me."

"As you say, I know that I am...perfectly safe with you."

She sat, clasped her hands, and set them on the desk. To anyone who knew Steers well, and there were almost none who really fit that criteria, she appeared calm and in control. She was actually none of these things. The man across from her was far more dangerous than the most dangerous of her cartel partners. He was no mere global criminal. And while he, despite what she had intimated to her other business colleagues, was not the head of an entire country, he was perhaps something more than that. He had heads of *countries*—all of them powerful and ruthless—beholden to him.

That was why she knew that he had not ordered her death when

Hao had attempted to end her life. If that had been the case, none of them would have been left alive.

Which means, of course, that I have a living traitor in the ranks.

"Our business arrangement has reached a crossroads, I think," she said.

"Well, with your mother back to advise you, I trust you now speak from a position of *superior* strength, Ms. Steers."

"You do me a great honor. And one reason I asked you here today was to explain why I did what I did with my mother. During my visit I became aware of her frailty. I did not wish her to die alone there in such a state."

"A most understandable reaction from a daughter," said the man graciously, but with a blank expression that ratcheted Steers's defenses even higher.

"I felt this was not something that you and I could come to terms on. The action I undertook was the only avenue I perceived that I possessed. My mother has received medical attention and is doing much better. I trust she has many more years left."

"How wonderful. Now to be clear, I neither appreciate nor condone what you did. It is bad for business. *My* business. If one can think they can freely take what is mine?" He spread his hands and smiled, an expression that did not come close to reaching his eyes. "Then I have no business. You, as an exemplary businessperson yourself, must understand this."

"I do."

"So where does that leave...us?"

"With my mother back and my father long dead, it gives me great reason to reflect on the future. I have no children. I am the last of the Steerses."

"And what have you concluded with your *reflections*, Ms. Steers?"

"That I want to sell my business to you."

The man hiked his eyes in some mild surprise. "All of it?"

"All of it."

"And the price?" he said, his expression becoming amused. "An astronomical sum, I am certain. You know something of the level of my wealth. You will take advantage, I am sure."

Steers stared directly at him. "The amount I wish for *myself* is... one American dollar."

CHAPTER

57

Nash had heard all of the conversation but couldn't comprehend any of it.

Her entire empire for a single dollar? That made no sense at all.

Later, he escorted the visitor back to the chopper. Nash managed to take a picture of the man's face after he boarded the aircraft and was facing toward Nash. He immediately sent it off to Agent Morris with a short message.

Who is this guy?

He got a response before the chopper was even out of sight. It was not what he expected, considering how important and powerful the man seemed.

I have no idea. But we will find out.

He went back inside and met Steers in the hallway.

"Did your meeting go well?" he asked.

She looked at him curiously—too curiously, he thought. She finally said, "Time will tell, Dillon-san."

"How much time, do you reckon?"

"Not enough, at least for me."

He was taken aback by this statement. "I'm not sure what you mean."

"Come into my office. This is really not a discussion meant for hallways."

She closed the door and they sat side by side, their knees nearly touching.

Steers said, "The man here today? There is no need to tell you his name. You would not recognize it. He remains always in the shadows. He never seeks attention. He is vastly wealthy, far more than I. He is powerful, again far more than I. Indeed, he has more wealth and more power than all of the other men who came here before *combined*."

"How can someone like that not be widely known?"

"If you have vast wealth, you are only widely known if you truly want to be. Many wealthy crave the attention. They want to be known and either adored or hated, or both. This man cares nothing for that. You see, one can accomplish so much more from the shadows." She looked off. "He is a supreme strategist. He wants to live forever and spends much money on achieving that goal. He is very, very close to top-tier leaders and ruling classes around the world, but particularly so in both the Middle and the Far East. For some powerful desert princes he is their primary investment and brand guru, as they try to remake their images across the world into something more acceptable. Whether it is buying up sports teams, creating a professional golf league, or building ski and golf resorts on the sands, they want people to look at that instead of all the other things they do that are not so pleasant or appealing. And his well-organized and crafty minions are placed around the world to seek and steal whatever useful secrets and intelligence they can. It is said that even Mossad fears him but also copies some of his tactics."

She paused and looked at Nash. "And though the public will never hear one word of it, he is very close to the leadership in *your* country. He has wrestled concessions from them on AI technology, the release of necessary GPU chips, the sharing of data, and investments in both the Middle East and your country in data center construction, in addition to other AI development facilities. He is also involved in nuclear power and green energy initiatives to provide the necessary electricity that these facilities require. In your country AI may be seen as a boon for many things, including the creation of unimaginable wealth. In the Middle East it is also seen as a boon, but they already have unimaginable wealth, so it is not that which they solely seek."

"What then?" asked Nash.

"It is the final ingredient they require to implement a complete police surveillance state across the entire region and thereby ferret out and crush dissent of any kind before it can mount any realistic challenge to them. They do not like dissent there. Past leaders, including family members of the current crop of rulers, have been assassinated by their enemies or overthrown by a dissatisfied public who see the wealth of their country consistently going only into a few elite pockets."

"That does seem to be a problem, around the world," noted Nash.

"He also had very close ties to China, but was forced, at least on the surface, to relinquish them in order to transact meaningful business with your country. But he plays both sides with consummate skill. He has the Middle East in one pocket and still keeps Beijing in the other. They are both places that wish a complete Orwellian police state." Her features deepened and then hardened. "And lest you think otherwise, *your* country's leadership is particularly intrigued by this feature, as are the wealthiest among you. After all, when you own the mountain your chief responsibility is to ensure that you do everything possible to prevent landslides. You see, landslides transfer what was once at the top to the bottom. Not a trip these people desire to take.

"And if AI takes many of the jobs, then the rank-and-file people will be solely dependent on the government, and/or on the largesse of the monied class, for their very survival. The power will be complete; the wealthy and holders of high positions will rule everything. So this man is a welcome friend and colleague wherever there is concentrated wealth and power around the world."

Nash looked and felt overwhelmed by all this. "How...how do you know all this?"

"I also have intelligence-gathering resources, even within his organization. Besides, he does not care if I know this. This plan is not being thought out with a distant date for implementation. It is being executed right now. For those who wish to fight back, I fear it is already too late."

"Don't take this the wrong way. But he sounds like a legitimate businessman with vast resources and connections in the government and business sectors."

She interjected, "So you want to know why he is involved with me, correct? Because, despite my wall of legitimate businesses, I am, at bottom, simply a criminal?"

"Frankly, yes."

Nash also knew that she was part of a conspiracy, presumably with this man, to flood the U.S. market with opioids and thereby weaken its democratic foundations.

So how did that jibe with this man working with *American interests?* he thought.

"Legitimate businessmen sometimes need what I can provide."

"And what is that?"

"When one is negotiating with another, what do you think is the most important thing to consider?"

"You need to frame things so that you can negotiate from a position of strength."

"And what are the ways one can do that?"

"You can make sure you have all your ducks in a row, have taken all steps to ensure you are operating at optimal capacity, have thought through every scenario, and allow yourself wiggle room as necessary. In sum, you tell the story you want to tell and back it up with facts."

"That is on *your* side. What of the other side? What can be done to them?"

Nash took a few moments as she watched him closely.

"You take steps to *weaken* the other side as much as you can. Which, I imagine, is where you come in."

"Yes, that is where I came in. The renting of the social fabric in your country was my mission. And I performed that mission to the best of my ability, which provided him and his partners enormous leverage in world affairs."

Nash thought, *So that's how his actions make sense. Work with America but also simultaneously weaken us.*

He decided to take a chance and just say it. "And yet I read an article where the deaths from opioid addiction are falling quickly here. It's said to be due to many factors."

"And one such factor is the drop in the use of fentanyl in the pill-making process," she said.

"And that was you?"

She looked past him, at the wall of books on the shelf. "One can play both sides, but only for a limited time. The truth will come out, of course."

"*You're* playing both sides, aren't you? The others from before and the man today?"

"The man today is a grand master in many games. I would wager that he will arrive at my duplicity long before the likes of Señor Ramirez or even the more cunning Señor Tecú do."

"And then what will happen?"

"He will kill me."

"That's your plan?"

"Are you so certain that I have a plan?"

"What about your mother?"

"What about her? Do you think she would care what happens to me?"

"It sounds like you're giving up, which is not like you. You are a fighter, a survivor."

"One cannot survive forever, Dillon-san. And unlike our visitor today, I do not wish to live forever."

"But making it to your eighties is a worthy goal."

She smiled. "You are still an enigma to me, Dillon-san, after all this time."

"I can say the same thing about you because despite everything, I'm convinced that you have a *conscience*. Something you allege you don't have."

Steers rose. "I must go and…finish some things. I will call if I need you."

He said resignedly, "I'll be there if you need me."

She walked out of the room, leaving Nash to stare after an enigma of his very own.

CHAPTER 58

"I SAW OUR VISITOR TODAY. BUT only from a distance," Masuyo said in a disappointed voice.

Steers set down her soup spoon and looked at her mother, who was, as usual, seated at the head of the table.

"I did not think you wished to greet the man who kept you a prisoner for years."

"That is not the point. You let that man into our home after what he did to me?"

"It was necessary, Māma."

"I do not understand you sometimes, Daughter. You are more powerful than you think. This is no time to shrink like a faded flower. You must be bold."

"Being bold *and* stupid is just being stupid," said Steers wearily as she picked up her spoon again and dipped it into her bowl.

"What did you talk to him about?"

Steers swallowed a mouthful of soup while she glanced at her mother. It seemed both women were appraising the other.

"You believe you need to know this?" said Steers.

"It was you who said that what you have is built solely on what I created. Thus, I believe I have every right to know all."

Steers laid down the spoon again, wiped her mouth with her napkin, and leaned back in her chair. "He is displeased with me. Not simply for having liberated you. Before this meeting he also made clear that he does not agree with the way my business is being conducted, largely with respect to this country."

Masuyo nodded and a cruel smile emerged on her lips. "You are not killing enough Americans to please him. I do not know what led to this, Daughter, or who you are listening to, but you are better than that." She tapped her forehead. "This houses your brain, nothing else. If he requires death, provide it. What do you care for this country anyway? America is our enemy! And look at Moscow. Do you think Putin wastes one minute of his time worrying about helping America? He wants to crush this country. Anyone who thinks otherwise is an idiot. But then again, idiots are useful, particularly if they are highly placed. And many are," she added knowingly. "Very highly placed indeed."

Steers visibly trembled, as though her rage threatened to break through all her outer calm. "Hiroko-san would disagree with you. Hiroko-san would speak of one's soul, of one's compassion, of one's good nature up here." She tapped her forehead.

Masuyo's lips curled into a sneer. "You embrace the advice of someone who never rose above the level of a servant? I do not know why you still have that foolish old woman around. But the fact that you do makes you a fool as well. And I did not raise you to be a fool. I raised you to be *victorious* above all others. You were named for a queen. Act like it, child!"

"All right, using my *brain*, I have partners who do not wish to kill their paying customers, since that is clearly bad for business. However, this man does not care about that. Indeed, as you just pointed out, he desires this outcome. Thus, I have conflict on both my flanks. An interesting challenge, would you not agree?"

Masuyo dropped her arrogant and domineering manner and assumed an engaged expression. "A challenging problem indeed. What do you intend to do about it, Victoria?"

"I have already done something about it."

"What have you done!" snapped her mother, giving Steers a ferocious look.

Steers rose, dropped her napkin on the table, and said, "I am tired. Have a good sleep, Māma. I very much intend to. Because tomorrow belongs to no one, especially people like us."

* * *

Two nights later Nash was lying on his bed thinking about his last conversation with Steers. Nash had wanted to ask about the prison but the timing did not seem right. Why did a man such as she had described run a prison in Myanmar? What would be the point?

He had not heard back from Agent Morris on his query about the man's identity. From this Nash concluded that Steers had been correct in her analysis of the man and his intense desire for anonymity.

As she had said: *You can accomplish so much more from the shadows.*

Thura and some of the security team were on duty now so that Nash and the others could sleep. Nash knew that Steers selling her empire to the man for really nothing did not protect her. Her cartel partners would not be at all pleased, especially after she had laid out such an impressive business proposal envisioning a central hierarchy to manage their various empires.

When they find out who their new partner is, they will try to kill her, without a doubt.

But that did not answer the question as to why Steers was getting out of the business altogether. And what about her mother? The woman who had created the empire in the first place? He doubted that she would have approved, which told him that Steers had not allowed her mother to be part of this decision.

And when she finds out, Masuyo will want to kill her daughter, too. You made many enemies with this perplexing decision, Victoria-san, and I wonder why.

His phone buzzed and he looked at the screen. Agent Morris had finally replied to his secure message. He opened the email and read it.

Nash now had a name for the gentleman who had visited them.

Connor Lord had been born... in America.

Okay. An American cozying up to Middle Eastern and Chinese dictators.

Lord had been an Army brat, like Nash, but his father's service had carried Lord to both the Middle and the Far East. When his father's service ended he had come home; his then-adult son had not. For the following twenty-five-plus years, Lord had been immersed in those twin regions of the world as a wealth builder and keen student of geopolitics. Never in the limelight, Morris noted in the email, and not in anything they could prove was criminal.

But always in the shadows, thought Nash.

Steers had not been joking about the man being good at chess. A fifteen-year-old Lord—who already spoke a half dozen languages, including Arabic, Farsi, Mandarin, and Japanese—had become a grand master, Morris reported. While still a teenager, he had beaten Garry Kasparov, and Anatoly Karpov the following year. But he had mysteriously left that competitive world before the age of twenty-one, Morris wrote. He had next turned his interests and his reportedly 215 IQ—

Nash gasped as he read this. He didn't even know the scale went that high.

Morris also said in the email that all efforts to learn more about the man had been met with walls of silence from those around the world in high places who surely knew Connor Lord. And that included those in the United States.

The shadows again.

Morris had asked Nash why he had made the inquiry. Nash wasn't sure what to tell the man.

Finally, he wrote, Steers offered to sell her entire business to him for a buck.

Morris' reply was swift. Are you drunk or high on something?

Nash wrote back, I wish. He put his phone down and stared at the ceiling.

None of this made sense, at least the way he was looking at it.

Shakespeare had written about rulers kissing away kingdoms, he vaguely recalled from some long-ago college class. But people didn't really do that. Once you had power you did everything possible to consolidate it, and then keep it.

He rose and found Thura, and spoke with him for a few minutes, then headed over to the main house. He let himself in using an electronic key card that allowed him access to the various buildings.

It was late and the enormous house was exceptionally quiet.

Quiet like a morgue.

He moved through one hall and then another. He stopped and stared down the hall where Masuyo had her suite of rooms.

Down another hall was where Hiroko had her room. He had visited with her often since they had come to live here. He had found her favorite chocolates at a shop in town and had brought her several boxes of them. They would have tea and she would speak with him in greater detail of Steers and her family.

As he stood there in the darkness, he recalled some of their discussions.

* * *

"I believe with all my heart that it is not too late for Victoria-san to become what she once was," Hiroko had said.

"You mean, the shy little girl who loved to draw," he said.

She looked at him sadly and said, "I think you know of what I speak. But with her mother having returned, things...things could once more become out of control."

"You mean Victoria-san could lose control because of her mother?"

"I fear that it could be worse than that."

"What do you mean?" he asked, dread ratcheting up through his senses.

"Masuyo does not take a second seat to anyone. To...anyone. I know of this, believe me."

"But she's old and probably not in the best of health after all those years in prison."

She shook her head. "Masuyo will outlive us all…unless…"

"Unless what?"

She shook her head again. "I cannot speak of it, Dillon-san. It is not for your ears. It is perhaps for no one's ears. Surely old Hiroko speaks of dreams, even of fantasies. But when one is old, one thinks of things that others cannot or will not."

And despite his attempts to draw her out, Hiroko had said nothing else.

* * *

Now, as Nash stood there, he suddenly heard a whimper filter through the hall, followed by a low moan, and then a stark cry for help.

He raced down the hall to Hiroko's room and tried to open the door, but it was locked. "Hiroko-san? Hiroko-san, are you all right?"

The cries grew louder, but they were unintelligible. And then he heard her thrashing around.

"Hiroko-san?" Nash cried out.

A voice behind him exclaimed, "What is going on? What is wrong?"

He turned to see Steers standing there in her nightdress.

"It's Hiroko-san. She sounds…ill. The door's locked."

She pushed past him and beat on the door. "Hiroko-san? Hiroko-san!"

When there was no response Nash pulled Steers out of the way. He backed up a few steps and then hurled his body against the door. The doorjamb broke off with the force of the collision and the door flew open.

Nash's momentum carried him into the room, and he staggered against some furniture, knocked over a table, and fell to the floor. By the time he regained his footing, Steers had come into the room and was staring over at a chair.

Nash looked, too, and he felt his skin turn cold.

Hiroko was in the chair. Her eyes looked at them but were clearly seeing nothing. Her head was angled to the right and rested on her shoulder, and her soft white hair hung limply in her face. Her body was still, her mouth open.

Steers checked the woman's pulse and then stepped back, her body trembling.

"My Hiroko-san…is…gone," she said in a voice that contained more anguish than Nash had ever heard carried in words before.

CHAPTER

59

Nash bent down in front of Hiroko. He looked at the foam on her lips and next observed the cherry-red color of her face. Then he glanced at the cup of tea on the table beside her. He lifted it and sniffed the contents. He detected an odor that should not have been there.

He stood and turned to Steers, who was still looking down in disbelief at the dead woman.

"I think…I suspect she was poisoned."

Steers glanced at him, and then at the cup and then at Hiroko's face. "I do not suspect that."

"But—"

She held up a hand to stop him. "I do not *suspect*. I *know* it to be true."

"Then you know who…?"

Steers's hands curled to fists and her chest heaved with emotion. She closed her eyes and the tears drained out from them. She shook her head sharply once, and then again, fiercely, as though to throw something repulsive off her.

"We have to call the police," said Nash.

She opened her watery eyes and stared up at him. "No police."

"But—"

"Dillon-san, I will say this only one more time. And though my respect for you is great, in my current state of mind I am capable of anything. *No* police. Do you understand me?"

He started to say something, but then stepped back and nodded. "I understand."

Steers knelt next to Hiroko's body and gently took the woman's hand in one of hers. With her other hand Steers stroked the lovely white hair, moving it out of the woman's face.

"Hiroko-san, you have served me faithfully and well. You deserved many, many more years of spirit and living and goodness. I am deeply ashamed to have failed you in allowing this to happen. You, above all others that I know, did not deserve this fate."

She then reached up and closed the woman's eyes.

"What do we do with...her?" asked Nash.

Steers rose. "I am not Buddhist as my upbringing in Japan would normally dictate, or a Shinto. Nor am I Protestant as was my father. And my mother is an atheist, so I am not bound by any of these traditions. But we must give her a proper pathway to eternity."

"I understand, but I meant, what do we do with the body?"

"I own land not far from here. It is completely undeveloped and will remain that way. I...I had intended to make it into a private park where I could walk...and think. We will bury Hiroko there. We will return her body and her spirit to the earth where they will reunite and form something truly special."

"Hiroko told me she was Chinese."

"She was. But while the government there preaches atheism, many Chinese practice an assortment of religions, Buddhism, Taoism, and even Catholicism. I learned that Hiroko-san became a Buddhist while living in Japan. And Hiroko-san believed, as Buddhists do, in reincarnation. The cycle of rebirth and death. But the ultimate goal is *nirvana*, where this cycle is broken and eternal peace is achieved."

"You certainly sound like a person knowledgeable about religion even though you don't practice one," noted Nash.

"One can have faith without a church attached," she replied tersely.

"So we do this now?"

She nodded. "We need to ensure that no one sees, not even Thura, and certainly not the other guards."

"The staff are all in their quarters, outside the main house. I can carry her to the garage and put her in the Suburban. And get some...shovels. But how will we explain her being gone?"

"Besides the attendants no one sees her except you, me, and my mother. I will explain to the attendants. Now go and get what you need and then come back here. I want to spend a few minutes alone with my Hiroko-san and I also need to...prepare her."

Nash hurried off to get the materials he needed. When he came back, Steers had positioned Hiroko on the floor, naked, with a sheet beneath her.

He averted his gaze, but Steers, observing this, said sharply, "Hiroko-san cannot see you, so she cannot be embarrassed. And I need your help."

They washed the body, including the hair, and then Steers carefully combed it.

"The nokanshi normally performs the preparation of the body, but that is not possible here. And in Japan everyone is cremated because there is no space for cemeteries. But that is also not possible for my Hiroko-san."

Steers left and came back with a white kimono.

"The kyokatabira," she explained. "It was what Japanese people wore when they went on their final pilgrimages. It will clothe Hiroko-san on her journey."

"Why do you have one of those?"

"We all die," said Steers. "It is best to be prepared, is it not?"

They dressed her in the kimono, and Nash then watched Steers carefully apply makeup to Hiroko-san's face. "This must be done precisely to ensure her onward journey," she noted.

"Where'd you learn to do that?"

"When I was a child a friend's grandmother died in Kobe. I

learned then." She sat on her haunches and looked at Hiroko. "Death has always...fascinated me. I am not sure why."

"Because you can't control it," he said promptly. "When it comes for you and how," he added.

She glanced up at him. "You are wrong, Dillon-san. There is one way to control *when* it comes. And *how*."

"I don't think Hiroko-san would like to hear you say that."

She dropped her gaze and went back to work on the woman.

Nash remembered the night she had threatened to kill herself, which was clearly what Steers had been referring to with her statement.

And who's to say a control person like herself will not make the decision of choosing when and how her death will occur?

After Steers was finished, Nash gently picked up the dead woman, carried her to the garage, and placed her in plastic that he had put in the rear of the Suburban. He had already loaded in shovels and some other tools. He had texted the security detail that he and Steers were taking a late-night drive.

Steers had rushed back to her room and hurriedly changed out of her nightdress and into jeans and a sweater. She rode not in the passenger seat but in the back of the Suburban with Hiroko.

She directed Nash to an isolated spot about three miles away.

He had told Steers that he would dig the hole but she insisted on helping.

"It is the very least I can do for her," she explained.

They shoveled until Nash's head was about level with the top of the hole. Nash was impressed with Steers's strength, stamina, and precise movements—no wasted motion, steady breaths, intently focused on the mission at hand. She had matched him shovel for shovel.

They laid Hiroko in her grave and placed the dirt over her. Nash then tamped the mound down to a level surface. He and Steers placed the grass that Nash had cut out in precise squares back on top of the leveled dirt. One would be hard pressed to tell that a hole had been dug here. In a few weeks' time all traces of disturbance would be gone.

A sweaty Steers stood by the grave, her hands clasped in front of her and her eyes closed. She was speaking words that sounded solemn and also Japanese to Nash. He just stood next to her and stared down at the last resting place of a good woman.

Steers found a large and unusually shaped stone nearby. Nash carried it over for her and placed it on top of the grave, at the exact spot Steers indicated.

"This way I will always be able to find my way back to Hiroko-san, you see," she said.

"Yes, I see," replied Nash.

They walked back to the Suburban and climbed in. Before Nash could start the engine she said, "Can we just sit here in the quiet for a bit, Dillon-san?"

"For as long as you want."

For the next thirty minutes Steers sat in her seat and stared at her hands and made not a sound, while Nash shot her glances and tried to surmise what was going on in her mind.

"I am ready now. We can go."

They drove back and Steers went to her room while Nash tidied things up in Hiroko's room. He put the contents of the suspect tea into a plastic container and closed the damaged door as best he could and then secured it. He carried the container to his room in the guesthouse and placed it in a locked drawer. He stood by the window and stared out into what was now the early dawn. It was calm and peaceful and rejuvenating.

But he knew Victoria Steers was feeling none of these things. The woman was undoubtedly all misery and sadness and, probably, regret for failing her beloved Hiroko-san.

And now mother and daughter had just lost the only buffer they would ever have. And Nash knew that Steers believed her mother had murdered Hiroko, the only true friend Steers had.

I have every reason in the world to hate Victoria Steers. And yet now I don't. And I hate myself for that.

Nash kept standing at the window and thought that no life should be as complicated as his.

And Victoria Steers's.

CHAPTER 60

THE NEXT DAY RHETT TEMPLE pulled up in his Porsche, and Nash let him through the front gate.

Temple got out of the car carrying a paper bag. "Hey, Dillon-san, how goes it with the evil queen?"

"I wouldn't talk that way, Rhett. There are listening devices everywhere."

"Oh, shit, I forgot." But Nash could tell the man was not remotely concerned about that.

"Yeah, always good to be careful."

Temple drew close to Nash and said in a whisper, "So I probably shouldn't let her in on the fact that you're actually Walter Nash then?"

Nash could not help but flinch. "What? Have you been drinking?"

In answer Temple pulled out a wineglass from the paper bag. "No, but you had. Your prints, all over this, Walt. Got them from your FINRA file. And prints don't lie." He ran his gaze over Nash. "But I have to tell you, it's an amazing transformation. I never, ever suspected. This Shock guy is the real deal."

Acid firing into his belly, Nash said, "I don't know what—"

"Angie saw you coming out of the bedroom next to mine the night Ryder came to see me. You had tea with my sister. And then you told her to go *night-night*, which Dillon Hope would have no clue about, but Walter Nash would. Remember, I told you that little trick when you and Judith came over for dinner and my father couldn't get Angie to calm down. And then after you had your 'tea' you got in your car, rolled it out the gate, and went to save your wife. Am I right? Judith is alive and kicking, isn't she?"

"You should try writing fiction, Rhett. You're good."

Temple studied him for an intense moment. "Okay, if that's the way you want to play it. I can just take the print results in to Steers and see what she says."

Temple started to walk past but Nash grabbed the man's arm to stop him.

Temple smirked. "Glad you came to your senses."

"Look, Rhett—"

"No, you look, Walt. You're a hell of a negotiator, the best really. But you need to have at least one card to play and you don't. So don't embarrass yourself, man."

Nash stared at the hand that had betrayed him. He had not continued to rub his finger and palmprints down with the pumice stone Shock had advised him to use to prevent this very thing from happening. But he was not ready to give up yet.

"You're good at making threats, I'll give you that. And I think you're terrified you won't actually find Walter Nash and so you're trying to throw me under the bus to get yourself off scot-free."

Temple grinned. "But the fingerprints—"

Nash placed a crushing grip on Temple's shoulder. "*Fuck* the fingerprints," he said in a low, menacing voice.

He squeezed harder and Temple moaned and tried to pry Nash's fingers off but couldn't.

"I could kill you right now, Rhett. You know that, don't you? You've seen what I can do. But you actually don't know the half of it." He increased the pressure on the man's shoulder and Temple dropped to his knees.

"Please," he moaned.

"What do you want?" said Nash.

Temple gasped, "What I want I already told you: I want to disappear. With all my money. To a place that crazy bitch can never and

I mean *never* find me. You do that for me, your secret is safe. I swear to God. Please, please let go. Please stop."

"How am I supposed to trust you? You've screwed me over before."

Moaning, Temple said in a halting voice, "I screw you, you can put Steers onto me. And we both know what she'll do when she finds me."

Nash looked down at his former boss. Such a little man in so many ways. But this was getting him nowhere. He let go of Temple and the man collapsed to the ground for a few moments, rubbing his shoulder and trying to catch his breath. "You…you could have broken my shoulder."

"I could have done a lot of things, Rhett. Desperate men do, you know. Crazy shit. Real crazy."

Temple slowly rose, rubbing at his shoulder. "You don't sound like your old self."

"I'm not Walter Nash, Rhett, not anymore. I can put you in contact with Shock. But you'll need to be willing to *transform* yourself. And there's no guarantee Shock won't kill you in the process."

Still wincing with pain, Temple shrugged and said resignedly, "What choice do I have?"

"Depending on what Shock says, we'll get you out of here and on your new journey to freedom."

"You know, it might be better to make it look like I died. I'm betting that's what you did with Judith. You went back to your old house after Angie saw you leaving my place. You killed those guys that Ryder sent there. And you and the FBI covered it all up, right?"

"That's quite a leap of logic," replied Nash, without answering the question.

"I don't really care. But if Steers thinks I'm dead, she won't bother coming after me."

"We can arrange for your death, sure."

Temple apparently did not like the way Nash had said that. He drew closer. "But just *fake* dying, Walt. Not the real thing. See, I know you hate my guts. I know you blame me for all this shit. You heard me with Judith. You heard me with the detective. I did my best to frame you."

"What should I expect from a guy who would throw his own father off a balcony?"

Temple took a step back. "That's bullshit. Wait, did Mindy tell—"

"Nobody needed to tell me anything, Rhett. Barton never would have kicked the bucket early, cancer or not. And the cops said he was murdered. And I know I didn't kill him. So that just leaves... you."

"Good luck proving anything," snarled Temple.

"Well, through DNA the cops can easily prove that baby is yours, not your father's. There's a motive right there."

Temple held up his hands in mock surrender. "Look, we both just need to take a deep breath and realize we have bullets in both our guns, symbolically speaking for me. The smart plan is to work together, not against each other, right?"

"Maybe."

Temple's expression changed. "And for what it's worth, I knew nothing about what they were going to do with Maggie. I hated that it happened. She should be alive. I'm . . . I'm so sorry that she's not."

"I actually believe you on that point."

"You do?" said a startled Temple.

"Yeah, or else I would have already killed you. By the way, I told Mindy to leave with Mandy so you couldn't beat her up anymore."

"Look, I lost my temper once with her."

"It looked like more than once."

"I'm...I'm not proud of what I did. But she's still there. I... promised not to touch her again. And I won't."

"Well, if you do, I'll beat your brains in."

Temple let out a nervous laugh, saw that Nash was not joking, and said quickly, "Give me a call after you talk to this Shock dude, okay?"

Nash watched him hurry back to his Porsche and drive away.

"What did he want?"

He turned to see Steers staring at him from the open front door.

CHAPTER 61

"He was just checking in," said Nash. "He might have some leads on Walter Nash that he needs my help in running down."

Steers walked toward him. "That may be a moot point now."

"You mean you don't care about finding Nash now? But it was your top priority."

"When circumstances change, so do goals and priorities. The man that was here to meet with me?"

"Yes."

"He is acquiring my business."

Nash pretended to be stunned by this revelation. "What? Why?"

"Because it is time that I no longer do what I have done for far too long."

"Will you be leaving here then?" asked Nash.

"I do not know."

"But you talked about this man wanting to kill you."

"One way to forestall that was by selling out to him. Then he can do what he wants."

"And he's agreed to this?"

"He will. I made the purchase price too appealing."

Nash knew that it was one dollar but he wanted to know more. He said, "But if you make it too cheap he'll probably think there's something wrong with the business, or else you're trying to trick or trap him somehow."

"Of course he will because that is perfectly natural."

"Again, I don't understand."

"As I told you before, you need not understand. Only *I* need to understand."

"And your mother? What does she say about this?"

"She says nothing."

"Because you haven't told her? She doesn't know?"

"I did not say that, did I?"

Nash took a step back. "Forgive me. I'm making inquiries about things that do not concern me."

"I understand your natural curiosity. And what I have done *will* impact you."

"You mean you won't have need of my services anymore?"

"Quite the reverse. You will be one of the few things between me and a premature death. So I ask that you exercise hypervigilance going forward, Dillon-san, and stand by me. The coming days and weeks could be quite…bumpy."

She walked back into the house, leaving Nash more confused than ever.

* * *

Nash called Shock and filled him in on Temple's discovering Nash's true identity.

"I threatened him with death if he tried to screw me. But I feel like an idiot for letting him find out the truth. You warned me about fingerprints."

"Ain't nothing we can do 'bout that now. So what does he want?"

"He wants you to do for him what you did for me," said Nash. "But you do not have to do this. In fact most of me wants you to tell him to fuck off and leave him to the wolves."

"But that may not help you," said Shock.

"You've done enough for me, Shock. More than enough."

"I'll take the dude on, Walter."

"Why?"

"Because it'll help you. That's good enough reason for me."

"But what if it's some kind of setup? I don't want you in the middle of it."

"I'll know pretty early on if the dude ain't legit and he's got another agenda. And I ain't gonna let no rich prick take me down."

"What will you do if he does have another agenda?"

"Ain't no need for you to know that, Walter. That will make you an accessory *before* the fact."

Nash gave him Temple's contact information and clicked off, just as he got a message from Masuyo that she wanted to go out. Now. But just with him.

He texted Thura, telling him this. He also instructed Thura to tell the rest of the security team to be especially attentive to their duties. He then headed to Masuyo's suite of rooms.

She was waiting for him and already had her coat on.

Nash walked her out to one of the vehicles and got her settled inside. She told him the address she wanted to travel to and they set off.

As he drove along, Nash said, "I have seen nothing of Hiroko-san of late. Her room is empty. Do you know anything?"

"I told you before that I do not answer ridiculous queries from my security people," she snapped.

"Sorry."

"What does my daughter say about her?" asked Masuyo.

"I have not asked her."

"If you *ask* me it is good riddance. The old, foolish woman was not a good influence on my precious daughter."

"I'm not sure she would see it that way."

"Then she is as foolish as the old woman."

The old woman who you murdered, thought Nash.

He drove to the address and parked in front of the office building. When he started to follow her inside, Masuyo told him to wait with the car.

"You're sure?" he said.

"If I were not I would not have said so," she replied brusquely and then walked inside.

Peering through the glass doors Nash waited until she was in the elevator before he slipped inside. He watched as the elevator rose to the eighth floor. Then he hurried over to the office directory and looked at the places on the eighth floor.

Dentists and doctors and lawyers and...

An import-export company, which the Mandarin characters translated to "Out of This World LLC," he found out with the aid of a phone app.

He took the stairs up to the eighth floor, opened the door, and peered out.

There was no one walking down the hall. Following the descending office numbers he made his way around a corner and peered down it. Halfway along the corridor he saw a set of wooden doors with the name of the company on a square of metal next to it.

He quickly walked toward it and noted that there was a button to ring if one wanted to be admitted. So they kept the door locked, he thought.

He took a picture of the doorway and sign. Then he rode the elevator back down and got into the car. He texted the picture to Reed Morris and asked him to find out what he could about the company.

He sat there and wondered why Masuyo would be visiting such a place. What did she have to import or export?

A half hour later, through the glass doors, he saw her exit the elevator. He got out of the car and held the building's door open for her and then helped Masuyo into the car.

As they drove off he said, "Back home or somewhere else, Mrs. Steers?"

She stared at him in the mirror with more intensity than his simple question warranted, he thought. Something else was clearly going on here.

"Let's go get a drink. And talk, Dillon."

"Yes, ma'am. Any place in particular?"

"You pick."

He drove them to a downtown restaurant that had an outdoor section. At this hour it was pretty much empty. They sat at a table and ordered their drinks. Masuyo had a martini while Nash opted for a tonic and lime.

"Still on duty," he said to Masuyo, who looked at him with contempt.

"I would think a man as large as you could hold his liquor."

After their drinks came and they had each taken a sip, Masuyo, who had not taken her eyes off Nash the whole time said, "For some odd reason my daughter has taken a fancy to you. I'm sure you are aware of this, Dillon-*san*. After all, you are the only one she refers to in that way."

"Except for Hiroko-san," he corrected. "And it is an honor for me," he said casually and he hoped disarmingly. "And keep in mind that I saved her from an assassination attempt. It's perfectly reasonable that she would be grateful."

"Why? Because you simply managed to do your job?" she said derisively.

"Gratitude can take many forms."

"I see that you have chosen to be both evasive *and* deceptive in your responses."

"I wasn't aware I was being either," he replied quietly.

"A man visited my daughter. A very powerful man. The same man that had imprisoned me for all those years."

"I was aware of his visit. I was not aware that he was connected to the prison."

"Well, now you are. My daughter made an arrangement with him. I would like to know the details."

"Surely, you can ask her."

"You do not know?"

"That is something that your daughter, in her boundless wisdom, would not confide in someone like me, Mrs. Steers."

Masuyo stared at him for so long that Nash barely managed to maintain eye contact. It was a withering look that seemed to drain all the energy and resolve out of him. He could not imagine having such a *person* as a mother.

Or as an enemy. But she surely is an enemy. For both me and her daughter.

"Then I need you to find out."

"How can I possibly do that?" he said.

"You can ask her."

"Clearly your daughter would tell you if you asked her."

"And if I wish that *you* do it?"

"I can try, but I cannot guarantee that I will be successful."

"Then if you're not, you can consider yourself terminated. And you will explain it to my daughter as your wish to leave and tell her nothing of my request." She paused and studied him. "But of course you will tell her the truth in an attempt to save face with her and blame me for your leaving."

"I will do my best, but again, the simplest way would be for you to ask her."

"I will await your results with interest," Masuyo replied, picking up her drink once more. "But do not take more than a day or two to provide them."

After driving Masuyo back home, Nash walked toward the guesthouse, thinking that Steers had deliberately kept the lines of command vague between his mother and herself and him.

And if I have to speculate, it was to prove my loyalty to her and also get her mother to prove her dominance. And to do that, she has to confide in me to a certain extent. And then Steers will expect me to report back to her. Which means I'm spying on her mother for her.

This was getting beyond his capability to process.

As soon as he walked into the guesthouse Nash received a reply from Reed Morris.

THE COMPANY IN QUESTION IS SUSPECTED OF BEING PART OF A CHINESE ESPIONAGE RING BUT NO HARD PROOF.

So it seems that Masuyo has gone rogue again.

CHAPTER 62

"I WOULD LIKE, DILLON-SAN, TO GO on a picnic," said Steers the next day, as he came to her office for the day's instructions.

"When and where?"

"Today and at the land that I own nearby. There is a stream nearby. I like the sound. And I can visit Hiroko-san."

"Okay. I'll have the kitchen make up a basket and Thura can drive you out. I can tell him to wait by the car so you can visit Hiroko-san in privacy."

"There is no need for that. And have the kitchen make up a meal for two."

"Who else will be going? Certainly not your mother?"

"No. *You* will drive me. We will have our picnic together."

A little taken aback, he said, "Okay."

Nash got things arranged, then he drove them out to the property. They walked to a clearing a few hundred yards from the spot where they had buried Hiroko. They spread out the blanket, and Steers and Nash got out the food and other picnic items. Nash was in his customary suit with his guns, while Steers, instead of her usual black, wore white capri pants and a long-sleeved aquamarine sweater, and sandals; her hair was in a ponytail that she wore a ball cap over. He had never seen her so casually dressed before.

She poured out iced teas while he plated the food. It was a nice afternoon with a cooling breeze and just enough sun. He slipped off his jacket and carefully laid his Glock and Beretta next to him on the blanket. She watched this all with amusement.

He caught this and said, "Did I do something funny?"

"No, but I was just thinking of Glocks on a picnic."

"Don't forget the Beretta."

They ate, and as the sounds of the nearby stream reached them Nash watched as Steers closed her eyes and seemed to sway with the delicate sounds of the water.

"A mental health day?" he said when she opened her eyes.

She took a deep breath. "Sometimes meditation is not enough. The body and mind require something...more."

"Well, not to bring more distress to your day, but I took the liberty of asking your mother about Hiroko-san and her disappearance when we went out yesterday."

Steers bit off a piece of chicken. "And?"

"And she told me she does not answer questions from staff. But she said if she was gone it was a good thing. She also has demanded that I find out and report back to her about the man who was here and who you said is buying your business, and what the details are. If I don't, she said, I'm fired. She gave me a day or two to get back to her."

Steers drank some tea, wiped her mouth, and sat back on her haunches. "And what do you plan to do?"

"I plan to do what you tell me to do."

"You drove her into town yesterday?"

"Yes, I did. She had a place to visit. It was afterward, when she wanted to stop for a drink, that she asked me about the man who visited you."

"Do you know the place that she visited?"

Nash sat back, surprised by this question.

Steers looked at him in a knowing way. "You are a very curious person, Dillon-san. You would not wait in the car. You would find out where she went." She paused. "Out of This World LLC?"

"You know about it, then?"

"It is actually quite simple. She suspects I am planning to sell my business, and she does not wish me to. Especially not to the man who had imprisoned her for all that time. Thus she is doing her own due diligence and perhaps plotting against such a transaction."

"And what do you think about that?" he asked.

She removed her hat and undid the ponytail so that her hair fell free and rippled across her shoulders in the breeze.

"Would you believe me if I told you I do not know what I think about it?"

"I would," he said. "Because I don't, either. And though you said it was simple, for people like your mother I would imagine that it's difficult to understand their agendas and motivations."

"And allegiances," she added.

"Allegiances?"

"They are important, are they not?"

"Yes. So, does your mother want to take over the empire?"

"That seems reasonable and logical, does it not?"

"Which might be why she wants me to report to her about it."

"She will also know that you found out what business she was visiting, and that you would report that back to me. So my mother's real goal in going there with you was to use you to let me know that she is taking steps."

Out of his depth, Nash said, "So what do I do?"

"You can tell her that I have decided to sell. And that the price is acceptable to me."

Since Nash knew the price was one dollar he said, "But you remarked that you made it perhaps too appealing to the buyer? Has he come back to you yet with an answer?"

"No, but he will. Right now he is fervently trying to figure out why I am selling to him at far below market value. At our next meeting I will explain to him that things are not always what they seem to be."

This remark made Nash think about Hiroko and her tale of the cows not actually being cows despite overwhelming evidence. But then again, Lynn Ryder *was* alive and kicking.

She added, "And I'm sure you too wonder why I am doing so."

"But you told me before that it was enough that *you* understood why."

"I did say that, yes. But I will tell you more if you tell me something first."

"What?"

"The *real* reason for Mr. Temple's visit?"

Nash sat back and sipped his tea to allow a bit of time to respond. He did not want to lie to Steers, but he also didn't want Temple to tell Steers his true identity, which he knew the man would do in a heartbeat if he thought it would help him.

"He feels as though his life is not headed in the right direction."

"He wants to leave his work with me, you mean?"

"I don't think he's made that a secret."

"And he wishes your help to do so?"

"He asked me for my advice."

"And you gave this advice?"

Now Nash began to feel the sweat forming under his arms as he sensed himself being outmaneuvered. "I...gave him the contact information for someone who could help him."

"Help him disappear, you mean?"

It was absolutely unnerving that the woman seemed capable of reading his mind. Nash was paralyzed and did not know what to say.

"You need not answer, Dillon-san," she said, clearly sensing his dilemma. "I am sure that whatever he was holding over you was worth your engaging in this favor for him." When he said nothing, she said, "We all have secrets, do we not?"

"I suppose we do, yes."

"You are still an enigma to me, but perhaps a bit less so now."

"Is that a good or bad thing?"

"I cannot tell you at present. It could be either or none, meaning it could not matter at all. Or it could matter for everything."

He said, "Was that a sufficient enough answer from me to get you to answer in return?"

"When you want something so badly, you can do one of two things. You can work very hard to get all that you desire along the way. Or you can do the same to get as little as possible in return."

"You opted for the latter? Hence the below market price?"

"We will need to see how it all plays out. But I will tell you this much in return for your candidness about Mr. Temple. Keep in mind that money is not the only thing one may receive in exchange. So a low price in one facet of an arrangement can actually bring a high price in another."

"Is that how you see it playing out?"

"If I knew the future, life would be without a care."

"But you *do* have cares."

"I have many things. And now let us go and visit Hiroko-san."

CHAPTER 63

Nash watched respectfully as Steers knelt in front of the rectangle of grass with the large stone in the center, closed her eyes, and said words he could not entirely make out. He thought he heard both Japanese and English, and perhaps a smattering of Mandarin.

She was there for nearly twenty minutes before rising and saying, "I will be back, Hiroko-san."

She and Nash gathered up the picnic elements, then carried them to the car.

On the drive home Nash said, "When do you expect to hear from the buyer?"

"He is a man who lives by his own timetable. There are only a very few people in the entire world who have any influence over him at all, and I am not one of them."

"And if he accepts, what then?"

"Then a new life for me commences, as it does for *him*."

"And your mother?"

"My mother will land on her feet, just like a cat. Indeed, it will be fascinating to see just how well on her feet she is able to land."

"And me and Thura?"

She looked at him. "No matter my new life, elements of my old one will follow me. I will need you if you are up to it and so desire."

"You mean I have a choice?"

"In some ways, significant ones, Dillon-san, you have always had a choice. But with that said, things will come to a head. And you will be truly free once more."

"And you?"

"We will see."

"If he completes the sale I assume the man will be no more danger to you."

"Oh, Dillon-san, do not make assumptions like that."

"Then you will need my services for the long haul."

"Perhaps. But perhaps not if things turn out the way I intend them to."

He didn't know what she meant by that. Or maybe Nash did know but was afraid to confront his own fears.

Then Shock's warning came back to him: This woman would kill him given the chance. He could afford her no quarter. If the opportunity arose, he should end her life because otherwise she would do the same to him. Yet there was a significant part of Nash's psyche that simply refused to accept this as true.

And if I'm wrong, it will cost me my life. And Maggie's death will never be avenged.

"May I ask you something, Dillon-san?" she said.

He broke from his thoughts and looked at her. "Yes, of course."

"The night you came to me back in Hong Kong, before you left for Myanmar. You said that I had a weakness, a flaw in my plan, with respect to you and Mr. Temple rescuing my mother. You would not reveal it before, and with good reason. What was it?"

"Can I be frank?"

"I hope you would be."

"I believed that you sent us there to take the blame for whatever happened with your mother. You were going to make the switch regardless, but you already had men in place who could free her. Now, you couldn't know those men would try to double-cross you," he added quickly, and dishonestly. "But we would be left behind, dead, to take the blame. Is that not so?"

"I must admit that that was my original plan. So the flaw?"

"That we would succeed in bringing back your mother

successfully, despite your intentions, which is exactly what we did. But I was counting on the fact that your normal business *instincts* would be overcome by...your gratitude, from our having saved your mother, and the respect a survivor such as yourself would have for other...survivors."

She nodded. "I see. Thank you, Dillon-san."

"And you said it was your *original* plan?"

"I...I would not have conceived such a plan had I known you then as well as I have come to know you now."

Nash nodded but thought, *But you really don't know me, not even now. I'm not sure I even know me anymore.*

When they got back to the estate, Steers went inside the main house while Nash parked the car, returned the picnic items to the kitchen, and checked in with Thura, who was still making rounds. When Nash later went to his room, his phone buzzed.

It was another email from Morris.

CONNOR LORD ON THE MOVE. PLANE ENROUTE TO THE US.

He understood how dangerous it was to send and receive messages this way. But since he was head of security, he had a little more comfort that no one would be watching him that closely. And Steers clearly trusted him. But then again, nothing was guaranteed. No, one thing would be.

She will kill me if she finds out who I really am, friendship and "Dillon-san" be damned.

He erased the message, then sat on his bed and took off his jacket.

Steers clearly had figured out Temple's plan to abscond. Whether she would allow him to do so or not he didn't know. It seemed to him that given her decision to abandon her business, Temple might be left free to go on with his life. But if Connor Lord learned of his involvement? Or maybe he already knew. Would Temple be locked in regardless?

And then he might reveal my true identity to his new boss just to gain favor. But I might be okay with that. Because if Steers is giving up, what does it matter if people find out who I really am?

His next thoughts turned to Judith. It had been a long time since he had seen his wife. And at least according to Agent Morris, Judith knew that Dillon Hope and Walter Nash were one and the same. That was a good thing for Nash because she would not worry about him. Or at least not think that he might be dead.

But Nash's feelings toward her had changed. His wife's long affair with Temple had destroyed something vital in their relationship, at least from Nash's perspective. And the fact that she had believed he could have abused his own daughter? He shook his head.

I can't say that I love her in the way I did before. And now it's pretty clear that she didn't love me in the way I believed she did.

This last thought came from the fact that she had been seeing Temple while Nash had been on the run. No doubt they were sleeping together. He hated her for that. But then having personally witnessed his wife's overwhelming grief at losing their daughter? He felt enormous empathy for Judith, too.

These competing thoughts were paralyzing for Nash.

And then he realized he had a similar dilemma with Steers.

This is an abyss I may never escape from.

He sat on the bed hovering between weeping and slamming his fist through the wall.

That was when he heard footsteps heading his way, fast.

He leapt up when Thura appeared in his doorway. The man looked shell-shocked.

Nash said, "What is it? What's wrong?"

Thura shook his head, pulled out his phone, and came forward.

"What is it, Thura?" Nash demanded.

Thura held up his phone, which had a picture of Masuyo on the screen. "I snapped this the other day when she wasn't looking."

"Why?"

"I told you my cousin was a guard at that prison for years. I sent the photo to him and asked him how much of a bitch Masuyo was when she was there. It was just for fun, man."

"And what did he say? That she was really bad?"

"No, man. Not that!"

"What then?" snapped an exasperated Nash.

"He said that Masuyo was never a prisoner there."

CHAPTER 64

It was a risk, but then again pretty much everything Nash had done for a long time had been risky.

He sat in the waiting area of the car repair facility where some warranty work was being done on one of Steers's vehicles. The space was empty except for the man sitting directly behind Nash and facing away from him. Both he and Nash were scrolling on their phones. The other man had on a cowboy hat and a jean jacket, and dirty corduroy pants with worn boots. His face held a few days' worth of beard. With all that and sunglasses on as well, he did not look anything remotely like FBI Special Agent Reed Morris.

"I'm taking a chapter from your book," said Morris softly. "Total transformation."

"The look suits you," replied Nash as he continued pretending to scroll on his phone, his face pointed down so no one could really see his mouth moving.

The only other person in the room was the man working the front desk of the shop, and he was on the phone arguing loudly with someone, apparently over a repair bill. A TV hung on the wall and was broadcasting a game show. The sounds helped cover Nash and Reed's conversation.

"Did you approach Elaine Fixx yet?" Nash asked.

"No, we thought with Steers's new CEO in place it would be too dangerous, and Fixx recently came out of a nasty divorce. We're really counting on you, Walter."

Nash proceeded to methodically fill the FBI agent in on all that had transpired since their last discussion and Nash's various emails.

"You think Masuyo is plotting out something with all this clandestine stuff?" said Reed.

"Apparently so."

"And Steers really is getting out of the business?" said Morris.

"Appears to be. But her partners won't be happy."

"We've been on Lord's trail ever since he came into the picture, but we've got no proof of any illegal dealings. To those in the know he's a reclusive billionaire genius who's started many businesses that have created great wealth for him and his partners."

"Steers said he's also wired in to the Middle East and Beijing."

"She's right. But that's not illegal. In fact, the Middle East guys are pretty popular now. And China is China. They're going to be in the thick of things regardless."

"And Russia?"

"Same answer. Just in a different way."

"One of Lord's businesses is running a prison in Myanmar."

"Right, the one that you and Rhett Temple rescued Masuyo from."

"Only now I found out that Masuyo was never at that prison."

"What?" exclaimed Morris in a voice loud enough for the front counter man to look up from his phone for a moment.

They both fell quiet and studied their phones until the man turned back to his call.

Nash explained what Thura had told him about his cousin who'd been a guard there.

"What the hell is that about?" whispered Morris. "Have you told Steers?"

"Not yet. I wanted to think about it for a bit first."

"So if Masuyo wasn't in the prison, where was she?"

"You said she was a loyal agent of China?"

"Yes. Dropped into Japan decades ago to disrupt that country's democracy before she turned to crime."

"Maybe her turning to crime was the plan all along," said Nash.

"Explain that."

"It's never made sense to me that someone like Masuyo, loyal to her country's ideology, would suddenly turn to building a criminal empire. What if she was placed into Japan to do just that? Marry a Westerner to throw off suspicion and then start building this global outfit that would end up benefiting Beijing?"

"To do what, exactly?" asked Morris.

"Exactly what she has been doing. Flooding the U.S. and other countries with drugs, crime, and violence. That by itself is more disruptive than anything she could have done as strictly an agent of the Chinese in Japan."

"And her family?"

"She had five kids. But only Victoria Steers is the child of the man she actually loved. The others were fathered by Joseph Steers."

"How did you come by that knowledge?"

Nash said, "Steers's nanny. That's why Victoria has always been her mother's favorite. And the nanny also believed that Masuyo actually killed her other children, but tricked Victoria into thinking she did it."

"Yeah, you mentioned that before. Do you really think this nanny was right?"

"She could be. Steers has compassion and empathy. Masuyo has none."

"But Steers had your daughter killed!"

"I've been trying to reconcile that," conceded Nash. He was now thinking of his wife and her inability to figure out why Maggie would have said those things about him.

I was innocent. Is Steers also somehow innocent? And do you want that to be true for personal reasons?

"So do you think Masuyo was back in China instead of at the prison?" said Morris.

"When I saw her in Myanmar she looked beaten down, dirty, thin. But that could all be staged. I *do* think she went back to China because her daughter was running the empire and doing it well. She also might have suspected that her enemies might try to kill her. And there *was* an attempt on the family's lives after Masuyo left."

"By taking down that plane, you mean?" said Morris.

"Yes. Her father died and Steers almost did, too."

"Why did Steers finally decide to break her mother out then?"

"I'm not sure about the timing."

"So, presumably Connor Lord had Masuyo brought back to the prison so she could—what?—be rescued by her daughter?"

"That has to be it. Which means they knew Steers was going to make an attempt. She had one inside person at the prison. He could have been working for Connor Lord, too."

"But why let Steers get her mother out, then, if they knew it was coming?"

"I think I have the answer to that. The Chinese might want Masuyo to return to power to get the fentanyl deaths back up. You alluded to it before, but now I'm convinced that their falling number was due in large part to Victoria swapping out fentanyl in the pill production for other, less fatal substances. The Chinese must be working with Lord to get Masuyo back in power to reverse that."

"So Masuyo was brought back onto the scene to take over the empire. But how does that mesh with Steers now selling her business to Lord?"

"I don't think the Chinese or Lord or even Masuyo saw that coming. Steers threw them a curveball, and Lord is one of the best chess players in the world. That must have done a number on his ego. I think she did it deliberately to throw them all off their stride. A bold chess move of her own. And, Reed, she didn't have to tinker with the pill production. She put herself in danger with that. That should count for something."

"All right," said Morris slowly, clearly not reading as much into this gesture as Nash obviously did. "I told you that Lord was on his way to the U.S. He's now on the West Coast."

"Which means we can expect another meeting with him at some point, I suppose," said Nash. "And whether he'll take over things for a buck."

"You think Steers knows the truth about her mother? That she may actually be working with Lord and the Chinese and against her?"

"When I tell her about the prison situation she will."

"But won't selling her business for a buck tell Lord that something is not on the up-and-up?"

"I think it's another curveball Steers has thrown. They have more firepower than she does, and she's trying to thread the needle."

"Think she's going to pull it off?"

"I wouldn't bet against the woman."

Morris didn't say anything for a few moments. "Even if she sells out we need to nail her, Walter, you know that, right? She's a criminal."

Nash didn't answer right away. "I understand the situation, Reed."

"I know you've been embedded with this woman for a long time. I've worked undercover before with some pretty bad people. And sometimes, things can get...confusing. And you saved the woman's life, and she feels like she owes you. And it seems like you've seen a different side of her," Morris added in an uncomfortable voice.

"I have not lost my objectivity, Reed."

"I'm just asking because our last call did not end well," Morris said cautiously.

Nash wanted to tell Morris that he was neither an agent nor an employee of the FBI. They might have fairly well-aligned interests, but that did not mean *perfectly* aligned. And sometimes things went sideways. But he did not tell the man that, because he had decided he was going to need the FBI. Maybe not entirely how they intended, but he was also not in a position to burn bridges. So like he had done in numerous business negotiations, he told the other party what he knew they wanted to hear.

"I have every intention of holding everyone accountable who should be."

CHAPTER 65

A MONTH LATER, STEERS'S JET CUT smoothly through the sky. On board the plane were the pilots, the flight attendant, Steers, and Nash. On Steers's orders Thura and the rest of the security team had remained at the estate.

Steers had told Nash that they were flying to LA. He had already assumed such a trip would take place after Agent Morris had told him that Connor Lord was now on the West Coast. But Nash, of course, had to play ignorant of that fact.

They had been served a meal and drinks, and the flight attendant had retreated to her jump seat in the cockpit with the pilots, leaving Steers and Nash alone. Steers fiddled with the sleeves of her blouse and then did the same with the scarf around her neck.

"Did you tell my mother that I am selling the business?"

"I did. And that the price was acceptable to you. And if she had other questions she should ask you. Has she?"

"She has no need to," Steers answered mysteriously. "As I am sure you deduced, I am to meet with my potential buyer on this trip." She sipped her tea and looked across the table at Nash with an unreadable expression. "His name is Connor Lord, just in case you are curious."

"Never heard of him. Who is he?"

"A formidable partner, a more formidable adversary. However, I have never actually been his partner, only his *subordinate*. Though I may very soon be his adversary."

"Should we have brought more men with us then?"

"That won't matter, Dillon-san. It is not nearly so simple. And the lion kills the hyena at his leisure."

"I actually see you more as a honey badger. And I believe that lions actually would prefer to take on a pack of hyenas than a single honey badger."

She self-consciously smiled at his quip, showing that it had pleased her.

"Do you think Lord was the one who tried to kill you back in Hong Kong?"

"Doubtful, or else I would be dead."

"So someone else then?"

"I have many enemies."

"Has Lord agreed to buy you out?" he asked.

"That is why we are going to see him. To receive his answer."

"You told me you lowballed it, but I still hope you're getting a lot of money," he said.

She looked at him curiously. "Why?"

"Well, for one, it's worth a lot of money. And, second, you might need the resources if he does becomes an adversary."

"Again, Dillon-san, it will not matter. He is too powerful, honey badger or not. I cannot create an alternate truth. I must accept reality."

"Then you're just ceding victory to him?" he asked.

She looked over his brawny physique. "What would you do when confronted with someone that you cannot defeat on your own?"

Thinking of Shock, Nash said immediately, "I'd find someone who could help me to beat my enemy."

She looked out the window. "I have been all over the world, many times. But if I had my wish I would never travel anywhere again."

"What would you do then?"

"I would have a little place where I could do my artwork and tend a small garden." She turned back to him. "When I was very young, Hiroko-san managed a garden at our home in the countryside in southern Kyoto. My mother did not care for such things, but my father grew up in a place called the Cotswolds in England, and his family had a large kitchen garden. He graciously allowed Hiroko-san to also have one. As a little girl I would work with Hiroko-san caring for the flowers and the herbs and the vegetables. I had my little spade and a bucket and a pair of blue gloves and 'Wellies' that my father bought for me. I would go there early in the morning and work until I was quite weary and sweaty. But I adored every minute. It was just me, Hiroko-san, and the earth. It was truly...glorious."

As Nash watched and listened to her he wondered how this seemingly soulful, thoughtful, and introverted person could have become what FBI Agent Reed Morris had first described to him as a global criminal who had no compunction about killing anyone. It was as though there were two vastly different people occupying her body and mind.

And which is the real one? Or is it both?

"You really cared for your father, didn't you?"

"He was...a good man. Who had different priorities in life from his wife. But then we both became..."

"Became what?" asked Nash.

"It is held deeply in the past and matters no longer." Steers looked away, seeming to realize that she had revealed too much.

He broke the silence. "After the sale of your business, will you go after that dream of tending to a kitchen garden and devoting more time to your artwork?"

She glanced at him. "If I get the chance, perhaps, yes. And what will you do, Dillon-san? Once this is all over."

Nash sat back and drew a shallow breath. He was confused and conflicted by everything.

No, just by her, really.

"I...I might travel a bit." He then blurted out, "And then I might come and see if you need help in your garden."

He had no idea where that had come from. His mission was to bring this woman to justice, not plant tomatoes with her.

She stared at him, her wide, deep eyes seeming to swell like a fruit ripening at fantastical speed.

She then looked away. "I trust you can do far better than *that*, Dillon-san."

"That may be your opinion. But I don't have to agree with it."

"Perhaps you should. You will find me dangerous company, I am sure."

"Well, you've always been dangerous company. That's right in my wheelhouse."

"Do not do this out of any sense of loyalty to me. I have not treated you well. As I told you before, I am not a good person. You have your life to lead. I suggest that you lead it."

"But before, you told me that you would need my loyalty, my ability to protect you."

"I did, yes. But I have rethought things, and I have decided that is too much to ask anyone to do."

"But what if Lord turns you down?"

She once more looked at him. Her eyes now seemed depthless. "My future does not depend on his answer, at least not solely. And regardless, I will be dangerous company."

As the plane flew along Nash finally worked up the courage to tell her. "Victoria-san, I have information about your mother."

In a distracted voice she said, "What sort of information?"

"Such that I do not understand, but that has been communicated to me by a credible source."

"What is it?"

"That your mother was never a prisoner in Myanmar. I believe that she was brought there solely so we could bring Masuyo to you. And since you told me that Connor Lord controlled the prison, that means he was part of this plan. That might impact your business with him." He paused. "I just found this out and thought you would like to know."

Nash didn't know what he expected her reaction to be. Steers had lost control only once in his presence, when she had been threatening to kill herself before Hiroko had intervened. So he didn't expect anything as extreme as that.

Steers closed her eyes and jerked her head sideways once and then twice, as she had done before, when she had been confronted with something extraordinarily difficult.

And then the woman rose without a word and retreated to her cabin for the rest of the flight.

CHAPTER 66

Upon landing at the Santa Monica Municipal Airport, Steers and Nash were met by a man holding up an iPad with her first name on it. They were led out to a black Chevy Tahoe, and the man loaded their bags into the rear cargo hold while a second man wanded them for weapons and listening devices. Nash's pistols were taken from him. He had started to protest, but Steers motioned for him not to.

They were the only passengers, but Nash noted that another large SUV fell in behind them on their way out of the small airport.

"Guess landing here made more sense than LAX," said Nash in a low tone that the two men in front could not hear.

"It's more private and we're heading northwest, toward Malibu," noted Steers. "Mr. Lord is not an urban sort of person. I have found that he treasures his privacy."

"I'm not sure *privacy* in this situation makes me feel better. Why not meet him in the middle of Dodger Stadium with lots of people around?"

She smiled and tapped his hand, as though in reassurance. "We will see what we will see."

"You have more confidence than I do," replied Nash worriedly.

"Sometimes that is all one has."

On the way they passed stark remnants of the 2025 fires, before the SUV turned in to a canyon in Malibu. Nash noted that the tail vehicle rode a precise two car lengths behind them.

They pulled through a set of gates and stopped in front of a large, three-story Mediterranean-style home with lush landscaping and a paved motor court.

"Does he own this place?" asked Nash after they had gotten out of the vehicle.

"I do not know," said Steers. "As I already told you, he does not publicize his wealth or assets."

"Smart guy. Only I'm betting you're smarter."

They were led through the front door and passed from one lovely room to the next until they exited out the rear of the home through a towering set of French doors into a beautifully landscaped rear yard. It held a lap pool, flagstone paving with grass growing in between, high-end outdoor furniture and umbrellas, a stone fire pit, and a table with three chairs set around it.

One chair was occupied by Connor Lord, wearing a white linen suit with a dark blue shirt and matching pocket square, loafers, and no socks. He slipped off a pair of sunglasses, folded the paper he was reading, placed it on the table, and stood. "Ms. Steers, welcome and thank you for making the journey to me."

When he glanced quizzically at Nash, Steers said, "It is fine, Mr. Lord. Mr. Hope has my complete confidence and he is fully aware of my *business*."

"Yes, your worthy hero that you told me about previously. Please sit. Coffee, tea, water after your trip?"

They requested coffees. An attendant promptly brought them out and scurried back inside. Nash could not see but could sense the presence of watchful eyes everywhere.

He looked over to see Lord gazing keenly at him.

"You must be commended for serving your employer so ably, Mr. Hope. When I heard of the attack in Hong Kong I was quite distressed."

"You have to be ready for anything, because one never knows," replied Nash.

Lord nodded. "One indeed *never* knows." He turned to Steers.

"I apologize for the delay. Your offer, I must admit, confounded me. So enticing a business prospect, and yet so unusual the stated price."

"No, it is I who must apologize, Mr. Lord. I should have been more straightforward. You see, I require no more money in my life. My needs are amply taken care of and I have no one to leave my wealth to."

"Nevertheless, the allure of fair market value has its obvious attractions, on many levels. Your generous spirit is evident. Thus, you could, for instance, demand a fair purchase price and then donate the proceeds to charity. That would amount to many billions. You would become, in one fell swoop, one of the greatest benefactors of humanity of all time."

"I will allow you to do so, if you see fit," she replied so immediately that Nash suspected she had anticipated this strategy by her opponent.

And then he realized what he was witnessing:

A real-life chess match between two grand masters.

And as good a businessman as Nash had been, he had to admit that he was out of his league now. He simply sat and watched.

"You would give me the credit?" said Lord. "How touching but, if I may speak frankly, it goes a bit against the bounds of human nature, does it not? Which compels one, again, to seek other rationalization for such an odd purchase price *and* likewise attendant behavior."

"Then I will freely give you the rationalization of *both*."

She pulled back the sleeve of one arm of her blouse and then the other, revealing the mass of damaged skin on each limb.

Nash shot Lord a glance to see the man's reaction. Though Lord was mostly stone-faced, Nash caught just a glimmer of revulsion, perhaps even of horror. But not pity, or empathy.

Steers said, "Two attempts have been made on my life, at least serious ones that almost succeeded. My plane was blown out of the sky, killing my father and leaving me like this. Which is why I told you I have literally walked through fire." She then lifted the scarf from around her neck. "And this was the second attempt," she said, pointing to the scar on her skin. "But for Mr. Hope's intervention, I would not be alive to have any business to sell."

"Those events must have been terrible to endure," Lord said, again without a trace of sympathy.

"They *were* terrible to endure. And they also provided great impetus to find another direction in life. For in my case the third time may not be the charm, but the end of me."

"But the connection to the price and what you could do with the—"

She did not allow him to finish. "But you *must* concede that I clearly lack the outward legitimacy that you enjoy, Mr. Lord, as a friend and advisor to many of the wealthiest people in the world, as well as an able partner to rulers and political leaders in myriad countries. Your public persona has been expertly crafted, and you are held in esteem by many. So were *you* to make such an enormous donation to worthy causes as you suggested I do, the media would rejoice and hail you as a magnanimous benefactor. I, on the other hand, as a suspected criminal agent who should be behind bars and would be but for lack of sufficient evidence, would be publicly eviscerated. My money would be deemed blood money and thus unacceptable. It would also lead to even more enemies on both sides of the equation that I do not need at this stage in my life. As to the lowered purchase price, it is true that *I* requested only one dollar, but that is *my* compensation, as I was clear with you about. The second part of the negotiation, which is the reason I came here today, will be for you to take part of what would be the fair market value of the business and give it to my partners as compensation for what they will no doubt see as my abandoning them."

Lord looked impressed. "Thus forestalling still more enemies?"

"The rationalization now leaps from the mind, does it not?" she said smoothly.

"So it only falls to what percentage would go to them?"

"I will allow you to make an offer on that. And that is also why I agreed to journey here today. I felt, in all fairness to you, that such terms should be discussed through a face-to-face meeting."

"Perhaps you will help me put together a thoughtful and mutually beneficial offer?"

"Which will forestall future enemies for yourself?" she noted. "Quite strategic of you."

"We will agree to agree on that point."

"I have a good working knowledge of their assets, cash flow, ROI, and funding needs, as well as intangibles that go along with any partnership, namely those of an emotional context," she said. "Before I offered to sell it to you, I had an appraisal done of my business. The total value was ten billion dollars." She looked at him. "Have you another opinion of its value? After all these years of working together, you clearly know as much about my business as I do."

"I would have no qualms over such a valuation. Indeed, some would consider that a bargain."

"I'm glad that we can agree on that. Now, seventy-six percent of a ten-billion-dollar purchase price would more than suffice as payment to my partners. However, if you wish to negotiate further I am ready, willing, and able to do so. I would only add that upon your purchase of the business these men will then become *your* partners. Their organizations carry the laboring oar on the operations that you will be acquiring. I have worked with them for many years. They are good men, but *tough* men. If you treat them right, they will do their job well without complaint and without the requiring of much oversight. But if they ever feel they have been betrayed or abused?" She held out her ruined arms. "Then the price I have asked for them will seem to you very cheap indeed versus the cost of the disruption to the business that they can engineer if they feel wronged."

"Seven point six billion then for the business?"

"Yes."

"Quite an attractive offer, although considerably more than one dollar," said Lord.

"As I said, I have no need of more money. All I wish to do is make sure my partners are taken care of. Then I can *safely* step aside. I have no desire to haggle over every penny."

Lord sat back, glanced at Nash, and then looked out over the mountainous terrain visible over the rear wall. "Thus, you are still giving me a substantial bargain."

"I am well aware of that. To the tune of two point four billion dollars."

"And the question remains: Why so generous?"

"At this stage of my life, I have other priorities."

"Such as?" asked Lord.

"Living as long as possible. And pursuing my garden and my artwork. I have spent most of my life doing neither. And frankly, I am tired. And having been nearly killed twice does give one pause, as I have expressed to you before. But as to the extra value given to you, I would also add that just as I seek to compensate my partners to the south with a generous payout to avoid…unpleasantness, I also seek to do the same with you."

"Forestalling blowback from all quarters, as it were?" said Lord. "Including, perhaps, from me for you taking your mother from my possession?"

"We can agree on that, yes. And a severed head does make an impression."

Lord smiled but then his expression grew serious. "I must admit that you make a very compelling case, Ms. Steers."

"The truth is often the source of fuel for enduring fires."

Lord shot her a patronizing look and said, "Please don't take this the wrong way, but that sounds like something off a fucking Chinese fortune cookie."

"That is exactly where I acquired it," she replied without missing a beat.

Nash couldn't help but laugh, as did Lord. However, Steers's expression did not change.

"But fortune cookie or not," said Steers, "the wisdom of the thing remains because in the end, no matter the hyperbole, or lies, or disinformation, the truth will win out because the truth is reflected in the lives of the individuals and how they each perceive the world. So at the end of the day you cannot convince a starving man that he is rich, or a dying woman that she will live. Thus, those who begin and end with the truth are far more likely to succeed."

"What will you do if the sale is consummated?" said Lord. "Besides your garden and artwork?" he added, with a bit of a sneer, noted Nash.

"I also have my mother to take care of."

"Of course, of course."

"Unless you will have need of her?"

With those seven words, Nash sensed that all the oxygen around them had not only been removed, but something harmful had replaced it.

He looked at Steers, who was focused on Lord. When he glanced at Lord, *his* eyes had narrowed and he sat up straighter in his seat. Nash also sensed the security team, perhaps playing off their employer's visceral reaction, move in closer from their hidden nooks and crannies.

Why the hell are you revealing that you know the two were working together to betray you? thought Nash.

Nash inched his hand toward his holster and then realized it was empty.

This is it and we don't have a chance. For the love of God, Victoria-san.

"I'm afraid I don't understand your query, Ms. Steers," said Lord in a tone that was about as ominous as any Nash had ever heard.

Steers, in a calm, almost placid voice, said, "You see, that was the other reason why I decided to sell you the business at such an *interesting* price point. My mother built the empire that I now oversee. And I wanted something for my mother to do because she is an indomitable person to whom a life of leisure is anathema. And it was clear from her words to me that she did not like the way I was running things. Not enough Americans are dying from the drugs I sell. Your partners in Beijing are not pleased, either. My mother, I can assure you, will have no compunction whatsoever about getting those deaths back up to the requisite levels. Although I will warn you that from experiences with my partners to the south, they will not be pleased to see their paying customers once again dying by the hundreds of thousands each year. That was what prompted me to pull back. But you, of course, may see it differently. I explained this to my mother, and she agreed that it was a unique challenge. Thus it may be a challenge you may choose to confront *together*."

All the tension seemed to release from Lord, and Nash could feel his pulse return to normal, the sweat under his armpits chilled, his fight-or-flight impulses faded, and he could breathe normally.

She just put him in check. But can she finish it?

Lord, for his part, eased back in his chair and assumed, at least to Nash, the manner of a snake that had just been about to strike but no longer needed to.

"Your wisdom, candidness, and competent advice reflect well on you, Ms. Steers. And having done my due diligence since last we spoke, I know that everything you just said is true. And in answer to your query, yes, I believe that I *can* use your mother in my operations. This may seem strange to you after where she was for all those years, and the role I played therewith."

Steers replied, "I have experienced enough in my life to find absolutely nothing strange anymore, Mr. Lord. I accept that *anything* can happen, and I find that my outlook is often proven correct. I will convey your wishes to my mother. She will be most pleased."

Lord nodded. "I am sure that her desire to return to the business will overshadow any difficult feelings accumulated during her, um, retention at my facility."

"I'm glad you said that, because in addition to the payment to my partners, it would, I think, be very advantageous for you to reward my mother as she assists in running the business."

"I think you are quite right about that."

"Does this mean that we have a deal?" asked Steers.

"If your partners will accept seventy percent as opposed to seventy-six percent, then, yes, we have a deal. And just so you know, the additional six percent will be going as compensation to your dear mother, partly to make up for her years of imprisonment."

"She will be doubly happy with your respect for her as a person, and for her abilities."

Checkmate, thought Nash as he marveled at the skillful maneuvering of the woman.

Lord said, "I told you before that you would be staying overnight with me. Dinner will be served at seven. Does that work for you?"

"We look forward to your hospitality and company," replied Steers. "And I very much look forward to closing this chapter of my life."

CHAPTER 67

The dinner was lavish and served professionally by the staff. Nash did not drink any alcohol because he wanted his wits about him. He watched Steers closely and saw that she ate little and drank only water.

After dinner Nash had been in his quarters for only a few minutes when a knock came on his door. It was Steers.

She held up her phone. On the screen Nash read: **Outside. Now.**

With two of Lord's men trailing behind them, Nash and Steers, using the flashlight features on their phones, went for a walk down the darkened canyon road.

"The house had audio and video surveillance throughout," noted Steers. "Including the bedrooms. I'm going to sleep in my clothes."

"You really outmaneuvered Lord, but tell me something. What's to stop him from killing you and taking over your business without paying anyone a dime? Despite what you said before, he might have been behind the attempt on your life in Hong Kong."

"No, he wasn't, Dillon-san."

"How can you be so sure?"

"Because it was my mother who attempted to kill me in Hong Kong."

Nash abruptly stopped and stared at her.

Steers, who had kept walking, said softly, "Continue strolling, Dillon-san, we have watchful eyes upon us."

Nash caught up to her. "Your mother?"

"She sees me as soft and not up to the business that must be conducted. I also saw her with Hao on several occasions, no doubt convincing him to do what he did. But it was impetuous, reckless on her part."

"My God, I knew the woman was ruthless. But—"

"It wasn't the first time. She also planted the bomb on my plane."

"What!" exclaimed a stunned Nash.

"*That* truth only occurred to me recently. I long thought it was other enemies of mine. I was wrong about that. It was her."

"But why?"

"My mother's loyalties lie elsewhere. Not even her own flesh and blood takes priority over that."

Nash was still confused. "But why a bomb on the plane? If your mother was allegedly already in prison that meant you were running the company by then, and it seemed that the Chinese were pleased with the job you were doing."

"But you do not know one critical point: *I* was not supposed to be on that plane, Dillon-san. Only my *father* was."

"So she wanted to only kill him then? And not you? But why?"

"My father loathed the family business. And I had succeeded my mother as the head of that business. Under the cover of this prison subterfuge, I'm sure she returned to China to do other work for her masters there. But she kept a close eye on things. And I know without doubt that she knew but did not like how devoted I still was to my father. I'm sure that she believed he would influence me in bad ways, much as she thought Hiroko-san did."

Nash, who had been told by Hiroko that Joseph Steers had not actually been Steers's biological father, said nothing. Whether she knew this fact as well, he didn't know. But Joseph Steers had clearly been, in all important respects, her father.

"Hiroko told me something similar, actually. About your mother fearing your father's influence on you."

"I think my mother began to think that with her out of the picture I would succumb to more and more influence by him. I only changed my travel plans at the very last minute, and Hiroko-san and I boarded that plane. I still remember the explosion, the sudden dive of the jet, the flash of light, the screams. And when we struck the ground, it was...I cannot describe it, really." She looked down at her arms. "I was on fire. The...pain. And I...I watched my father die."

"I can't imagine how horrible that must have been," said Nash emotionally.

"If Hiroko-san, an elderly woman by then, had not pulled me out of the wreckage and obtained help, I would have assuredly perished as well."

"If you both had been killed, then what would have happened to the business?"

"My mother would have simply stepped back in to run it," replied Steers. "She would not have shed a single tear." She looked off for a moment. "I thought by rescuing her that she would...change toward me. That we could finally have a...relationship. But I was a fool. She does not love me. She does not even care about me. I must thank you, Dillon-san, for telling me of her deception in Myanmar. Quite frankly, my mother's imprisonment had never made much sense to me. And no one had explained any of it to me. She was there, and then she was gone. I was only notified of it later. And why would she be taken and sent there of all places? My father did not understand, either. And then the successful attempt on my father's life so soon after? When considered in all its aspects, and after realizing she was never a prisoner, things readily began to make sense to me. It was my mother still controlling things even though she was no longer with us."

"But why a prison?" asked Nash. "Why not just have her return to China?"

"Because it gave them maximum leverage over me, knowing that I would do whatever they told me to in order to keep my mother safe. It was quite brilliant in its conception and execution. And it worked, Dillon-san. But now I have turned that influence against them by selling my business to Lord."

Nash remembered that he had thought something similar, before he knew that Masuyo had not actually been a prisoner in Myanmar.

"Back to my original question: What stops Lord from killing you?"

"I have many legitimate businesses and properties. Their sale must be done in an aboveboard and orderly fashion or else none of my assets and operations will legally convey. And a man with Lord's stellar reputation will do everything in his power to shield his connection to the business in which I am engaged. He is a private man, but he also loves the idolatry shown to him by his wealthy and powerful peers. He has been China's intermediary with me all this time, but to the rest of the world he is legitimate and well respected. That would all collapse if he were tainted in any way by a connection to someone like me.

"This will all take time for the lawyers to complete and the necessary documents to be signed. It is far more complicated than a typical business transaction, because of the additional layers of complexity necessary with the sale of an illicit, underlying company. And my partners to the south also must be appeased. Beijing and Lord know this. To not do so will invite a war that Beijing does not want. That is why Lord so readily agreed to my terms. His hands are tied on this. Otherwise, I would never have come here."

"Why did you mention his possibly being in need of your mother?"

"To absolutely confirm my suspicions about Lord and my mother working together all these years. His reaction provided me the necessary answer."

"And what is this prison he runs? Do you know what it's actually for?"

"I have learned that it is a place where people who have fallen out of favor with those in power in their respective countries disappear to. For the Russians, the Middle East princes, strongmen in Africa, even enemies of the cartels. Indeed, as I said, I had come to believe that my mother had been taken so that Beijing could maintain control over me, as her successor. Now I know that was all a lie."

"But why not just kill them, rather than imprison them?"

"Oh, Dillon-san, a quick and easy death compared to decades in a place like that? Which do you think is the greater punishment?"

"I see your point."

"And this way, if there is international scrutiny, which there sometimes is, the parties can honestly say that they do not have possession of these people. 'Come and check our prisons. See, they are not here.' From a moral perspective it is abominable. From a business angle, it is brilliant, and Lord is paid enormous sums to keep those people there."

"So I guess you'll soon be able to start a new chapter of your life."

Steers stopped and turned to him. "This is only the first step. A critical one, but still only the first."

A startled Nash asked, "Then what comes next?"

"For that, we shall both have to see."

CHAPTER 68

STEERS AND NASH FLEW BACK home the next day. After they arrived at the estate Steers went directly to speak with her mother.

"I do not like you galivanting off without a word to me, Daughter," said Masuyo irritably. "It shows disrespect to me."

"I believe you already know where I went and for what purpose."

"How could I possibly?"

"Because you are my mother and you know all," replied Steers evenly.

Masuyo studied her daughter for a moment. "And what has come of all this *activity*?"

"The sale has been agreed to and the legal documents are in the process of being completed. The official closing of the transaction will take place in a matter of weeks. And, with Mr. Lord in full agreement, you will once more be running the empire that you created, with Mr. Lord as, hopefully, your silent partner."

"I do not care for others negotiating on my behalf. I would much prefer to do it myself."

"Well, as the result of *my* negotiations, you will receive six hundred million dollars, to start. And I trust that you have kept some of your previous fortune and not given it all back to your masters in Beijing. It was quite a large sum, and they hardly deserved all of it."

This earned Steers a hard, vicious slap to the face from her mother.

"The mouth you have acquired, Victoria. It shames me that you speak to your mother in such a way."

Steers didn't touch the growing red spot on her cheek. She simply stared at the woman until Masuyo broke off eye contact and rubbed her wrinkled hand.

Steers continued on as though nothing had happened. "The deal also includes substantial sums for my partners. That will appease them when they learn I have stepped away. I came up with a new proposal for running things that I presented to them and which they subsequently approved. I would encourage you and Mr. Lord to go over it, and then implement it if you agree with the protocols I developed. It will save you large amounts of money and make the operation far more productive and efficient, and also safer from prying eyes."

"We will of course look at anything that promises to do such things," said her mother. "Regardless of the *source*," she added spitefully.

"And I trust you have ingenious plans to facilitate more drug deaths in America."

"It was not just your eliminating fentanyl and other lethal opioids from the precursors, Daughter. It is this Narcan. It has saved many lives and we will have to somehow deal with that. Perhaps pay off the manufacturer or take over the company, or line the pockets of politicians willing to impede its availability and distribution. There is always a way forward with Westerners. All they care about is money, especially the Americans."

"I take it you have no issue working with Mr. Lord?"

"I am aware that he has the full confidence of Beijing. I do not need to know more than that. I have *never* lost sight of my duty or where my loyalties lie. I wish others could say the same," she added bitterly, giving her daughter a piercing stare.

Steers said, "He has the full confidence of a great many people. But it makes one wonder which direction he will go when a conflict occurs. Because a man can have too many masters, can't he?"

"You can now let me worry about that, Daughter. Unlike you, I expect Mr. Lord to listen to what I have to say."

"I hope your expectations pan out. But one never knows."

"And what will you do now that you have stepped away from all that I have given you, worked my fingers to the bone for, shed blood for?"

"You shed no blood, Mother. It was *I* who shed the blood. And it was my father who shed the most, before he died."

"I speak symbolically, of course. As to your father, his fate was largely up to his own ineptitude. A bomb on a plane? The very height of incompetence," she added in disgust.

"I wonder how you know that it was a *bomb* that brought the plane down? Nothing about it was ever reported. And you were in prison at the time. And I never said a word."

Masuyo said smoothly, "What else can bring down a plane in such a way? And now I must turn my attention to the *business*."

"Come now, Māma. Take some time to rejoice. This is what you have been dreaming about ever since gaining your freedom. Well, I have now realized your dream for you. I do not require thanks, only seeing my mother do something she was created for. And your masters will surely enshrine you in some hall of pride when you are dead and buried."

Masuyo barked, "You make flippant remarks over such an important matter? You think this will be an easy task? I am no longer a young woman. I have been through much hardship. I have lost my husband and all of my children save you. And you are now clearly a complete disappointment to me."

"Not a complete one, Mother. I vanquished my siblings, as you desired me to do. As you forced me to do."

"How dare you say that I had anything to do with their deaths? That was you, Daughter. Only you. I do not care what that idiot of a woman might have told you."

However, now Masuyo did not look as confident. Indeed, she gazed at her daughter with something akin to...fear.

Steers stared back for a moment of intimidating quiet. "Hiroko-san never once lied to me. Never once. There are *very* few I can say that about. So what she told me, I believe. All of it."

Masuyo regained her imperious look. "And where is she now? Tell me that. She has abandoned you. She was probably fearful when I returned. Fearful that I would once more talk sense into you, ridding you of her inane influence. For all I know she killed herself." Masuyo tried to appear triumphant but the look of unease was still in her eyes. "She is gone, Victoria. Your old nanny is finally gone. And it is for the best, trust me."

"You are wrong, Mother. Hiroko-san is right here with me." Steers touched her chest. "She will always be with me, right up until the moment I draw my last breath." Steers bowed and said, "I wish you to receive all that is coming to you, Māma."

"I trust you will now be going off with that...man."

"What man?"

"You know perfectly well that I am referring to Dillon Hope. I have seen how you look at him. A Westerner. Are you mad!"

"Forgive me, Māma, but you married an Englishman."

"I married him to further the cause of my *mission*. I never loved the man. Never. This may be hard for you to hear, but it is the truth and it's high time you heard it. But I have also seen how Dillon Hope looks at you. He is smitten, Victoria. If you do not see that you are blind."

"And you do not want men to be attracted to me?"

"I want the right kind of man to be attracted to you."

"He saved my life."

"After perhaps endangering it."

"The plot to kill me in Hong Kong is resolved, Māma."

"Meaning what!"

"Meaning I know who was behind it."

The two women once more paused their conversation to gaze at one another.

"And what will you do with that information?" asked Masuyo quietly.

"As I said, it has been resolved."

"You worry me, Victoria. You are acting erratically. That will not serve you well in the days ahead."

"We will have to see about that, won't we?"

"Do you plan to go off with this man Hope?"

"What if I do?" said Steers.

"Then you need to know something about him."

"I know all I need to know."

Masuyo gazed at her maliciously, clearly sensing an advantage. "Do you really? Well, when he brought me back to Hong Kong, he knew my real name was Dai Lu. He read it off the sign the man was holding, in Mandarin no less. Did you tell him this, Victoria? Because if you did not, how could he possibly know that, Daughter?"

Steers stared at her mother for a long moment, and then, as she had done before in the face of information that surprised her, Steers closed her eyes and shook her head, as though trying to throw off the impact of the words. Then Steers turned and left the room without answering.

CHAPTER 69

"So that's it, man?" said Thura.

He and Nash were sitting in the kitchen of the guesthouse. Nash had filled him in on the sale of the business by Steers.

"Apparently so."

"So I have to leave this country?"

"No. Through Ms. Steers's contacts you obtained a work visa for the U.S. before we came here. You can next apply for a green card, which will grant you permanent residency. I'm sure she'll help you with that. Eventually, you can apply for citizenship."

"Without a job?"

"You got into this country with a specialty occupation visa. And you have plenty of money saved. That will also be in your favor. And I'll do all I can to help you get another job."

Thura smiled and patted Nash kindly on the arm. "Man, am I glad I ran into you over there. Changed my whole life."

"It didn't start out that way," said Nash. "You probably thought I was going to cost you your life."

"So what about you? What are you going to do?"

"Haven't really figured that out yet."

"And the nasty old woman?"

"She's going to be very busy helping to run the business with the man who owned that prison she was supposed to be in."

A confused Thura shook his head. "Them two working together now? That is some messed-up shit."

"Yes it is," agreed Nash.

"And she was never in that prison. Did you tell Ms. Steers?"

"I did."

"What'd she say to that?"

"Not much," replied Nash.

"So what's she going to do now that she sold out?"

Nash didn't answer right away because he didn't know what to say.

You're no longer objective about this, Nash. It's what Shock and Morris have been trying to tell you. You've let your personal feelings for the woman interfere with your judgment. But how can you just ignore what you've seen? Everything she's been through?

Nash pulled himself back from these uncomfortable musings to tell Thura, "I don't know. She keeps things very close to the vest."

"What would you do if you was her?" asked Thura.

"Get as far away from her mother as possible. After that, I don't know."

* * *

A few weeks later Nash spoke with Shock, who told Nash that he was at his training academy with Rhett Temple.

Nash filled him in on Steers selling her business and not really caring about Temple anymore.

"So I can cut him loose then?" said Shock.

"How's he doing up there?"

"Belly-achin' 'bout how tough it is. Just makes me kick his ass harder."

"If you can stand it, Shock, keep him up there for a few more months, charge him triple what you quoted, and continue to kick the shit out of him. And hopefully, before long, his next home will be a prison."

"Done. Tomorrow I think we'll see how many times we can make him puke."

Nash went out to his car, drove off, and called Agent Morris.

"The sale's been officially completed, and Connor Lord is now in control of the Steers crime empire, with Masuyo as second-in-command and I'm sure a vocal one."

"We'll have to let this play out now and build up a case against both of them."

"I won't have access to that," Nash said. "They didn't invite me to the party."

"We have other ways now that we know who and what to look for. Between you and me, Lord is an interesting piece of the puzzle. As I said before, he has connections to some heavy political hitters around the world. And now that he's taken over Steers's business, we could bring down a whole ton of bad actors in high places that we used to think were untouchable."

"Well, you have the names of her former partners. And Steers told me that Middle Eastern sheiks and princes also use that prison to hide enemies. And I'm sure some or all of them are in bed with other criminal elements. I mean, the oil and gas won't last forever."

"So what will you do now?" asked Morris.

"For now, hang close to Steers. There's more there for me to learn."

"Just so you know, we're pulling the trigger fairly soon, Walter. DOJ figures they're building an ironclad case against the woman. She'll go away for life, or maybe she'll even get the death penalty. You did find that stuff belonging to your daughter. You testify to that, she's cooked."

Nash felt like the man had plunged a knife into his chest. "Wait, testify?"

"Yes. You're going to be the lead government witness in the case against Steers."

"I didn't agree to do that," Nash said heatedly.

"I'm sorry, but I just assumed you would know that would be required. Physical evidence is important, but we'll need your testimony to really nail her."

"Again, I never agreed to testify against her."

"But if you don't, all of this is pretty much for naught."

"I don't work for you, okay? I work for myself. I thought I made that clear."

"I don't think you grasp the situation. And we paid you a lot of money, in case you've forgotten," Morris added aggressively.

"I think I grasp the situation a lot better than you do. And don't throw the money in my face. I lost my daughter because of your screw-up."

"Look, I'm sorry. I...I didn't mean that. And I know you're under tremendous pressure, but you need to listen to reason."

"No, Reed, you just need to let me do this my way."

Nash ended the call, pulled off the road, and sat there, his heart hammering into his ears.

A minute later his phone buzzed. He thought it might be Morris calling back, but it was Steers. She needed to go somewhere and wanted him to take her. He had not spoken with her very much since they had returned. And when he had, the woman had seemed cold and distant. He wondered if it had to do with her suddenly realizing that with the sale of her empire the woman's life was going to change, perhaps drastically.

Or is it something else?

CHAPTER 70

Steers said nothing to him as she got into the rear seat of the car.

"Where to?" asked Nash.

"Just drive," replied Steers.

He pulled through the gates and onto the road.

"Left," she said.

He glanced in the mirror at his boss. She had reflective sunglasses on so he could not see what she was looking at.

"How did things go with your mother?" asked Nash. "I presume you've talked to her by now, since several weeks have passed since our visit with Connor Lord, but you never said."

"As expected, except for one thing."

"What was that?"

"Dai Lu?"

To his credit, Nash managed to keep driving straight down the road. "Excuse me?"

"It is my mother's real Chinese name, but you knew that, Dillon-san."

When he looked in the mirror she was holding a gun pointed at the back of his head.

"Drive me to where Hiroko-san lies."

He turned right at the next road, and a few miles later he pulled to a stop at the lonely patch of land where Hiroko was buried nearby.

They got out of the car.

Steers said, "You will remove *both* of your guns and place them on the front seat."

"I can explain this."

"You will do what I asked you to do, Mr. Hope, or whatever your real name is."

He noted that her voice trembled, but he saw that the hand holding the gun on him was rock steady.

He took out his pistols and laid them on the seat.

"We will now go into the woods," she said.

"Why not just shoot me here?" he said.

"We will go into the woods and *discuss* this," she replied. "You have earned that right. Otherwise, I *would* simply shoot you."

She followed him down a path toward Hiroko's grave.

When they reached it Steers said, "This is fine. You may turn around and face me."

Nash turned and looked at her. She took off her sunglasses and he now saw the tears sliding down her cheeks.

"I suppose your mother told you that because she was so worried about your safety?" he said in a mocking tone.

Steers just stared at him, the muzzle of the gun pointed directly at his chest.

"Or maybe she wanted to throw a secret she knew into your face, to cause you pain one last time? Which version would you vote for, Victoria-san? The former or the latter?"

"You still call me *Victoria-san* even though you have betrayed the trust that we had? That I thought I had with you? From day one you have been planted in my life to spy on me. To take me down, is that not correct, Mr. Hope? I suspected you had an ulterior motive very early on, but then things seemed to change and, as you know, I became far more comfortable with you, more trusting. But now I know that my first reaction was the correct one."

"If it were that simple, I would have let them kill you back in Hong Kong. I wouldn't have taken you to the hospital. I would have just let you bleed out in the car."

She flinched and bit at her lip and her eyes briefly closed before snapping back open. "Then you will tell me right now why you did not let that happen."

He sat down next to Hiroko's grave, picked up a twig, and twirled it between his fingers, then looked up at her. "I have every reason in the world to hate you more than anyone else on earth. More than your mother even."

"I did not even know you before, so how can this be?"

"It's true, we'd never met. But you stole, brutally and violently, the most cherished thing I had in my life."

"How could I have done any of this? You are not making—"

She stopped, and her features appeared to be frozen in place. It was not the look of mere surprise, but profound shock.

"You are…"

He stood and looked down at her. And her gun, which was still pointed at his chest.

Nash touched, in turn, each of the tattooed links of chain on his head.

"Me. My wife, Judith. And my daughter, Maggie. Now deceased. At your hands."

"You are… Walter… Nash?" Steers said breathlessly.

"I am… Walter Nash," he said, and after all this time it felt like he had just released an enormous burden from his soul.

She slowly lowered her gun until its muzzle pointed straight down. Then she let it fall to the ground.

"I thought you were going to shoot me, Ms. Steers."

"I am trying to understand you, Mr. *Nash*."

"That shouldn't be too difficult after what I just revealed."

"But back in Hong Kong you let me live, when you had every reason to want me to die. It makes no sense."

Nash looked down at the stone that lay on Hiroko's grave. "You're right. It doesn't make sense… because I can't make sense of it." He glanced at her. "After spending all this time with you? Well, I suppose my perception of you became… complicated. But I do hate you. For what you did to me. To my wife. And most especially to my daughter. For that I want you to be punished. Severely."

Steers shook her head, again, as though trying to fling off the imprint of this stunning exchange. But when she grew still Nash watched as fresh tears slid down her cheeks. When she spoke, her voice was tremulous. "I told you long ago that I am not a good person. That I have hurt a great many people for no reason other than money or my own self-protection. You should have let me kill myself," she added dully.

"It was Hiroko-san who would not let you take your own life. She cared for you. She loved you." He glanced down at the grave. "Until her dying breath she did. A person must be truly evil to not have one person to mourn their passing."

"But Hiroko-san cannot mourn my death now, Mr. Nash. She is gone."

He looked at her. "No, but *I* can."

In the gentle breeze that rippled through the woods the pair stared at each other over the width of the woman's grave.

"I have never been deceived by anyone as I have been deceived by you. And a great many have tried, including my own mother."

"It is not a role I wanted to play. But I didn't have a choice. You were the reason I did not have a choice."

"Me?" she said blankly.

"Yes. Do you really think I wanted to become"—he ran a hand over himself—"this?" he added fiercely.

She said slowly, "That must have taken much time, discipline, and... motivation. And I suppose *I* was the motivation."

"No, not you. It was this." He slipped out his wallet, extracted an item, and held up the picture. "*This* was my motivation."

Steers stared at the picture of Maggie Nash that he had taken from his wife's locket and retrieved from a secret hiding place when they had returned to the United States. "A truly beautiful young woman."

"Not anymore," replied Nash icily. "Not anymore. Thanks to you."

His phone buzzed. He took it out and looked at the screen. "It's Thura. May I answer?"

She nodded.

"Hello, Thura, I'm—"

"F-fuck, D...Dillon."

"Thura, what is it?" exclaimed Nash.

"T-they...sh-shot...ever-body. B-bad."

"What? Who, who shot everybody?" Nash glanced at Steers, who was looking panicked.

"M-men...all d-dea—"

"All dead! Thura? Thura! What's happened? Who's there?"

He heard a gunshot and then another voice came on the line and said, "You give us her, you get to live."

Nash ended the call, grabbed Steers's arm, and said, "We've got to go. Now!"

They fled back to the car.

CHAPTER 71

Steers climbed into the front passenger seat as Nash started the car, shifted it into gear, and punched the gas. A minute later they reached the main road and Nash gunned it.

"What happened? What did Thura say?" exclaimed Steers.

Nash eyed the rearview mirror. "He said men came in and shot everybody. Apparently they're all dead. I heard a gunshot while I was talking to Thura. I think he was killed by that shot. Then a man came on the line."

"A man? What did he say?

He eyed her and lied: "He said we're dead too." Then he looked up ahead. "We need to get rid of this car. They'll be able to track it. Do you have your phone with you?"

"No, I left it at the house. Did he say anything about my mother? Is she dead as well?"

"He didn't mention her. But she was there when we left the house."

Thirty minutes later Nash stopped the car in a parking lot. Just in case, he took the time to wipe all their fingerprints off the vehicle. Then they rushed over to a nearby rental car agency. Fifteen minutes later they sped off in a Nissan Rogue SUV.

Nash had already taken the SIM card out of his phone and crushed it. He next stopped at a store and bought a new card for his phone, then set it up using his backup identity. He also purchased a throwaway phone for Steers.

"Will they be able to track your renting this car?" asked Steers when he got back to the car. "Or the phone purchases?"

"No. I used a credit card with a duplicate identity that I set up a while ago. The same ID I used to set up my phone."

They drove off and Nash hopped on the interstate.

"Where are we going?"

"Right now, away from here. We can settle on a destination later."

As they drove along Steers stared out the windshield. He shot her glances from time to time and finally said, "You said you and Lord were good to go?"

"I believe I intimated that I was safe until the transaction officially closed. Now that it has... well, things have obviously changed. But we don't know for sure it was him behind this attack."

"Well, he's right at the top of my list."

She glanced at him. "We need to part company, Dil—Mr. Nash. Your chances of survival are much greater without me along."

"Do you have any other properties that they might not know about that we can go to for now until we regroup?"

"Why do you still desire to help me, after all that I have done to you? It would make more sense that you would simply shoot me."

"Look, just cut that shit out," barked Nash. "For now, we need each other to survive."

"I *do* have such a property. I have kept it as a safe house of last resort."

"Can we drive to it? Planes and trains are out."

"Yes, but it will be a long drive."

"Where is it?"

"In New Orleans."

"The Big Easy. Interesting choice," he commented.

"I like the weather. And it's private."

"Private is good, especially now."

They stopped at a department store and bought some clothes and other essentials, which Nash put on his backup credit card. He also stopped at a gun store and bought an extra pistol and a box of ammo for it, as well as additional ammo for the Glock and the

Beretta. Unfortunately, Steers had left her gun back at the gravesite when they'd fled. Then they headed south.

After three hours on the road they got off the interstate and had dinner at a pizza place in a strip mall. He had pasta and a beer, and Steers had a salad and water. They paid in cash.

As they walked out he said, "Not exactly high cuisine and amenities, I know."

"Food is food. It does not really matter to me."

Back on the road, they drove for another three hours. It was well past dark now, and Nash was weary.

"I would drive, Mr. Nash, but I never learned how and am not licensed."

"Just call me Walter, okay?"

"And you may call me Victoria if you wish."

They constantly checked for news on their phones of what might have happened at Steers's estate. Finally, when they had pulled into a rest stop, the story broke.

Nash quickly read through it.

"Okay, a delivery guy showed up and saw a body in a pool of blood. He called the cops." He looked up at Steers. "The live-in staff included Thura and four other security guards, the cook, two maids, your three attendants that came with us from Hong Kong, and a gardener."

"And my mother," pointed out Steers. "Do they not identify or quantify the number of bodies?"

"Not yet. And they make reference to the owner not being there, meaning you. There is no mention of me, but that probably won't last once they start looking into things."

"Do you think they will arrive at the conclusion that you and I did this and then fled?"

The thought had occurred to Nash. "Not out of the realm of possibility."

"Which means the police will be looking for us."

Nash said, "Maybe I can do something about that."

He got on his phone, downloaded the encrypted app that Agent Morris had previously provided him, and then sent an email detailing what had happened.

"Who did you send that to?" asked Steers.

"Somone who can help us."

"The FBI perhaps?" she said.

He shot her a glance. "Someone who can help us," he repeated.

They got back on the road and kept driving. Finally, Nash had to pull off. They checked into a motel and took the only room available.

Nash grabbed dinner at a burger place and brought it back for them.

Steers was in the shower and came out a bit later with wet hair and wearing a long-sleeved T-shirt and shorts that she had purchased when they'd stopped for clothes. Her feet were bare and her features tight as she eyed the twin beds.

Nash sat on one of the beds and checked his emails. He read off the one he'd received from Morris.

Understand and are monitoring the situation and will keep you apprised. We will do all we can to keep cops off your back.

Nash figured that was the best they could do under the circumstances.

He parceled out the food on a small table. They drew up their chairs and ate in silence, until Steers said, "What did your person write back to you?"

"That they're aware of the situation, are monitoring it, and will keep us informed."

She nodded but made no comment.

In the bathroom Nash washed up and changed into a T-shirt and sweatpants that he'd bought.

Twenty minutes after Nash had turned out the lights she said, "Once we get to New Orleans, what then?"

"We catch our breaths, get some data, process it, and then make decisions, hopefully good ones."

"All right." She paused and asked, "Is your wife alive?"

"What does it matter to you?"

"I would hope that she is alive, that is all."

"Why?"

"Because she did nothing wrong. It was Rhett Temple who put her in danger. But I do want you to know that Lynn Ryder did not ask me before she sent her team out. But she did let me know about it shortly afterward. I ordered her to instruct the men not to harm your wife."

Nash turned to the side and looked in her direction. It was so dark in the room that he could barely make out her figure lying on the bed.

"Well, I'm not sure they got the message, because I killed all three of them before they could murder her."

She said nothing for a few seconds. "That would have required a great deal of skill."

"I was fortunate to get us out of there alive."

"So she *is* alive. I am happy for you."

Nash turned away from her. "Sure, thanks," he said curtly. He was confused and frustrated and tired and not very hopeful about how this was all going to play out.

"Can I ask you a question?" he said.

"Of course."

"Lord has your business. Why does he want you dead?"

"As I said, we have no way to know that Mr. Lord is behind this."

"Who else?"

"My partners from the south perhaps?"

"No."

"Why not?"

"Because you got them billions. They'll be cheering you, not looking to kill you."

"For some it's not always about the money."

"How about you? It can't be about money. You sold your empire for zip."

"You are wrong. I received my *freedom*. That is worth more to me than *billions*."

"Well now you're running for your life," he pointed out.

"As I said before, we will see what we will see."

"I don't understand you."

"I can say the same about you," she retorted.

"My motivations are pretty clear."

"Not all of them, no," she replied.

"Think what you want."

Nash closed his eyes. His thoughts turned to Thura, who was almost certainly dead. All the man had been through, only to die like that.

I'd be dead, too, if Steers hadn't ordered me to take her for a drive.

And she could have shot me out in the woods. But she didn't. Even after she found out who I really was. The man she'd been looking for all that time.

Steers's voice interrupted these thoughts. "I know what you must think, Walter, and all I can say is I'm sorry for everything you and your family have endured. If I could have, I would have made different choices."

"You *could* have made different choices, Victoria. There was no one stopping you. You have to own this. Just you. Nobody else."

Exhausted, he fell asleep.

In her bed Steers continued to stare at the ceiling.

CHAPTER 72

THEY WENT TO A DRIVE-THROUGH for breakfast and then got back on the road. The news was now full of the slaughter at Steers's estate, and speculation was rampant about the missing owner.

Had she killed everyone? the news media wondered. Or was it enemies of Victoria Steers, a woman who was allegedly involved in criminal activity?

There was, as yet, no word about the identities of the victims, so the fate of Masuyo was unknown. There was also a side story about another woman presumably missing from the household based on a search of the premises.

This must be Hiroko, thought Nash. Steers had ordered her room to remain intact. The search apparently was on for her, too. And Nash wondered if the search for her would end at her grave in the woods.

Where Steers and I buried her.

The miles flew by. They spent one more night at a motel off the interstate, where they awkwardly had to share a bed.

They each had turned in opposite directions, but the bed was small and Nash was closer to her than he wanted to be. He could smell the shampoo she had used during her shower. He was starting to feel things that were making him sick. He finally put his hand over his nose to cut off the scent.

For her part Steers kept her eyes shut tightly and her body rigid, careful not to move in case she ended up touching him.

The following day they arrived in New Orleans. Steers's house was in the Garden District behind a high wall. She gave Nash the code to input at the gate and they drove through and into the front courtyard.

Nash parked the car in one of the garage bays after Steers keyed in the code. Steers used a biometric reader to open the door leading from the garage into the house. The alarm started to beep and she quickly disengaged it at the pad just inside the door.

As they walked through the home Nash saw that the rooms were spacious and luxurious, and everything was clean and well tended to.

"I have people who come in each week," she explained. "But they will not come while we are here."

"Have they seen you on previous trips?" Nash asked.

"No. That would defeat the purpose of a safe house of last resort. I used a shell company on the deed."

Nash made some coffee for himself and tea for her. She drank hers in her room while Nash sat in the kitchen nook. He had emailed Morris and had just received back an astonishing reply.

> We have taken over the investigation from the police. A man named Thura survived. He is badly wounded and they're not sure he will pull through. But he managed to tell the cops that he called you and told you what happened, so you and Steers are in the clear, for now, at least on these killings. Masuyo is not among the dead. I know what happened to Hiroko, since you told me about it, so we won't be pursuing that.

Nash emailed him back, telling Morris it seemed likely that with the sale of her business to Lord complete they had decided to kill her. He ended by asking Morris to thank Thura for warning him and that he hoped to hell his friend pulled through.

Nash sat back and sipped his coffee, his eyes and his nerves tired and frayed, respectively. His mind was going so fast it was hard to concentrate on any one thing. He was so lost in thought that he didn't notice Steers standing in the kitchen doorway until she spoke.

"Do you have news from your 'friends'?" She eyed the phone in front of him.

He glanced over to see that she was wearing a white nightgown, her hair was pinned up, and she was barefoot. Her face was flushed and he thought that she might have been crying.

"Thura survived but he's in bad shape. He was able to tell them what had happened, so the FBI doesn't think we're involved. Your mother was not among the dead."

She sat in a chair opposite him. "I am glad Thura is alive."

"For now," Nash said. "Maybe if I'd been there things would have turned out differently."

"Only in that you and I would be dead," said Steers.

"You're probably right, but... I should have been there."

"I ordered you elsewhere. Do not waste time feeling guilty."

"I choose to *waste* time feeling human," he countered heatedly.

Steers waited a moment. "And my mother not being among the dead makes it likely that our initial thought was correct."

"She's with Lord."

"I clearly fell out of favor when I sold my business. But there might be other things going on as well."

"So why did you sell then, since you had to be aware that could be one of the likely consequences?"

"Life is not the most important thing there is to a person, Walter."

"I don't think most people would agree with you."

"I actually only had one choice, regardless of the consequences."

"But you could have disappeared. You *chose* not to do that."

"You do not disappear from these people," she said with a touch of weariness.

"I disappeared, and you couldn't find me."

"I am not you. And how exactly would I change this?" She rolled up one sleeve, revealing her damaged skin. "By lifting weights, or having tattoos inked over *this*?"

He looked away. Clearly this was getting them nowhere. He suddenly decided to go there. "I found the box at your building in Hong Kong. With Maggie's things inside."

He paused and studied her reaction. There was really none, he concluded. She just stared over his shoulder, her features impassive.

"Why would you keep those things? As, what, souvenirs?"

"Even I am not that...sociopathic, Walter."

"Then why?"

She said, "I choose to live in the present and to take on the future, what little I might have left. You can stay in the past, if you wish, but I would not recommend it."

Steers rose and walked out.

Later, Nash went to his room and started to unpack his things. That was when he noticed that the pistol he had purchased was missing, along with its box of ammo.

They did Uber Eats for dinner that night, with Nash using his credit card. They ate in the small dining area. Nash had his pistol in a belt clip and noticed that there was a small bulge under the shirt that Steers wore.

That's where the gun went.

He looked up to find her staring at him. By the woman's features, it was clear that she had deduced what he was thinking.

"We *both* must be prepared for what might happen," she said.

All the warnings about Steers from Shock and Agent Morris came flooding back to him. And the woman sitting across from him once more seemed like the intimidating person whom Nash had met for the first time in Hong Kong. Crafty, cool, and deadly. And it occurred to Nash with startling clarity that it might well come down to him against her.

"I agree," he said. "For *whatever* might happen."

CHAPTER 73

Nash, wearing a ball cap and sunglasses, had picked up a week's worth of groceries from a store that Steers had told him about. She also wanted some specialty items from there.

Steers made dinner for them that night with some of the ingredients he'd purchased for her. She told him the dishes were from recipes that Hiroko had taught her.

"She was quite proficient in the kitchen. When I was a little girl I always loved to smell her cooking something."

Steers served an appetizer called gyoza. "It is like a pot sticker or dumpling. This is yaki gyoza."

Nash had watched her make the meal, after she had declined his offer to help. But it still seemed surreal, having a moment like this in the middle of everything they were facing.

Nash took a bite of the dish. The pork, cabbage, garlic, ginger, onion, and soy sauce flavors did not overwhelm one another, but rather complemented each other. "It's delicious," he said.

She smiled at his compliment. "It is a testament to Hiroko-san's talents."

They next had soba and udon noodles in a thick fish broth, and then, as their main dish, karagge, which she told him was deep-fried seasoned chicken.

They had both opted for sparkling water over alcohol.

As the two ate they talked about things that had nothing to do with their current plight. Nash had been to New Orleans before on business trips and once had traveled there with Judith and Maggie for a holiday. They had also attended a concert in the city.

The memory of the trip with his family evidently weighed so heavily on him that Steers said, "Are you all right, Walter?"

He glanced up at her. "I was...just thinking about some stuff."

She nodded. "It is quite unusual that we sit here, diametrically opposed on so many issues, and share a meal and speak of trivial things."

"Life doesn't have to make sense. It just...is," he replied.

"Have you had any communication with your wife?"

"No. I doubt that I ever will."

"Once this is over, surely you will be reunited."

"Once this is over, you and I will most likely be dead, Victoria," he replied, more sharply than he probably intended. But then again, maybe not.

She bowed her head at this comment.

After that each then fully retreated into their own thoughts.

The rain fell heavily two nights later. Nash tossed and turned in his bed. Usually he slept well when it was raining. But the way the pellets of water were hitting the slate roof of Steers's home sounded almost like the jarring impact of pistol shots.

At two in the morning he finally gave up, put on his pants, and padded barefoot out into the main living space. He sat in a chair in the dark, closed his eyes, and tried to make his mind shut off. However, with everything facing them, Nash found that impossible.

Then, during a lull in the storm, he thought he heard something. He sat very still and listened. There it was again. Like someone grunting or perhaps moaning.

He rushed back to his room and grabbed his Glock. Nash then came back out into the hall and eased over to Steers's bedroom door, which was down the hall from his.

He put his ear to the wood but heard nothing. He tapped on the door and said quietly, "Victoria?" There was no answer. He slowly eased the door open, mindful that she was armed after having taken the gun he'd purchased on their way here. And if he surprised her from perhaps a nightmare?

He opened the door just enough to see that her bed was empty. The bathroom door was open, and he could see that it was dark inside.

He went downstairs, where he heard the noise again. He knew that homes in New Orleans did not have basements because of the high water tables. But then he recalled that the stairs up to the front door had been very high.

Because there's an aboveground floor below this one.

He looked around for a passage leading down and finally found it in the small library. It was a pop-out door that looked like a wall, and it even had a large painting hanging on it to aid in this deception.

He eased the door open and encountered a set of carpeted spiral stairs. He skittered down them, reached the landing, and turned right, following the sounds that were now reverberating clearly.

The hall was lined with doors that were locked. He kept going and reached the end of the hall, where there was a door that had a glass panel above. A light was on inside. He peered through the glass.

And there was Steers. And in front of her was the same boxing dummy that he had seen back at her building in Hong Kong. Steers was clad in a white T-shirt and shorts, the damaged skin on her arms and part of her back revealed. Her feet were bare. She was holding a pair of knives, and he watched in fascination as she attacked the dummy. Steers wielded the blades with exceptional skill, he noted, and she drove home the knives on every critical area of her opponent.

Then she set the knives down and wiped off the sweat using a towel draped on a bench. She then assumed a martial arts fighting stance and once more went after the dummy. Her powerful kicks and hand strikes were first-rate, as good as if not better than the ones of which Nash was capable.

She kept going full-bore until she was dripping in sweat and then she bent over, gasping for breath.

It was then that Nash opened the door and walked in.

When Steers saw him she straightened and backed away, looking like she had just been discovered in some compromising position.

He eyed the dummy and then her. "I had no idea you had such fighting skills."

She quickly regained her composure and finished toweling off. Glancing at her exposed arms, she used the towel like a cape to cover them.

"You don't have to do that," he said. "I have no issue with your injuries. We all have them, some are just more evident than others."

"It is not about you, it is about me," she replied quietly.

He nodded and eyed the dummy. "I trained on one of these. For well over a year. But it seems that you have been doing this sort of thing for far longer."

"My mother thought it useful. She herself was a master of wushu." When Nash looked puzzled she added, "What you might call kung fu, although wushu encompasses more than simply one form of martial art."

He picked up one of the knives. The handles were of intricate design, and the blades were both serrated and slightly curved, and perfectly balanced. "These look custom."

"They are."

Steers took the knife from him, picked up its twin, and placed them back into a box with cushioning inside that held precise cutouts for the weapons. She turned back to him. "How did you happen to access this floor?"

"Just followed the sounds of you killing your opponent. The pop-out door in the wall took a little sleuthing. The chair rail molding didn't line up precisely. That was the giveaway."

"So, you could not sleep?"

"I guess there's a lot on my mind."

"A cup of tea perhaps? It helps me when I have a lot on my mind."

He followed her back upstairs to the kitchen. She boiled the water and made tea for them, letting it steep for several minutes.

Once they had their cups in hand, she led him out to the enclosed rear porch that overlooked the small backyard. The storm was still raging, and they watched the lightning strikes mar the sky, and listened to the resulting cracks of thunder as well as the sounds of rain hitting all around.

Though the storm was violent, Nash seemed to calm when starkly confronted by it. As he glanced at Steers he could tell by her features that she seemed more relaxed, too.

"When storms like this happened in Japan when I was a little girl, I would hide under my bed," Steers finally said. "Hiroko-san would come and find me and hold me so very tight." She paused. "Until my mother took me from her and made me run out into the storm, to show my mettle, I suppose." She then seemed surprised that she had voiced this vulnerability, even if it had been from her youth.

"I was pretty much scared of everything when I was a kid," confessed Nash. "Here my father was this big, tough combat soldier who all men both feared and respected. And I was his wimpy son."

"You are no longer that little boy, Walter. And no one would call you a wimp now," said Steers, glancing at him. "This I have seen for myself."

"Well, maybe I'm more like my father than I thought."

"I was very much like my father," said Steers. "When I was young. But as I grew older I became much more like my mother."

"Strong, tough, indomitable?"

"I think the more accurate term is *cold-blooded*."

"I doubt that Hiroko-san would call you that."

Steers shook her head. "Hiroko-san would never acknowledge who I *became*."

She had put on a long-sleeved shirt to cover her arms, but now she edged one of the sleeves up and stared down at her ruined flesh. Her expression was so pained that, despite everything, Nash felt compassion for her.

"You're not your mother, Victoria."

"Oh, but I very much am, Walter. By now you have surely seen this for yourself."

"You gave up your criminal empire. Do you think your mother would have done that? Or *pretended* to shoot someone in the head instead of doing it for real? Would you have blown her or your father out of the sky by putting a bomb on a plane? Or poisoned Hiroko-san?"

In lieu of a response Steers stood and walked over to one of the windows. She raised it so the wind and rain were able to enter their space. She stood there, her head against the glass, while the heavy winds drove the rain into the room.

Nash watched in silence as her clothes and skin grew wetter and yet she didn't move, as though the woman was rooted to that spot no matter what the storm threw at her.

He wondered if she was imagining being forced to run out in the middle of a storm to prove to her mother that she was strong enough to do what Masuyo wanted done. Always what Masuyo wanted done. Like killing her other children.

Is she good? Is she evil? Should I hate her? Should I…?

He ceased these musings when she turned away from the storm.

"Are you all right?" he asked.

She glanced at him, her face a mask of confliction. The woman looked close to just losing it, thought Nash. When he thought she might start to scream or cry or…something, she simply passed by him and headed up the stairs.

Nash sat there for an hour, watching and listening to the storm's continued raging. Then he closed the window and headed to bed, but he stopped by her door on the way. He quietly opened it and peered inside.

In the explosive beams of the lightning spears, he could see that she was asleep. Her arm had slipped off the side of the bed and dangled there. The shirtsleeve had slid up, and her damaged flesh was revealed. He stepped inside the room and drew closer to her. In that ruined skin he saw many things, but chief among them a woman who was burned from flesh to soul, and not simply by a plane crashing.

Nash gently lifted Steers's arm and laid it next to her. Then he walked back to his room feeling both more defeated and more confused than he ever had.

And that was when the email landed in his mailbox.

CHAPTER 74

It was from Judith. Morris must have given her his new contact information on the secure portal.

The note was long but was summed up best by her telling him that she was sorry for having doubted him. And that she wished things could be different. She was in a safe place under an assumed name and life, and while not ideal, Judith was doing okay. She ended by telling him to stay safe and that she respected what he was doing and that she loved him. Very much.

He read it over three more times and was surprised that he didn't feel more emotion from her words. It was like an email from a friend, not a lover or a spouse.

Too much has happened in the interim for us to ever...be what we were before.

He set his phone aside and looked out the window. Dawn was not that far off, and Nash wondered what it would hold. People were after them. As the anonymous man on the phone taken from Thura had suggested, he could turn Steers over to Lord and company, if that was indeed who their pursuer was, with the result that Nash perhaps could survive this.

But I can't do that to her. I'm not sure what I can do for her, but I can't do that. She's had enough betrayals.

He fell asleep for a few hours, then rose, dressed, slapped his gun in its holster, went downstairs, and made coffee and had breakfast. An hour later, when Steers had not appeared, he boiled a cup of tea and took it to her room. He knocked and she told him to enter.

She was sitting up in bed. She looked freshened and her hair was damp, probably from a shower. She had changed into a nightdress that covered her arms.

"Tea," he said.

"Thank you," she replied, averting her gaze. Every fiber of the woman seemed to quiver with suppressed emotion.

He set the cup next to the bed and looked down at her. "It's actually nice outside. We might want to go for a walk, with sunglasses and hats on of course."

"Yes," she said. "That would be…fine."

He had turned to leave when she called out to him. "About last night, Walter."

He turned to look at her.

"I apologize for allowing you to see me in such a *confused* state."

He drew back to the bed. "You mean in a *human* state?"

She glanced at him, her look suddenly close to anger, he perceived. For being usually so calm and in control Steers sometimes could be…*mercurial*, he thought.

"I think you know exactly what I mean."

He sat down in a chair and studied her. "In my mind at least admitting or showing weakness is not actually a weakness."

"Perhaps in *your* world that may be true," she retorted.

"It could be in your world, too, Victoria."

"How is that remotely possible?" she snapped.

"Well, that might be up to you."

She rubbed at her temples. "You speak in platitudes that sound quite nice and perhaps convincing on the surface, but have no meaningful connection to *reality*, at least *my* reality."

"Again, much of that depends on you."

She hiked her eyebrows and said, "You actually believe I have any control over *this*?" She fanned her hands in front of her.

"I don't know, do you?"

She swept away the covers, swung her long legs to the edge of the bed, and her bare feet touched the floor. When she rose Nash rose, too.

Her features were fixed for battle. They faced off right there.

CHAPTER 75

"You are the most infuriating person of my acquaintance," she snapped.

"Not my intent," he replied calmly.

"You were sent to spy on me, and you no doubt have fed your masters everything they need to put me in prison for the rest of my life. Is that not so?"

He just watched her, warily, since he now knew of her formidable fighting skills.

She didn't step forward, she stepped back, which instantly put Nash more on his guard.

"Is that not so?" she said again.

"Perhaps."

"So why have I not been arrested then?" she demanded.

"That's a funny question coming from you. I thought you wouldn't bring it up for fear of what I might say."

"None of what you just said makes any sense," she barked.

"I think it does. If you ruminate for a bit you might agree."

She drew a deep, filling breath and stood as tall as possible in her bare feet. Still, he towered over her. She seemed to take offense at this because Steers lunged forward and pushed him. However, he outweighed her by at least a hundred pounds, so her thrusts barely budged him; indeed, the collision resulted in her falling backward against the bed. This apparently incensed her even more because she then struck him with a hard roundabout kick that landed solidly against his shoulder.

Nash grimaced and absorbed the blow, but he held his ground, staring at her with a calmness that further infuriated her.

She screamed and kicked at him again, but he was ready and caught her by the ankle. He lifted her leg up even higher and then pushed her backward. Steers toppled onto the bed, but she was up in an instant, and she launched herself against him. She threw fists and elbows and knees and legs; her breathing was labored, not really by her physical efforts, Nash knew, having seen her training before, but seemingly from raw emotion.

He blocked all the flung blows, and this seemed to ratchet her anger to a whole other level.

Nash was breathing more heavily now, too, because Steers was no slack opponent. He watched her cautiously as she fell back and seemed to regroup. Her features had gelled into a mass of hatred. Nash truly felt it was probably pointed more inward than at him.

He said as calmly as he could, "You've more than proven yourself, Victoria. Given time, you could probably beat me. But this is not helping either of us."

She exclaimed, "I am not trying to *help* you. You are trying to destroy me."

"If I am, I'm certainly taking my time about it," he replied.

"You are cunning. You are patient. You are a bastard."

"Maybe I am all of those things. But what are you, really? You keep telling me who and what you are. But I don't believe it. So why don't you try again?"

Instead, Steers charged him, but this time Nash was ready for her assault. He stepped forward before she could strike and wrapped his muscled arms around her arms and torso, and clamped her legs tightly between his powerful ones. And then he lifted her completely off the floor.

She struggled to free herself, but Nash was far too strong. She tried to head-butt him and managed to once, but then he dipped his head next to her neck so she couldn't do that again.

She screamed and struggled. He held her tighter. She screamed even louder, fighting to free herself, but he would not let go. He breathed in her scent and then felt wetness on his neck.

He realized it was probably her tears.

"Please stop, Victoria. Please," he said, in a hushed voice that still managed to surge with emotion.

At these words she ceased struggling and hung limply in his arms, her feet dangling nearly six inches off the floor, her chest heaving.

He lifted his head and looked at her. Her eyes were reddened, her features crumpled.

"I'm...sorry," she whispered. Steers looked him in the eyes and then her gaze dipped to his mouth. She looked up again and then Nash's gaze lowered to her mouth.

Their lips met spontaneously and then each hungrily gripped the other. He carried her to the bed and set her down, then lifted her nightgown over her head. She helped to undress him, quickly, ferociously. He put his gun on the nightstand. She flung his pants and then undershorts across the room and pulled him down on her.

But then Nash abruptly lurched back.

"Walter?" she gasped.

He was rocking back and forth on his knees, his eyes closed, and he was shivering, as though he had been immersed in ice water.

"Walter?"

He backed away off the bed, put his feet on the floor, and grabbed up his clothes. He slipped on his undershorts and his pants.

"Walter, what's wrong?"

He whirled on her. "What's wrong? This whole—" He swept his arms around, dropping some of his clothing in the process. "This... this whole thing is wrong. Wrong!" he screamed. He picked up his gun and looked down at it. His expression calmed, his brow relaxed. It was as though he had found a measure of inner peace, or at least an answer to his dilemma.

"Walter?" she said cautiously.

"I'll... I'll be... back in a... minute. I just... just need some time to..."

He racked the slide on the gun and turned to leave.

Sensing what he might be about to do, Steers wrapped herself in a sheet and said urgently, "No wait, Walter, I need to show you something first. I should have done it long before now. But I realize it speaks to exactly what you are dealing with. And I have to show you. I have to!" she exclaimed. "Please look at me. Please."

He did not look at her. Instead, his finger slipped to the trigger of the gun and he started to raise it with the muzzle pointed at his chest.

She jumped off the bed, rushed toward him, and gripped his arm. "Please, Walter, please. Listen to me. For just a few moments. Please."

"Why should I?" he said coldly, the gun now aimed at his heart.

"Because you are a kind, decent man who has been thrust into a hell not of your making. I will not take up more than a few seconds of your time. Then... you can..." She glanced at the gun.

His breathing slowed and he gazed at her. "What do you have to say to me that would make a damn bit of difference?" he said in a bare whisper, as though that was all he had the lungs for.

"May I?" she asked, looking at the gun. "As Hiroko-san did for me that night? Please?"

A long moment passed as the two stared at each other.

Finally, he allowed her to take the gun from him and she carefully placed it back on the nightstand. Then she grabbed her phone and returned to Nash, tapping keys on it to access something.

"This will be a shock, Walter. And I want you to be prepared."

Now alarmed, he gazed at her. "Victoria, what is going on?"

Steers tapped some more keys, checked the screen, and then held it up to him. With her other hand she clutched his shoulder tightly, as though she was single-handedly trying to buck him up against whatever was coming.

"Please just try to remain... s-stable, W-Walter," she said.

When Nash looked at the phone screen, he immediately saw that it was a picture. And though a long time had passed, he had no trouble at all recognizing the person.

He drew his gaze from the phone and stared at Steers, the tears bubbling in his eyes.

"Maggie? She's alive?"

"Yes."

CHAPTER 76

Their lovemaking now was slow and sensual, instead of the previous attempt's feral and frenetic display. Nash's pelvis methodically rose and fell between her legs before he pulled her upward and she sat astride him, seamlessly moving her hips up and down against him. When they were both done, she slumped against him, breathless. With her in his arms, Nash fell to one side and they lay next to one another on the bed. She let out a throaty moan and rubbed his arm. Then she rose on one elbow and turned to him.

"This was much more pleasurable than how it started out between us," she noted.

He managed a weak smile. "The first attempt was more of a war."

Her large sad eyes took him in fully and she said, "We should get ready, Walter, and then... discuss things."

Forty-five minutes later Nash and Steers sat in front of the flames from the gas fireplace in the living room after a hastily prepared meal that they ate quickly and with little conversation. The weather had turned cloudy, with a damp chill.

Steers had explained very little about Maggie's being alive and, in truth, Nash would not have been able to process it if she had elaborated. The fact that they had made love after the stunning revelation was probably good. He had not wanted to think at that moment. If he had, Nash was certain he would have convinced himself that Maggie was in fact dead.

But now, the time had come for an explanation from Steers.

He looked at her. "Maggie?"

"I had mentioned long ago that your CIA was interested in me?"

"I remember that, yes. But you didn't get into details."

"I could not at the time. But…they were not just interested. They made me an offer, an offer I could not refuse."

"What sort of offer?"

"A future. Not a bright one, really, but better than what I had."

"Why come to you with an offer? They must have known the authorities were already after you."

"The truth is, I made discreet overtures to certain parties that led the CIA to secretly approach me. My mother believed she could make me just like her. But she could not. And you have always been right about that, Walter. I am not her."

"It's good to hear you say it, Victoria."

"It is good to hear me say it," she replied.

"So you, what, started working for the CIA?" he said.

"Yes."

"Ironic in that the FBI engaged me to be a mole against *you* while you were a mole against everyone you were working with."

"I do not believe that your FBI knows of any of this."

"And the sale of your business?"

"That was necessary because it placed Connor Lord squarely in the bullseye. The CIA wants him for many reasons, they told me. He can bring down many major figures."

"The FBI told me the same thing."

"His purchase of my organization was the first time he actually took over any overt criminal enterprise. That was why I dangled it like a carrot and then made sure he would accept my terms. The CIA told me that if we managed to pull this off, it will be one of the most important operations they have ever been party to."

"If Lord is this master chess player and genius, why do you think he agreed to take over your operation? He must be aware of the risks."

"He is also a narcissist, which can be a weakness of enormous degree. He feigns contentment lurking behind the scenes, but Lord has always thirsted for more power, and the opportunity to be center stage. And I used that against him. And I hope that it also will be his undoing." She paused and studied him. "So that is why I could tell you nothing. I am so very sorry."

"I understand."

"Lord told me that the FBI had recruited you, in your position at Sybaritic, to spy on me and the Temples. How he found out, I do not know. He wanted you taken care of. Not killed. He wanted something more so that the FBI would no longer work with or trust you, and indeed might abandon their investigation entirely. That is why I did what I did with your daughter. It was the only thing I could think of. After Maggie was taken and her AI-altered image appeared online, I was supposed to capture and then torture you to make you tell me what you had disclosed to the authorities. But I had no interest in that, and you managed to elude me and the police. And afterward, while I made noises about trying to find you and kept imploring Rhett Temple to do the same, it was all window dressing to placate Lord. I...I had done enough harm to you."

"But then you sent Lynn Ryder over and made a big push to locate me."

"I became desperate. I needed to know what you had told the FBI. You see, it had occurred to me that if they brought down my business before Lord was attached to it, everything I had worked for with the CIA would be ruined. I just wanted to take you out of the equation until I could complete the transaction with Lord. I of course had no inkling you were right there the whole time."

"And those men being sent to my wife's home? Would they have killed her even though you said not to? They came into the house with knives out and looked ready to murder her."

"I ordered Lynn to have those men abduct your wife, that is all. As soon as I did, however, I regretted it. You see, those men did not work directly for me. They worked for Lord." She looked away. "I...I should have thought it through more, but I suppose I panicked. I had so little time to make a decision. It...it was...a poor choice. And if I failed, the CIA would, of course, have disclaimed all knowledge of our arrangement. I would be in prison for the rest of my life, and Lord would be free to continue to wreak havoc."

"Rhett finally figured out my real identity," said Nash.

Steers looked at him pensively. "That does surprise and intrigue me. How was he able to accomplish what I could not?"

"A perfect storm of clues, mistakes on my part, and lucky deductions on his, unfortunately. But I struck a deal with him. You see, I also know that he murdered his father, so I had that to hold over him, too."

"He killed his father? I did not think he had that in him."

"I didn't either. But Rhett is cagier than most people think. Ironically, it wasn't the FBI who told me your mother's real name was Dai Lu. It was Rhett. He overheard some of your associates talking about it."

"I see."

"Your mother was actually using my knowledge of her real name as leverage. And when she told you I knew her Chinese name? You had me drive you out to Hiroko's resting place, at gunpoint."

"I was not planning to kill you, just find out who you were really working for and then let the CIA deal with it. But when you told me you were Walter Nash?" She shook her head. "I have truthfully never been more surprised in my life. Even more so than when I found out my mother was not a prisoner in Myanmar."

"I still don't understand how Maggie is alive. They found her remains. Bones, teeth."

"They found *some* remains, but they were not hers."

"But they ran tests. DNA doesn't lie."

"The CIA made certain the tests would come back as a positive match. The ring and strands of hair that were also found we took from Maggie to leave with the bones and teeth to further substantiate that those were her remains. She has been in safekeeping with your U.S. Marshals all this time. Things have been explained to her. She knows that you are alive, and also what you have been doing."

Nash was taken aback by this revelation. "She knows about me?"

"Yes."

"Does Judith know that Maggie is alive?"

"I do not know. But I do know that the CIA does not like to share information with anyone." She paused. "I communicated with my handler earlier. I was also told that Maggie wanted you to know that she could not be more proud of you for all that you have done."

Nash felt the tears creep to his eyes. At bottom, regardless of the muscles and tats and lethal skill set, he was, in some respects, still the overly sentimental Walter Nash.

Steers rubbed his arm. "I know how you have suffered. If there had been any other way…"

He brushed his tears away and attempted a smile. "I've been working with the FBI for a while, so I got a crash course in government secrecy and skullduggery, Victoria. But what about our neighborhood security guard, Billy Adams? He *was* killed."

Steers gazed once more into the flames. "The fake police, who were the ones to abduct Maggie, were sent to me by Lord. However, I arranged that Maggie would be immediately turned over to my people for interrogation…and disposal. Those people were agents of the CIA. So Maggie was then safe. However, the fake police, unbeknownst to me, placed a listening device at the guard shack. They heard your conversation with the guard, and your urging him to go to the authorities about what he had seen. Again, without my knowledge, they used your vehicle to kill him. I truly did not intend anyone to die or you to be blamed for it."

Nash nodded slowly. "And your mother and the prison? Why did Lord bring her back so that you could 'rescue' her?"

"To me it evidenced a master chess move of stunning creativity.

Lord, you see, allowed me to visit my mother in prison as a reward for disposing of the threat you represented to both of us, but for different reasons. He did not want his plans with China thwarted, and I did not want my pact with the CIA disrupted. As I informed you before, with my mother in prison, or so I thought, that was significant leverage over me to do Lord's bidding without restriction."

"They might have sensed you wanted to get out."

"This, too, I have thought is more probable than not."

"But what happened then? What was this master chess move?"

"My mother returning to the business allowed her to spy on me, a capability Lord did not have previously."

"Like a Trojan horse," said Nash.

"As you know, Beijing was not happy with me. They deemed a leadership change in their best interests. So my mother would use whatever intelligence she could gather to eventually dethrone me. *That* is a master chess move because it is both tactical and strategic, and it achieves multiple goals from the same set of actions."

"But why not just kill you and insert your mother or Lord at the top of the chain?"

"As you now know I have partners all over the world, and they are men who are unafraid of Connor Lord or even Beijing. Were the Chinese to do what you suggested it would have caused a dramatic and violent rupture in that partnership. Beijing and Lord are far too intelligent to go down a road filled with such potholes. She stroked his arm. "I was fooled by my mother until you suggested that she was distracting me from what she was really doing." She gazed at Nash in reverence. "You actually read Masuyo better than I did, Walter. And that is not an easy undertaking."

"But she *is* your mother, Victoria. And, regardless of the circumstances, it's not easy to think badly of a parent. I had no such allegiances to your mother."

"After that I had her watched most carefully. And my suspicions were confirmed. My mother is brilliant. But she is also arrogant, and sometimes arrogant people are not as careful as they otherwise should be. They make mistakes, and she made enough to where the truth became apparent to me."

"So you planned to turn that to your advantage?"

"After Hiroko-san's murder at my mother's hands, that became my one desire in life. And it also meshed quite perfectly with my plan to lure Connor Lord in and then trap him. Now the authorities are closing in, and all I have to do is survive."

"I would have thought the CIA would put you in protective custody right after the sale went through."

"If that had been done, Lord would have instantly seen the truth and taken steps to counteract anything we might have planned. I had to remain in the relative open in my 'retirement.' What happened at the estate was unforeseen by any of us, occurring far earlier than any of us would have predicted. With that said, I sense my mother's impatient hand in it."

Steers fell silent, and Nash looked to the window as the wind picked up.

"Clearly now they suspect that you are working for the authorities," he said. "They tried to kill you. They are hunting you. What is the CIA doing about that?"

"They are aware of the attack, obviously, and are working out a suitable plan."

"If you are killed, is their case weakened?"

She nodded. "Yes, considerably."

"How long before arrests are made?"

"Soon."

"It may not be soon enough for us."

"That is a definite possibility, yes."

"It seems the CIA is better at concocting the entrance into a scheme than they are at the exit."

"This, too, I have thought."

Nash rose and said, "Go pack. We need to leave here. Now."

She looked up at him in surprise. "Now?"

"I used to be a businessman who just ran numbers for a living.

I now have a new set of skills for keeping myself and those in my charge safe. But my old job instilled in me a great sixth sense about potential problems in every deal I ever did. And right now, Victoria, it's blaring a foghorn."

"But where will we go?"

"I have somewhere in mind. And it offers more than just a hiding place."

"What else does it offer?"

"Help. Which is something we both really need right now."

CHAPTER 77

Rhett Temple ran as hard as he could on the treadmill, sweat flying off him and spittle coming out of his mouth. Still Shock stood next to him shouting at him to go faster, to put more balls into it. Temple became so exhausted he slowed to nearly a stop, was flung off the equipment, and slammed into the wall behind.

"Shit!" he bellowed, picking himself off the floor and pointing a finger at Shock. "You are trying to kill me, old man."

Shock eyed him with disdain. "I told you I was gonna do that your first day here."

"I bet you didn't treat precious Walter like this."

"Didn't have to. He worked way harder than you do without me on his ass."

"Right, sure he did." Temple toweled off and said, "Look, when do I get the tats and shit?" He made a muscle. "I'm strong enough. I can kick ass, shoot like a pro. Now, I need a new identity, and I'm out of here with a mountain of money and a life of leisure."

"You don't know half the shit you need to know, you pussy," countered Shock.

"No, I know all the shit I need to know, and now it's time to say our goodbyes. I've got the rest of my life to lead and a world to do it in."

"My house, my rules."

Temple got up in Shock's face. "No, because I know Nash is alive and what his new identity is. There are people out there who would love to know that. So it's *my* rules."

"He's been exonerated. The police ain't lookin' for him no more."

"I'm not talking about the police, and you know it."

Shock took a step back. "Thought the man was your friend."

"Nash was pushed in my face by my father as the example of what I should be. Well, to hell with my old dead father and fuck Walter Nash."

"Like you did Walter's wife, right?"

Now Temple took a step back. "Hey, if a lady comes sniffing around is it my job to say no? I don't think so. Not how the world works." He wrapped the towel around his neck. "So get hopping on the docs. I mean it. Or little Waltie goes bye-bye."

He walked out of the room, leaving a concerned Shock staring after him.

* * *

Temple skipped his final meal and sat in the same room Nash had used when he had been training at Shock's facility. He had been in touch with Mindy, and also with the folks at Sybaritic. To all of them he was simply traveling around the world blowing off some steam and having some fun. You could do that when you were rich beyond all reason. Who could tell you no?

Despite his angry encounter with the man, Temple had to hand it to Shock. In a fairly short period he was stronger, faster, more nimble and limber, and he could process and analyze things he never even knew existed before. He had become a fine shot and could take apart weapons and put them back together relatively quickly. Yeah, he hadn't busted his ass all the time, and never put in any extra training beyond what Shock had required, but it was enough. He wasn't looking to be Rocky Balboa going into the ring against some asshole Russian. He just wanted to disappear in style and kick the occasional butt when he wanted to, probably to impress some ladies.

He had learned all about the killings at Steers's estate. He also knew that Nash and Steers were not among the dead. He had no idea where they were. Maybe someone had killed them. That would ease his troubles immeasurably. In any event, Steers, if she was still alive, no doubt had bigger fish to fry than him and would probably stop looking for him.

I can drop out of sight and then go live my life however I want to.

His wealth was all there just waiting for a new identity to send it to. He had set up shell companies and blank wall enterprises in a labyrinth that would have made Steers proud.

It was all there, the finish line in clear sight.

But there was one stumbling block.

Mindy.

She confessed to Nash that I killed my father. What if she gets nervous, lets something else slip? What if the cops go to question her? Can she hold out? No, she'll blab to try to save herself. And put me in prison for life with all my billions beyond my reach forever. You can't have that, Rhett. No way.

And then something else occurred to him. Shock was going to put together his new identity. But then he'd know what that was. And he could tell Nash, if Nash showed back up. And they could easily find him that way if Mindy did tell all.

So any new identity from that guy is totally worthless. Which means I have no reason to hang around this place another minute.

He waited until it was late and Shock was asleep.

Then he slipped out with everything he'd brought with him. He'd also taken something that belonged to Shock but that he needed. Temple got into his Porsche and drove out of the gate.

Fortunately, Temple knew some people who could give him a new identity and maybe throw in a few tats as well for good measure. Temple had grown a Fu Manchu that might not impress many ladies, but he had the bucks to amaze them all he needed to. The training and rigorous diet he'd undergone had carved his features into a markedly different configuration. He had looked in the mirror several times and couldn't swear it was him. Which was good. No, which was great.

He hit the gas, and the Porsche leapt forward.

Temple had some things to do and not a lot of time in which to do them.

He had killed before, now he just had to do it again. He had once grown sick at the sight of a murdered man. But no longer. He had muscles and fighting skills and he would get the tats, badass ones. The best money could buy.

Yes, he was a new man. And he had to get this done. Because the woman was standing in his way, after all he'd done for her. A quarter of a billion bucks, a beautiful home, plus an adorable kid, and all she had to do in return was keep her mouth shut.

And the bitch couldn't even do that.

Well, unfortunately for you, here comes judgment day, Min, in the form of...me.

CHAPTER 78

NASH WAS DRIVING AND STEERS was dozing in the passenger seat when his phone rang.

He instantly recognized the number. "Shock?"

Steers stirred, sat up, and looked at him curiously.

"Hey, Walter, look, man, we got a problem."

"What?" said Nash, tensing.

"Your boy's gone. Lit out sometime late last night."

"Rhett's gone? How?"

"I was asleep. When the dude didn't show for training I went lookin'. He's gone. He was all pissed off thinking he'd done enough. Wanted me to give him his new ID and tat him up and all. Dude has progressed but he ain't nowhere near where he needs to be. But guess he decided on an alternative. And there's another thing. And it's got me worried."

"What's that?"

"He took one of my guns with him. Any idea where he might have gone that he needed a weapon?"

Nash stared out the window and tried to process all of this. Then a thought occurred to him. He eyed Steers and then said, "I think I might. Look, we were on our way to see you."

"*We*?"

"Yes, *we*. You heard what happened?"

"Yeah, it's all over the news. Does the *we* include Victoria Steers?"

"Yes, it does. I'll explain when I get there. But after what you just told me I've got to go somewhere else first. Luckily, we're not that far away. If Rhett left sometime last night it'll be the afternoon before he gets there, if he drives straight through. Then he'll have to wait until nightfall, and we'll be waiting."

Nash clicked off and looked at Steers. "Rhett is going to kill his stepmother."

"Because she knows that he killed his father?" said Steers.

Nash shot her a glance. "Yes, how did you figure that?"

"What other reason would he have to murder her? He has enough money to forestall any other danger, except someone telling the truth." Steers sat up straighter. "And what are you going to do about it?"

"Stop him, if I can."

As they drove along, Steers's eyes widened and a smile crept across her features. "We may actually be able to do better than that, Walter. Far better."

"What are you talking about?"

"I don't think we need to go to your friend's place after this little detour."

"But we need help, Victoria."

"I think we can get it somewhere else. From a very unlikely source, in fact."

When he glanced at her curiously Steers started to explain.

And now Nash's eyes widened. When she'd finished, he said, "How did you come up with that so fast?"

"When you have lived the life that I have, you must think fast and well, or perish."

* * *

Clambering over the wall of the estate late that night, even with the backpack he carried, was far easier this time for Temple than it had been on the night he'd dumped his father off the balcony. From there he made his way to the rear door. There was no security here right now. He'd made sure of that. The only people here were Mindy, their daughter, Angie, and the staff in their quarters, which were far away from the main house. He'd fired Colin the butler before he'd gone to Shock's facility. He sensed something like this was coming down the road ever since Nash had told him that he knew the truth about Barton Temple's death.

He tried to make it seem like he'd figured it out, but I know it was Mindy. That was what they were talking about outside the night he came to dinner. I saw them from the window. Well, by doing that you signed your own death warrant, lady.

He had to play it smart. The house had an alarm system, and as he looked through the side door he saw by the red light that it was engaged. If he opened the door and then disarmed the system, *his* code, not Mindy's, would be recorded, and the cops would know he had probably been there or given someone else the code to get in.

But he knew the house well, and thus he climbed up a copper downspout to the top floor and exited onto the same exterior balcony from which he'd pushed his father to his death. The doors going into the office were armed, but he knew the windows were not.

In fact, he had left one of them unlocked before leaving to go to Shock's because, again, he knew this day might come.

He slipped through the window and into the office, where he pulled a crowbar from the backpack to force open a small safe set in the floor under the rug. He emptied the contents into the backpack. He then rifled the desk drawers and collected some cash, watches, and a couple of rings, which he also put into the backpack. His plan, obviously, was to blame Mindy's murder on a botched burglary. He walked down the darkened stairs and reached the floor where Mindy's room was.

His gloved fingers were curled around the gun he'd taken from Shock's place. He had initially planned on shooting her. But now Temple knew he couldn't bring himself to do that. It was Mindy, the mother of his child.

I'm an asshole but I'm not that big an asshole.

He had now settled on a pillow over her face. No blood, and it would be over quickly. He had on a thick jacket in case she struggled, so none of his skin would end up under her nails. And the place was full of his prints and DNA, and that could not be used against him for one very compelling reason.

It's my house.

He did feel bad about making Mandy an orphan. Well, not strictly since he was her father. A paternity test had confirmed that. But he would make sure the little girl was well taken care of.

I'll give her everything a kid could want. Except maybe a father.

As he thought this, something jolted inside of Temple.

Except a father. Just like my old man did to me. I'm my father. The circle is complete. Lucky, lucky me.

He shrugged this off, put the gun away, and eased open the door to Mindy's room. She was in the bed, facing away from him.

As he studied her, Temple started to get cold feet. It was one thing to kill his father in anger after decades of abuse. But Mindy hadn't done anything to him, except give him a couple sessions of great sex. If he could just make sure she would keep her damn mouth shut. But she had already spilled the beans to Nash. And since he had been exonerated, he might go to the police with what he'd been told. Then they would come here, question Mindy, she would fall apart, say it was all his plan—which, Temple conceded, it was. And that would be that. Life in prison instead of living as a billionaire playboy.

He shook his head. He couldn't take the chance.

I have to do this, whether I want to or not. Buck up, Rhett. Be the killer your old man said you never were.

He stepped inside, eyed a large pillow on the chaise lounge, and picked it up. He crept to the bed right as Mindy rolled over so she was facing the ceiling. He froze but then realized she was still asleep.

He raised the pillow up and plunged it down on Mindy's face.

But when she started to scream and struggle, Temple took the pillow away.

I can't do this. I could throw my old man off that balcony, but I can't do this.

Then the lights came on. An arm went around Temple's neck and he was violently jerked away from the bed.

CHAPTER

79

Rhett Temple landed hard on the floor, but he quickly regained his footing.

Walter Nash stared at him from next to the bed.

"What the hell!" exclaimed Temple.

Nash glanced at Mindy, who was sitting up and glaring at her stepson.

"You were going to murder me," she snapped at Temple.

"You're out of your head, Min. What, are you sniffing glue now?" Temple turned to Nash. "And what are you doing here? You broke into my house."

"No, he didn't. I let him in," said Mindy.

"Why?" barked Temple.

"Because he was afraid you were going to come to kill me. And he was right. Then we heard noises and he told me to pretend to be sleeping. Then you came in and tried to smother me. And he stopped you."

"Come on, Min, you are way off base. I'm...I'm not a killer. I had already pulled the pillow off you. You must have realized that."

"You killed your father," she shot back.

Temple roared, "And you were right there when I did it. So I go down, you go down, too!"

Nash said, "We can go round and round on this if you want, Rhett. Or we can cut to the chase and do something productive."

Temple glowered at him. "Meaning what, exactly?"

"Meaning you can work with us, or else you'll suffer the consequences."

"Work with you? Doing what?"

Nash glanced at the door to the bedroom. "Okay," he said.

Victoria Steers appeared there.

When Temple saw her, he immediately took a step back. "Son of a bitch! I spent all this time and money trying to get away from her, and you just ruined everything. Well, my turn to do the same to you, asshole." He called out to Steers. "Hey, guess what, he's Walter Nash. The guy you've been looking for all this time? He's right there, lady. I found him, just like you asked me to. So I am out of here for good. Bye-bye."

However, Nash blocked his exit.

In a tone of disbelief, Mindy exclaimed, "*You're* Walter Nash?"

Steers stepped fully into the room and looked at Temple. "This I already know."

Temple shot Nash a look. "She knows! What the hell is going on?"

Nash said, "Things have changed."

"Meaning what, exactly?"

"You want a get-out-of-jail-free card?" he asked.

"No, what I want is to kick your ass. And now I can." He swung a haymaker at the other man's jaw.

Nash ducked under it and let the momentum of Temple's attack carry the man right into the wall. He bounced off it and came back at Nash, swinging and kicking.

Nash blocked every blow. "This is counterproductive, Rhett," he said.

"You're not the only one with muscles and moves now, bro," retorted Temple.

He kicked once more at Nash but Nash caught the leg, forcing Temple to hop on one foot.

"Are you going to listen to reason or not?" asked Nash.

"I'm done listening," said Temple. He reached into his jacket and pulled out his gun.

The foot caught Temple on the side of the head. Nash let go of his leg at the same time, and Temple spun around and dropped to the floor unconscious, his gun falling to the floor. Nash scooped it up.

Mindy looked at Steers, who had struck the blow, and exclaimed, "Holy shit. You're like some kind of kung fu girl." Mindy then smiled broadly. "That was awesome."

Steers looked down at the senseless Temple, strode into the bathroom, came out with a glass of water, and dumped it on Temple's face.

Gagging and sputtering, he came to and sat up, looking around in a daze.

He glared at Nash. "You sucker-punched me."

"I did nothing to you. She did," added Nash, pointing at Steers.

She said, "Do you want to live or do you want to die, Mr. Temple? That is the question you have to answer."

He scrambled to his feet. "Of course I want to live, who doesn't?"

"Then you must listen to Walter."

"Is it just Walter, or Walter-*san*?" Temple said sarcastically.

Nash sat on a chair and said, "We know you murdered your father. We know you were going to kill Mindy tonight."

"You know shit!"

Nash held up his phone. "I have it all recorded on here, including your confessing to killing Barton. Up to you. The police, or you work with us?"

Temple started to blurt something out, but then seemed to recalculate. "I'm listening."

And Nash explained about his and Steers's roles with the FBI and CIA, respectively, and the sale of her business to Connor Lord. When he was done Temple looked at him and then Steers.

"Since when is a mole at the *top* of the pyramid?"

"That is irrelevant," said Steers. "It is what it is."

"Well, then I'm outta here." He started for the door, but Nash quickly rose and blocked him again.

"No, you're going to stay here. In fact, you're going into Sybaritic and take back the CEO position from the woman you appointed."

"But won't that piss off the new owner, this Lord guy?"

"Probably, but you'll just have to prove your loyalty to him."

"And how the hell am I supposed to do that?"

Nash said, "You're a lot smarter than your father ever gave you credit for, Rhett. You think quickly on your feet and you have excellent survival instincts."

"Well, I appreciate you saying that, *Walter-san*. But what am I supposed to do as the CEO?"

Steers answered. "Ingratiate yourself to Lord. Tell him how things can be run better with me out of the picture. Oh, and you'll also have to convince my mother."

"Your mother is a fucking psycho," barked Temple.

"She *is* mentally disturbed, but you can use that against her. I will show you how."

"And with what endgame? You told me the CIA has everything it needs to bring Lord down."

"This will buy us some more time, Mr. Temple. And distract Lord from finding me. And one can never have too much evidence."

"Okay, you want me to risk my life and help you? Why should I?"

Nash said, "Well, for starters, you screwed my wife. Second, you ruined my life. So it's time you started working on your salvation."

Mindy interjected, "He screws everything, including his own stepmother."

"Shut up, Min," snapped Temple. He looked at Nash. "Those two points don't really do it for me. What else you got?"

Nash held up his phone. "Well, then, you won't have to go to prison for the rest of your life. Hard to be a true billionaire behind bars. Take it or leave it."

Temple rubbed his face. "Shit, this is so..."

"Difficult?" said Steers. "Yes, it is. For all of us. But we are giving you an opportunity to avoid the serious consequences of your actions. Most people do not get that chance."

"Yeah, but the most likely scenario is I get killed by these people."

"You'll have a chance," said Nash. "That's all I had."

Temple eyed him and let out a long breath, and with it the man finally seemed to really calm down. "Okay, I get it, you got fucked, Walt, and I was part of that. And you lost your daughter too."

Nash had not told him about Maggie being alive. He needed the man to feel as guilty as possible. "So you'll do it?"

Temple looked at Steers, then back at Nash.

"Why not just turn me in to the police? Like you said, you have the evidence. I'm up to my armpits in crime. Yeah, it was because my old man lost his fortune and hoodwinked me into this shit. But so what? Nobody's going to be crying tears for me. And I'm part of the reason Maggie was killed."

"I don't think you're really like your father, Rhett. You showed courage and fairness in Myanmar. I know you love your sister, Angie. And you told me about your mother and what Barton did to her. I think who you are is a byproduct of how Barton treated you. But that doesn't mean he gets to define you now. He's dead. You're not. He has no more chances to get it right, but you do."

A long moment passed and Rhett Temple, his expression, surprisingly, one of contriteness followed by resolve, said, "Okay, I'm in. So how do we beat this Lord guy? And the dragon lady?"

Steers stepped forward to face him. "I will tell you *exactly* how."

CHAPTER 80

One week later, Rhett Temple marched into the offices of Sybaritic Investments and said hello to Ellen Douglas, the matronly receptionist.

"Mr. Temple, we haven't seen you in quite a while. You look different," she added, running her gaze over his more muscled and toned physique. He had shaved off the Fu Manchu.

"I've been at a spa, Ellen. Good for the body and soul." He nipped a cookie off the platter set on her desk. "How are things here?"

"They seem to be fine."

"Neisha Mirza?"

Douglas's lips curled in displeasure. "She...seems to have her own way of doing things."

"I'm sure. But don't worry, Ellen."

"What do you mean?"

Temple grinned. "I mean...I'm back!"

He bit into the cookie and banged his still-activated security pass against the sensor, and the door clicked open. Temple strode down the hall and then poked his head into one office.

"Rhett!" said Elaine Fixx. She rose from her desk. "What are you doing here?"

"I own the company, Elaine."

"No, I mean, I thought you'd basically retired and were traveling the world."

"Well, now I'm unretired. I'll be back in two minutes. Stay right there."

"What?"

But he had already walked off.

Temple marched to his old office, knocked on the door, and opened it before receiving an answer.

The woman behind the desk, Neisha Mirza, rose. She was in her forties, tall, poised, and intimidating.

"What are *you* doing here?" She did not sound or look pleased.

"Nice to see you too, Neisha. I'm here because I always like to deliver good news face-to-face."

"What good news?"

"I'm taking over as CEO. Your services are no longer needed."

"How is that good news for me?" snapped Mirza.

"Well, I didn't say it was good news for *you*."

"You're actually trying to fire me?" She stared at him as though the man had lost his mind.

"No, not trying, I *am* firing you. I have other plans for the place. Big plans. Big goals. Goals that you have not accomplished, or so I was told…by someone. Which is the only reason I'm here."

Now Mirza did not look so confident. She said, "I…I was unaware of—"

He cut her off. "Neisha, at this level, you always need to be aware…of everything. If you're not, things don't tend to end well."

"I was told that—"

"There has been a changing of the guards. I'm sure you've been watching the news. Steers is probably dead."

Mirza looked like she might be sick. "I did see that, but I didn't think—My God."

"God won't help you, unfortunately. You need to help yourself. Starting with leaving here. Quickly. Before certain other people show up."

Alarmed, she glanced around her office. "But…I…my things."

"I'll have them packed up and sent to your place. We appreciate your service." He stepped forward and put a hand on her arm. "And Neisha, this is not something you need to talk about to anyone. In fact, doing so would be very unfortunate for your...survival. And, reading the tea leaves, if I were you, I would get on a plane and fly as far away as possible as fast as possible. And if you've ever fantasized about becoming someone else, now would be a good time to realize that fantasy. I don't have to give you this warning. In fact, I'm taking a risk doing it. But I've been in your shoes before and I know none of this is fair. But such is life. Hell, if I didn't have to be here, I wouldn't. Unfortunately, I don't have a choice in the matter."

She paled and grabbed the edge of the desk to steady herself. "But—"

He gripped her arm harder. "I will take care of everything on this end. But if you don't do as I say, I cannot guarantee your safety. And I don't say that lightly, Neisha. You know the lay of the land. And when these people are displeased, it is not good for the target of their displeasure. And, like I said, I would not be back here if I didn't have to be. But I have a new boss. And I can tell you that his wish is for you to disappear off the face of the earth, because you were hired by Steers, who he probably had killed. What I'm offering you is a way to disappear, on your own terms. But the grace period is limited. Twenty-four hours. Think you can manage it?"

She grabbed her purse from a desk drawer, fled past him, and raced down the hall.

A few moments later he walked slowly back to Fixx's office; she was standing in the doorway. "What did you say to Mirza? She just hauled ass out of here."

"I just told her I hoped the criminal investigation against her wouldn't be too tough."

"Wait, what? How do you know there's an investigation?"

"Because I was the one who filed the complaint. Now, I want you back in Walt's old job."

She looked askance at him. "So you're promoting me after demoting me? Twice?"

"Third time's the charm. Pack your stuff. Now go."

After Fixx sped out of the room Temple walked back to his

office and sat down in a chair. His bravado was hiding more than a little anxiety. His conversation with Nash and Steers had been, to say the least, eye-opening. He was in serious trouble, he knew that. And it was coming from the law on one hand and Connor Lord and the Chinese on the other. The former could land him in prison for life. The latter could propel him into a grave for eternity.

He pulled out his phone and looked at the number. He drew a deep breath and made the call. The phone rang, and Temple waited for someone to answer.

Okay, here we go, killer.

CHAPTER 81

"Mr. Temple, welcome," said Connor Lord.

They were at the latter's estate in Malibu, standing around the same patio table as had Steers and Lord on her trip there with Nash.

"Thank you," said Temple. "Nice to meet you."

"I was curious as to why you wanted to *meet*," continued Lord after the men had sat. "I thought you had removed yourself from the business. At least that is what I was told."

"I tried to remove myself, but it kept calling me back."

Temple knew this was the biggest business pitch of his life and if he screwed it up, he was dead. But instead of filling him with anxiety, the challenge actually calmed him.

"You'll need to explain that."

"I came prepared to do that and a lot more, which I think you will find beneficial to both our interests."

"Go on, please."

Steers had drilled him with facts and background on Lord. Chess prodigy, super-high IQ, ruthlessness to match any cartel boss concealed behind a smooth, civilized, even aristocratic façade. But Temple had one advantage here.

This guy is, minus the brag and bluster, exactly like my father, who I knew better than anyone.

"First things first," said Temple. "Victoria Steers left you with a good business but also a lot of potential problems."

"I know the FBI piece. But that has been resolved."

"Even though they said Walter Nash was framed?"

"He has also not reappeared. I have it on good authority that he is not working with the Bureau any longer. He could well be dead."

"He could be," conceded Temple. "But you need to know that I fired Neisha Mirza and appointed myself as CEO of Sybaritic."

Lord lifted his teacup and took a sip. He was dressed in a dark two-piece suit with a light blue shirt. His pocket square matched the shirt. His complexion was perfect, his teeth the same. His hair had a high-dollar cut. His shoes cost thousands. He was the poster boy for a pampered existence.

Not just like my father, just like me, thought Temple.

"And why would you do that?"

"Because I can do a much better job than she could. And I want to prove it to you. And since I know how intelligent you are—"

"Excuse me, but how do you know this?"

"If you weren't, you would not have survived this long in the world we both inhabit. And when Steers spoke of you it was with respect...and fear. I never heard her talk that way about anyone else."

Lord nodded. "All right. You've made yourself the CEO. What now? Please keep in mind that your answer will be a factor in my decision on allowing you to remain CEO."

And living, thought Temple.

He leaned forward, and his voice dropped to a conspiratorial level. "As an intelligent man, you're no doubt wondering why I said the business has potential problems."

"Please elaborate."

"Your partners. Their business goals do not necessarily align with yours."

Lord shrugged. "I know that they believe we're killing too many of their customers."

"And Steers caved to that belief by pulling back on the fentanyl in the product. Consequently, for that reason, and others, deaths associated with the drug have dropped substantially. Which I know is not in line with your expectations."

"Nor mine," said a voice.

Temple turned to see Masuyo standing there. She had somehow crept up on them.

"I believe you two know each other," said Lord, who did not, to Temple's mind, look pleased at the woman's sudden appearance.

But it actually was very good for what Temple was attempting to accomplish. He rose and bowed to Masuyo. "Mrs. Steers, how are you?"

She sat down in one of the chairs. "That is no concern of yours. Now sit and explain."

Temple retook his seat. "If you put fentanyl back in the precursor process it will anger your partners. But even if you can overcome that, there are other issues standing in the way."

"Such as?" demanded Masuyo.

"Narcan, which can reverse an overdose. And better counseling and treatment methods. The fact that users often take the drug in pairs, so one can administer Narcan to the other if they overdose. They're also cutting pills into smaller quantities, lessening the effects and halving your profits. But besides all that, for me at least, the biggest problem is this: Fentanyl is a depressant."

"Why is that an issue?" said a puzzled Lord.

"Your overall goal, as I understand it, is to disrupt this country in a grand way. From the bottom to the top."

"And you know this how?" snapped Masuyo.

"I worked for your daughter for a long time, Mrs. Steers. If I didn't pick up on that, I'm too stupid for this job. Now, I have no dog in this hunt. You want to screw this country over? I don't care. I'm rich enough to live in another country, or a dozen if I want to. The French have better food, wine, and women, in my humble opinion."

"And your point?" said Masuyo irritably before Lord could interject a query. To Temple's mind, the man was clearly growing frustrated with her. Which might be a good thing for him, Temple thought.

"To disrupt, I mean really disrupt, you don't want people to die quietly and alone. They're found, buried, and that's it. Yes, there is some disruption for the families and the like, but what I have in mind is far greater, and it will achieve your and your partners' goals at the same time."

"Tell us," ordered Masuyo.

This was it, thought Temple. The holy grail if he could sell this. "You would agree that if I can do this a reward would be in order?"

"What sort of reward?" said Masuyo—again, before Lord could ask.

"I don't need more money, if that's what you thought it would be." He paused and then took off his jacket, undid his cufflink and rolled up his shirt sleeve, exposing the long scar on his arm.

Masuyo watched him closely, as did Lord, who looked mildly repulsed by the wound.

"Your daughter had this done to me," he said. "She actually wanted to kill me, but my father talked her out of it. So my reward, with your permission, is to kill her."

He slowly rolled down his sleeve and reinserted the cufflink. He looked at Masuyo. When she said nothing he looked at Lord. "And I will deliver her head to you, as proof."

"As proof of her death?" said Lord. "There is no need for that."

"No, as proof of my loyalty to *you*. Steers did things her own way, and not always in a way that benefited the mission." He looked back at Masuyo as he said this. "She got you out of that prison, but it seemed clear to me, from the brief time I was there, that you two butted heads almost right away. Tell me if I'm wrong."

Masuyo did not answer, which was an answer in itself.

He looked again at Lord. "Someone tried to kill her not too long ago. I heard on the news that they mowed down everybody in that house, only she wasn't there." He turned to Masuyo. "Apparently she and Dillon Hope were out when the attack occurred. That is too big a coincidence. Which means someone tipped her off."

Masuyo bristled. "Are you accusing me of something, Mr. Temple?"

"There's only room for one leader, right? And it seemed to me that you had lost faith in your daughter to be that person. So you stepped in."

"Then, instead of warning her, you think I had something to do with that attack at her home?" Masuyo said, drilling him with a dark look.

"Let me put it to you this way: When my father was killed, I made it my business not to be anywhere near where he died, at least that was provable. And I know you're a lot smarter than I am, Mrs. Steers. So when bodies started tumbling at your daughter's estate I was not surprised to find you were not there."

He let that statement fall and then said nothing else. He used his peripheral vision to see Lord's reaction. The man looked suspicious, which was exactly what Temple was going for.

So Masuyo had instigated the attack, without getting approval from Lord first, deduced Temple.

Masuyo sat up straighter and then receded back into her chair, her manner not nearly as commanding.

Lord said, "So what is your plan to appease our partners and also achieve our *goals*?"

"Methamphetamine," replied Temple.

"It is an old, tired drug," said Masuyo dismissively, clearly trying to regain the advantage. She glanced sharply at Lord. "This is all he has, really?"

Temple plowed ahead. "It *is* an oldie but a goody. For starters it's a *stimulant*, not a depressant like fentanyl. Mexican labs already churn out the stuff, then distribute it throughout California and the southwest, where it's pipelined to the rest of the country. They don't need pseudoephedrine anymore to make it; they did a chemical workaround. And it's more potent than the old version. They took a page from the cigarette manufacturers and tweaked the formula to make it even more addictive. One pop, you're pretty much hooked for life. Narcan has no effect on it. Methadone works on fentanyl but not on meth. There is no real treatment, no FDA-approved drugs to help beat the addiction. They try to detox you and get you through in-patient rehab, family therapy, and the like. But it's a long road with a low success rate. Meth comes in a pill, crystals, powder, and liquid, which is a really dangerous way to take it. You can snort, smoke, swallow, or inject it. The effects last for hours and even days. People forget to eat, drink water, sleep. They have delusions, hallucinations, they get violent, they tear shit up, howl at the moon, run into traffic, attack people, pick at their skin. It floods the brain with dopamine; the pop is unbelievable and people will kill their mother and their own children to get another hit."

"Interesting facts, Mr. Temple, but your point?" said Lord.

"My point is, you can combo meth with xylazine, an animal tranquilizer, and get some more deaths out of it, but you'll also create some turbocharged crazy shit happening all over the country. Long-term effects are cognitive decline, depression, heart valve issues, stroke, brain bleeds, and meth mouth, meaning your teeth fall out as your gums rot. So, at a massive scale, all that will end up bankrupting the health care system in this country."

"But it is not immediately fatal," countered Masuyo. "That is the whole point."

"Well, I don't know about that, since nearly forty thousand died from overdosing meth last year in this country. But, again, why have death as the main goal? As I alluded to before, nobody sees the body except the police, the funeral director, and the family. The media reports on it occasionally and you have some sob stories here and there. But I don't call that true disruption, just sweeping it under the rug, really. With meth you got people climbing trees, attacking Grandma and their own babies, stealing and trashing stuff, walking onto interstate highways, invading homes and businesses. Police gunning them down. Hospitals full of berserk nutjobs. People scared to go outside. Needles and glass pipes and drug paraphernalia everywhere. And again, one pop and you're hooked, so maybe you start getting people to take hits without even knowing they are. You got a lot more addicts that way. And a lot more chaos." He paused and then fixed his gaze on Lord.

Temple continued: "I guess it comes down to which do you think is more *disruptive*. People lying quietly in graves and urns, or the fucking zombie apocalypse? And it'll get your partners off your back because they won't be losing so many customers, and because meth is so addictive those customers will keep coming back until the country goes right down the toilet, while you make more money than you ever have before because meth is cheap as shit to make and easy to get past police checkpoints."

He stopped, spread his hands, and said, "That's it. That's my plan."

He saw Masuyo quivering with some emotion but then Lord said, "A well-thought-out plan, Mr. Temple. I am impressed." He looked at Masuyo. "Aren't you?"

Masuyo didn't answer right way but then said, "It seems to have reasonable potential."

"So if it works out I can kill your daughter and bring *you* her head?"

Masuyo turned to him and said, "It would give me great pleasure."

"What are the next steps?" asked Lord.

"A trip to what I like to call ground fucking zero," replied Temple.

CHAPTER 82

A WEEK LATER, AT AN ENORMOUS warehouse facility a few miles south of San Diego and near the Mexican border, Rhett Temple, having just landed in his private jet a half hour before, strode through a side door with several armed men. Behind them came Connor Lord and Masuyo, who had just helicoptered in from Lord's place in Malibu. Lord's security detail also accompanied them.

The inside of the building was vast. On the rear side were loading docks, where a dozen semis were loading up with the products flowing from the warehouse. Workers scurried here and there, and forklifts rumbled over the cement floor, passing between enormous shelves rising fifty feet into the air, and all of them piled high with boxes full of merchandise.

In another section were long columns of huge refrigeration units crammed full of fruits, vegetables, and other perishables.

Lord said, "I was aware of this facility because it was part of the assets that I purchased, but I had not yet visited. From its sheer size I can see why you call it ground zero for the operation."

Temple said, "It was actually purchased through my company, Sybaritic. I've been here many times over the years. In addition to fentanyl and other synthetic opioids, your daughter, Ms. Steers, trafficked in the more traditional contraband. LSD, heroin, coke, crack, GHB, and Ecstasy. And *meth*."

Temple led Lord and Masuyo over to a stack of watermelons. He pulled one off the top, asked one of his security detail for a knife, slit the watermelon open, and laid the two halves on a work table.

Temple put on a double pair of nitrile gloves. "This watermelon has already been cut open. But then it was resealed so meticulously with a process we developed that no one could ever tell." He pried out a dark seed. "That's actually an Ecstasy pill. All the seeds are. We also put in GHB, fentanyl, pills laced with heroin, LSD. Don't think even the drug-sniffing dogs can ferret this out."

He next led them over to one of the warehouse shelves. He pulled off a box and opened it, revealing rolls of toilet paper. He unwrapped one roll and undid the toilet paper. "You can't really see it, but there's coke laced throughout the paper. We tried stuffing packs of pills and powder into the cardboard holder, but the cops figured that one out."

They followed him to another shelf full of boxes.

He opened one and pulled out a bottle of perfume. From another box he lifted out a can of mineral water.

"Liquid meth is in both of these. When they get to where they're going the meth will be extracted from the perfume and the water."

"And does anyone actually drink the water after that or use the perfume?" asked a smiling Lord.

"Well, the extraction process is not one hundred percent, so you do so at your peril," said Temple, adding a chuckle.

Masuyo said darkly, "Let's hope additional overdoses come from those who do so, then."

Temple tossed the gloves in a hazardous waste receptable, then led them all into a small office and closed the door. "This place is two million square feet and employs an army of people. Now, a ton of legit stuff is moved out of here as well, so as to keep up appearances and also because it's profitable. We actually provide warehousing, delivery, and other logistical support for some of the biggest retailers in the country. We pay taxes, field local baseball and softball teams, give out scholarships, all the feel-good stuff. The community here is poor and we're one of the biggest employers. We're not far from the border, so we have to play everything close to the vest, but that proximity also works in our favor. We've built innumerable channels and methods for getting the drugs from Mexico to here. Then we work our magic packing the drugs into the products." He opened the office door and pointed across the hall to a solid, alarmed door. "Behind that door is where all that happens. Then the products come out here, are stored, and then readied for shipping. We don't sit on anything long. We get it in and we get it out. And we get paid." He looked at Lord. "Your money now, Mr. Lord."

As Temple shut the office door, Masuyo added sharply, "And mine." Her comment drew a look of annoyance from Lord.

"Impressive operation," said Lord.

"It was one of the first projects I worked on when I became *associated* with Steers. This is the main location for moving her entire product into the U.S. I've been here so many times over the years I've come to know just about everyone who works here. A good crew. They work hard."

Masuyo said, "They will need to learn to work harder."

This comment drew another scowl from Lord.

Temple said, "The workers here really are top-dollar and loyal as they come, ma'am. When I visit I hand out cash to them for a job well done."

Masuyo looked at him with a patronizing expression. "You clearly have a different management style than I do."

Lord said sharply, "Well, *his* method appears to have worked remarkably well."

Masuyo would not even look at him. She kept her pursed lips and stern gaze pointed at Temple.

Lord said, "I compliment you on your approach, Mr. Temple." He paused, his eyes dancing with anticipation. "And now, I have a little surprise for you."

Temple did not look happy. "Surprise? I'm not really into surprises."

"Oh, you're going to love this one."

He nodded at two of his security detail, who hurried off.

A minute later they brought back to the office two people whose hands were shackled and who had hoods over their heads.

"Who's this?" asked Temple nervously.

On a nod from Lord the men swept the hoods off, revealing Walter Nash and Victoria Steers with gags in their mouths.

CHAPTER 83

A STUNNED TEMPLE BLURTED OUT, "WHERE the hell did you find them?"

Lord smiled. "You may not be aware that I quite enjoy a rousing chess match, Mr. Temple. And in chess one must see the whole board, at all times. Every possible scenario. I knew that the reason for Ms. Steers selling her business to me for such a low price had certain components to it. She is a supremely smart businesswoman, so why be so generous to me? Despite what she had told me in explanation, I did not believe it. So I kept an eye on her. The attack at her home had nothing to do with me. That came from another." He glanced at Masuyo. "Which caused me to lose her trail for a while. But we recently regained our advantage. Real estate paper trail, the home in New Orleans. Some CCTV at gas stations and other retail outlets reviewed by AI facial recognition software, and presto, there they were. I gave them a short leash because I wanted to understand their plans. We followed them to a hotel not too far from your estate, where I am sure they were busy planning how to do me harm. They of course could not go back to Ms. Steers's estate, as they were possible suspects in the murders that took place there. And they well knew that someone wanted them dead and would be watching." He put a hand on Nash's shoulder. "And let's dispense with the fiction that this man is Dillon Hope. Hello, Walter Nash."

Nash looked wide-eyed while Temple said, "How the hell?"

"Isaiah York's business? Transforming one man into another man? I believe that you, Mr. Temple, tried to do the same thing, with less successful results. You see, it all comes down to the smallest of details. I also had spies in your household. Fingerprints on a glass? Difficult to keep that totally secret. Plus you haven't changed your email password in a very long time, and intercepting your phone calls was fairly easy."

"Shit," mumbled Temple.

"Your confrontation with Mr. Nash outside of Ms. Steers's home was also duly observed when you told him you knew the truth." He added leisurely, "I could have pulled the trigger at any time, but decided to wait until it was most advantageous for me."

"And for me also," added a gloating Masuyo.

Lord gave her a condescending look before staring back at Temple. "I have also come to learn that Ms. Steers has been working with a certain American intelligence agency to bring me and my partners down. This could not be allowed, of course, and I knew the time had come to end the chess match. So, acting on my orders, my men captured them and flew them here." He looked at Temple. "Now, is there anything you'd care to add to this? As an incentive you should understand that I know they approached you with a grand plan that they hoped would deliver them to victory. I would just say that your telling me the truth is the only chance for survival that you have, small though it is."

Temple glanced at both Nash and Steers with a defeated look. They stared back at him with hopeless expressions. "Well, since you seem to know pretty much all of it, yeah, they wanted me to work with them to get back at both of you."

"And your answer to their proposal?" asked Masuyo, a thin smile playing triumphantly over her lips.

Temple shook his head. "They showed up at my house and threatened me with the truth about my father's death while...I was there taking care of a little problem with my stepmother." He looked at Nash. "I guess he guilted me. Even though my old man deserved it." He pointed at Steers. "She had a plan that she laid out. Said it was foolproof. All I had to do was my part."

"Which was what, exactly?" asked Lord.

Temple reached into his jacket and produced a recording device. "This."

He tossed the device to one of Lord's men, who dropped it on the floor and crushed it with his heel.

"I was to bring you here and get you on tape with all this stuff, saying incriminating things. Send it to the cops and you all go down." He pointed around the room. "And there are hidden cameras all around filming us right now. We were going to use that, too."

"I thank you for your honesty," said Lord. "But I had this entire facility swept for surveillance devices before I ever agreed to step foot in here. Everything was remotely disabled, and/or jammed." He paused. "But I now worry about what to do with you after this betrayal."

"*I* have no such worries," interjected Masuyo darkly.

Temple sighed and spread his hands. "You know, I really don't give a shit. My whole life someone's been telling me what to do. My old man made my life miserable." He pointed at Nash. "And I've been compared to this guy for years and always ended up on the short end. I tried to disappear, worked my ass off for that, and of course it didn't work, either. Got all the money in the world but I've really got nothing. I'm beyond sick of it. They told me I could be a hero by helping them. And you know what, being a hero sounded good. But it didn't pan out, did it? Of course it didn't. And now I'm screwed. But to be honest, I've been that ever since I came out of my mother's womb."

Masuyo looked at Lord. "I am tired of listening to him whine. Just kill them all and be done with it. And then we leave this place."

Lord looked at his men and nodded.

However, they had made a mistake in not shackling Nash's or Steers's legs. Nash executed the kick to Temple's head perfectly. The man spun around and collapsed to the floor, spitting blood out of his mouth.

Nash didn't stop there. He caught one of the security detail flush on the chest with a mule kick and sent him cartwheeling over a stainless steel table stacked with boxes.

One of the other guards pulled a gun, but Steers struck him with a kick to his hand. His weapon flew away and Nash lunged for it.

He reached it and stood, but before he could swing the gun up, something hit him in the gut.

Temple was standing right in front of him, blood dripping from his face from the blow delivered by Nash. Nash looked down to see the hilt of the knife against his belly. Temple slowly walked the knife up toward the sternum and then moved it side to side just as Shock had instructed in order to sever the aorta.

Blood now oozed over the front of Nash's shirt.

Temple held Nash's fading gaze and said, "I'm sorry, Walter. I'm sorry it didn't work out. I really wanted to be a hero, for once, but it just wasn't meant to be, man. It's just not my destiny. All the shit we went through, Sybaritic, my old man, fucking Myanmar." He glared at Steers. "Her!" His expression softened as he looked back at Nash. "At least you'll be heading upstairs. Me? I don't think so. I only see fire in my future. Hopefully, I won't run into my dad."

He pulled the knife free, and since that was the only thing holding up Nash, he slipped to the floor and lay still.

Steers managed to loosen her gag and scream, "Walter!" She lunged toward him.

Two of the guards grabbed Steers and pulled her back.

Temple slipped the bloody knife into his pocket and motioned to one of his security detail. "Let me have your gun."

"No!" exclaimed Masuyo. "Kill him."

Six guns were instantly pointed at Temple.

Temple said, "Keep your hair on, *Dai Lu*. Nobody's shooting your scrawny ass."

He motioned to the guard again. The man looked questioningly at Lord, who cautiously nodded his assent.

He passed his weapon over to Temple. Surprisingly, he immediately held it out to Masuyo.

The older woman looked at the gun and then at him. "And what do you expect me to do with *that*?" she asked stonily.

"I'm giving you the honor of killing your daughter. I thought it would please you. You don't want to waste the effort pulling the trigger on me. I'm not important enough. Any one of your muscle can do that. But I assume your daughter is special." He glared at Steers again. "And since she ruined my life I wouldn't mind seeing her eat a round and go bye-bye while I'm still breathing."

Masuyo smiled and took the gun from him. But then, just as surprisingly, she held out the pistol to Lord, who looked sharply at her.

"Here, Mr. Lord. I have killed enough people. *You* may do the honors."

Lord did not reach for the gun. He seemed about to say something to Masuyo, but then he looked around at the security men and Temple, who all stared back at him expectantly.

"Is there something wrong, Mr. Lord?" said Masuyo icily. "Surely, you have killed someone before?"

The up-to-now-masterful Lord looked nervous. He slowly reached out for the gun and gripped it. It was clear how the man held it that he was not used to wielding a firearm.

Temple walked over and grabbed Steers by the hair, forcing her to stand straight. "Aim directly for the fucking heart," he instructed Lord. "If she has one."

A gasping, teary Steers glanced at Masuyo, "Māma, please."

"You are no daughter of mine," she snapped. "You are weak and have placed yourself into this situation through your own stupidity. And now you must pay the price for your incompetence."

Lord looked down at the weapon and then was surprised when the same guard took the gun from him, demonstrated how to hold and aim it, and then handed it back. "Round's already in the chamber, sir. Just aim and pull the trigger."

He stepped back. Lord looked at Masuyo, who said, "We have wasted enough time. Do it."

Lord squared his shoulders, gripped the weapon with both hands, took aim, and looked at Steers.

Her face was now one of stone. She used her shoulder to push Temple roughly away. "I have no need of your *assistance*," she said imperiously.

Steers pointed her shackled hands directly at her heart.

"Not even a *weak* man like yourself could fail in this endeavor," she taunted, even as she looked down at Nash's body. She closed her eyes and the tears drained from them.

"Goodbye, Walter."

Lord aimed at her chest and pulled the trigger.

The gun fired and Steers flinched with the impact. Blood immediately spread across the front of her shirt where a hole had now appeared. She looked once at her mother, and then her eyes rolled up into her head and she fell next to Nash.

"And now, Mr. Temple, it is your turn," said Masuyo, as she nodded at one of her men.

Temple moved to stand in front of her. "Take your best shot, lady. And I'll see you in hell."

A moment later every door in the warehouse exploded inward.

CHAPTER 84

FBI SPECIAL AGENT REED MORRIS strode down the long hallway, his heels clicking rhythmically on the cement floor. He turned left, then stopped at the cell door. The uniformed man next to the door nodded, unlocked the portal, and Morris went inside.

At the table Connor Lord was outfitted in a prison jumpsuit and shackled to a bolt in the floor.

Morris sat down, opened a file he was carrying, and noted the date, time, and people in the room into a recorder that sat on the tabletop.

Lord said, "I have already requested an attorney, so you can ask me nothing." He could not have looked any more smug.

"I'm not here to ask questions, because I have no need to. You've been charged with murder."

"I have no idea what you're taking about," said Lord. "I was in a warehouse when your agents burst in. We were taken there by Rhett Temple. Who, by the way, killed Walter Nash and Victoria Steers."

"We've already talked to Temple. He's agreed to a deal."

"How was he able to make a deal?" said Lord. "He murdered Walter Nash right in front of us."

Morris cleared his throat and looked grimly at him. "He's going to prison for the rest of his life for that crime. And he's cooperating with us to put you away for the rest of your life."

"This is ridiculous. He killed Nash. And Steers."

"Steers's death is not something that will ever make me lose any sleep. But Walter Nash was a hero who ultimately sacrificed his life to do the right thing. And he was also my friend. I only wish we had arrived in time to save him. But you are going to pay for your crimes."

"I have no idea what you're talking about. What crimes? I was in a warehouse at the request of Mr. Temple. If there is something illicit going on there you must talk to him," said Lord. "I know nothing whatsoever about it."

"Before you bought her out, you had been working with the late Victoria Steers. But you weren't alone in that. You had major backing from Beijing."

"That is preposterous."

"Actually the Chinese say the same. In fact, they have disclaimed any ties to you at all. Indeed, whatever property you owned in China has now been confiscated by their government, or so we've been told. And the U.S. government has impounded all of your property and assets in this country. The same for our global partners, including all your friends in the Middle East who are doing their best to forget who you are because they are about to be hit with severe sanctions. And a certain prison in Myanmar? It's been visited by Interpol agents, and its prisoner population was found to be, well, interesting, to say the least. It's now been closed and a major investigation started. So right now, you have zero assets. But rest assured, you will be provided with a public defender. And Beijing will not escape this scot-free. They will take a hit on the world's stage, for sure."

Lord said, "But with Victoria Steers dead, how can you prove anything? Who will take the word of a murderer like Rhett Temple?"

"Steers previously recorded all her testimony against both of you. And Nash provided a treasure trove of evidence as well."

"My lawyers will never allow that evidence in. And if Steers can't testify in person, that's too bad."

"No, it *will* be admissible because we also have video of you shooting her."

"That is absolutely impossible," exclaimed Lord.

"Why, because you swept it for bugs and used jamming signals?"

Morris smiled. "That would work for most surveillance operations, but not the one we employed. DHS and NSA have some amazing backdoors to every tech manufacturer in the world, Mr. Lord. Trust me when I tell you that we have the goods. All through warrants, all legal and admissible. We have you dead to rights for the murder of Victoria Steers. That will allow her video testimony to come in."

Morris looked down at his file. "Bail will never be granted, so you'll be in prison for the duration before trial, which might be years away." He rose and closed his file. "FYI, we've already made dozens of arrests of your major coconspirators, closed down fourteen major distribution centers, confiscated five billion dollars' worth of contraband, and shut off the financial pipelines for half of the world's major drug suppliers. And these folks are falling all over themselves to cut deals and testify against you and Masuyo Steers. And Beijing is fully back on their heels and offering all sorts of goodies to us too. All in all, a nice day."

"Then why did you want to meet if there is nothing you need from me?" demanded Lord.

Morris leaned down to stare at the man. "Because I wanted to tell you to your face that you are royally *fucked*." He lifted his middle finger to the man. "And that's for Walter Nash, who most definitely got the last laugh."

He walked out.

CHAPTER 85

Maggie and Judith Nash sat side by side in the front row of a small church in southern California.

Next to them was a closed casket set on a church truck.

The mother and daughter had been reunited weeks earlier, and the moment had been emotional and sob-filled. They had clung to each other for hours.

Behind them sat Shock, his large body bowed and his features full of grief. "I'm so sorry," he said to them as he leaned forward.

The women turned to him, teary-eyed, and they each placed a hand on one of Shock's broad shoulders.

"Isaiah, you did all you could for him," said Judith. "Without you helping he never would have survived as long as he did."

Shock said, "He was just like his daddy, you know. His motor ain't ever quit. And all he talked about was you two. How much he loved you and all."

"He never quit, on anything," said Judith. "And I can't believe I was...unfaithful to him."

Maggie shuddered when her mother said this. But she put her hand on top of Judith's and gripped it. "We all make mistakes, Mom. All of us."

"I'm so sorry, Maggie. For everything."

"We still have each other. That's what Dad would have wanted. Okay?"

Shock said, "And you got me, too. No lie."

Then he slipped his hand into his pocket and took out the necklace and locket that Judith had worn around her neck and then left at the spot where she believed her daughter's remains had been discovered. "They found this with Walter's things. I know he would want you to have it back, Judith."

She took it from him, opened the locket, and looked at the picture of her daughter on the day she was born. "Thank you, Isaiah."

They all rose, went to the closed casket, and put their hands on it. Judith's legs started to buckle. Shock quickly gripped her by the shoulder and held her up.

Two FBI agents came forward from the back of the church and led mother and daughter out to waiting cars. Shock walked out to his rental car and stood there. The casket was rolled out and placed into a hearse, and it was driven away as Shock, Maggie, and Judith somberly watched.

There would be no burial. They had been told that Nash's remains had already been cremated, and the urn was inside the casket. His ashes, the agents had told Judith and Maggie, would be given to them before they left to fly home.

They had new identities, and the money that the government had contracted with Nash to pay him had been transferred to accounts over which they would have control. They were now wealthy in dollars. But they were impoverished in everything else. Both women started to sob as they were driven away.

After they left, the church was quiet for about ten minutes before a tall man stepped out from a side room and surveyed the space.

Then Walter Nash walked over and sat in the front pew.

I just attended my own funeral. But... it has to be this way. For a lot of reasons.

His anxiety heightened, Nash did the old breathing exercises his father had taught him. They had long served him well, but this time they did not seem up to the task. Neither did thinking of the painting with the girl and dog. Nothing seemed to be able to plug the hole in the dead center of his chest. He was physically strong but weak everywhere else.

"I know how hard this is for you, Walter."

Nash turned around. Shock came out of the shadows and sat down next to him.

"It's harder for Judith and Maggie," said a shaken Nash. "Far harder."

"Yeah, but don't shortchange yourself on grief, Walter. You lost a helluva lot, too." He paused. "I know why you couldn't tell them the truth."

"I tried to convince myself that it would be all right. That I could tell them. That I could go and live with them as a family again, under assumed names. But that's a pipe dream. And if all three of us go into hiding? And we're found out? I couldn't take that risk. If the world thinks I'm dead, then no one will bother to hunt for them to make them reveal where I am. Better I'm always separate from them, Shock. It's just safer all around."

"Logic don't make it any easier to swallow," said Shock. "But I appreciate you lettin' me in on the fact that you made it through okay."

"You can take care of yourself, Shock. That I know better than most."

"You ever need anythin', man, I'm here for you. No lie."

"Because of the promise you made to my father?"

"No. This ain't got a damn thing to do with your daddy. I will be here for you, Walter, because of you, no one else."

Shock put out a big hand, which Nash shook.

Then the man rose and left, leaving Nash sitting in an empty church wondering what came next.

CHAPTER 86

Masuyo had been sent to a federal prison in Texas to await trial. The prosecution was contemplating seeking the death penalty against the woman for her myriad crimes, which had resulted in the deaths of hundreds of thousands of Americans.

She looked small and frail, like she had in that prison in Myanmar, though there her *infirmity* had far more to do with hair and makeup, the requisite dirty clothing, and her own acting skills.

Masuyo was being held in solitary confinement and thus was surprised when she learned that she had visitors. She was even more surprised when she was told the name of one of the visitors.

"Dai Lu?" she had asked the guard escorting her to a secure visitors' room.

He had nodded but offered no other comment.

Believing that Beijing had finally sent someone to aid her, Masuyo's heart filled with hope and added a spring to her otherwise shackle-burdened walk.

Two people were waiting for her in the visitors' room.

A big man with long hair and a full beard and thick glasses, and a tall, thin woman with close-cropped blond hair and wearing large sunglasses.

The guard locked Masuyo's shackles into a bolt on the floor and exited the room.

Masuyo stared across at the pair and said eagerly, "Who are you? Why did you want to see me?"

When she saw that the woman was looking over her shoulder,

Masuyo glanced that way too and saw that the surveillance camera that was hanging on the wall had been pointed to the ceiling.

Masuyo turned back around and hissed, "Who are you?"

The woman took off her sunglasses. Victoria Steers said, "Hello, Māma."

Masuyo sucked in a breath. "You are dead."

"Yes, you're right. To the world I am dead."

Masuyo smiled triumphantly. "But now you have placed yourself in my power, you stupid child. You will get me out of this prison, or I will tell the world that you are really alive. And all your enemies will gather and crush you."

"There is no need for histrionics," said Steers calmly. "We actually came here to free you from this place. Walter has come to support me in that endeavor."

Masuyo eyed the man closely and nodded. "Yes, I see him now behind the beard and long hair. Two peas in a pod, Daughter. Well, how do you plan to free me?"

The visit here had been arranged with the FBI's and the CIA's full blessing, although Steers was awaiting her own punishment by the American authorities and was technically under arrest and in custody. This visit was a reward for Steers's helping the U.S. government. It had also been approved to avoid a potentially embarrassing incident for China, which the current U.S. administration intended to hold over Beijing's head to gain the upper hand on certain disagreements between the two superpowers.

In response, Steers reached up and lifted the back of the blond wig. When she brought her hands back down, she was holding a small plastic tube with a screw-top. Inside the tube was a small quantity of liquid.

Masuyo looked at the tube and then up at her daughter. "What is this? You play stupid games when time is of the essence."

"They seek the death penalty against you," said Nash.

"I am aware of that."

"It's by lethal injection," interjected Nash.

"Not exactly what you did to poor Hiroko-san, but close enough," added Steers.

"What?" snapped Masuyo. "You talk of that foolish old woman *now?*"

"Hiroko-san was not foolish. *You* are the foolish one," retorted Steers. "All your life you worked and sacrificed for your masters, and at the one moment when you truly needed them, they abandoned you. Do you see now, Māma, finally, how *you* are the fool?"

"I am...I am sure they are at this moment conceiving of...of a plan—"

"There is no plan. There is nothing. Except for this." She held up the tube. "You can either await the executioner's injection at some point in the future. Or take the honorable way out and secure your death how, where, and when you and only you choose it. I give you this opportunity though I owe you nothing. No-thing," she said again.

"So you, too, abandon your mother in her hour of need?"

"Hiroko-san was my mother. I called you Māma as a mere technicality. You were never a mother to me. You were the opposite of a mother. You are vile and disgusting and you raised me to be the same."

Steers paused and looked at Nash, who nodded in support. Then she looked back at the woman. "But in this you have failed, Masuyo. I am not you. I will never be you. I am Victoria, my father's daughter."

"Your real father—"

"My father was Joseph Steers, a good man whom you murdered for no reason other than that you are evil beyond all comprehension."

Steers set the tube in front of her mother and sat back looking expectant. "It is your choice, *Masuyo.* You can let them kill you. Or you can make your own choice."

She and Nash rose.

Masuyo crumpled and gasped, "No, Daughter, do not leave me here alone. Please. I will do whatever you tell me—"

"I *tell* you to make a choice. Now."

"Only cowards take their own lives."

"Goodbye, Masuyo. We will never see one another again. And your executioner will decide your time of death. I hope it is the most agonizing wait of your amoral life." She reached for the tube.

But before Steers could take it, a desperate Masuyo grabbed the tube, unscrewed the top, and swallowed the contents. She looked up wide-eyed at her daughter.

"You have chosen wisely," said Steers.

Using a handkerchief Steers gingerly took the empty tube and top, and put them in her bag.

She bent down so she was eye to eye with Masuyo and said, "For what you did to dear Hiroko-san, may you receive your just punishment for all of eternity."

CHAPTER 87

Rhett Temple paced back and forth in the small room, anxiously checking his watch and looking at the door.

When it opened he halted his pacing and glanced over.

Walter Nash came in, and the men sat down in the two chairs that constituted the only furniture in the room.

"Well, I'm glad that's over, and we made it through," said Temple.

"It's never really going to be over," noted Nash.

"No, I guess not," said Temple dully.

Nash eyed the spot on Temple's face where he'd kicked him. "All healed up?"

"Yeah."

"Had to make it look real."

"Right, I know. Hope I didn't hit you too hard with the knife to the gut."

"Your performance was Oscar-worthy, Rhett. And the knife hilt having real blood to eject onto me? Definitely sold the image of me breathing my last. And you using the maneuver Shock taught us both to cut the aorta? A classic touch."

"The FBI provided the knife. And a video on how to use it. But I have to hand it to Steers. It played out just like she said. Talk about outmaneuvering a chess champ. It was the greatest battle of wits I've ever seen because Lord knew a lot more than I thought he did. But she must have already figured that in. And that is...well, special."

"She's a formidable person. Both by design and necessity."

Temple looked down at his hands. "Full confession, Walt, I...I forced Mindy to go along with what happened to my dad. She's not to blame. It was all me. But he just made me so mad. I wanted his help to save Maggie's life. To talk to Steers and get her back safely, but he just... didn't give a shit. That's when I just lost it and attacked him. And then? I did what I did because I didn't see another way out."

"What happened to your father wasn't right, Rhett. Although I appreciate you trying to help Maggie, I really do. But Barton made choices in life, and he got you into all this. And he contributed to the deaths of many people. I, for one, do not lament his passing."

Temple slowly nodded. "Yeah, good old Dad." He shook his head and said, "So what happened to Thura?"

"He thankfully recovered from his injuries and is living in France, in high style due to Steers."

"Does he know that you're alive?"

"No. It's better that way. For him. He's suffered enough."

"So... what happens to me?"

Nash sat back and studied him. "None of this would have worked without your doing what you did."

"But I still have to pay the piper, right?"

"There's nothing I can do about that. But you can afford the best lawyers."

"Right, yeah." Temple added a hollow chuckle to these words.

"And I've talked to the feds, Rhett. Based on all you did and the risks you took and how you were forced into the business in the first place, there is a definite inclination from them to go light on you. I think you'll have a lot of decades left to enjoy."

"Seriously?" said Temple, looking both surprised and hopeful.

"Yes. But you have to own the mistakes of your past, Rhett. Only you don't have to let those mistakes dictate your future. It's really up to you. But I wish you only the best. I mean that. I know we never saw eye to eye on a lot and with what happened with Judith." He paused and gathered himself. "I think you have it in you to redeem yourself. But only you can make that decision. I would just suggest that you choose to be the Rhett Temple who loves his sister Angie and wants to do right by her, more than the guy who wants to strut around with his billions. And you have a daughter, who deserves to have a father who loves her."

The men rose and shook hands. Then Temple wrapped his arms around Nash and held him tightly even as he wept, his body shuddering against Nash's.

When Temple stepped back and rubbed his face dry, Nash said, "Take care, Rhett. And do some good with all that you have."

Then Nash walked out.

CHAPTER 88

The prison was in the middle of nowhere, not a scrap of cover to hide any inmate trying to escape. The walls were brick, tall, and weathered. Guards carrying rifles manned the four stations at each corner of the parapet. It was a grim, foreboding place that seemed to have sucked away any hope, any happiness for a hundred miles in all directions.

A car pulled up and stopped in front and a man got out.

Walter Nash leaned against the fender and waited. And reflected.

Temple was right. Steers really had fought the battle of wits of her life leading up to the events at that warehouse. He had respected the woman greatly before that had happened. Afterward, that respect had reached a whole new level.

And now here he was. Waiting. For her.

Twenty minutes later the front gates of the prison opened and out walked a woman with a buzz cut and a long, lean frame.

Walter Nash pushed off the fender and walked toward Victoria Steers, who stood there with a small bag containing the few items she had brought with her to prison.

She looked surprised to see him, a fact that Nash noted.

"You thought I wouldn't be here?" he said.

"I didn't think they would tell you."

"I have a friend who kept me in the loop."

He took her small bag and escorted her to the car. Before he drove them off Nash turned to look at her. She was thinner, her face drawn, but the hair really caught him.

"Your idea?" he said, pointing to the ultra-short cut.

"Inside there you do not have ideas. You just do what they tell you to."

"You want to get some food? You look like you could use a good meal."

"Thank you, yes."

"Anything in particular?"

"It doesn't matter, so long as it's not in there," she said, glancing apprehensively at the prison.

After their meal he drove her to a small residential apartment building two hours from the prison and in a small town with rugged mountains in the distance. He walked up the stairs with her and unlocked the door to the apartment.

They stepped inside and Steers looked around. "Who furnished it?"

"I did, but the government footed the bill. I hope it's comfortable."

"It is very nice, Walter, thank you."

"And there are new clothes in the bedroom closet, things for the kitchen and bathroom. I tried to be thorough."

"I have no doubt of that."

He led her to a back room, opened the door, and turned on the light. The room was empty except for an easel with a canvas on it, a stool, and a cabinet on wheels loaded with art supplies. He pointed to the sole window, which looked out onto the courtyard, where a single magnificent oak soared to the sky.

"I thought that would be an inspiring subject to paint."

She walked to the window and looked out at the specimen. "It truly will be, Walter. But I must work up to it. I have become rusty."

"Like riding a bike, for someone like you."

As he looked her over, he noted the lines etched more deeply on her face, how she held her arms rigidly and had shuffled along when walking, which he concluded probably came from being shackled to move from place to place. There was an elevated distance in her gaze, as though objects near her did not really come within focus. In her voice, he had detected the diminishment of her spirit that no doubt came when one's liberty was taken away.

"How about some hot tea?" he suggested. "It's chilly out there."

"Yes, tea would be good," she said listlessly.

They sat in the kitchen. He poured the hot water over the tea bags, and they let it steep for a few minutes. There was a small balcony accessed by a sliding door off the kitchen. On the balcony was a raised planter that Nash had put together and filled with dirt.

"You mentioned the garden you worked at with Hiroko-san back in Japan. This is nothing like that, but you can get your hands dirty come the springtime."

"It was very thoughtful," she replied. "Very thoughtful."

"I wanted this to be... as... hopeful a day as possible, Victoria-san."

"I am to be called Jenny Lee now," said Steers as she took a sip of her tea. "I received this information from the authorities. "

"Well, I can tell you from experience that a new name and life isn't so bad."

"I have always liked the name Jenny. I am sure I will get used to it."

"I understand they've lined up work for you?" said Nash.

She nodded. "Ironically, as a drug counselor. I received some training while in prison. I will receive more before I start. It is close by here, they tell me."

"Actually, close enough to walk or ride a bike," said Nash. When she looked at him in surprise he said, "I asked them. And I got you a bike, with a basket and a bell. It's in the laundry room off the kitchen."

She smiled at him. "Thank you, that was very kind."

She drew up a sleeve. "They wanted me to have surgeries to fix my damaged flesh. It was the only time I refused them while in that place."

"Why did they want that?"

"It is an identifier of Victoria Steers. They wanted to do it for my protection. Against my enemies still out there."

"Why did you refuse then?"

She looked up at him, and in her expression Nash saw a little bit of the old Steers: defiance, pride, resoluteness.

"Because I do not deserve to be protected. I am what I am. And if I live many years in peace, or die soon and violently, it will be on those terms. *My* terms."

They both stared off for a few moments and then Nash asked the question he had been waiting to ask: "Did you know Connor Lord had figured out so much?"

"You must assume that a man such as he will know as much as you know, if not more."

"So when you let him capture us? He could have killed us. Not taken us to the warehouse."

"I was counting on the fact that at that point, I knew a little bit more than he did. About himself."

"I don't understand."

"He was the new head of what was my empire. Some would have doubts as to his capabilities. By showing everyone that he bested me? He would have removed all lingering uncertainty about his fitness." She looked earnestly at him. "But it was your idea to have an FBI agent inserted into the security detail at the warehouse. And have Temple request from this man his gun."

"Well, we had to make sure it wasn't a real gun that would be used to shoot you, but the Lynn Ryder version of firearms." He eyed her chest. "The CIA has interesting technology—inserting the detonation device into your clothing and not on your skin. Because Lord's men searched us thoroughly for weapons and surveillance devices. And Rhett had Lord fire at your heart and not anywhere else."

"Yes, it was a team effort," she replied in a desultory voice. "And since I suspected Lord was watching us, I had the CIA slip these items to me in a women's dressing room while I was shopping."

"The feds desperately wanted to get Lord on a charge of murdering you. But you told Rhett to give the gun to your mother. How did you know she would pass it on to Lord?"

"Because I know my mother."

"You'll need to explain that."

"From the moment Lord took over, she had been seeking ways to undermine him, with, no doubt, the eventual goal of pushing him out. By giving the gun to him and challenging him to kill me, she was attempting to show him up in front of the others. The fact that he hesitated and had to be shown how to fire the weapon? It humiliated him in front of everyone. Which was her goal. But I'm sure it was a struggle for her."

"Why?"

"Because I know how desperately she wanted to kill me herself."

Nash shook his head and said, "I know mother-daughter relationships are difficult, but I think Masuyo took it to an entirely new level."

She played with the handle of her cup. "Did you...see your family?"

Nash looked off for a moment. "Yes, at my funeral. Only they didn't see me."

"But—"

"It was the only way, Victoria."

"Jenny," she corrected. "We must be consistent."

"Yes," he said. "They have their lives to lead, and the resources to lead good ones."

"But without you there, I fail to see how good it could be."

They eyed one another over the width of the small kitchen table he'd ordered online. He had painstakingly put all the furniture together upon arrival and set up the apartment for this very day. Nash felt he owed her that. And perhaps a lot more.

But now he sensed that she was not speaking of his family being without him.

Steers was speaking of him not being with her.

"It's just the way it has to be, *Jenny*," he said, perhaps answering her actual query. He eyed her curiously. "Why did you keep Maggie's things in that box?"

Steers met his gaze. "I planned to return them to her. Indeed, I was told she now has the items. The ring, I know, must be special."

"I see. Thank you."

She set her teacup down and looked out the window at the bleak day. "And what of you, Walter?" she asked.

"Actually, it's Dillon," said Nash, drawing her gaze to him. "At least for now, between you and me. We have to be consistent," he added with a tender smile designed to bring the woman a bit of relief from all that she was no doubt feeling.

"Yes, Dillon," she said. She bent down and lifted her pants leg. Revealed was an electronic monitor.

"How long do you have to wear it?" he asked quietly.

"They told me probably for as long as I remain alive." She looked up at him. "It is no more than I deserve. I was surprised that my prison term was not of longer duration."

"You sacrificed a lot. Everything, really. That worked substantially in your favor. They showed Rhett the same preferential treatment. He's out now too."

"It does not make up for what I did. You know that as well as anyone."

"I know that you were brave and honest *and* brutal on yourself. And that anyone else who had to endure the life you did would not have managed to get to this point."

"That excuses nothing," she replied bluntly.

"But redemption is possible, Victoria. And I use your real name because I want you, Victoria Steers, to realize where you started and where you ended up. Hiroko-san said that you were a shy, curious, full-of-energy, and stubborn little girl who loved to draw pictures. I believed Hiroko-san because she was a good person who knew you better than perhaps you came to know yourself. Had your mother not proceeded to control and destroy your life, you would not have turned out like you did." He reached across the table and took her hands in his. "I need you to understand and then believe those words. *You* need to understand and believe the *truth* in those words."

"I can promise to you that I will try, Walter-san. I will try my very best to do so. Because a chance at redemption is all that I have left."

He gripped her hands even more tightly. "No, that's not so. With your job you will be helping many desperate and hurting people. That work will have worth and value, and it will be you who does it. Now, that is a way to reach redemption for your past, yes. But it is also a way for you to move forward in your life. To be the person you started out being."

She nodded slowly. "To go forward, I need to go back in my life. To...to where I cared."

"I don't think you ever really stopped caring. You cared for Hiroko-san; I saw that for myself. You cared for your father."

"And I care for you," she said. "I *care* for you, Walter Nash."

"And I care for you," he replied.

Later, he left her in front of the easel as she was contemplating how to begin transferring the image of an eighty-foot-tall tree onto a three-by-three-foot canvas. Nash had promised to return to visit her soon. He hoped he could keep that promise. He desperately wanted to.

Nash stopped and looked back at the building where on the third floor resided a woman who was easily the most complicated person he had ever known. Her future would not be easy.

Nor will mine.

But they both had a chance. Nothing guaranteed, but a chance.

And in this world, that was likely as good as it was ever going to get.

He drove off toward a sky teeming with dark clouds directly overhead, but with a horizon that might actually be brightening.

ACKNOWLEDGMENTS

To Michelle, thanks for all the encouragement and support with the Walter Nash series. It means a lot.

To Grand Central Publishing, for continuing to be superb partners in all that I do.

To Aaron and Arleen Priest, Lucy Childs, Lisa Erbach Vance, Frances Jalet-Miller, Kristen Pini, and Natalie Rosselli. You are the gold standard of literary agencies.

To Mitch Hoffman, who pushes me to keep getting better with each book. Thanks for always having my back.

To Pan Macmillan, for continuing to push the envelope and find me new audiences.

To Praveen Naidoo and the stellar team at Pan Macmillan in Australia and New Zealand, for all your creative energy and hard work.

To Caspian Dennis and Sandy Violette, for always being so supportive, kind, and brilliant.

And to Kristen White and Michelle Butler, who do everything else while I'm making stuff up.

ABOUT THE AUTHOR

David Baldacci is one of the world's bestselling and favourite thriller writers. A former trial lawyer with a keen interest in world politics, he has specialist knowledge in the US political system and intelligence services. His first book, *Absolute Power*, became an instant international bestseller, with the movie starring Clint Eastwood a major box office hit. He has since written more than fifty bestsellers featuring, most recently, Walter Nash, Travis Devine, Amos Decker and Aloysius Archer. David is also the co-founder, along with his wife, of the Wish You Well Foundation, a non-profit organization dedicated to supporting literacy efforts across the US.

Killer twists. Heroes to believe in. Trust Baldacci.

If you enjoyed *Hope Rises*, then go back to where it all began with this extract from *Nash Falls*, the first instalment in the Walter Nash series . . .

CHAPTER

1

WALTER NASH DID NOT WANT to attend the funeral. Who wanted to bury their father, even if the two were not close? Yet when he had been a little boy the pair had experienced many wonderful times together, the stuff of Hallmark movies and greeting cards.

Then, as the years crept by, Nash had the misfortune of becoming someone that his tough-as-nails, take-no-prisoners Vietnam veteran father had been unable to respect, or apparently even like. After that, his father, Tiberius—universally referred to as Ty—had led his life and Nash his, and the two never saw one another for the most part, although they resided in the same town: his father in an ordinary cluster of old homes, Nash behind a security gate that kept out all others, including probably those who lived in the ordinary cluster of old homes.

Nash worked on his tie while he appraised himself in the mirror. Forty years old, a stitch over six feet three and lanky, but too thin with a bony, undeveloped chest and lackluster shoulders, and stick arms and legs; he'd never focused on muscling up. Unless you were an athlete, soldier, cop, or bouncer, what was the point? His brown hair was still thick and wavy, although graying slightly at the temples.

He and his wife, Judith, and their nineteen-year-old daughter, Maggie, lived in a sprawling nine-thousand-square-foot, two-story, stone-and-stucco house with a finely appointed finished lower level, and a total of five bedrooms and seven bathrooms for just the trio of them. There was also a three-car sideload garage, with his big burgundy Range Rover, Judith's silver Mercedes-Benz S-Class sedan, and Maggie's forest-green BMW convertible occupying the bays. The property was completed by a large, landscaped backyard anchored by an in-ground pool with iridescent tiles.

Maggie had been a college pregnancy, compelling Walter and Judith to hasten down to the local courthouse to say their wedding vows with a judge they did not know, and in the absence of both their families. A true honeymoon had never followed. They'd purchased a condo instead. It made far more sense, Nash had decided. For him honeymoons were simply very expensive photo album fillers. He had later sold the condo and paid off both their college loans with the profits.

Nash was a senior executive VP at Sybaritic Investments. He had risen to that title after years of hundred-hour weeks and brief or no vacations, and living at thirty-five thousand feet as he went from one state or country to the next, crunching numbers, analyzing business opportunities, negotiating terms, and putting together complicated deals that required legions of lawyers and mounds of paper, and a cool hand while under enormous pressure.

All of his hard work and sacrifice had paid off. He now earned a seven-figure salary plus substantial bonuses.

Although he adored them both, Nash was not overly close to his wife or daughter; it was simply not in his nature to be particularly intimate with anyone. They did not seem put off by his aloofness. Indeed, his wife and daughter welcomed him on those occasions when he did join in.

The truth was he had never made friends easily. An introvert, he was proficient and talented with numbers and moving money from here to there, and assembling business prospects together in ways that were visionary and value enhancing. He could articulate all sorts of substantive and meaningful things having to do with such tasks, and also be a motivating and fair leader with his team. However, in truth, he preferred to be alone.

He had had one friend, though, one that he missed terribly to this day. He was a labradoodle named Charly. They'd gotten him from a breeder when Maggie was four. A year ago, as age and illness had robbed the senior dog of any quality of life, they'd had to put Charly down. Nash had become so disoriented and breathless during the procedure that he had thought he was having either a panic attack or a heart attack.

Did that make me pathetic? Shedding tears for a dog when I didn't come close to that level of grief for my father's passing? Yes, it probably did.

Yet, in Nash's defense, Charly had demanded nothing of his owner other than the ability, time, and space to adore him. And Nash's father? Well, the man had done pretty much the opposite of that, much to his only child's continued bewilderment.

Nash did take pride in providing his small family with a prosperous living. Judith had gone to college to study to become a teacher. However, with the pregnancy they had decided that she would stay home with Maggie. But now that their daughter was grown, Judith had talked about getting her teaching certificate and maybe starting out as a substitute teacher before seeing if she wanted to go full-time. Whether it was teaching or something else, Nash supported her a hundred percent.

A lovely, tall, and athletic woman, she kept fit and healthy, optimistic and energetic. She liked to garden, and was an excellent cook. She had been an attentive and hands-on mother to Maggie, volunteering liberally at school, being a member of the PTA, and also being steadily active in neighborhood functions, all while Nash was in London, Singapore, or Doha negotiating and closing yet another deal.

He knew he couldn't have done what he did without her support. Nash had always considered theirs a true partnership. Judith had also been a game participant in all the corporate functions and other duties expected of spouses whose significant others were climbing what could be a very slippery business ladder.

A weekly cleaning crew looked after the house, and they had people to maintain the pool and yard. Judith also went on fun trips each year with her girlfriends. He and Judith occasionally went away on their own, or with Maggie, and when they did, it was always quite pleasant. Their sex life was right where it should be, he thought, for people of their age with two decades of marriage and a child behind them.

He had sensibly started Maggie's college fund on the very day she had been born, but his daughter had decided to take a gap year after graduating from high school. She had been accepted at a handful of quality universities. However, Maggie had recently informed her parents that she wasn't even certain that she wanted to go the college route.

She had started to make noises about becoming an *influencer* and a *creator* on social media and using some of her college funds to do that. Nash knew that she spent a lot of time in her room on her computer, like most people her age. She also had a sophisticated digital camera and an expensive Yeti microphone along with some editing equipment. He could hear noises coming from her room at odd hours.

He did not mind helping his daughter realize her dreams. She was full of positive spirit, and was also tall, like both her parents, and lovely, having taken after her mother in that regard. However, the parade of boyfriends that had come through their home during her high school years! They had run the gamut from cocky jocks to awkward nerds, and even some well-past-college men whom Maggie had met in ways she had never fully explained. Nash had sent the older gents away using his executive voice to let them see the potential liability of dating someone so much younger than themselves.

So if this influencer thing was partly a popularity contest, then Maggie might have a shot. But he also didn't want to support her to such an extent that she ended up incapable of supporting herself. Relying on others was not a good idea.

Before their falling out his father had once told him: "You rise or fall on your own, sonny boy. Then you have no one to blame or thank except yourself."

This made Nash think of the titular head of his company, its CEO, Everett Temple, who was five years younger than Nash. His lofty position was due entirely to his father, Barton Temple, who had founded Sybaritic and many other companies over the decades. Everett was worth at least $200 million, again solely due to daddy.

And Everett, who insisted on being called Rhett, thought himself the very smartest person in the room, because to see himself as anything less would be akin to confessing that his "success" had nothing to do with him. At least that's what Nash conjectured, and he doubted he was wrong. Because very often Nash *was* the smartest person in the room, even if he never intimated that he was.

I surround myself with people just as smart or even smarter than me. That way, they collectively make me look brilliant.

But who knew what tomorrow would bring?

CHAPTER

2

As NASH FINISHED GETTING READY, he thought about his mother and the breast cancer that had taken her five years before. And long before Nash had been born, Agent Orange in Vietnam had gotten its miserable clutches into his father, filling the man with carcinogens that had, for decades, wreaked havoc on his once powerful body.

His father's first wife had killed herself for reasons that had never been explained to Nash. He had married Nash's mother when he'd been thirty-seven and they'd had Nash a year later. As an Army brat Nash didn't have to move around much, because by the time he had come along his father was navigating the downhill portion of his enlisted ride to a full military pension. They had come here when Nash had turned three, and he had been here ever since, except for when Nash had left to attend college.

When Nash was a child, he and his father had spent a great deal of time together, doing things that fathers and sons normally did. Years in Little League baseball where, due to his clumsiness brought on by growing too much too fast, Nash played outfield and his father called out advice nonstop, or else screamed at the coaches, the ump, and other parents, sometimes throwing fists as well as insults. They had gone canoeing a few times and camped out once, but not for long as poison sumac waylaid Nash and nearly sent him to the hospital. By the time he was thirteen his father had taught him how to shoot like a pro and handle firearms exceptionally well. Nash, though, had absolutely refused to go hunting with his father. He could never see himself killing another living thing.

They also attended sporting events together where his father sucked down beers and Nash a soda. His father was the sort of fan who shouted and gesticulated no matter how well or poorly his team was performing. During these times Nash ate a hot dog and cheesy fries, and thought of other things. For the most part those times had been good; his father had been a fun, willing participant in the important moments of a little boy's life.

As a child Nash had attended his father's military retirement ceremony. He had experienced great pride during the ceremony as he watched his father in his full military regalia, his chest brimming with hard-earned ribbons and medals, being celebrated by other brave, tough, and strong men.

He'd also seen, when they would go to the beach on vacation, the permanent wounds grafted onto his father from his combat days. He had felt proud of his dad and sorry for him at the same time, that he'd had to go through that and suffer so.

These blissful times had ended when Nash had opted to play tennis instead of the manly sport of high school football. It had been for a simple reason: While already over six feet at age fourteen, Nash was very thin and underdeveloped, and he didn't want to get his head knocked off. Playing a sport that could damage your brain for the rest of your life, for no compensation in return, had never struck him as a productive or intelligent use of his time.

His father, who Nash knew had been a football legend back in Mississippi, had completely changed toward his son after Nash had made his decision not to pursue football. There were no more fun times. No more father-son outings. There was only a wall between the two that Nash had never really understood because he couldn't believe something so frivolous as choosing one sport over another could have such drastic and inane consequences.

Then high school was done, college had begun, and then Nash had married, become a dad at a young age, graduated with high honors with a degree in business, and begun forging his identity as a husband, father, and businessman extraordinaire.

His widowed father, who had lived only eight miles away, in the same little vinyl-sided house in a hardscrabble neighborhood where Nash had grown up, had not spoken to his son right up until the day he had died. He hadn't even allowed Nash to come to hospice to say his goodbyes. He had never even told his son he had been taken to hospice. In fact, Nash had only heard of his father's death from the man's elderly neighbor.

So today was here and goodbyes would be made, and then what exactly?

His black dress shoes polished, his hair combed, and his slender jaw set as firm as he could manage, he walked out the door to join his family. Then they would drive off to pay final respects to a man who, for decades, had not respected his son in the least.

He was actually looking forward to tomorrow coming as quickly as possible. Then it would just be another day at the office where he could be reasonably sure of what to expect, for Nash was a man who, for the most part, loathed surprises.

And another day of his predictable life left on earth would be checked off to be followed by another day that was pretty much a facsimile of its predecessor.

Or so Walter Nash thought.

THE ONLY MAN FOR THE JOB

Discover David Baldacci's gripping series, featuring undercover operative Travis Devine.

Meet Travis Devine. Framed. Blackmailed. Accused of murder. It's just another day on Wall Street for the 6:20 Man.

The 6:20 Man is back! Can Travis Devine solve the haunting murder of a high-ranking CIA agent before his own time runs out?

Trying to escape a skilled predator who wants him dead, Devine finds himself on a job perhaps even more dangerous than the one he's running from . . .

In a town full of secrets who can you trust?

Discover David Baldacci's historical crime series featuring straight-talking WWII veteran Aloysius Archer.

ONE GOOD DEED

Poca City, 1949. Aloysius Archer arrives in a dusty southern town looking for a fresh start. After accepting a job as a local debt collector, Archer soon finds himself as the number one suspect in a local murder. Should Archer run or fight for the truth?

A GAMBLING MAN

California, 1949. Archer is on his way to start a new job with a renowned private investigator. Arriving in a tight-lipped community rife with corruption, Archer must tackle murder, conspiracy and blackmail in a town with plenty to hide . . .

DREAM TOWN

Los Angeles, 1952. Private investigator and WWII veteran Aloysius Archer returns to solve the case of a missing screenwriter during the Golden Age of Hollywood.

REMEMBER MY NAME

Amos Decker is the Memory Man

Once read. Never forgotten.

Discover David Baldacci's bestselling series featuring the Memory Man, Amos Decker, an extraordinary detective who — because of a life-changing brain injury — remembers everything, including painful things he would give anything to forget.

You took my sister.
I've hunted you for 30 years.
Now . . . your time's up.

Discover David Baldacci's bestselling series featuring Special Agent Atlee Pine

LONG ROAD TO MERCY

Thirty years since Atlee Pine's twin sister, Mercy, was abducted from the room they shared as children, Pine starts the pursuit of a lifetime to finally uncover what happened on that fateful night.

A MINUTE TO MIDNIGHT

Seeking answers in her home town, Pine's visit turns into a rollercoaster ride of murder, long-buried secrets and lies . . . and a revelation so personal that everything she once believed is fast turning to dust.

DAYLIGHT

When Pine's investigation coincides with military investigator John Puller's high-stakes case, it leads them both into a global conspiracy from which neither of them will escape unscathed.

MERCY

FBI agent Atlee Pine is at the end of her long journey to discover what happened to her twin sister, Mercy, and must face one final challenge. A challenge more deadly and dangerous than she could ever have imagined.

Discover David Baldacci's standalone historical drama

Strangers in Time

Every second counts.

Orphaned with no prospects, Charlie Matters steals what he needs, living day-to-day until he can enlist in the war effort. Returning to London after being evacuated five years before, Molly Wakefield faces a city changed beyond recognition, and the devastating news that neither of her parents are there.

Charlie and Molly's paths converge at 'The Book Keep', where they find an unexpected ally in the owner, widower Ignatius Oliver. But the trio's newfound peace is jeopardized as past secrets catch up with them.

Can they help one another survive this turbulent time? Or will they be ripped apart from the last people they hold dear?

Discover David Baldacci's standalone courtroom drama

A Calamity of Souls

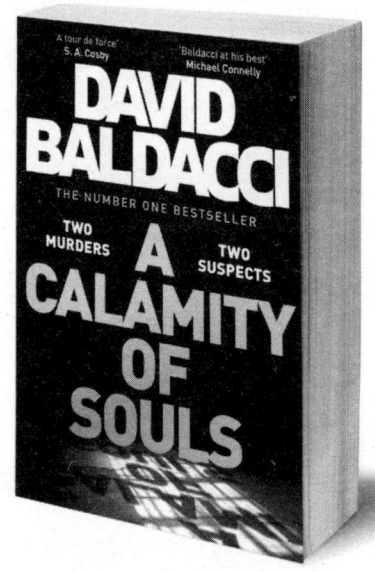

Two murders. Two suspects.

Set in the tumultuous year of 1968 in southern Virginia, a murder case sets a duo of Black and white lawyers against a deeply unfair system as they work to defend their wrongfully accused defendants.

Lee and DuBose could not be more dissimilar. On their own, neither one can stop the prosecution's deliberate march towards a guilty verdict and the electric chair. But together, can they fight for what once seemed impossible: a chance for a fair trial and true justice?